the flight of

GEMMA HARDY

ALSO BY MARGOT LIVESEY

Learning by Heart

Homework

Criminals

The Missing World

Eva Moves the Furniture

Banishing Verona

The House on Fortune Street

the flight of

GEMMA HARDY

A NOVEL

MARGOT LIVESEY

HarperCollins*Publishers*Ltd

Published by HarperCollins Publishers Ltd

First Canadian edition

HarperCollins books may be purchased for educational, business,
or sales promotional use through our Special Markets Department.

HarperCollins Publishers Ltd
2 Bloor Street East, 20th Floor
Toronto, Ontario, Canada
M4W 1A8

www.harpercollins.ca

Library and Archives Canada Cataloguing in Publication
Livesey, Margot, 1953–
The flight of Gemma Hardy / Margot Livesey.

ISBN 978-1-44340-613-0

I. Title.
PS8573.I89F55 2012   C813'.54   C2011-905718-2

Designed by William Ruoto
Printed and bound in the United States
RRD   10   9   8   7   6   5   4   3   2

For Roger Sylvester, 1922–2008

Home is the sailor, home from the sea
And the hunter home from the hill.

—"Requiem," Robert Louis Stevenson

the flight of

GEMMA HARDY

PART
I

chapter one

We did not go for a walk on the first day of the year. The Christmas snow had melted, and rain had been falling since dawn, darkening the shrubbery and muddying the grass, but that would not have stopped my aunt from dispatching us. She believed in the benefits of fresh air for children in all weather. Later, I understood, she also enjoyed the peace and quiet of our absence. No, the cause of our not walking was my cousin Will, who claimed his cold was too severe to leave the sitting-room sofa, but not so bad that he couldn't play cards. His sister Louise, he insisted, must stay behind for a game of racing demon.

I overheard these negotiations from the corridor where I loitered, holding my aunt's black shoes, freshly polished, one in each hand.

"In that case," said my aunt, "Veronica and Gemma can walk to the farm to collect the eggs."

"Oh, must I, Mum?" said Veronica. "She's such a—"

The door to my uncle's study was only a few feet away, across the corridor. Hastily I opened it, stepped inside, and shut out whatever came next. Not long ago this room had been the centre of the house, a place brightened by my uncle's energy, made tranquil by his concentration as he worked on his sermons, but last February, skating alone on the river at dusk, he had fallen through the ice, and now I was the only one who spent any time here, or who seemed to miss him. Just inside the door was a pyramid of cardboard boxes, the remains of my aunt's several recent purchases. But beyond the boxes the room was as he had left it. His pen still lay on the desk beside the sermon he'd been preparing. At the top of the page he had written: "Sunday, 16 February A.D. 1958. No man is an island." A pile of books still sat on the floor next to his chair; the dead coals of his last fire crumbled in the grate. To my childish fancy, the room mourned him in a way that no member of his family did, certainly not my aunt, who dined out two or three times a week, played bridge for small sums of money, and since the season started, rode to hounds whenever she could. At breakfast that morning, she had said I must no longer call her Aunt but ma'am, like Betty the housemaid.

Setting the shoes on the floor and trying not to imagine how Veronica had finished her sentence—such a copycat? such a moron?—I read over my uncle's opening paragraph. "We each begin as an island, but we soon build bridges. Even the most solitary person has, perhaps without knowing it, a causeway, a cable, a line of stepping-stones, connecting him or her to others, allowing for the possibility of communication and affection." As I read the familiar phrases I pictured myself as a small, verdant island in a grey sea; when the tide went out, a line of rocks surfaced, joining me to another island, or the mainland. The image bore no relation to my present life—neither my aunt nor my cousins wanted any connection with me—but I cherished the hope that one day my uncle's words would prove true. Someone would appear at the other end of the causeway.

I stepped over to the bookcase and pulled down one of my favourite books: *Birds of the World*. Each page showed a bird in its natural habitat—a puffin with its fat, gaudy beak, peering out of a burrow, a lyre-bird spreading its tail beneath a leafy tree—accompanied by a description. Usually I read curled in the armchair beside the fire, conjuring an imaginary warmth from the cold embers, but today, not wanting to reveal my presence by turning on the light, I settled myself on the window-seat. Pulling the heavy green curtain around me, I flew away into the pictures.

LONG BEFORE VERONICA'S REMARK, even before my uncle's death, I would have said that the only thing I shared with my oldest cousin was an address: Yew House, Strathmuir, Perthshire, Scotland. At fourteen, Will was a thick-necked, thick-thighed boy who for the most part ignored me. Sometimes, when he came upon me in the corridor or the kitchen, an expression of such frank surprise erupted across his face that I could only assume he had forgotten who I was and was trying to guess. A servant? Too small. A burglar? Too noisy. A guest? Too badly dressed. I had seen the same expression on my uncle's face when he watched Will play football, as if he were wondering how this hulking ruffian could be his son. But their blue eyes and long-lobed ears left no doubt of their kinship. My uncle had once shown me a photograph of himself with his brother, Ian, who had died in his early twenties, and my mother, Agnes, who had died in her late twenties. "Thank goodness she was spared the Hardy ears," he had said.

With Louise and Veronica, however, I had a history of affection. Until last summer the three of us had attended the village school, walking the mile back and forth together. Although Louise was two years older, I had often helped her with her arithmetic homework. I had also endeared myself by giving her my turns on Ginger, the family pony, an act of pure self-interest that she took as a favour. But in July my aunt had announced that her daughters, like their brother, would go to school in the nearby town of Perth. Suddenly they had other friends, and I walked to school alone. Meanwhile the dreaded Ginger had been sold, and Louise now had her own horse. She had tried to convert me to her equine cult by lending me *Black Beauty* and *National Velvet*. So long as I was reading I understood her enthusiasm, but as soon as I was in the presence of an actual horse, all teeth and hooves and dusty hair, I was once again baffled.

As for Veronica, who was only six months my senior, she and I had been good friends until she too developed alien passions. Now she was no longer interested in playing pirates, or staging battles between the Romans and the Scots. All her attention was focused on fashion. She spent hours studying her mother's magazines and going through her wardrobe. She refused to wear green with blue, brown with black. Any violation of her aesthetic caused her deep distress. When my aunt bought a suit she didn't approve of, Veronica retired to bed for two days; my appearance, in her sister's cast-offs, was a kind of torture. Her father had teased her about these preoccupations in a way that held them in check. Without him, she too had become a fanatic.

Despite these changes I had, until the previous week, believed that Louise and Veronica were my friends, but the events of Christmas Eve had forced me to reconsider. For as long as I could remember, the three of us had spent that afternoon running in and out of each other's bedrooms, getting ready for the party given by the owners of the local distillery. Last year I had drunk too much of the children's punch and won a game that involved passing an orange from person to person without using your hands; I had been looking forward to defending my victory. But on the morning of the twenty-fourth, when I had asked Louise if I could borrow her blue dress again, my aunt had paused in buttering her toast.

"What do you need a dress for, Gemma?"

"It's the Buchanans' party tonight. Don't you remember, Aunt?"

I jumped up to retrieve the invitation from the mantelpiece where it had stood for several weeks and held it out to her. "Yes," said my aunt, "and who is this addressed to? The Hardy family. That means Will and the girls and me." She reached for the marmalade. "You'll stay here and help Mrs. Marsden. You can start by doing the washing-up."

"Anyway I won't lend you the dress," Louise added. "You'd just spill something on it."

If she had sounded angry I would have argued, but like her mother, she spoke as if I were barely worth the air that carried her words. Without further ado the two of them turned to talking about where they would ride that day. Abandoning my toast, I marched out of the room.

Mrs. Marsden, the housekeeper, was the only member of the household whose behaviour towards me had not changed after my uncle's death. She continued to treat me with the same briskness she had always shown. She had arrived in the village the year after I did and rented the cottage on the far side of the paddock. Then my aunt had an operation—she can't have any more babies, Louise announced cheerfully—and during her convalescence Mrs. Marsden had become a fixture at Yew House. She had grown up in the Orkneys and could, sometimes, be lured into telling stories about the Second World War, or seals and mermaids. Helping her, I told myself, was infinitely preferable to being a pariah at the party.

But as I watched Louise and Veronica trying on dresses, ironing, and doing their hair, I had felt increasingly left out. Although Mrs. Marsden's own wardrobe consisted of drab skirts and twinsets, she was regarded as an excellent judge of fashion, and the two girls ran in and out of the kitchen, asking, Which necklace? The blue shoes or the black? When I momentarily forgot myself and seconded her in urging the blue, Louise did not even glance in my direction, and I saw her nudge Veronica when she thanked me. Suddenly I was no good even for praise. By the time they came in to display themselves one final time, I was peeling chestnuts for the stuffing and determined not to utter another word, but that didn't stop me from staring.

In the last year Louise, as visitors often remarked, had blossomed. She carried her new breasts around like a pair of deities seeking rightful homage. Privately I called them Lares and Penates, after the Roman household gods. Veronica was, like me, still flat as a board, but her lips were full and her hair was thick and wavy. In their finery, with their glittering necklaces and handbags, the two sisters could have been on their way to the Lord Mayor's Ball. That Louise could scarcely walk in her high heels, that Veronica had applied so much of her mother's rouge that she seemed to have a fever, only heightened the transformation.

"You both look very nice," pronounced Mrs. Marsden. "The green is most becoming, Louise. Veronica, your hair is lovely."

I was reaching for another chestnut as my aunt sailed in, wearing blue velvet, her golden hair piled high. "My gorgeous girls," she said, putting an arm around each. She was still praising them when Will appeared. At once she released her daughters. "My dashing young man."

None of them seemed to notice that my uncle was missing. The previous year, when I wasn't passing oranges and playing games, I had watched him as he danced. Later, from memory, I had drawn a picture of him, looking like a Highland chieftain in his kilt and sporran; it had stood on his bookshelf until my aunt threw it on the fire. Now he was gone, and all they could think about was their fancy clothes. In my fury the knife slipped from the chestnut into my finger. My gasp drew a flurry of attention.

"Hold your hand above your head," ordered Mrs. Marsden.

"Move the chestnuts," said my aunt.

"Bloody idiot," said Will, snickering at the double meaning.

His sisters made noises of disgust until my aunt hushed them. "Let the dogs out last thing," she told me. "And be sure to leave the porch light on."

Heels clicking, skirts swishing, they disappeared down the corridor.

Mrs. Marsden bandaged my finger and said she would finish the chestnuts. She must have felt sorry for me, because she told a story about an Italian prisoner of war who had been brought to the Orkneys in 1942 and fallen in love with a local girl. He couldn't speak English, so he courted her by singing arias. After the war he was sent back to Naples. "We all thought we'd seen the last of him," said Mrs. Marsden. "But a year later Fiona heard a familiar voice. She looked out of her bedroom window and there he was, kneeling in the road, singing and holding a ring."

By seven-thirty everything that could be prepared for the next day's dinner was ready. Mrs. Marsden untied her apron with a flourish and wished me Merry Christmas.

"Where are you going?" I said stupidly.

"Home. I have to get ready for tomorrow."

"Can't you stay?" I imitated Veronica, opening my eyes wide and clasping my hands. "We can play cards, or watch television. You could have a drink."

Mrs. Marsden stopped buttoning her coat at my second suggestion—she did not have a television—but at my third she continued. On several occasions I had overheard my aunt complaining to her that a newly purchased bottle of gin or sherry was almost empty. Once Mrs. Marsden had rashly retaliated by mentioning Will. Now she told me not to talk nonsense and picked up her handbag. With a creak of the door she was gone.

Alone I tried to settle to patience at the kitchen table, but I could not keep my attention on the cards. When Will's rowdy friends came over, Yew House seemed small, but now the empty rooms stretched around me, too many to count. And the dogs, the affable but dull William and Wallace, were no help. I put the cards away, let them out, and then shut them in the cloakroom. Taking advantage of my solitude, I made a hot water bottle and climbed the stairs to bed. Through the window on the stairs I saw the first snowflakes falling.

Until last summer my bedroom had been next to Louise's. Then, on the pretext of redecorating, my aunt had moved me to the maid's room under the eaves. In the warm months I had enjoyed my eyrie, sitting for hours looking out at the treetops and daydreaming. But in winter the ice on the inside of the windowpane thickened by the day. "Heat rises," my aunt said when I asked for an electric fire. I had learned to undress, pull on my pyjamas, and jump into bed at top speed. There my teeth chattered until the sheets grew warm and I could lose myself in the pages of a book. Even this pleasure was often curtailed by my aunt's command to turn off the light. I would lie in the darkness, listening to the noises from below: Louise and Veronica talking, Will playing his radio.

On Christmas Eve I had tried to enjoy the luxury of reading undisturbed, but the house was full of other, more sinister sounds: rustling, gnawing, pitter-pattering. That weekend the newspaper had reported the abduction of a girl from her home in Kinross. Even in the murky photograph it was obvious that she was the opposite of me, fair-haired, rosy-cheeked, the sort of child anyone would want. Still, a villain might make a mistake, especially in the dark, and William and Wallace were notoriously friendly.

Picturing my bedside lamp like a beacon signalling my solitude, I set my book aside and switched it off. At the first sign of an intruder I would run down the backstairs and hide behind the curtains in my uncle's study. The idea of being trapped in my small room made my stomach ache. In the darkness, the noises at first grew even louder, but after a while, when there was no breaking glass, no footsteps, I forgot to listen for my kidnapper and turned to more realistic fears. I knew from my uncle that in Scotland one could go to university at seventeen, and I had come to think of this as the age at which I would, magically, become an adult. But how was I going to endure the next seven years, and how, when I left Yew House, would I earn my living? In Veronica's comics girls ran away from home and discovered long-lost relatives and unexpected talents. I had none of the former and doubted the existence of the latter. I was good with numbers, could recognise most common birds by flight and song, was capable of passionate attachments and of daydreams so vivid that my immediate surroundings vanished, but I was hopeless at sports and had crooked handwriting; I could not act, or play an instrument, or cook, or sew. The fires I laid smoked. I could swim but had twice failed my life-saving exam. Lying there on Christmas Eve, clinging to my hot water bottle, I had understood more urgently than ever before that I was alone in the world.

Finally I had climbed out of bed and made my way downstairs. In the sitting-room the Christmas tree drooped beneath its burden of balls and tinsel. Around the base lay a pile of gifts. I knelt down and read the labels. Present after present was addressed to Will, or Louise, or Veronica. Near the bottom I came upon a single, hard, rectangular package: *To Gemma from her cousins.*

The next day I had feigned a cold and remained in bed, coming down only to watch the Queen on television. Why should I play audience while my cousins opened their many gifts, and pretend gratitude for whatever dreary book my aunt had bought me? Even in this thought I gave myself too much importance. When I finally opened the package on Boxing Day I found a book about horses; Louise had received two copies for her birthday.

Now, a week later, alone in my uncle's study, I listened to the leaves of the holly tree scratch against the window and turned the pages of *Birds of the World.* Each picture suggested a place I might someday visit—a steamy forest filled with tropical flowers—or reminded me of one I dimly remembered—a snowy landscape with matching white birds. I imagined myself wrapped in furs rather than the curtain, padding across the ice towards an albatross or a snow eagle. Suddenly the study door was flung open. Will appeared, loutish in his brown sweater and corduroy trousers. His game of cards with Louise must have ended. He didn't notice me in my hiding place as he shambled over to his father's desk and sat down.

"If only I had more players like Will," he said, leaning back in the chair, "we'd win the season. The rest of you spineless wonders should take a leaf out of his book. That tackle he made in the first quarter was bloody brilliant."

My cousin, I realised, was pretending to be his football coach. I watched in fascination as he squared his shoulders and praised himself. It had never occurred to me that Will had an imaginary life. When he began to talk about making the Scotland team, my amusement escaped in a gust of laughter. He jumped to his feet, looking wildly around. Perhaps he thought his play-acting had summoned his father's ghost. Then he spotted me behind the curtain.

"What are you doing here, spying on me, you miserable little twerp?"

Before I could answer he seized my arm. "Don't you know that we all hate the way you sneak around, pretending to be such a Goody Two-shoes? All you do is scrounge off us. You eat our food, sit on our chairs, you pee in our toilets, and you don't do one thing to earn your keep. Even the dogs are more useful than you are. Everything you're wearing"—he jerked the sleeve of my cardigan—"belongs to my mother, and that means it belongs to me."

"And your sisters," I said, in the interests of both accuracy and anger.

His fingers pressed tighter. "So you ought to say thank you every morning when you get dressed, every time you sit down to eat, every time you—"

"Thank you, thank you, thank you, Master Will, most brilliant of humans, best of football players. You didn't even make the junior eleven."

I got no further before he let go of my arm, grabbed *Birds of the World*, and brought it down, two-handed, on my head, as if he were trying to break the book in half. I fell off the window-seat, landing hard on my hip. I cried out and, as Will's foot found my ribs, cried out again.

"What on earth is going on here?"

From my position on the floor, my aunt towered over her son, and they both towered over me. "Wretched girl, stop making such a row."

"Will hit me." For once—both my fall and Will's blows had hurt—I didn't care about telling tales.

"She was spying on me. I came in here to think about Daddy and she made fun of me. I tried to tell her how much she owed him. If it hadn't been for him she'd still be wandering around on some iceberg, eating seal blubber. And she said she was glad he was dead."

At this, despite the pain, I jumped up, kicking and punching, trying to reach his eyes. "You liar. I never said anything like that. You are the one who forgets your father. You behave as if he never existed, as if he wouldn't hate your muddy sports and your pathetic jokes about beer. You don't care about anyone but your fat, stupid self."

A thread of snot dangled from Will's nose and his eyes bulged. He shoved me hard, and I again fell to the floor.

"You poor boy," said his mother. "I don't know what your father was thinking when he brought such a minx into our home. Please, darling, don't exert yourself further. I will take care of punishing Gemma."

She stepped out of the room and returned a moment later with Betty, the maid. "Lock her in the sewing-room," she commanded. "She'll stay there until she is sorry for her bad behaviour."

Betty was a hefty girl, and I was slight and unaccustomed to fighting, but at the news that I was to be shut in I struggled with all my might, kicking her ankles, even sinking my teeth into her hand. I had almost pulled free when Will, ignoring his mother's remonstrations, joined in. The two of them dragged me from the study, down the corridor, and up the stairs. Gleefully they thrust me into the sewing-room, and slammed the door.

The only sources of light in the small room were a single window, far above my head, and a single bulb hanging from the ceiling. The window, close to dusk on this overcast day, made little difference, and the light switch was outside, in the corridor. In the gloom the sewing-machine glinted, black and malevolent, and even the tall shelves, stacked with sheets and towels, had a threatening air. Mrs. Marsden always kept the door open when she sewed and still complained about the chill. I sat down and tried to calm myself by picturing the birds I had just been studying, but I could not summon even a modest fairy-wren. For five minutes, perhaps ten, I managed to pretend that I was sitting there by choice. Then my hand reached for the doorknob, and in an instant, I was on my feet, pounding on the door, crying for help.

At last footsteps approached. "Be quiet," said my aunt. "You won't be allowed out until you prove you are sorry. To attack your cousin like that."

"It was his fault. He hit me first."

The only answer was the sound of her footsteps retreating down the corridor. "Please, ma'am," I cried. "Don't go. I'll be quiet. I'll be good. I never meant to insult Will."

I am not sure what else I promised—in my desperation I was shameless—but nothing made a jot of difference. Her footsteps continued unfaltering, fainter and fainter, towards the stairs. I heard them no more. In the shelves, among the linens, something moved. A figure stood there, tall and gaunt. It stepped towards me.

chapter two

THE STORY OF MY parents was, according to my uncle, a tale of heroism and true love; to my aunt, an example of stupidity and stubbornness. They had met in 1943 when my mother, Agnes, a WRNS, was posted to Iceland, and my father, a man who had grown up in the shadow of glaciers and geysers, was working on the new docks in Reykjavik. After only four months Agnes had returned to Scotland, but they had kept faith, sent letters, and made romantic arrangements that involved looking at the North Star. They had planned to meet after the war, but then my mother found herself back in Edinburgh, taking care of her father, who had had a stroke. My uncle described the tall, stern house near the Botanical Gardens, and their small, stern parents.

"They could have hired a nurse," he told me, "but our mother wouldn't hear of strangers in the house. She was never the same after Ian's death."

My uncle was already married and in his first parish in Aberdeen; he hadn't known of my father's existence for nearly a year. Then a church council meeting brought him to Edinburgh. On the second day of his visit he had insisted Agnes take a walk with him in the Gardens.

"Even to get your grandmother to consent to that was a tussle. What if something happens? she kept asking. It was then that I began to realise what your mother's life was like and why she was so pale. The only times she left the house were to do the shopping, or fetch the doctor, or go to church. It was May and the azaleas were in full bloom. Agnes kept going from bush to bush, smelling the flowers, exclaiming."

My uncle and I were walking too, along the track that led to the footbridge over the river. It was a still afternoon in early autumn, and nothing seemed to move except the two of us, and the sheep, grazing in the nearby fields. We stopped in the middle of the bridge. My uncle leaned over the railings and I looked through them.

"The summer before the war," he went on, "my father took us fishing on Speyside. Ian and I were hopeless, but right from the start, Agnes had the knack. She could find the fish when no one else could. She told me how one day when she wasn't on duty your father took her out in his boat and showed her the schools of herring. 'They made their own waves,' she said. I should have walked her home from the Botanical Gardens right then, and put her on the next boat to Iceland. Look."

A heron was standing in the shallows, head hunched, waiting for its prey.

My parents wrote faithfully, and eventually, in 1946, three months after my grandfather's funeral, my father travelled to Scotland. They were married in my uncle's church. He asked if I knew what *radiant* meant, and when I shook my head he explained it meant giving out light, like the lamp in the sitting-room that was shaped like a lady wearing a crinoline. That was how my mother had looked on her wedding day. My father too. They had sailed to Iceland that night. From her new home my mother wrote wonderful letters. She had fallen in love with the country and with my father's small fishing village. She learned Icelandic and made a garden among the rocks. She and my father had come back to Edinburgh only once, in 1948, so that I could be born in a Scottish hospital.

"The last time I saw her," said my uncle. "She couldn't have been happier."

I was born in April, and that summer, when I was still too young to crawl and the seas were calm, my mother and I often went out in my father's boat. I pictured the two of us in the bow, watching the waves while my father in the stern cast his nets. But one day the following spring, shortly after my first birthday, we stayed home and went for a walk instead. My mother slipped on some seaweed and, protecting me, hit her head on a rock. She picked herself up, brought me home, made a cup of tea, and took two aspirin. By the time my father returned, there was a lump the size of a hen's egg on the back of her head, but she insisted she was fine, just tired. My father put me to bed and made supper. In the morning she didn't wake up.

For the next two years I lived with my father; a neighbour minded me while he fished. Then one pleasant August afternoon he didn't come home. The neighbour said he must have found an enormous school of fish. He was following them, filling his nets; he would be back tomorrow. The next afternoon I saw the blue hull of his boat rounding the harbour wall. I ran to meet it, but the man at the tiller was a fisherman from the next village. When he stepped ashore, I hurled myself at his knees, demanding my father. He knelt down so that his face was level with mine and said something that made no sense. My father had drowned.

I came to meet the boats the next day, and the next, and the next. Whatever the weather, I insisted on going down to the harbour. I ran up to each man in turn. Surely one of them would be my father. Several times I tried to stow away on a boat, but I was always discovered. If only I was allowed to look, I knew I could find him.

I am not sure how many days or weeks later a strange man arrived, speaking in a language I didn't understand. I hid in terror behind the neighbour. She showed me a photograph that stood on my mother's chest of drawers and pointed first to the man in the photograph, then to the man standing a few feet away. "Your uncle," she said.

Later he told me that as a boy he had once tamed a fox cub and that the process of befriending me was similar; mostly he sat and waited for me to approach, or did things—sang, played bowls—that he thought might interest me. Then one day my uncle and the neighbour explained that I was going to a place called Scotland, where he and his family lived. I would have a brother and sisters, an aunt. The next day we packed, and the day after that we drove to the city and boarded a boat bigger than any I'd ever seen.

The voyage took two days, and I spent every minute of daylight on deck, hoping to see my father, his head or his arm, even a sea-boot, above the waves. When my uncle asked me to come to meals, I explained why I couldn't. He had found a sailor to translate for us, but the man's English was uncertain; it took several exchanges before my uncle understood. Then he sat down beside me to scan the watery horizon. Sometimes, for a minute or two, a seal or a cormorant raised my hopes.

I wept bitterly when land appeared. For the first time I believed my father was dead. Worse was to follow. As we drove along streets of grey buildings, it dawned on me that we were leaving the sea behind. I remember little of the drive to Yew House. We stopped several times for petrol or food and once for me to go behind a wall. The mossy stones were not so different from the ones at the back of our house.

Every trip I had ever made had begun and ended with the sea, but as the sun set, we drove into a small village with no water in sight. My uncle pointed out his church.

"No," I said: my first English word.

We drove along a narrow road between fields of black-faced sheep and up a drive lined with rhododendrons, shadowed by beech trees and firs. How dreary it seemed, closed in with trees, how silent without the sea to sing a lullaby.

I still cherished some small hope that this was only temporary; my uncle had come to visit me; now I was going to visit him. But when we reached the stone house at the top of the drive and my uncle led me past a rowan tree and through the front door, I knew I would never see my father again, never walk down to the jetty to greet the fishing boats and laugh at the crabs scuttling over the rocks, never see the beady-eyed gulls waiting to pounce on fish scraps, never watch the snow fall day after day after day.

I was inconsolable, and this, surely, was the beginning of my difficulties with my aunt. I howled every time she approached. I refused to talk to her, or to my cousins. I spoke only with my uncle. He neglected his own children to teach me English and that winter nursed me through first measles and then tonsillitis.

Gradually I forgot my Iceland home, forgot my father and our village that was almost part of the sea. I went to school, played with my cousins, dogged my uncle's footsteps, and enjoyed his praise of my reading and writing and sums. I had a home, and a family. It had taken me almost a year to understand that with his death, I had, once again, lost both. The true nature of my relations with my cousins and my aunt, like the branches of an elm in winter, became clear.

chapter three

W<small>HEN</small> I <small>OPENED MY</small> eyes I was looking not at the sewing-machine and the shelves of linen but at the sloping ceiling of my attic room with its mossy paint. I was still blinking cautiously as Mrs. Marsden appeared at the foot of my bed.

"You're awake," she said. "What a fright you gave us. Dr. Shearer was here and he thinks you had some kind of fit. You kept talking to him in some strange language and trying to put on your shoes."

The notion of my doing and saying things of which I had no memory made me dizzy all over again. "I don't remember any fit," I said. "I just remember my aunt telling me to be quiet and being left alone in the cold and dark. She knows I hate being shut in. How could she be so cruel?"

"Cruel," exclaimed Mrs. Marsden. She had turned on the light and it shone on her fair hair, which was as usual pulled into a tight bun. "What nonsense. Your aunt gives you a home, food, and clothes. Without her you would be in an orphanage."

"At least there would be no one to say I'm worse than a dog. All the other children would be orphans too, and when people were stupid or unkind, they'd be punished."

Mrs. Marsden shook her head. "You don't know what you're talking about. Orphanages are dreadful places. The children have no toys or books or drawing things. They work all day and are scolded for the smallest fault. You know how clumsy you are and how you take half an hour to lay a fire because you're daydreaming. You would always be in trouble. Now lie still and don't talk while I go and tell your aunt that you're awake."

Who would I talk to? I wanted to say, but even this brief conversation had exhausted me. I was happy to lie back and close my eyes. Mrs. Marsden was right—I didn't know the first thing about orphanages— but I couldn't go back to being the docile girl who had allowed Will and Louise to bully her. As I drifted towards sleep I vowed I would no longer let myself be treated like an unpaid servant.

WHEN I AWOKE AGAIN a man with cavernous nostrils and gold-rimmed glasses was bending over me, one hand wrapped around my wrist. "Well, young lady," said Dr. Shearer, "how are you feeling?"

"Fine."

"You didn't seem fine last night." He held up his hand and made me count fingers. Then he asked the names of the queen—Elizabeth II— and the prime minister—Harold Macmillan—and where I lived. I answered quietly, not quarrelling with the simple questions; Dr. Shearer had been a friend of my uncle's and, on his rare visits to the house, always greeted me kindly. Once in the autumn when I was walking home from school he had stopped in his red sports car to give me a lift. "Hold on," he had said, and then we were flying down the road, past the fields of startled cows and sheep. When we skidded to a halt in front of Yew House, he had said I was the perfect passenger.

"Can you sit up?" he asked now.

I tried, but little dots appeared before my eyes. Gently he told me to lie down again. Could I tell him what had happened? I described my encounter with Will, how he had attacked me, how my aunt had taken his side and locked me in the sewing-room. "It was freezing and she wouldn't even turn on the light."

"Heavens, Doctor," said my aunt from the doorway. "You'd think I was an ogre. She flew at Will like a wildcat only because he reminded her of how much she owes our family. I would be failing in my duty if I didn't make sure that Gemma understands that she won't have the same advantages as her cousins. She will have to work for her living as soon as she's able."

She came into the room and stationed herself at the foot of the bed. It was as if a peacock had invaded the nest of a sparrow. Everything about her—her hair, her pullover, her lipstick—was too large and vivid.

"She might go to university," ventured the doctor. "She might marry."

My uncle had always spoken as if all four of us would go to university. Now my aunt acknowledged, grudgingly, that this was possible. "But she's a plain little thing, and bad tempered to boot. Even if she finds a husband, she'll have to work, like Betty."

"Oh, come now," said Dr. Shearer. "Betty has a good head on her shoulders. If she hadn't left school at fourteen, she'd have made a capable nurse. Many women make their own way in the world nowadays: teaching, working in offices. Gemma will have the advantages of your example, and a thorough education."

He stepped over to the window, barely more than a single stride for him, to check the latch. Turning back to my aunt, he remarked that the room was chilly. If my condition turned into flu or pneumonia, who knew how long I might be in bed. My aunt said she'd always understood that the dry heat of an electric fire was the worst thing for an invalid, but if the doctor insisted, she would send one up. She had something to ask him, she added.

"Give me five minutes with Gemma," said Dr. Shearer.

She glanced at her watch and folded her arms.

"I meant," he said, "five minutes alone."

Her eyes narrowed. "I don't want her telling you stories. Charles used to say she had a vivid imagination, but sometimes I think she doesn't know the difference between truth and falsehood."

I struggled to sit up, but the doctor's hand on my shoulder restrained me. "Please, Edna," he said, "trust me to know my business. No one likes to answer questions about their digestion in public."

This was not, in fact, the case at Yew House. Until a couple of years ago my cousins had reported daily on whether they'd done number one or number two; the latter earned a sweet. But my aunt seemed reassured and left the room. As soon as the door closed, Dr. Shearer pulled over the chair.

"I was a great friend of your uncle's," he said, "and I've seen some of what's happened to you since his death. Tell me, are you happy here?"

"How can I be happy when I'm treated as if I'm stupid and a burden? No one here cares whether I live or die."

The doctor did not contradict me. "Would you like to go away to school if such a thing were possible?"

Remembering my conversation with Mrs. Marsden, I said yes, I'd even go to an orphanage. "At least I'd have orphan friends who wouldn't despise me."

Dr. Shearer smiled. "I don't think that will be necessary. There are boarding schools where they have scholarships for girls like you who are bright but have no money. I happen to know of one, and I'll ask your aunt if you can apply."

He took off his glasses and polished the lenses, first one, then the other, with a handkerchief before returning them to his nose. "Mrs. Marsden told me that when they found you in the sewing-room you were lying on the floor saying, 'Please don't touch me. Please don't hurt me.' Did you see something? A mouse? A rat?"

"There was a figure," I said slowly. "Like a person, but very tall. I couldn't see its face."

"The sewing-room is small." The doctor's hairy nostrils quivered. "Whoever it was must have been almost as close to you as I am now. How is it that you couldn't see its face? And surely you must know whether it was a man or a woman?"

His question brought back a story, a story I still remembered even though the teller, surely my father, had long vanished. "In Iceland," I said, "a person made of snow visits houses when something bad is going to happen. Sometimes it appears as a man, sometimes as a woman. Whoever was in the sewing-room didn't want to be seen clearly."

"Did it speak?"

His newly polished glasses reflected my own pale face. The figure had spoken; it had used my name—not Gemma, but the name my father and mother had called me, which no one ever used anymore—and it had told me to be careful. I stared at my miniature self in the shining lenses behind which lay the doctor's kind eyes. If my uncle had been there I would have told him everything, but if my uncle had been there the figure would never have come. He had kept certain things away, just as the rowan tree beside the front door of Yew House kept witches at bay. And the doctor, however kind, was not my uncle.

"No," I said. "It didn't speak."

"Did it threaten you?"

"I was frightened but it didn't do anything frightening." I closed my eyes, hoping for another glimpse of the figure, another phrase, but all I could see were the shelves of linen rising into the darkness. The doctor was still watching me when I looked up again.

"Perhaps," I suggested hesitantly, "it was trying to take care of me."

chapter four

I STAYED IN BED FOR several days, enjoying my solitude. I was not, by nature, someone who liked being alone—after even an hour or two I yearned for company—but I wanted to hold on to whatever had happened in the sewing-room. So I read and dozed and ate the soups and milk puddings that Mrs. Marsden carried up to me. When she wasn't too busy she would perch on the edge of the bed and tell me an Orkney story: one day she described a woman who married a seal; another, the big storm that blew all the henhouses off the island.

When at last, on a bright, mild afternoon, I dressed and came downstairs I felt as if I had been away for months; I was surprised to find the lower floors of Yew House, and their inhabitants, unchanged. Louise was out riding; Veronica was sitting by the fire, studying one of her mother's magazines; Will, recovered from his cold, was trying to teach the dogs a trick that involved their pretending to be dead; my aunt was on the sofa, drinking a cup of tea and writing in the notebook where she kept her lists.

"Oh, Gemma," she said vaguely, "I hope you turned off the fire. God knows what the electricity bill will be this quarter."

"Yes, Aunt." The word slipped out before I could stop it.

My impertinence made her look up from the notebook, but her eyes did not reach my face. "Why are you wearing Louise's pullover?"

Mrs. Marsden had come into my room the day before and set a pile of neatly folded clothes on the chest of drawers. I had given no thought to the slight oddity of her returning my washing until I discovered that the pile included several garments that Louise had recently outgrown. I said the pullover was in my room.

"And how did it get there? Elves?"

"With my clean clothes." I hoped to implicate Betty, who did the laundry.

"Go and take it off at once and bring it to me. Louise's clothes belong to her and to Veronica. They are not for the taking."

"So what do you expect me to wear?" I demanded. "At the Sunday school party Mrs. Lunn said I looked positively Dickensian."

Before my aunt could answer I left the room. Usually I climbed the stairs two at a time but today I mounted them slowly, carrying my defiance like a banner. I had liked the blue pullover, but its loss was nothing compared with the knowledge that I had an ally. When I returned downstairs, wearing a grey cardigan that had belonged first to Louise, then to Veronica, and that even on my small frame barely buttoned, I headed to the kitchen. "Can I help with supper?" I asked.

As she handed me an apron Mrs. Marsden looked askance at the ragged cardigan. "Is that all you could find to wear?"

I described my arrival in the sitting-room.

"Oh, for heaven's sake." She shook her tidy head. While I scrubbed the potatoes, she told me the story of the film she'd seen the night before at Perth Odeon. "And then the hero— Mind you take out all the eyes."

"Oh, Mrs. Marsden," said my aunt from the doorway. "I was just wondering what time we're having supper. I've invited Mr. Carruthers and his wife for sherry."

Bob Carruthers, the new master of foxhounds, was a frequent and popular guest at Yew House. He arm-wrestled Will, talked to Louise about riding, admired Veronica's outfits, and flattered my aunt absurdly, calling her Diana, mistress of the hunt. As for me, he always asked how the hockey was going. "I don't play," I would remind him. I much preferred his wife, who was expecting a baby in March and shared my passion for *Anne of Green Gables*.

"Seven-thirty," said Mrs. Marsden, briskly stirring the white sauce.

My aunt picked up the pepper grinder and studied the base, as if she had never seen such intricate workmanship. I knew she was hoping that Mrs. Marsden would ask if the Carruthers were staying to dinner and that Mrs. Marsden was determined not to make the invitation easier. Presently she set down the grinder and left the room.

Mrs. Marsden turned to me. "Do four more potatoes. Better now than at seven."

DEFIANCE WAS APPEALING, BUT it did not warm my cold room, it did not clothe me, it did not fill the long hours after school and chores. On Saturday I walked to the edge of Strathmuir and turned in the direction of Perth. A mile to the west a small hill rose beside the road. On the summit, my uncle had explained, were the remains of a Roman fort. The Romans had made several attempts to subdue this part of Scotland but had never succeeded, any more than the Vikings or, more recently, the Germans. As part of their campaign, however, they had built a number of outlying forts. "Imagine making this with a pick and a shovel," my uncle had said. With several parishioners he had excavated a small area and found some fire-stones and a few fragments of pottery; he dreamed of a huge project: scores of people digging under the supervision of a real archaeologist.

On one of our walks to the fort he had described the town of Bath, and how it had been built around the hot springs where the goddess Sulis lived. Sulis's followers, my uncle said, used to throw lead tablets into the water inscribed with requests for children or good harvests, or sometimes curses.

"What sort of curses?" I had asked. We had reached the foot of the fort.

"Fierce ones," said my uncle cheerfully, "and very specific. Cursed be he who stole my gloves. May his corn fail for five years. May he who lamed my horse have only feeble girl children." He laughed and lifted me over the wall. "It's not very Christian, but who doesn't wish they had a god on their side, ready to smite their enemies?"

The idea that just by saying certain words you could harm someone fascinated me. I had asked if the curses worked; my uncle had said he didn't know.

Now I stood looking at the rough mound, covered with heather and bracken, and tried to picture the soldiers who had lived here. "They were a tough lot," my uncle had told me. "Down south on Hadrian's Wall, the soldiers slept on sacks of wool and practised their archery, but up here there was nowhere to go, nothing to do, and yet they couldn't be off guard for a minute. They'd be eating their porridge or milking their goats and suddenly these half-naked people would appear over the nearest hill and rush towards the fort, shooting arrows tipped with poison or flame. At night they'd see fires out in the heather, hear strange music and wild cries."

Girls did not play much part in these stories. When I asked if there were any women warriors, my uncle described Joan of Arc, a poor shepherdess, not much older than I was, who had persuaded people to follow her into battle and save France from the English. After that I had pictured myself wearing armour and carrying a shield, successfully holding at bay marauding hordes.

I scrambled up the slippery hill. At the top the wind stung my eyes and blew my hair straight back. The blue and white bus was winding its way along the road to Perth. To the north the hills were white with snow. However hard I looked I could not see the sea.

Standing there, watching the bus grow larger, then smaller, I thought about running away. I could take the bus, or walk, it was only ten miles to Perth, but what would I do when I got there? No one would ever mistake me, as they might Louise, for a grown-up and give me a job in a shop. I pictured myself standing in a doorway asking for money, as I had seen the Gypsy women do. But what would I eat? Where would I sleep? My room was cold but outside was colder. And what would I do when my shabby clothes wore out? If the police caught me they would take me back to Yew House and things would be even worse. I must bide my time, I thought, until I was seventeen. I must endure.

A mournful chorus roused me. A V of geese was heading towards the fort, flying so low that I could hear the whistle of their wings. I waved but they gave no sign of seeing me. Perhaps, I thought, they were going to Iceland.

I was walking down the hill, barely keeping my balance on the loose stones, when a figure sprang out from behind a rock and, at the same moment, someone shoved my shoulder; I was sprawling in a clump of heather and then, on the grass, sliding fast. As the sky tumbled and rocks grazed my arms and legs, I saw four figures leaping around me, whooping, brandishing sticks and fists. For a moment I thought the Picts had got me; my uncle had taught me to identify with the cultured invaders rather than the barbarian Scots. Then one of them hastened my descent with a helpful kick, and I recognised my cousin.

THE MONDAY AFTER MY visit to the fort I came home from school to find an envelope bearing my name on the hall table. I stared in wonder at the words: Miss Gemma Hardy, Yew House. I could count on one hand the number of letters I had received. As suddenly as the boys had ambushed me, the idea leapt out from some crevice in my brain that the writer was a friend of my mother's, a person who loved me even without knowing me, who had been searching for me for years and had at last tracked me down. I was still scrutinising the illegible postmark when my aunt appeared.

"Oh, Gemma. Those must be the forms from the school Dr. Shearer recommended. If you do well in the exams they'll give you a scholarship. They even have provision for girls to stay during the holidays. Will and Louise can help you study."

The loving friend vanished. Instead I was torn between delight about the school and irritation at the notion that my doltish cousins could teach me anything. But both these feelings also fled when something almost as unusual as the arrival of a letter occurred: my aunt put her arm around me. Unthinkingly I curved my shoulders to fit her embrace. It was so long since anyone had touched me with even a semblance of affection.

My teacher that year was Mr. Donaldson. He had moved to the village only last August and was still a figure of mystery. A tall, saturnine man, some days he arrived in the classroom just as the bell rang and gazed out of the window, scarcely seeming to remember whether we were studying geography or arithmetic. Other days he was rapping his ruler on the desk as soon as assembly was over. "Page sixty-two. Who can describe the events leading up to the invasion of the Spanish Armada?" Behind his back the older girls sang, "Donald, where's yer troosers?" but we were all a little afraid of him. He wore a fat gold ring on his little finger, which Isobel, the brainiest girl in our class, said was a sign that he belonged to a secret society. He was one of the few bachelors in the village whom my aunt never invited to dinner.

The day after the letter arrived I stayed at my desk when the final bell rang. I was waiting for Mr. Donaldson to notice me, but he was having one of his vague days, staring out of the window at the slate roofs and the lemon-coloured sky. That morning during history—we were studying the quarrel between Mary, Queen of Scots, and Elizabeth I—he'd announced that in Switzerland women still didn't have the vote. Now, in the silence following the other girls' departure, I could hear him humming faintly through his yellow teeth.

Finally I approached his desk. "Mr. Donaldson," I said, offering the envelope. At last his eyes left the window and took in my presence. Silently he reached for the letter. I stood watching as he read, confident that he would know what needed to be done.

"Whose idea was this?" he said.

"Dr. Shearer's. My aunt thinks it's a good plan. She wants me to be independent as soon as possible."

"But you're only nine."

"Ten. I need someone to watch me take the exams else I won't get a scholarship."

Mr. Donaldson was pushing back his chair. "I'd like a word with her."

He fetched his raincoat and briefcase from the staff room and I collected my coat, the last one hanging in the cloakroom. I had inherited it from Veronica, and it was already worn down to the nap at the elbows and cuffs. As we crossed the playground, I saw that Mr. Donaldson's coat was almost as shabby; a button dangled from one sleeve. He led the way through the village, his long legs scissoring. I trotted beside him.

"Remind me, Gemma," he said, "how did you end up with your aunt?"

Breathlessly I explained about the deaths of first my mother and then my father and how my uncle had brought me to Yew House.

"He sounds like a remarkable man," said Mr. Donaldson.

"He was," I said, pleased as always when anyone praised my uncle.

His pace did not slow when we reached the outskirts of the village and we hurried past the cows. My favourites, Marie Antoinette and Celeste, were near the fence. Silently I promised them extra handfuls of grass tomorrow.

"Do you always walk home by yourself?" said Mr. Donaldson.

"Yes. My cousins go to the school in Perth." I did not add that my aunt drove them to the bus stop in the village and that they often passed me with a jaunty wave.

As we turned through the gateway, I saw Mr. Donaldson glance at the lion on each gatepost. At the top of the drive we both paused. "Very posh," he said, staring at the clean, curtained windows of Yew House. I had agreed to his request to talk to my aunt unthinkingly—obeying teachers was second nature—but now I worried he might spoil my plans. As I led the way to the back door, I tried to warn him.

"Mr. Donaldson, I hope you won't upset my aunt. She doesn't care for me, but it's not her fault. She never cared for my mother either."

He looked down at me, his yellow teeth glinting. "I'm not good at being tactful," he said, "but I hope your aunt will be upset by what I am about to tell her."

In the kitchen Mrs. Marsden was rolling out pastry. "You're late," she said. "Did you get kept in after school?" And then, catching sight of my companion, "Henry."

"Good afternoon." He doffed his cap. "I'm here to see the dragon."

"Lucky you," said Mrs. Marsden, and I understood that they knew each other in some unexpected way. "She's in the sitting-room. Let me tell her you're here."

As Mrs. Marsden left the room, Mr. Donaldson turned to me. "This concerns you, Gemma, but I think it would be best if you weren't present."

I wanted to argue, but the habit of the classroom was too strong. I ran up the stairs to my icy room and tried to do my homework and ignore the sounds, mostly my aunt's shrill voice, from below. Usually Veronica, or occasionally Louise, would call me to supper, but that evening no one came. When I finally tiptoed downstairs I found a plate waiting for me on the kitchen table.

THE NEXT DAY MR. DONALDSON asked me to stay after school. This time there was no wool-gathering. As soon as the other girls left the room, he waved me over to his desk. "Your aunt is a very stubborn woman," he said. "I don't know if she spoke about my visit"—I shook my head—"but she did not give a fig for my opinions and told me so. I can see that your position in her household is not easy."

He eased his gold ring up and down his finger and announced that he was going to say something I might find strange. "I want you to fail the exams."

"But why?" I said. "Why would I fail an exam on purpose?"

"Because Claypoole School is not a good place for you. I am sure Dr. Shearer recommended it in good faith, but I have heard that the scholarship girls are little better than scullery maids. I know you want to get away from your aunt, and I promise I'll try to find another school, but you must fail the exams."

I listened dumbfounded. Doing well at school was one of the few touchstones of my life, something that connected me with my uncle, and that my aunt could not take away. I might be small and plain and clumsy but I could get 98 percent in arithmetic. The idea of deliberately failing made no sense. Before I could say any of this we both heard the clatter of the janitor's broom in the corridor.

At once Mr. Donaldson was on his feet. "Do your worst, Gemma. And, please, keep this conversation to yourself. Your aunt could make my life very difficult."

On the way home I stopped at the church. My uncle was buried in Edinburgh, but sometimes I came to the graveyard and sat on the oldest grave—the inscription so blurred by moss and weather as to be unreadable—to consult him. I set down my satchel and stared up at the steeple.

"Please, Uncle, tell me what to do. Being at Yew House without you is awful, but Mr. Donaldson says I have to fail the exams."

In the branches of the larch trees the sparrows shrilled, protesting the oncoming night; in the street a car sputtered. I listened and listened, but my uncle said nothing.

DURING THE NEXT WEEK Mr. Donaldson was even more absent-minded than usual. As for my aunt, she didn't mention his visit save to say that Miss Gregg, the Primary 3 teacher, had agreed to supervise me. I had run into teachers in the village often enough to know that they could be different outside the classroom. Now I discovered that, like their pupils, they could change as soon as the last bell rang. Miss Gregg, who was a martinet in class, behaved as if staying behind in the empty school was a treat. We would go from classroom to classroom, searching for the warmest one. Once we had settled, she would produce her knitting. She had learned to knit only last year, and the clicking of her needles was frequently interrupted by exclamations of "Drat" or "Botheration" as the blue scarf grew and shrank.

I did not follow Mr. Donaldson's advice. I could not. The idea of writing the wrong answer when I knew the right one was like stepping in front of a speeding car. Besides, Dr. Shearer had known my uncle and was fond of me. Why should I ignore his advice and follow that of a stranger? Since Mr. Donaldson's visit to Yew House I had overheard some of the older girls talking about him in the playground. One claimed he had been a spy during the war, another that he had crashed his car while drunk and that was why he didn't drive.

The first exam was scripture and the first question was "How did the three wise men find Jesus?" Before I could stop myself I had written, "A star led them to Bethlehem." For a moment I stared at my neatly written sentence—do your worst, Gemma—then I hurried on to the next question.

Each exam took an hour, and by the time I finished, it was nearly dark. Miss Gregg, who lived in the lane behind the school, would always ask if I was all right walking home, and I would assure her that I was. Which was true as long as I was in the village, but then came the moment when I passed the last streetlight and the darkness thickened. Even the cows were of little help. I would walk resolutely, trying not to examine the shadows too closely. Sometimes I sang the songs my uncle had taught me—"I love to go a-wandering," "Clementine," "John Brown's Body." Sometimes I daydreamed about Claypoole School. I would have friends, join clubs, start to learn French and Latin, chemistry and biology. I pictured other girls like myself who had no parents and needed to make their own way in the world.

The road that led past Yew House was little travelled even in daylight, and often I walked the whole way home without seeing a single vehicle. The evening after the history exam I was nearing the cows when I heard the noise of an engine. I stepped onto the verge and, glad of this brief companionship, waved cheerfully at the headlights. The car came to a halt a few yards ahead. As I hurried over, the passenger door opened. The burly figure of a man, cap pulled low, cigarette glowing, leaned towards me.

"Get in, lassie. It's a cold night. I'll take you wherever you need to go."

Although his face was shadowy, his voice was hoarsely familiar—we must have spoken in the village or on one of my walks—but I could not summon a name. I heard a faint tapping sound and guessed he was patting the passenger seat. Still something made me hesitate.

"Are you going to visit my aunt?" I said.

"Yes. Where does she live?"

I was thinking his answer was odd when, from the field, Celeste, or perhaps Marie Antoinette, mooed. "I'll walk," I said. "Thank you."

As I stepped back, the strange man grabbed my sleeve. I did not stop to think. I jerked free and began to run back towards the village. Now that the kidnapper was here, I was not as frightened as I had been lying in bed, imagining him. The man seemed stupid. The road was too narrow to turn around and I did not think he would get out of his car. I stopped at the gate into the field, ready to climb over at the first sign of pursuit. Presently the sound of the engine changed and the lights began to move away.

The kitchen was empty when I arrived home and it did not occur to me to tell either my aunt or Mrs. Marsden about the man. Only later, eating baked beans on toast alone at the kitchen table, did I wonder what would have happened if I had got into the car.

chapter five

MISS GREGG SENT OFF my exams with a note stating that she had supervised me. I probably wouldn't hear for a while, she warned, but barely a week passed before my aunt called me into the sitting-room and handed me a second letter. In return for working in the kitchens and helping with housework my fees at Claypoole School would be waived. They had recently lost a working pupil. Could I come as soon as possible?

"I passed," I said jubilantly. "I was worried about geography."

"So," said my aunt, "you'll leave on Saturday."

"Saturday!" In my daydreams I had left Yew House over and over, but the idea of actually doing so, at such short notice, was startling. I had no friends but that did not mean I did not have attachments. I wanted to say goodbye to the fort and the cows. I wanted to visit my uncle's church and tell him what was happening. "That's only four days away."

"I can count," said my aunt. "They say as soon as possible and you don't have much to pack. Bring down your washing for Betty to do in the morning."

In a daze I climbed the stairs. Even my icy garret, now that departure loomed, seemed dear. When I returned to the kitchen, my arms full of clothes, Mrs. Marsden gave me a rare smile. "So you're off to the Borders. I hear it's a lovely part of the country."

"I don't want to go," I said, and, before she could ask why, I poured out the thoughts that had filled me since my departure became a reality. How I did not want to be farther from my uncle, how the valley was my home.

Mrs. Marsden listened, a tin of salmon in one hand, a tin opener in the other. "Everyone wants a home," she said when I finished, "but Yew House can't be yours. Your aunt hates you. Better to face that now and start to make your own way in the world. Remember what you said about preferring an orphanage. At the school you'll be just like everyone else. Now put those clothes in the basket and come and wash the leeks."

I did her bidding, but in bed that night I could not stop thinking about her claim. I had never thought to add up all the things my aunt disliked about me and put them into that one small word: hate. It was not just, as she often said, that I was plain and clumsy and prone to daydreaming. She hated me and nothing was going to change that. With this revelation came another. If I was going far away, to a place where my uncle had never been, I must take some part of him with me. Bob Carruthers had come for dinner and I could hear him and my aunt laughing in the sitting-room. Although his baby was due any day, he seemed to spend more time than ever in her company. I slipped out of bed and made my way downstairs to my uncle's study. By the light of his reading lamp, I surveyed the room I might, after Saturday, never see again. I would have liked to put everything—the desk, his chair, the green curtains, his books—in my suitcase. I stepped over to the bookcase and pulled out *Birds of the World*. But as soon as I felt its heft, I knew there was no chance of smuggling it into my luggage. After a quick look at the lyre-bird, I returned it to the shelf. What I needed, I thought, was a photograph of my uncle. The half-dozen pictures on the mantelpiece were spoiled by the presence of my aunt and cousins, but off to one side was a small one of him as a newly ordained minister. With his tidy hair and solemn gaze he did not look much like himself, but it was better than nothing. I was heading for the door when it occurred to me that Betty, who was in charge of packing my clothes, might report my theft. I put it back to retrieve on Friday night and stepped into the corridor. At the same moment my aunt, in the sitting-room, squealed.

"Oh, Bob, I never—"

In the abrupt silence that followed I saw that I was not alone. Will was standing at the bottom of the stairs. Before I could decide whether to advance or retreat, another squeal propelled him down the corridor, and through the sitting-room door.

"What are you doing to my mother?" I heard him cry. "Don't you know she's a widow?"

Quickly I ran to the stairs and climbed them two at a time, as quietly as possible. From my room I heard the front door slam, a car start, and then my aunt and Will, their voices raised. The next morning, passing her in the corridor, I noticed that my aunt's cheeks were glazed with make-up.

ON FRIDAY NIGHT I put a torch by my bed and banged my head twelve times against the pillow but there was no need. The prospect of departure kept me awake long past my usual hour. In the last few days I had visited the fort, the river, and the church. That morning at school Mr. Donaldson had announced that today was Gemma Hardy's last day and presented me with a copy of *Robinson Crusoe* inscribed *To Gemma, from her classmates and teacher. With all good wishes for her future. February 1959.*

At the end of the afternoon he had again asked me to stay behind. He stood over my desk, waiting until the last girl had left the room. Then in a low voice, quite unlike his normal teacherly tones, he said,

"As I have no choice but to wish you luck at Claypoole, let me give you some advice. Try not to be noticed. You will be one of many girls. There is no reason why you should put yourself forward. If there is anything I can do, please know that I consider myself your friend."

He handed me a brown paper bag. My surprise at the contents—a pad of writing paper and half-a-dozen envelopes already stamped and addressed to him—must have been obvious. Hastily he explained that I didn't need to write; he just wanted to be sure that I could. "Of course I'll write," I had said. "If you like," he had said, and busied himself with his briefcase.

It was almost midnight when I crept out of bed and tiptoed downstairs. The prospect of departure filled my mind with new thoughts. For the first time I wondered what had happened to my parents' possessions. I remembered my uncle describing how my parents' neighbour had shown me a photograph of him and my mother. Where had it gone? My aunt always claimed that I owned nothing, but this photograph, if it still existed, was mine. Perhaps other things too? I pictured the day I arrived at Yew House. Surely my uncle had unloaded something—a trunk? a large suitcase?—from the boot of the car. And surely whatever it was must have come from my parents' house.

I had never seen anyone but my uncle open the drawers of his desk. Now, with apologies to him, I set down the torch and slid open the top drawer; it was full of sermons. The next contained correspondence. The next, bills. At last, in the bottom right-hand drawer, was a cardboard box with my name printed on the lid. Inside, lying on top of a pile of papers, was a photograph of a man and a woman, my uncle and my mother. On the back were the words *Botanical Gardens, Edinburgh. May 1941.* I sat down and stared at my mother in her summer dress, my uncle in his black trousers and white shirt. They were sitting side by side on a grassy slope, laughing, with a bank of azaleas behind them. I had known my mother was dead for all of my conscious life, and in the last year I had gradually come to terms with my uncle being in the same strange state. But, looking at their bright smiles, it seemed unimaginable that they were not nearby, laughing, talking, playing backgammon.

The sound of the holly leaves scratching at the window brought me back to myself. I set the photograph beside the one of my uncle and closed the box. There was no time now to investigate the rest of its contents and no space for it in my suitcase; if I carried it openly, my aunt would accuse me of stealing. My mind skidded over the alternatives. The box was small enough to fit on the top shelf of the sewing-room or at the back of the boot cupboard, but when would I ever return to Yew House? Mrs. Marsden's cottage was only a few hundred yards away but she was tied to my aunt in ways that made her unreliable. As for burying the box in the garden, I had no confidence that I could dig a hole deep enough, let alone ensure that the contents remained dry.

Only one solution presented itself. I tiptoed to the cloakroom, pulled on my Wellingtons and a coat of Louise's, and let myself out of the house. I had never before been out this late and the air smelled of dampness and animals. In the cloudy sky the almost full moon looked ready, at any moment, to burst into the open; in the nearby woods an owl hooted, fell silent, hooted again. Clutching the box, I half walked, half ran down the road to the village.

Mr. Donaldson rented rooms in a house near the church. I even knew which window was his because once, in the autumn, I had seen him sitting there, smoking and listening to the wireless. I had no thought of what I would do if he was asleep but luck was with me. A crack of light shone through the curtains and, when I tapped on the window, his startled face appeared. Two minutes later the door opened and he stepped out, wearing his shabby coat. Putting a finger to his lips, he led me into the street and the shadowy interval between two lights.

"Are you mad?" he whispered, glaring at me. "If anyone saw you here I could be in serious trouble."

I had expected anger; children weren't allowed out this late. Now, bewilderingly, I recognised fear. "I'll tell them it's all my fault," I said, and explained about the box. "Will you keep it for me? I don't have a safe place."

"Are you sure it belongs to you?"

"Look, it has my name on the lid. Please."

For a few more seconds he continued to glare. Then, wearily, he unfolded his arms and reached for the box. "I'm not the ideal person to keep anything safe for anyone but I'll do my best. If things go arse over tip I have a sister, Isobel. She lives in the town of Oban."

He padded back towards the house. A moment later the light that had welcomed me went out. I ran back to Yew House as fast as my Wellingtons would permit.

PART
II

chapter six

THE SKY WAS STILL dark when my aunt's sharp knock hurled me into the new day. Downstairs, to my surprise, Veronica was seated at the kitchen table. We ate porridge and toast and talked as we had used to do, about teachers and girls at school and whether a ponytail was better than pigtails. With no one to braid my hair I had been forced to adopt the former, which, Veronica claimed, didn't suit me. She produced a brush and comb and, as a parting gift, made me two neat braids. She was lecturing me about my eyelashes—"They're so pale"—when my aunt called from the hall that it was time to leave.

"Goodbye, Gemma," she said, flinging her arms around my neck. "I hope you have a happy life."

"I hope you do too," I said, and kissed her cheek.

Pretending to fetch my scarf, I went upstairs one last time, and slipped the photographs into the old handbag of Louise's I had been given for the journey. In the hall Mrs. Marsden was waiting with a paper bag. "You'll need some lunch," she said, and, before I could thank her or hug her, retreated to the kitchen. Betty had already put my suitcase in the boot of the car and, liking the idea of departing in state, I climbed into the front seat only to have my aunt order me into the back. As we headed down the drive, she explained that I would change trains in Edinburgh and be met in Hawick by the school van. The sky was lightening and in the frosty field I could make out Celeste and Marie Antoinette huddled near the gate. I pressed my face to the window and waved.

In the village we stopped beside the post office and Mr. Carruthers, his cap pulled low, his scarf pulled high, got into the front seat. For a moment I wondered if he could have been the man who accosted me, but when he greeted me—"So, Gemma, you're off to see the wide world"—I knew that, whatever his crimes, he had not tried to drag me into a smoky car. For the remainder of the journey I caught only stray phrases of his and my aunt's conversation as we headed past the fort, past the curling pond, past the boundaries of my familiar world.

At Perth station I ran ahead of my aunt to the ticket office, and stood waiting as she asked for one child to Hawick.

"One way, or return? First or second class?"

"One way, second class," she said, sounding pleased about both choices.

The train was already at the platform and while Mr. Carruthers carried my suitcase to the guard's van, she stared down at me. Against her blue coat her golden hair shone; dark crumbs of make-up dotted the creases around her eyes. Perhaps Veronica had lectured her too about her eyelashes.

"Well, Gemma, we've reached the parting of the ways. You're an ugly child—my poor sister-in-law was a plain Jane—but I hope you'll study hard at Claypoole and be a credit to me. You must—"

"I'll always try to be a credit to my uncle," I broke in, "but you've treated me like a leper. If I win every prize in the school it won't be because of you."

Without waiting for an answer, I turned and marched towards the train. Behind me I heard Mr. Carruthers cry, "The ungrateful brat," and his footsteps in pursuit. Then came my aunt's voice and two sets of steps walking away.

I chose the first empty compartment I came to. As soon as the train pulled out of the station, I knelt on the bristly seat, switched on the little lights on either side of the mirror, and studied my reflection. With my hair pulled into braids, my face had a naked, startled look. My eyelashes were pale, Veronica was right, but my eyes were the same shade of grey as the feathers of the geese that flew over the fort, and my nose was small and straight. I might be plain but I did not think I was ugly. I would make friends at the school. I would try not to show off, or be a copycat. I would learn French and hockey and take piano lessons. I sat down in a corner seat and, lulled by the sight of the wintry fields and the sound of the wheels—one way, second class, one way, second class—fell asleep.

I woke to the wheels making a different sound and the dull red struts of the Forth Rail Bridge flashing by. In one of his sermons my uncle had compared living a good life to the endless task of painting the bridge. As soon as the painters got all the way across, he explained, they had to begin again. Far below I glimpsed the choppy waters of the Firth of Forth flowing into the North Sea.

In Edinburgh the guard carried my suitcase to a platform at the far end of the station and installed me on a bench. My train to Hawick left in an hour. "You're a wee lassie," he remarked, "to be travelling alone."

"I have my book and I have my lunch." I held up each in turn, smiling, but the guard's ruddy face did not smile back.

"My youngest daughter can give you three inches," he said, "and I wouldn't let her loiter about the station. Stay here and don't speak to anyone not in uniform."

My aunt's briskness and a sense of adventure had carried me through the last few hours. Now I was alone on the windy platform, and the thought came to me that no one within fifty miles knew my name, or my whereabouts. I too could disappear, blown away like the dry leaves I saw skimming down the tracks. Perhaps other people had had the same feeling. The bench was covered with initials. Among several hearts I made out the command FLY AWAY. If I had had my penknife to hand, rather than rolled into a pair of socks in my suitcase, I would have carved YES below. I stamped my feet for warmth and even that sound disappeared into the emptiness.

But in a few hours everything would be different. And for now I opened the paper bag to discover my favourite egg and cress sandwiches, a bottle of Ribena, an apple, and two chocolate biscuits. I put these last in my pocket for later, and set to work on the sandwiches. I was dropping the crusts into the bag when I saw a note.

Dear Gemma,
The best of luck at your new school. Be good!
I hope our paths cross again one day.

Kind regards,
Audrey Marsden

Reading the words—she had printed them as if I couldn't read cursive—I was doubly glad I had not gone to her the night before. She had been kind to me when no one else had, but a small part of me counted her a coward. I tore the note into pieces, stepped to the edge of the platform, and released them into the wind.

I was eating the apple in neat bites when a train steamed up to the platform and, with one last exuberant shriek, came to a halt. No one in uniform was nearby, so I asked a tall man in a smart green coat if this was the train to Hawick. "Indeed it is," he said. Claiming a mysterious slipped disc, he commandeered a boy of about Will's age to carry my suitcase. Once we were settled in a compartment and the train was under way, the three of us exchanged destinations. The man was going to Carlisle. The boy was going only one stop. He had come into the city to apply for a job at a fishmonger's but they had said he didn't have enough experience.

"That's ridiculous," said the man. "A lad your age, they should train you."

I regarded the boy with new interest. In profile his upper lip jutted over his lower, like the trout my uncle had occasionally caught. I asked if he liked fishing.

"Not really," he said. "Too much hanging around, but I like cleaning my dad's fish. Everything's very organised—bones, guts." He wriggled his fingers. "Do you like fish?"

"Yes." Over the years I had grown accustomed to my landlocked life but suddenly I longed for the sea. Why hadn't I asked Dr. Shearer or Mr. Donaldson if there was a school on the coast? Then the man asked where I was going and I explained about Claypoole.

"Isn't this the middle of term?" he said, his voice lifting in surprise.

"They're short-handed, and I did well on the exams." My boasting made it sound as if I would be helping in the classroom, not the kitchen, but kindly he did not press me. He said he'd left school at fourteen and always wanted to travel; so far the only place he'd gone was Africa during the war. "I'm always suggesting to the wife that we go to Madagascar or New Zealand."

"Would you like to go to Iceland?" I asked.

He shook his head. "Bit chilly for me."

"I wouldn't mind it," volunteered the boy. "I like the idea of dogs and sledges."

"I think that's Lapland," I said, "though they do have lots of snow."

After the boy got off, the man remarked, like the guard, that I was young to be travelling alone. "Couldn't your mum come with you?"

Living in the village, I had seldom had to deal with such questions. Now I said cheerfully that my parents were dead and I was an orphan.

The man's eyes widened, and he began to stammer out apologies. Quickly I reassured him that this had happened a long time ago. For the rest of the journey we played I-spy and I could see him pretending not to know the answers. We stopped at a town called Galashiels. Twenty minutes later we pulled into Hawick. Cautiously the man lowered my suitcase onto the platform and wished me luck. I waved as the train pulled away but he did not wave back.

When the train was out of sight I left my case and made my way to the front of the station. A maroon van was waiting. As I approached, a door opened. "You must be Hardy," said the man who climbed out. "I'm Mr. Milne."

"Gemma Hardy," I corrected, studying this first ambassador of the school. Mr. Milne was only a few inches taller than me and, with his large head of grey hair and his round belly, he resembled nothing so much as a garden gnome. His dungarees had many intriguing pockets and were very clean.

"Is this all you have?" he said when he saw my case. "Some girls bring everything but the kitchen sink."

Like my aunt, he made me sit in the back; unlike her, he talked to me. The town of Hawick, he said, was famous for its woolen mills. His wife worked at one that produced lovely cardigans; they cost a pretty penny. Then he told me how to get to the school and, thinking I would need to reverse this journey someday, I paid close attention. First we drove five miles to the village of Denholm. There we crossed the river Teviot and drove two more miles to the village of Minto. Claypoole had been the ancestral home of Lord and Lady Minto until both their sons died in the war, the older in North Africa, the younger on an Atlantic convoy. They had sold the estate in 1946 and moved to Edinburgh. The school was owned by Miss Bryant, the headmistress—Mr. Milne's voice underlined the name—and her sister-in-law, Mrs. Bryant, who'd been widowed a few years ago. "I've never known a woman," he said, "who can make a shilling go further."

When I left Yew House that morning there had been snow on the stony hills and frost whitening the fields. Here the hills were green and softly rounded, and the fields were surrounded by hedges rather than stone walls. Even the sheep were larger and cleaner. In Denholm crocuses and snowdrops bloomed in the gardens of the whitewashed cottages. On the far side of the Teviot a line of willows led to a crossroads; we turned right up a hill. Almost at the top we swerved into a driveway, past a little gingerbread house. "That's where we live," said Mr. Milne. "In the lodge."

The house that came into view around the next bend rewarded all my daydreaming. Claypoole was built of a pleasing light grey granite. The two wings of the school stood at right angles to each other and were linked by a curving balustrade supported by elegant pillars. Row after row of windows shone. Mr. Milne parked beside a flight of steps. These led down to the back door, which, he explained, I would normally use. Today, however, we would enter by the front door. He rang the bell and led me into a large oak-panelled hall. Several armchairs were grouped around the fireplace, and at the far end a beautiful, red-carpeted staircase spiralled up to a glass dome. How grand everything looked, and how comfortable. A girl, dressed in a green tunic and brown knee socks, appeared. I stared at her wonderingly while Mr. Milne asked her to tell Miss Bryant that the new working girl was here.

She hurried away through the nearest door and he pointed out the picture over the fireplace; it showed the house as it had been in 1900. "You can still see the remains of the carriage house," he was saying when something made me turn. A tall, grey-haired woman wearing a beautiful navy suit was descending the spiral stairs. Miss Bryant, I was to discover, liked to make an entrance. I glimpsed a high, bony forehead, an elegant nose, and scarlet lips, the upper unusually thin, the lower unusually full. Later I heard one girl claim that she was fifty; another that she was barely thirty. Both seemed plausible.

"Thank you, Mr. Milne," she said. "The suitcase goes to the Elm Room."

Without a backward glance he disappeared. "So you are Hardy," Miss Bryant continued. Her accent, like her age, was elusive, neither Scottish nor English but some blending of the two. "Your aunt has warned me that you are prone to lying and daydreaming. At Claypoole you will find that, between your lessons and your other duties, there is no time for either. You understand that you are here as a working pupil?"

"My aunt should have not said that."

"Stop glaring at me, and address me as Miss Bryant. Let me ask again: Do you understand that you are a working pupil?"

"Yes, Miss Bryant. But my aunt—"

"It is up to you to prove her wrong and to prove us right in offering you a place. Your work does not begin to pay for your board, let alone tuition. Ross will show you what to do. You'll start in Primary Seven on Monday."

I was about to blurt out my pleasure—I must have done exceptionally well in the exams to be moved up two years—when a tall, red-cheeked girl with a chest even more formidable than Louise's stepped into the hall.

"Ross, this is the new girl, Hardy. She will take over Montrose's duties."

Ross studied me, her glance shifting rapidly from my leather shoes to my pigtails. "Montrose minded the fires," she said. "This one won't be able to carry the scuttles."

I stood up straight and said I was strong for my age.

Ross smiled, not pleasantly; her two front teeth were longer than the others and one was chipped. Miss Bryant's expression did not change. "Arrange things as you see fit," she told Ross. "Be sure she works hard."

She departed with the same clip of heels and swish of skirts that had accompanied my aunt's entrances and exits. A moment later the chandelier and the wall sconces went out, leaving us in gloom. Ross seized my arm. "Got any grub?"

Before I could answer she plunged her free hand into my pockets, first left, then right, and triumphantly retrieved the chocolate biscuits. "My favourites. Come on. Let's dump your coat and you can start in the kitchen. I hope you're not a whiner."

"I don't whine," I said, trying to pull free. "Please let go of my arm."

She only tightened her grip.

SOON I WOULD DISCOVER that the main building of the school, like Gaul, had three regions. The hall where I had entered was in the grand part, which contained the dining-room, the library, several classrooms, and the rooms where the Bryants and the senior teachers lived. On the lower level was a warren of kitchens, cloakrooms, and, facing the garden, more classrooms. At the top of the house were the dormitories. But on that first day it was all confusion. Ross dragged me down a dark staircase and along a corridor to a room that smelled of shoes. She threw my coat on a peg, and dragged me along another corridor to the kitchen. Three broad-shouldered women—sisters, I later learned—and several girls were at work. Ross brought me before the largest of the women, who was standing at the stove, face flushed, bosom heaving, as she stirred a gigantic pot.

"Cook, here's the new girl. What should she do?"

"Potatoes," said Cook, without ceasing to stir.

In the scullery Ross handed me a grubby apron, tipped a mound of potatoes into the sink, and fetched two huge saucepans. Single-handed, I was to peel the potatoes for 120 people. I wrapped myself in the apron and set to work as Mrs. Marsden had taught me, washing each potato in the icy water, peeling it thinly (the vitamins were right below the skin), and carefully taking out the eyes. However many I peeled, the mound grew no smaller.

"Cripes," said Ross, "you're a slow-coach. These need to be on the stove by five sharp." She pointed to the clock over the door—it was already four-thirty—picked up a knife, and began to peel potatoes in a slap-dash fashion.

"What happened to Montrose?" I asked.

"You don't want to know."

I tried another line of questioning. "Are you an orphan too?"

Ross hooted with laughter. "Shut up and peel the frickin' potatoes."

CLAYPOOLE HAD BEEN BUILT to be occupied by a few lords and ladies waited on by an army of servants. Now the proportions were reversed; a dozen working girls struggled to take care of more than a hundred regular pupils, and the teachers. Happily the laundry was sent out, but we were entirely responsible for the housework and we helped to prepare and serve meals. All the food had to be transported by lift up one floor to the dining-room, where portraits of men and women in evening dress gazed down benignly on girls in ugly uniforms, eating ten to a table. I was not among them. My job was to carry out plates of food as fast as I could. At first I felt shy in my role as waitress—Ross had set me to serve the younger girls—but they ignored me except when I accidentally slammed down a plate. At last everyone was served, and Cook handed me my portion of mince, potatoes, and turnip. I sank onto a milk crate too exhausted to eat. Only my limp pigtails testified that my breakfast with Veronica had taken place hours, not weeks, ago.

"Get a move on," said Ross. "We clear the tables in five minutes."

"I'm not hungry."

"You'll get nothing else till breakfast and that's just bread and jam."

When I still didn't move she seized my plate and devoured the contents. I watched wonderingly. Whatever my tribulations at Yew House, meals had been a constant. Not so at Claypoole. Working girls got the last of everything. By the end of three days I had learned to eat at top speed. Someone was always hovering, ready to snatch whatever I left. Often I saw Ross and the other girls scooping food from the dirty plates the way I had done at Yew House for the dogs. But that evening all I wanted was to lie down and figure out how I had ended up here.

Before bed, however, came another Herculean task: the washing-up. A stout girl named Smith and I were assigned to the cutlery. "Hurry up," she kept saying, and ignored my requests for a clean tea towel. Only when every plate and every knife and fork had been washed and dried and the tables laid for breakfast did Ross lead me to the Elm Room. The other dormitories—Beech, Poplar, Pine, Willow, Holly, Maple, Oak, Birch, Fir, and Lime—were filled by age, but the working girls were housed together, although I was ten and Ross nearly seventeen. She led me up three flights of stairs, first the dark one we had come down, then a broader, more elegant flight to the floor where the regular pupils slept, then a narrower and steeper one. The Elm Room was just wide enough to accommodate two rows of beds beneath its sloping ceilings. By the light of a single bulb several girls were playing cards.

"Here's the new girl," said Ross.

"I'm Gemma." Despite my weariness, I longed to make a good impression.

A couple of the girls grunted and one—she had olive skin and sharp features—approached. "So this is what they got instead of Montrose. A little rat."

"Beggars can't be choosers," said Ross. "I doubt she'll last the year."

The girl gave my left pigtail a fierce tug and drifted back to the card-players.

Ross steered me to the bed by the door, the noisiest and draught-iest in the room. My school uniform was already lying there: a dark green tunic several sizes too large, a light green shirt clearly too small, a brown belt, and brown knee socks. Veronica would have gnashed her teeth at the sight of such ugly garments. The colours reflected the school crest: a brown acorn and a green oak leaf. The motto, predict-ably, was that small things lead to large ones.

While I unpacked into the small chest of drawers at the foot of my bed, Ross explained that Sunday was the easiest day of the week for working pupils. Serving breakfast was followed by church, followed by lunch, followed by cleaning the classrooms. Supper was an hour earlier so that we had a free hour before bed. I laid out my pyjamas and dressing-gown. Ross fingered the latter, a cast-off of Louise's made of nice, thick flannel. "Watch out for Findlayson," she said. "She'll have this off you in the bat of a pig's eye."

She picked up the dressing-gown and led me back downstairs. In the bathroom I washed my face and hands with cold water and bitter yel-low soap, and brushed my teeth. At the next basin Ross did the same, spitting out the toothpaste with gusto. Back upstairs the Elm Room was already dark. The school matron turned off the light at nine-thirty on the dot; only in case of fire or flood were we allowed to turn it on again. I undressed, glad to be shielded from the girls' scrutiny, and climbed into the narrow, lumpy bed.

Gone were the owls and the wind in the trees, my cousins' chatter and my aunt's laughter. The girl in the next bed was already snoring. Someone else was laughing, or perhaps crying. I heard floorboards creaking, and a muffled gasp. The thought that had come to me as I waited for the train in Edinburgh returned even more acutely; not one person in this room, or indeed within a hundred miles, wished me well. But on Monday there would be lessons. I would meet the teachers and the regular girls and start to make friends.

When the only sounds around me were sighs and snores, I climbed out of bed and, carrying my suitcase, tiptoed down the stairs. Locking myself in one of the toilets, I used my penknife to make a slit in the lining of the case and slipped my precious photographs into hiding.

chapter seven

I WOKE TO THE CLANG of a bell and the groans of the other working girls dragged from sleep. Rain was drumming on the roof, and in a bucket beside my bed, water pinged steadily. The uniform, as I had guessed, was a disaster. The buttons of the shirt gaped and the sleeves stopped several inches short of my wrists. Meanwhile the tunic slipped off my shoulders and hung well below my knees. The socks drooped. The tie was absurd. Only the cardigan fitted.

"Look what the cat dragged in," chortled the sharp-featured Findlayson.

Smith, the stout girl of last night's washing-up, giggled.

After the sparse breakfast Ross had predicted, the entire school walked to the village church under the supervision of the prefects. The Bryants drove in a sleek black car; the teachers followed in assorted vehicles. The rain was heavy, and before we reached the bend in the drive, my coat was soaked and my hair dripping. Everyone else had a raincoat with a hood. The girl next to me, her name was Gilchrist, hummed tunelessly and ignored my questions—how old are you? how far is it? what's your favourite subject?—until I fell silent. I soon understood why the older girls marched ahead. The radiators were at the front of the church where the parishioners sat, and the teachers and seniors occupied the pews immediately behind them. Then there were the younger girls. We working girls shivered in the rear. Wedged between Ross and Gilchrist, I was grateful for their warmth.

My uncle had given lively sermons, often drawing on recent events, and led the hymn singing in his pleasant tenor voice. His successor, Mr. Cockburn, had been inferior in every way, but his sermons had been brief, his singing passable. Now, as the organ started to play, a large man, his surplice like a tent, mounted the pulpit. Mr. Waugh did not even pretend to sing the first hymn. As soon as it ended he shouted, "Let us pray," and proceeded to yell requests at the heavens.

The sermon too was delivered at full volume. The text was the commandment to honour thy mother and father, and Mr. Waugh explained what one should do if they weren't available, namely, honour one's minister, one's teachers, and grown-ups in general. And how should one do this? Why, by working hard, doing as one was told, never speaking out of turn, being clean and neat. On my left Ross dozed; on my right Gilchrist fidgeted; overhead the church clock chimed. Mr. Waugh began his sermon soon after ten-thirty and was still going strong at eleven-fifteen. My feet went from cold to numb. Standing for the closing hymn I stumbled and, save for my companions, would have fallen.

Outside it was still raining. Almost trotting, Ross led us working girls back to the school. We were passing the lodge when the Bryants' car swept by, spraying us with water. In the kitchen a woman wearing a yellow raincoat, whom I'd spotted near the front of the church, was waiting to address us.

"Girls," said Mrs. Bryant, with a broad smile, "one of our governors is coming to lunch. Cook has made something delicious, and I want everyone to put her best foot forward. Clean aprons all round." Clipboard in hand, she continued to issue instructions. "And you, new girl," she concluded, "get a uniform that fits and stop slamming the plates on the table."

Mrs. Bryant, I soon learned, had perfected the art of using a single expression—a smile—to convey a whole range of emotions: rage, disapproval, anger, boredom, sarcasm. Only when she was with her sister-in-law did her face relax into a kind of vacancy, which perhaps signalled genuine pleasure.

Lunch passed, mercifully, without incident. For the rest of the day I swept corridors of which I could not see the end, and mopped floors, which looked just as dirty when I finished. My only brief respite was dusting the library. Later I would overhear parents who were being shown around exclaim over this book-lined room with its tall windows, but working girls weren't allowed to use it. When Ross discovered me reading *The Thirty-Nine Steps* she moved me to scrubbing bathrooms. Still I clung to the idea that tomorrow lessons would begin, and, thanks to Mrs. Bryant, Matron issued me a new uniform.

The sole adult living among the dormitories, Matron had no eyebrows—she drew them on each morning—and almost no capacity for surprise. Only utter mayhem could make her look up from the romances she read incessantly, and almost nothing could make her finish a sentence. "I don't see what . . . ," she said, surveying my drooping tunic. "But if Mrs. Bryant . . ."

She led me to a wardrobe filled with tunics and intimated that I should choose the two that fit me best and were in the best repair. Then she produced two shirts only a little too large. As for the socks, I would have to use garters. Finally she handed me an Alice band.

ON MONDAY MORNING ROSS detailed Findlayson to take me to Primary 7. She led me to a classroom on the lower floor, knocked once, and, with a quick grin, ran off down the corridor. "Come in," said a voice. I stepped inside to see the teacher at her desk, writing. While I waited for her to acknowledge me I examined the rows of girls. Even beyond the uniform, they looked oddly similar. Each girl's hair, I realised, irrespective of length, was scraped back, like my own, in an Alice band. Only at weekends were girls allowed to wear their hair as they wished.

At last the teacher raised her head. "Who are you?"

"I'm Gemma Hardy."

"And what class do you think you're in?"

"Primary Seven."

"Two doors down," she said, and returned to her writing.

Closing the door I saw the label, PRIMARY 6, and understood, yet again, that I must be on my guard at all times. At my knock the door of Primary 7 flew open. Beside the blackboard stood a woman wearing a black gown, holding a pointer. Like Mr. Milne, Mrs. Harris had neither neck nor waist; a small sphere, her head, was balanced on a larger sphere, her body. She asked the same question as the last teacher; once again I introduced myself.

"Hardy, you're five minutes late." Her voice was surprisingly high-pitched.

"I went to the wrong classroom."

"I am not interested in excuses. Bring the late sign, Andrews."

A girl rose from the front row, went to a box in the corner, and returned carrying a piece of cardboard emblazoned with the word LATE. She slipped the string over my head and I was made to stand at the front of the room for the first period: arithmetic. My cheeks were burning but I did my best to focus on the sums Mrs. Harris was writing on the board. Several times I raised my hand to answer a question; she never looked in my direction. The bell rang for second period and she gestured to an empty desk in the front row.

"Turn to page twenty-seven of your English books."

I raised my hand again. "I don't have a book."

"What a nuisance you are, working girl. Share with Balfour for this period. At break she'll take you to fetch your books."

Reluctantly the girl at the next desk slid over. Mrs. Harris stood at the blackboard parsing sentences, asking questions round the room. At last her head swiveled towards me. "Give the rules for using a semi-colon."

I knew a semicolon was a combination of a comma and a full stop, but I had no idea when to use one. "My old school hadn't got to that yet," I said.

"First late, now a dunce."

"It's not my fault we did things differently."

Suddenly Mrs. Harris was standing over me. She bent down so that her large face was inches from mine. Except for a single crease beneath each small dark eye, her skin was very smooth. "What did I say?"

"First late, now a dunce?"

"No." Her eyes grew still smaller. "When you first arrived what did I tell you?"

"You're not interested in excuses."

"Exactly. No one cares about where you went to school before today. You must catch up as quickly as possible. You're a working girl, aren't you?"

"Yes, Mrs. Harris."

Her chin sank into her gown and emerged again like that of a tor-toise. "Girls, we've never had a working girl in Primary Seven before. We must do our best to educate her. Andrews, you know which card to get. Balfour, the rules for using a semicolon, please."

Balfour reeled them off, or so I gathered from Mrs. Harris's ap-proving nod. Standing once again at the front of the room, this time with the card DUNCE around my neck, I was too miserable to listen. Most of the girls—I counted fourteen—ignored me, but one girl in the third row gazed at me steadily. Her brown hair stuck out untidily beneath her Alice band and her velvety eyes reminded me of Celeste's.

Another bell rang, and Balfour led the way down the corridor at breakneck speed. Later I discovered she was a vigilante on the hockey pitch.

"Why is everyone's hair the same?" I asked as I trotted behind her.

"It's a school rule, ever since a girl set fire to her hair with a Bunsen burner."

"Is Balfour your Christian name?"

"Idiot. Miss Bryant thinks that calling us by our surnames is better for discipline. Like in boys' schools."

I could have happily spent the day in the book room, with its brimming shelves, but Balfour led me to the section marked PRIMARY 7 and started handing me books pell-mell: English, grammar, scripture, geography, history, arithmetic, nature, writing. Several of the books were tattered; one fell into two parts. As Balfour reached for another copy, the bell rang. "Hurry," she said. "If we're late Mrs. Harris will kill us."

We ran down the corridor, each clutching an armful of books and reached the classroom just as our teacher turned the corner. Everyone stood as she came into the room. The next subject was geography, and to my relief the topic was fiords, which I had studied last year, but the lesson had barely begun when there was a knock at the door and Ross appeared.

As I SOON LEARNED, working girls were the lowest form of life at Claypoole. We were constantly being taken out of lessons to prepare meals and then being punished for being late for class, or for not finishing our homework. Mrs. Harris seldom called on me and barely heard when I gave the correct answer. I knew the other working girls experienced the same treatment but, it seemed to me, with greater cause. Several of them could barely read the hymns we sang each morning in assembly.

The regular fee-paying pupils were mostly from middle-class families; many had parents who worked abroad in Hong Kong or Nigeria or Kenya. While I cooked and cleaned and slept in one-twelfth of a bare, leaky room, they lived in a much more comfortable fashion. Their dormitories had radiators, rugs on the floor, and pictures on the walls. Their doors closed. They received parcels of food. On Saturdays they wore their own clothes and were allowed to go to the shops in Denholm. These differences made friendship between a regular pupil and a working girl virtually impossible. A girl who failed to say please or thank you to Cook had to write out a hundred times, "I will be polite to Cook," but anyone could say anything to us.

Even the regular pupils, however, were carefully monitored. The school grounds were surrounded by a high wall; no one could come in or out without permission. Nor was it easy to communicate with the outside world. The only telephones belonged to Miss Bryant and Matron. Every Sunday evening an hour was given over to letter writing, but the letters had to be put, unsealed, in the mailbox in the hall. Girls who wrote anything critical about Claypoole soon found themselves in Miss Bryant's office.

Of course a few people knew about the school—Mr. Donaldson, after all, had warned me—but private schools were not subject to inspection, and Miss Bryant was very skillful in managing her educational experiment. The working girls were presented as a stroke of philanthropic genius. Here was a way to give scholarships to a dozen girls. The school would raise us up to be hospital orderlies or maids or, like one star former pupil, work for the post office. The entrance exams I'd prided myself on passing were irrelevant. I could have claimed that Moses gave the Sermon on the Mount and Henry VIII invaded Scotland; once my aunt had determined to send me to Claypoole, my fate was sealed. Pupils were cheaper than maids. The other working girls were the daughters of farmers, factory workers, or disabled soldiers. Several, like Ross, came from homes that made being at the school a relief. Their main recreation was to periodically, for no obvious reason, gang up on one of their number. For several days they would play tricks on the victim, ambush her in the bathroom, sing stupid rhymes, make fun of her bra and a mysterious article of clothing called a sanitary belt. Then, just as suddenly, the attacks would cease. Presently a new victim would be chosen.

The week after I arrived, Drummond was the victim. A stolid girl with beautiful red hair, she was almost as old as Ross but much less forceful. Even the simplest question—is it still raining?—brought her to a standstill. Now I watched, mesmerised, as the girls surrounded her and undid her shirt.

"Look, Hardy," called Ross, "this is a bra. And this"—I glimpsed pale skin, a nipple—"is what's under a bra."

Drummond shrieked and half-a-dozen girls pulled her to the floor and fell on her, tickling and pinching. All I could see were two feet in brown socks, kicking. As quietly as possible I climbed into bed and pulled the covers over my head. At last Matron came to turn out the light.

"Girls," she said mildly, " . . . detention."

If such a thing were to happen to me, I thought, I would die, but the next morning I saw Drummond laughing with another girl as she knotted her tie. I was staring at her in amazement when Ross sidled up. "Got an eyeful last night, didn't you?" she said.

"Why doesn't she report you?"

Ross grabbed my wrist and bent my arm behind my back. "What do you think happened to Montrose?" she demanded.

THE FOLLOWING DAY DRUMMOND was in charge of taking me to feed the pigs. We carried the buckets of scraps across the small stream at the back of the school and past the tennis courts. Just beyond was an enclosure with five pigs. They rushed over, grunting, as we emptied the slops into their trough. Drummond jumped back, but I leaned across the fence to scratch their woody skin. They were the nicest beings I had met at Claypoole.

Walking back to the kitchen, I asked Drummond why she didn't report the girls.

"What for?" she said, eyebrows raised.

"For taking off your clothes, tickling you."

"It's all in fun." She swung the empty bucket. "They didn't hurt me."

"But"—I did not know how to voice the shame that must surely accompany such an attack—"they held you down. They took off your bra."

"Look," said Drummond, "there's a rabbit. My foster parents kept rabbits. Did yours keep anything?"

"No," I said.

The rabbit twitched its nose and hopped away. If only I had a friend, I thought, just one, the school would not be so bad. We would hide in the library and build secret huts and visit the pigs. Among the girls I had met so far there seemed no possibilities, but perhaps next term another working girl, close to my age, would join the school. Clinging to this prospect, I followed Drummond across the bridge. Only much later did I understand that my arrival at Claypoole had coincided with the great tide of changes sweeping postwar Britain: attitudes to children were shifting; the British Empire was dwindling; working girls were already hard to come by.

chapter eight

Every weekday at Claypoole began with assembly in the library. While the teachers sat along one wall, the girls lined up by class to sing a hymn, listen to a lesson, say the Lord's Prayer, and hear any announcements. Miss Bryant presided over the occasion from a dais at the front; at the back, beneath a portrait of Lord Minto, the music teacher, or one of her senior pupils, played the piano. The whole affair took less than ten minutes, except for those unfortunate days when Mr. Waugh strode in just as we said amen and delivered an impromptu sermon. Afterwards, if his duties permitted, he would visit a class. I had been at the school for a fortnight when he flung open the door of Primary 7.

Scripture, like arithmetic, was a subject where I felt confident. I knew the Gospels thoroughly and was acquainted with Genesis and Job. On the day of Mr. Waugh's visit we were studying the parable of the talents. A master, going on a journey, gives ten talents to one servant, five to another, and one to a third. The first two servants invest and multiply their talents; the third buries his single coin for safekeeping. When the master returns he praises the first two and, to my fury, scolds the third and takes away his talent. My uncle had claimed that the parable was not about money but about the gifts we'd each been given—whether for recognising a willow-warbler, or baking a Victoria sponge—and about how not using them was a sin. Still I argued that the third servant was just following instructions, protecting his master's property; the other servants, with more talents, could afford to take risks. My uncle had quoted me in his sermon.

We stood while Mr. Waugh offered another lengthy prayer. Then he asked a girl in the second row to read the parable. As Kendall stumbled through the verses, I watched the veins in his nose swell and the buttons of his jacket grow alarmingly taut.

"Mrs. Harris," he said, "this girl reads like a five-year-old."

"Yes, sir. Elocution isn't part of the curriculum. I'll make sure she practises."

I was smugly registering that she had made an excuse when Mr. Waugh asked for another reader. I raised my hand.

"Sir," said Mrs. Harris quickly, "she's a working girl."

"She can't be worse than the last one. I will stop her after a verse or two if she's hopeless. Stand up, girl."

I stood, and in my best voice read the parable. Mr. Waugh's buttons relaxed. When I finished he said, "Competent. Sit down," and began to expound on the importance of servants—and weren't all children servants?—doing what was asked of them promptly and cheerfully. I raised my hand again and, when he inclined his head, repeated the arguments I had offered my uncle about the third servant.

"Come here, working girl."

I approached, my head almost level with the buckle of his overworked belt.

"Face your classmates."

I did and found fourteen pairs of eyes fixed on me. No, thirteen. The girl who had watched me sympathetically when I wore the label DUNCE was studying her Bible.

"Here, girls, you see what it is like to receive no education. The mind, without guidance, cannot grasp the principles of right and wrong.

This girl cannot receive the truth even when it is offered. Doubtless her parents were illiterate, perhaps even criminals, and—"

"That's not true. My parents were both very educated and my uncle was a minister like—"

Mr. Waugh seized my shoulders and shook me until my teeth chattered. When at last he stopped, I sank to the floor. Standing over me, he proclaimed that although young and small I was already filled with sin. "Can you tell me which sin?" he said.

"Ignorance," called out one classmate. "Pride," called another.

"Ignorance is not a sin and can be forgiven, but pride is one of the worst. Anything else?"

"Blasphemy, sir," said Balfour. I recognised her smarmy tone.

Mr. Waugh clapped his hands. "Exactly. When you argue with a minister, you are arguing with God's representative. What could be more blasphemous? Jesus tells his listeners what the story means, but this girl is deaf to His explanation. Any other sins?"

While I stared at the floorboards, a few girls made suggestions, which Mr. Waugh repudiated. Then he announced, triumphantly, one final sin: lying. My uncle was not a minister, or if he was, he had never held such views. Of all sins lying was the worst, for it was the foundation of the devil's house. The working girl was a liar. As he uttered this last sentence, something hard pressed against my ribs: the toe of his shoe.

"Mrs. Harris," said a small, breathless voice. "I need to get my inhaler."

"Sir, excuse me. MacIntyre, go with Goodall to make sure she's all right."

The girls stepped past me, and in doing so forced Mr. Waugh to step back. Perhaps it occurred to him that a large minister trampling a small girl was not a pretty spectacle. He told me to get up, and go and wash my face.

For the rest of that morning I stood at the front of the room, a sign saying LIAR around my neck. At one point my knees shook so hard that a couple of girls in the front row started to giggle, but the girl with the brown eyes came up to ask Mrs. Harris a question about the composition. As she passed me she smiled, and on the way back to her desk— "You already know that, Goodall"—she smiled again. She walked, I noticed, with a slight limp.

THAT NIGHT IN BED I gave way to despair. After all that had happened since I left Yew House, I was still only ten years old, still less than five feet tall. My journey south had shown me how conspicuous I was as a child travelling alone. And now I was utterly friendless. Even my memories of my uncle, without the familiar landscapes to frame them, were less vivid. I recalled again that last afternoon when he had invited me to go skating. "Fancy a spin on the ice?" he had said. But I had stayed behind to build a fort with Veronica. A sob escaped me.

"Shut up," a voice hissed.

"Stow it," said someone else. A floorboard creaked menacingly.

I shut up.

The next morning at assembly I was made to stand before the entire school while Miss Bryant asked God to help me improve. Now everyone, I thought, even the girls I hadn't met, believed me to be a liar. Any last hope I had of making friends was doomed. But later that day one of the prefects, a plump girl who often played the piano at morning assembly, smiled at me in the corridor, and at lunch Cook gave me an extra portion of shepherd's pie and settled me near her at the kitchen table. As I ate, I caught a whiff of cigarette smoke—she smoked a pack a day—and suddenly I remembered I was not utterly friendless. On Sunday, when we had our precious free hour, I would make use of the notepad and envelopes Mr. Donaldson had given me.

Claypoole School
Minto
The Borders

Sunday, 15 March 1959

Dear Mr. Donaldson,
 This is a terrible place. I am sorry I didn't listen to you and fail my exams although the school would have taken me anyway. All they wanted was another scullery maid. I spend most of my time peeling potatoes. We are like servants, only worse, and the teachers are sure we're stupid. Most of the other working girls talk like Betty, the maid at Yew House, and they are stupid. They're older than me and a couple can't even read.
 I would run away if I had a home to run to, or any money, but even if I could make my way to Yew House, my aunt would send me back. Please will you come and get me as soon as possible.

Yours very sincerely,
Gemma Hardy

Only as I sealed the envelope did I realise that I had no way to post it. I could not put it in the box in the hall, and we did not pass a pillar-box on our way to church. The older girls went to the village on Saturday afternoons, but they were strangers. For several days I kept the letter in my arithmetic book. Then it occurred to me that I could ask Mr. Milne to post it. He always winked at me as he dropped off groceries in the kitchen. Surely it would be no trouble to slip an envelope into one of the many pockets of his dungarees. The next day I waited for him to leave the kitchen.

"Mr. Milne dropped this," I said, holding up a piece of paper.

"Well, don't just stand there," said Cook. "Run and give it to him."

He was halfway up the back steps when I called his name. "Did Cook forget something?" he said.

Framed by the dark yews that lined the steps, his grey eyebrows drawn together, he looked more like a fierce goblin than a friendly gnome, but this was my one chance. "I'm Hardy, the new working girl," I reminded him. "You met me at the station last month."

He gave a brief nod; I plunged on. "Would you post this letter? It's my uncle's birthday tomorrow and I missed the collection."

Mr. Milne's eyebrows parted. "Give it here," he said. "I'll make sure it goes in the two o'clock post." Just as I had hoped, he put the letter in the top pocket of his dungarees.

That night I fell asleep picturing Mr. Donaldson reading the letter over breakfast, clicking his yellow teeth and making a plan. But I knew the ways of adults; I was patient in my imagining. It was already Thursday. Even if he got the letter in time, he wouldn't come this Saturday. But the next, I calculated, nine days away, for sure.

As if sensing my imminent departure, Claypoole began to show its better side. Our dormitory was less frigid. Daffodils and pussy willow lined the school drive, and our Sunday walk to and from church became a pleasure. Mrs. Harris made a joke in geography about temperate climes. In only a fortnight, Ross told me, the regular pupils would go home for Easter and we working girls would spring-clean the school and tidy up the garden. We were crossing the playing fields as she spoke, on our way to clean the gym.

"Look," I said, pointing with the mop I was carrying. "There's a magpie."

"What's a magpie?"

"That black and white bird with the long tail. They eat the eggs of other birds."

"A bird? I thought from the way you spoke you'd found half a crown."

A week ago her sarcasm might have silenced me; now I didn't care. "And that"—I waved my mop again—"is an oyster-catcher. They usually live by the sea." Ross remarked that the bird's orange legs made it look like Miss Gibson, the French teacher.

THE FOLLOWING WEDNESDAY AT assembly Miss Bryant said, "Form Five will leave for lacrosse at two o'clock today. Hardy, come to my study after first period."

I hung my head to hide my delight. Mr. Donaldson had written; perhaps he was already on his way. Fortunately the first period was arithmetic, and even in my distracted state, I was able to solve the problems. As soon as the bell rang I asked to be excused. Several times I had swept the corridor outside Miss Bryant's study. Now, as I stood before her white door, the brass doorknob shone so brightly that I could see my tiny curved self in its sphere. I knocked boldly; a voice bade me enter. Inside a beautiful blue carpet led to a mahogany desk. With luck I would never see Miss Bryant again. Still, after a hasty glance, I did not dare to look at her directly.

For several seconds she studied me in unblinking silence. "So," she said, "you have an uncle called Mr. Donaldson. Your aunt was surprised to hear that."

She picked up an envelope from a pile of papers. It looked like my letter but so, I reminded myself, would any letter of Mr. Donaldson's. "Mr. Milne," she went on, "gave me this last week."

"But he said he'd put it in the two o'clock post." In my indignation I at last looked up; I saw her eyes narrow, her lips, thin and full, tighten.

"Mr. Milne has worked for me long enough to know that pupils don't always act in their own best interests. Why else would you try to send a letter secretly? You are not the first working girl to find the rules hard."

I understood then her mastery of the situation. For five days she had allowed my hopes of rescue to grow, knowing that my disappointment would be all the greater.

She handed me the letter. "Read it."

My mouth was suddenly so dry that my lips stuck to my teeth. Sounding like Kendall, I stammered out my sentences. When I had finished, Miss Bryant rose from behind her desk. Noiseless on the thick carpet, she circled the room.

"You think Claypoole doesn't care about exams," she said softly. "You are wrong. You wouldn't be here, none of the working girls would be, if our examining board had not judged you teachable. Perhaps in your case they made a mistake. Exams do not capture the moral life. When I spoke to your aunt I told her you might be too tough a nut for us to crack. Would you like to know what she said?"

She cocked her head, as if I had a choice. "She said, 'Miss Bryant, under no circumstances can I have that girl back. My children aren't safe under the same roof. If she can't stay at Claypoole, she must go to an orphanage.' These are strong words, and I take them seriously. You are small for your age, but you are a rebel. Even now"—she continued her steady circling—"I can feel you arguing with me. You forget that you don't know everything, or indeed much of anything. Your letter could have harmed Mr. Milne. Certainly it has harmed Mr. Donaldson. Your aunt has talked to the headmaster of the school, and Mr. Donaldson will be let go at the end of term. Doubtless much of your relationship with him is imaginary, but it is up to teachers to contain the imaginations of their pupils. Apparently there were problems at his last school. It will not be easy for him to find another position."

I pictured Mr. Donaldson's expression when I had appeared at his door and knew she spoke the truth. "Please, Miss Bryant," I said, "none of this is Mr. Donaldson's fault. He didn't even get my letter."

Miss Bryant paused in her orbit near my left elbow. "Did I ask you to speak?"

"It is everyone's duty to speak when they see injustice." It was something my uncle used to say, and quoting him made me feel stronger. "Mr. Donaldson needs a job. He's not rich. Please," I said. "I'll do anything."

"Right now," said Miss Bryant, "you will be quiet, but I am glad you understand that you made a bad mistake in writing that naughty letter. Let me remind you of some facts. You are ten years old. You have been here for five weeks. Mrs. Harris does not have one good thing to say about you. Ross says you are lazy and careless. Only Cook claims you are helpful. So for the remainder of term you will work in the kitchen. During the Easter holidays you'll be assigned extra tasks. If throughout this period you work hard you will be allowed to rejoin Primary Seven after the holidays. Most likely, though, you will fail the exams in June and be kept back a year. Do you understand?"

I did not. I was so upset about Mr. Donaldson that I had barely heard a word. "Punish me as much as you want, Miss Bryant," I said, "but please let Mr. Donaldson keep his job." I fell to my knees and clasped my hands.

She gave a small sigh, like the sound of a swing door closing. "You still don't understand. Mr. Donaldson has already lost his job, and you will do what I say."

"And what if I don't? What will you do then? Kill me?"

For a few seconds Miss Bryant's mask cracked—I glimpsed amusement or perhaps surprise—then, once again, she was impervious. "This is the temper your aunt warned me about," she said. "You think yourself hard done by, but you forget you have shelter, food, clothing. To give you a glimpse of how much you still have to lose, for the next fortnight you will have nothing to eat but bread and water. You are dismissed."

I thought about touching my forehead to the carpet, practising patient opposition like Gandhi, but I knew that nothing I said, or did, would make a difference. My pleading interested her; it did not move her. She sat down at her desk and turned to her next task. The carpet swallowed my fourteen footsteps. I opened the door as quietly as possible.

Outside Ross was leaning against the wall, arms folded. "Someone's been a bad girl, very bad, I'd guess, from how long she kept you."

"Why do you stay here?" I asked as she led me towards the stairs. "You're almost a grown-up. You could leave, get a job."

She did not answer, and I thought she too was going to ignore me, but halfway down the stairs, where no one could come upon us unexpectedly, she stopped and turned to me. With a stair between us, her face was level with mine. "I did leave once," she said, "a couple of years ago." She had hitchhiked to Edinburgh, sleeping one night in a sheepfold on the moors, and tried to find work in a hotel or a shop, but everyone wanted references. Her shoulders hunched as she relived her unhappy experiences. "I even tried"—her voice grew still lower—"to be a pros-ti-tute but I didn't have a clue how to go about it."

For a moment I had no idea what she was talking about. Then I understood she had meant to do that terrible thing I read about in books: sell herself. Staring into her muddy brown eyes, I briefly forgot my own troubles. If she had been short of sympathy, so had I. She was awkward, plain, slow at book learning, and she knew those things about herself. She was as much alone in the world as I was and she had never, even for a few years, experienced the kind of love I had had from my uncle.

"Next year," she went on, "when I'm eighteen Miss Bryant will give me a reference. I can work as a chambermaid."

"Is that what you want to do?"

"Who'd want to be a chambermaid?" Her chipped tooth glinted. "So did you have a plan?"

"I thought there was someone who would help me, but all I did was get him in trouble. Miss Bryant says he's going to lose his job."

"Girls have to watch it. We can get blokes into trouble just like that." She snapped her fingers. "Mr. Milne is here because there was a fuss about a girl at his last job. And some of the other staff have had wee accidents. That's how they ended up at Claypoole."

Listening to Ross, I understood how clever Miss Bryant was; like Nero or Claudius, she had created her own empire of fear and favour. "Will you help me send a letter?" I said. "I can't bear to think of Mr. Donaldson being fired and not even knowing why."

It was as if I had hurled a brick. "You're nuts," Ross spat. "Stark, raving bonkers." She seized my arm and dragged me down the remaining stairs to the kitchen.

For the rest of the day I was so busy doing Cook's bidding that I scarcely had a moment to think. Not until I was lying in bed, my bones aching with fatigue, did it occur to me that Mr. Donaldson had come to the village only to teach; when he lost his job he would leave. He and my box would vanish. I really was alone in the world.

chapter nine

Miss Bryant was right. My previous life had had its meagre pleasures. Now, when the other working girls went off to lessons, I was left to scour ovens, scrub pans, grate cheese, and chop onions. Mr. Milne, as he came and went, always greeted me loudly. I stifled the impulse to punch his belly and looked straight past him. Only the pigs, to whom I carried the slops morning and evening, were pleased to see me. I named them after my favourite characters: Anne, Heidi, Pippi, Thumbelina, Katie. While they ate, I leaned over the fence to scratch their rough skin but I couldn't linger long. Throughout the day, usually when I least expected her, Mrs. Bryant appeared with her axelike smile, ready to find fault and hurry me on to the next task.

Besides the endless work, the other part of my punishment was to spend hours each day surrounded by the fragrance of fried onions and baked puddings. As I ate my bread and water, I reminded myself of the stories I had read in Will's comics about prisoners who had been forced to eat their shoes, or things found crawling under logs. All these deprivations, however, were trivial compared with my concern for Mr. Donaldson, and the knowledge that I was falling further and further behind in my studies.

On Tuesday afternoon Mrs. Bryant dispatched me to clean the windows in the library. There were six of them, stretching floor to ceiling, the upper panes far out of reach, but I had learned not to question my duties. I was kneeling by the first one, wearily rubbing the glass, when a voice said, "Hello."

I jumped to my feet, afraid I had been caught in yet another crime, and found myself facing the girl who had interrupted Mr. Waugh. Her pale skin only made her eyes look larger and darker. Several strands of thick brown hair had escaped her Alice band, and a greyish stain marked the bodice of her tunic. When she stepped closer, I saw that she favoured her right leg. "I'm Miriam," she said, holding out her hand. "You're Gemma, aren't you?"

"How did you know?" No one had used my Christian name since I left Yew House.

"You told us the day you arrived. I agree with what you said about the third servant. People shouldn't be punished for no reason." She was still offering her hand. Slowly I held out mine. "You're cold," she said. "You poor thing." She began to rub my chilly fingers with her warm ones.

"I'm a working girl," I said quickly, wanting to fend off any misunderstanding.

"I know." Her brown eyes didn't waver. "I'm sorry you have to work so hard. It doesn't seem fair."

"What are you doing here?"

"I can't do gym"—she gestured towards her leg—"so I have library duty. I check to make sure the books are in alphabetical order. It's just something to keep me busy."

"How old are you?"

"Thirteen, nearly fourteen. I was ill for a year, and then I did badly on arithmetic. That's why I'm older than the other girls. How old are you?"

When I said nearly eleven, Miriam nodded and said she thought so. "It would never do to have a working girl in Primary Six. You seem very good at sums."

So even my being moved up two years—how pleased I had been when Miss Bryant broke that news—was part of her scheme. But

Miriam's smile dulled my dismay. "I am good at sums," I said, "but in other subjects I'm falling further behind every day. I'll never catch up."

"Yes, you will. The holidays are nearly here, and you'll see, everyone slacks off. I'll help you. Now we'd better get back to work. Mrs. B. often comes to check on me. She knows I'm easily distracted."

I wanted to ask more questions: Why would she be at Claypoole in the holidays? Would she really help me? But she limped away to the far corner of the room and set to work as if alone; I followed her example. I was polishing the fourth window when the door opened quietly. Mrs. Bryant liked to steal around in the hope of catching wrong-doers. Miriam and I both curtseyed.

"Back to work, girls." Smiling silently, she observed our handiwork before offering advice. "Goodall, it will go faster if you pull out all the books that are out of order first. Hardy, has no one taught you to clean windows? The edges must be done thoroughly. You'll need a kitchen stool for the upper ones. But even with a stool," she added, "you are too small. You should not have been given this task."

She uttered this last remark as if some stranger had sent me to the library. After making a note on her clipboard, she told me to finish the current window and go and clean the music room. As soon as the door closed, I whispered to Miriam, "Will you really help me catch up?"

"Yes, but please don't talk now. You'll get us both in trouble."

If sorrows never come singly, perhaps that is also true of acts of kindness. That evening Cook summoned me to put the food away. It was a task normally performed by older girls, and I felt additionally persecuted when she handed me a tray of eggs and led the way to the larder, a locked room at the back of the kitchen. But as I set the eggs on the shelf, I smelled a familiar fragrance. There sat a steaming bowl of stew.

"Look what you found," said Cook. "The idea of giving a girl your age nothing to eat all day. I'll be back in five minutes."

She stepped out of the room. As the door closed behind her my heart began to race—the larder was no bigger than the sewing-room—but I perched on a crate of onions and tried to eat slowly. My uncle had told me that prisoners or castaways when rescued often ate too fast and became sick. The stew was a standard at the school, and the regular girls complained about the turnips and greyish meat, but I savoured every mouthful.

MIRIAM'S DESCRIPTION OF THE holidays proved correct. The Bryants disappeared to their house in the nearby town of Coldstream, and most of the other teachers left to visit relatives and friends. Several of the working girls, including the dreaded Findlayson, also went home. The rest of us were allowed to mingle more freely with the few regular pupils, like Miriam, who stayed at the school. Ross organised the spring-cleaning every morning. Later in the day, if it was fine, she made up teams for rounders and hockey. While these games were in progress Miriam and I would sit over our books in the common room. She was not a great scholar, but she was a patient teacher and made sure that I understood each lesson. She forced me to recite the two Shakespeare sonnets they'd studied in English until I was word-perfect. When she was satisfied with my efforts she showed me the scales she knew on the piano.

In return I tutored her in arithmetic. She was afraid of numbers the way some people are of spiders. The sight of them made her want to hide. What I loved about them, their clarity, was for her duplicity. Behind an innocent 2, or 5, or 9, she spied a mass of traps and pitfalls. Mrs. Harris had told her she was stupid so often that she had given up trying to work through even the simplest problem and instead guessed wildly, expecting to be wrong. I tried to be as patient with her as she was with me.

Sometimes as we studied, Ross loitered nearby, and once when we were doing long division I asked her to join us. I knew from watching her attempts to double a recipe for Cook that she struggled with both reading and arithmetic. "I did this stuff ages ago," she said, but she sat down at the table. Miriam slid over a page torn from her notebook and a pencil. I set a problem, 132 divided by 11, which I knew they would both find hard. Miriam managed to take 11 from 13. Ross chewed the end of the pencil.

"Come on, Ross," I said smugly. "What's the first step?"

"I don't need to learn your stupid baby sums." Flinging down the pencil, she ran from the room.

"Good riddance," I said as the door banged behind her.

But Miriam's eyes grew wide. "She scares me."

From my first day at the school Ross had dominated my life. She bullied me in small ways, telling me to hurry up, not to be such an idiot, and she protected me in large ones. I had never stopped to wonder what I had done to earn her attention, nor whether she might want anything in return. Now I assured Miriam that there was nothing to worry about; like the rest of us, Ross hated Miss Bryant; she had even tried to run away.

"I remember that," said Miriam. "She looked so hang-dog when the police brought her back. Still, people don't always say what they mean."

"So," I prompted, "eleven from thirteen leaves two?"

MIRIAM TOO HAD LOST her mother, although not until the summer she was four. I envied her her hazy memories of being sung to sleep and of tending some tall blue flowers in the garden. Since then she had been brought up by her father, a livestock auctioneer. They lived in Galashiels, the town I had seen from the train.

"All the farmers say that if anyone can get you a fair price for a cow it's Goodall. He likes cattle more than children."

He had enrolled her at Claypoole when she was eight, the autumn after she broke her leg. She'd been visiting a farm with him when a horse kicked her.

"I hate horses," I said. "Big, stupid animals. Did it hurt?"

Miriam smiled. "I like that you hate them too. Half the girls here are horse-mad. At first it didn't hurt much more than the time I fell off the garden wall, but it got worse each day instead of better."

Her father, she explained, was afraid of doctors—he insisted they'd killed her mother—and he hadn't taken her to one until she finally collapsed on the stairs. "He felt terrible when they showed him the X-ray. I was on crutches for four months."

She went home only twice a year, for a week at Christmas and two weeks around her birthday in July. Don't you mind? I asked, but she said no. The house was freezing, her father was mostly gone, and she'd come home from her first term at Claypoole to find that her beloved spaniel, Spencer, had been put to sleep. She looked so sad as she said this last part that I told her one of Mrs. Marsden's stories about a selkie, a seal-woman. "She had brown hair and brown eyes like you," I said. "Her name was Selina and she applied to be a housekeeper to a man with one daughter."

MIRIAM WAS ALMOST FOUR inches taller than me, and three years older, but most of the time I forgot these differences, and I was sure she did too. One evening, though, when I described my aunt and how she'd gradually banished me from the family, Miriam suggested she might be jealous. "Like Titania with Oberon," she said. We had been reading *A Midsummer Night's Dream*.

"Jealous? What could she be jealous of? I didn't have a changeling boy, or anything else she wanted." I scratched my calf, wiped my forehead. How could Miriam be so mistaken?

"I'm only guessing," she said calmly. "As you get older, Gemma, you'll understand things that don't make sense now. Think how much you've changed since you left Iceland. You're going to change that much again in the next ten years."

She had never before pointed out my youth, and I was stung. "I'll be older soon," I said. "My birthday's next week. Tell me the things I don't know."

Miriam patted my knee. "Don't be grumpy. I'm just saying that people's feelings aren't like arithmetic; they don't always add up. As for telling you, I don't know if I can. Some things you can learn from other people and books; some you have to live through. I'll never know what it's like to live in Iceland and have feet and feet of snow."

She said all this so nicely that I stopped being upset and told her about the "No man is an island" sermon my uncle had been working on when he died. "He said words are the stepping-stones between one person and another. Sometimes they're under water and you have to wait for them to surface again."

"I like paddling," said Miriam. Then she quizzed me about Puck's role in the play.

THE NEXT WEEK, WHEN the Bryants were away and Ross had the other girls playing hockey, I led Miriam to the working girls' bathroom. "There's something I want to show you," I said. While she laboured up the stairs I ran ahead to pull my suitcase from beneath the bed. For a moment I was terrified that my precious photographs would be gone—my penknife had been stolen the week after I arrived—but I reached into the lining, and there they were. I took only the one of my uncle and mother together. Downstairs Miriam was leaning on a basin, breathing hard. I asked if she needed her inhaler.

"No, I just took the stairs too fast." She had by now explained to me about her asthma and how, when an attack came, it felt as if a giant hand was squeezing her chest. The inhaler helped loosen the hand.

"How pretty your mother is," she gasped. "And your uncle looks as if he's just about to laugh. You can see they're brother and sister, can't you?"

I had not dared to look at the photograph since I came to Claypoole. Now, gazing over Miriam's shoulder, I saw my uncle's kind smile, my mother's bright eyes, and behind them the azaleas in bloom. "Do you have a picture of your mother?" I asked.

"It's on the wall above my bed in Galashiels. When I go there in July I'll bring it back to show you. We'd better go downstairs and look busy."

Despite her dreaminess Miriam was good at remembering that we had to be careful. She set off towards the library and I carried the photograph back to its hiding place. No one could ever replace my uncle, but as I slipped the suitcase under the bed I cherished the confidence with which Miriam had spoken of a shared future. That evening in the common room she handed me a small package. "Happy birthday, Gemma."

When I removed the wrapping paper I found a pocket guide to Scottish birds.

"Sometimes you're not quite sure what a bird is," she said shyly. "I thought this would help and that the other girls wouldn't try to steal it."

"Thank you. It's exactly what I wanted." I told her then about my favourite book, *Birds of the World*, and how I had had to leave it behind at Yew House. "But this is much more useful," I added.

MIRIAM STILL WORKED IN the library over the holidays and she had persuaded Mrs. Bryant to let me assist her after I finished my other tasks. We were alphabetising the history section one afternoon when she asked if I knew about Cecil.

"Who's Cecil?" I said.

"The Mintos' younger son. He died in the Second World War." When she first arrived at Claypoole, she went on, there had been several sightings of a young man in a bloody uniform wandering the lower corridors. She herself hadn't seen him until last year, when she'd discovered him in this very room, sitting in a chair by the window, reading. She pointed to the window in the far corner. I asked if he'd said anything and she said no. "He just smiled at me, and went on reading."

"So how did you know he was a ghost?"

"I didn't. He was wearing ordinary clothes, a white shirt and dark trousers, and I thought he was someone's brother, visiting the school. But one minute he was turning a page and the next there was just the book, lying on a chair."

I reached for a history of the Tudors, and asked what he'd been reading, and whether she'd seen him again.

"*Kim*. It's a novel by Rudyard Kipling. Sometimes I get this feeling that he's waiting for me, and I come here and find him. But that hasn't happened in months." She held up a biography of Oliver Cromwell with a portrait of a long-faced, unsmiling man on the cover. "This could be my father," she said.

"He looks cross, but finish telling me about Cecil. Does he ever talk to you?"

Miriam slipped the book into place. Then she fussed with her Alice band in a way that made her hair stick out even more. "I'm worried you'll think I'm balmy," she said.

I was about to tell her what had happened in the sewing-room, but something cautioned me not to, almost as if the figure itself had appeared to tug my sleeve. "I don't think you're balmy," I said. "What does he say?"

"Ordinary things. Last summer we spoke about how warm it was and how nice it would be to have an ice cream. He likes strawberry; I prefer vanilla. Another time he talked about being on the convoys; how he'd seen whales and icebergs. He said when a submarine showed up on the radar everyone on the ship held their breath."

"Didn't he die on a ship?"

"Yes." Miriam blinked slowly. "But it seemed rude to mention he was dead. Like asking a grown-up how old they are."

I stepped over to the fiction shelves *H–N*. When I pulled out *Kim*, the gold-edged pages were covered with dust. "Did you read it?"

"I tried. I waited until I thought he must be finished and then I borrowed it but I got stuck after twenty pages. Maybe you could read it and tell me the story."

Before I could slip the book into my tunic pocket Miriam began to briskly straighten volumes. Out of the corner of my eye, I saw the door inch open.

IN ALL OUR CONVERSATIONS I never spoke of Mr. Donaldson; I could not bear to voice the enormity of what I'd done. Then, on the last day of the holidays, it was unusually warm, and Ross sent me to weed the herbaceous border on the lower terrace. Miriam came to help. A cuckoo was calling nearby, sweet and insistent. We both called back, and it fell silent. As I dug up a dandelion, I told her how the maid at Yew House had believed that dandelion milk cured warts.

"I should tell my father," she said. "He has warts. I don't mean to be nosy, Gemma, but I can't help wondering what you did to make Miss Bryant so cross."

I could easily have offered a small fib—I'd been cheeky, or untidy—

but, to my amazement, the words I had thought myself so reluctant to utter were bubbling forth. I told her the whole story, beginning with Mr. Donaldson's visit to my aunt and his advice to me and then describing how I had found the box and taken it to him for safekeeping. When I described what had happened with the letter, Miriam exclaimed.

"Oh, Gemma, anyone could have told you that Mr. Milne is Miss Bryant's slave. Cook would have posted the letter. Miss Bryant has something on her too, I don't know what, but she enjoys having little secrets."

I had been braced for Miriam's censure, but the news that there had been a safe way to send the letter was more than I could bear. I drove my trowel into the soil until she pointed out that I was uprooting a primula. "There must be something I can do," I said, restoring the dishevelled plant. "Mr. Donaldson shouldn't lose his job because of me."

"Start weeding," said Miriam, edging away.

Suddenly Miss Bryant was standing over us. For several minutes she watched in silence from behind her large dark glasses. I crawled along the border, piling up the weeds in small heaps. Miriam tugged at a shoot of willow herb.

"Stand up, girls."

We did, offering awkward curtsies to her black stare. Her blue dress with its white collar and belt was like one my aunt had worn the previous summer.

"I have been observing the two of you," she said, "and I see that you've formed an unhealthy relationship. Goodall, your father is not paying for you to fraternise with working girls. Tomorrow you'll move into Form One. Miss Seftain will coach you on what you've missed. Your father will be pleased that you're catching up with your age group at last. Hardy, this border will be finished before you re-enter the school. Be sure to dig up every inch of dandelion root so they don't grow back."

A few weeks ago I would have told her that I was due in the kitchen at four. Now I bobbed my head and resumed my digging. I did not dare to watch as she led my friend away, but I took some small satisfaction in leaving, unmolested, a piece of each dandelion. Let the plants grow back, boisterous and yellow.

chapter ten

THE SUMMER TERM BEGAN, and in the classroom, thanks to Miriam's coaching, I held my own. Mrs. Harris no longer picked on me at every opportunity. In the kitchen I had learned to be slap-dash and make mounds of carrots and potatoes disappear into saucepans. Even Mr. Waugh's sermons were less tedious, now that we no longer shivered in the pews. When he visited Primary 7 I kept my head down and hoped he wouldn't guess that I disagreed with every sentence he uttered.

As I swept the classrooms on Saturdays, I often studied the map of the British Isles that hung on the wall of each room, wondering if Mr. Donaldson had joined his sister in Oban. The town was on the west coast of Scotland, north of Glasgow, opposite the island of Mull. Then one day in geography, when we were reading about rain forests, I suddenly thought, What was to stop him from going farther afield? I pictured my precious box mouldering under a palm tree, or being eaten by kangaroos. But I had no one to whom I could confide my fears.

Since Miriam had moved to Form I, I seldom saw her, and when I did her face was pale and her leg seemed to drag more heavily. At lunch or supper we would exchange looks as I set down her plate. I miss you, I would think. Her eyes said the same thing. In one of our conversations during the holidays I had told her about my parents, gazing at the North Star and sending messages back and forth across the ocean. Maybe we could do that, she had said. In maths, you could send me the right answer. We had tried it one Sunday. During the first quarter-hour of Mr. Waugh's sermon I had thought about Sulis, the goddess of the hot springs at Bath. When the clock chimed I closed my eyes and tried to imagine myself inside Miriam's head. At first there was only the fuzzy dimness of my eyelids. Then I caught a glimpse of a black and white dog: Spencer, I thought. But that evening, while the other girls played Ping-Pong, she told me she'd been remembering the afternoon we visited the pigs, and she'd pictured me thinking about Iceland. Maybe it's like tennis or poetry, she had said, we have to practise.

Now each night I fell asleep trying to send her a message: ask me home for the summer holidays. If only her father would invite me, I was sure Miss Bryant would agree. One less mouth to feed. Miriam and I would be together, and during the long hours while her father was at work, I could track down Mr. Donaldson.

One Saturday, when instead of cleaning the Form I classroom I was standing, broom in hand, before the map, a voice behind me said, "Lost your fancy friend, haven't you?"

Arms akimbo, Ross stood a few feet away, dressed in the ugly overalls we wore for cleaning. It was easy to picture her ten years from now, washing some office floor. "I was trying to find the school," I said.

"Here, moron." As she raised her hand, I smelled the cleaning fluid we used in the toilets. "Here's Hawick, and Denholm. Minto is too small."

"I was looking too far west. Where did you used to live?"

She pointed to the large, dark circle of Glasgow. "When I first came here I couldn't stand the quiet. I thought some animal was going to jump out and eat me."

"What kind of animal?"

"A fox? A wolf? Whatever lives in the woods and eats girls. So where's the cripple from?"

"The cripple?"

Even as I asked, the word twisted inside me and found its meaning, but before either of us could speak again, Mrs. Bryant stepped into the room, smiling. "Ross, you're needed in the upper corridor. Hardy, you've got five minutes to finish this room."

TWO DAYS LATER, WHEN I climbed into bed, my bare feet encountered something cold and feathery. As I jumped out, screaming, everyone in the room burst into gleeful shouts.

"Look what the cat's brought in," said Findlayson.

"Cry-baby," called Smith.

They were still laughing and shouting comments when Matron appeared. "Girls, if you . . ." The light went out.

I fetched some toilet paper, retrieved the sparrow, and threw it out of the bathroom window. Since I had shown her the magpie, Ross had several times asked me the names of birds. With the help of Miriam's book I had taught her to distinguish a swallow from a swift, a rook from a crow. Over Easter a pair of blackbirds had built a nest in a flowering currant bush near the back door, and often she followed me when I slipped out of the kitchen to check on their progress. She might have allowed this to happen, I told myself, but she was not the executioner. Findlayson, I guessed, or Drummond. As I lay under the counterpane, I thought, Invite me for the summer. Invite me for the summer.

IT SEEMED THE WORST kind of coincidence when, in assembly the next morning, Miss Bryant summoned Goodall to the front. I had never seen a regular girl publicly scolded, but now Miriam was made to stand on the dais, as I had once been, while Miss Bryant pointed out her unbrushed hair, the stains on her tunic, her wrinkled socks and muddy shoes. "This girl," she concluded, "is a disgrace to Clay-poole."

"I'm very sorry, Miss Bryant," Miriam said in a low voice. "I'll try to do better."

"You won't try. You will. For the rest of the term you'll get up fifteen minutes early to make sure that your uniform is clean."

"Yes, Miss Bryant." Miriam gave a small, crooked curtsey.

That evening as I peeled the interminable potatoes Ross jerked my apron strings. "Your friend got a right old ticking off. Just because her dad pays fees doesn't mean she can behave any old how."

She was grinning so broadly I could see past her chipped tooth to her tonsils. Suddenly I knew, as clearly as if she had told me, that it was she who had drawn Miss Bryant's attention to my friendship with Miriam, and she who had put the sparrow in my bed. Quite possibly she had also engineered Miriam's current punishment; she was one of the few girls free to roam the school. As I reached for the next potato, I grinned back. "She should have minded herself," I said.

While we peeled and halved the potatoes, I kept talking as if nothing had changed. Had she seen Miss Seftain's blouse? It looked like raspberry jelly. Did she think the lacrosse team had a chance against the visiting school? We finished the potatoes and went to check on the blackbirds' nest. The dusty brown female regarded us patiently while I explained that the eggs would hatch any day. Then both parents would feed the chicks. We could help by finding worms and leaving them nearby.

"You get the worms," said Ross cheerfully.

She seemed to have forgiven me, but my policy of appeasement was too little, too late. The other girls sensed that she had withdrawn her protection. Someone tipped pepper on my food; someone spilled ketchup on my shirt; someone stole my Alice band so that for a whole day I was reprimanded for not wearing it. I did my best to avoid the Elm Room and to be as unobtrusive as possible. The only place I felt safe was the classroom, where Mrs. Harris, in her tyranny, tolerated no competition.

Then one night, soon after Matron turned out the light, Findlayson appeared on one side of my bed, Drummond on the other.

"Little Miss Smartie Pants."

"Little Miss Know-it-all."

"Thinks she's so much better than the rest of us."

At the first touch of their hands I screamed, "Help, Matron. Help me. Someone help me."

"Christ, what a racket," one of the older girls said.

"Better gag her," said another.

I screamed even louder—someone seized my ankles—and fought as hard as I could, kicking, scratching, biting, but this was not like fighting Will, a single enemy of superior strength, this was a barbarian horde: wild, lawless, pitiless. Someone dragged off my pyjama jacket. Someone forced my mouth open and stuffed in a sock. Someone tugged my hair. And the worst of it was not the pain, or even the shame, but the bodies shutting me in, holding me prisoner, smothering me. Eventually, as I had in the sewing-room, I slipped away.

WHEN I CAME ROUND I was lying in bed in a small, bright room. Matron was sitting by the window, reading one of her romances, a faint smile on her lips.

"My, you gave us . . . How are . . . ?"

Her blue eyes gazed down at me and I gazed back, silently. Without calculation, I had hit upon the perfect response. Matron asked a few more of her abbreviated questions. Then she brought me a poached egg on toast, which I ate with pleasure. I could feign muteness but not loss of appetite. Afterwards I mimed that I would like to borrow a book and settled down to read about Catherine, a nurse, and Robert, the handsome laird, who seems determined to ignore her.

Later that day the doctor came from Hawick. I had heard the older girls describe Dr. White, with his intense gaze and dimpled chin, as a heartthrob. I did whatever he asked—raising my pyjama jacket for his stethoscope, sticking out my tongue—in silence. Meanwhile Matron explained, in her fragmentary fashion, that she'd found me lying unconscious at the bottom of the stairs.

"She seems healthy," he said, "except for the bruises. Perhaps she fell on the stairs? Or perhaps someone scared her. People sometimes become mute from shock."

"Perhaps she saw . . ." Matron's painted eyebrows rose.

"The Claypoole ghost? Actually I was thinking of her fellow pupils. Let's keep her in the infirmary for a couple of days."

"But she's a working girl." His suggestion had surprised her into a complete sentence, and now it was the doctor's turn to be surprised.

"A working girl?" he said. "She's what, nine? Ten at the most. Even the Victorians didn't send children to work so young."

Matron explained how hard it was to find working girls these days.

If you didn't talk, I began to realise, people assumed you couldn't hear.

An hour later I was deep in Catherine and Robert's adventures when I looked up to see Miss Bryant herself approaching, her eyes narrowed, her thin upper lip almost invisible.

"I don't know what's going on in your head," she said in a soft voice, "but playing dumb isn't going to get you anywhere. You have no broken bones, no serious illness. You may have one more day in the sickroom and then it's back to work." Before I could not answer, she turned on her heel and left the room.

That night I woke to the tick of bare feet on floorboards. I was bracing myself for a battle with Ross, or some other girl, when I caught a familiar wheeze.

"Gemma, are you all right?"

"Miriam." I pulled her down beside me. The bed was just wide enough for the two of us. I could smell her shampoo, sweet and flowery, lingering in her thick hair. Her father, she'd told me, had said her hair was like a horse's tail, and when I stroked it, it was surprisingly coarse. "How did you know I was here?"

"I heard the girls talking. They said the working girls hit you so hard you couldn't talk."

"I can talk, but I decided not to. There's nothing I want to say to anyone but you."

"Did they hurt you? What happened?"

Even to Miriam I could not describe the girls' attack. To remember it was to relive it and to relive it brought me back to that excruciating edge. Instead I said she had been right about Ross. I had been stupid not to understand that, like Mr. Milne, her allegiance was to Miss Bryant.

"That makes sense," said Miriam thoughtfully. "Even if someone is cruel to you, if they're the only person in your life, you'll love them."

How could that be? I wondered. I had hated my aunt and now I hated my tormentors at Claypoole. "But you don't love your father," I said indignantly.

"Maybe he's not cruel enough."

This was so bewildering I pretended I hadn't heard. "Did you get my messages?" I asked.

"What messages? Oh, you mean telepathy. I think that only works for a very few people. Your parents may have been among them. Or maybe they were just sending the same message over and over."

Her voice was gentle and I knew that, once again, she was remembering my age, but I didn't stop to argue. I told her my idea that her father should invite me to stay in July. We could be together, we could grow flowers and read, and I could try to find Mr. Donaldson. I had pictured her exclaiming with pleasure, saying why hadn't she thought of that, but she said nothing. I sat up, trying to make out her expression in the darkness.

"I wish it were that easy, Gemma. I can ask, but he'll probably say no. He thinks children are a bother and more children are more of a bother."

As she spoke her breathing grew louder, her voice fainter. I had noticed before that the hand often squeezed her chest when we spoke about her father. "Do you have your inhaler?" I said.

She shook her head. One of the worst things about the asthma attacks, she had told me, was that she couldn't call for help. I jumped out of bed and pulled her to her feet. Slowly I led Miriam, limping and gasping, through the dark corridors to the Birch Room. We parted in silence. I listened to her stumble across the floor, then a soft thud: her sitting or falling on the bed.

chapter eleven

THE NEXT DAY MATRON gave me breakfast and sent me back to Primary 7. I think she was a little sorry to lose me. She patted my shoulder, told me to come back if I felt poorly, and allowed me to borrow the book I was reading about Milly, a music teacher, and Edward, a postman. I smiled my thanks. What had I needed speech for? The first period of the day was arithmetic. When Mrs. Harris started to go round the room, asking girls for their answers, I readied myself to go to the blackboard to write mine, but she skipped over me as if my desk were empty. Miss Bryant must have warned her.

In the Elm Room that evening the working girls pretended to ignore my return—they were playing a noisy game of snap—but as I undressed I caught Findlayson eyeing me uneasily, then Drummond, then Gilchrist.

"You all right?" said Gilchrist.

I went to brush my teeth. No one followed.

For a few days the girls questioned me at odd moments, jumped out from behind doors. Once, when Findlayson sprang up beside my bed, I screamed, but otherwise I managed to remain silent. Soon they lost interest and I became what I had wanted: almost invisible. In assembly I did not pretend to sing although I silently repeated the Lord's Prayer, which my uncle had laboured to teach me during those early months at Yew House. Only Cook was concerned. One afternoon she took me into the larder and said, "Hardy, tell me what's wrong. Did those brats bully you? Are you hurt?"

In the notebook I had started carrying I wrote, *Thank you. I'm fine!*

That evening I hid in one of the bathrooms and wrote my long-rehearsed letter to Mr. Donaldson.

> *Please tell everyone it's all my fault and I would be happy to tell them that too. They won't give me a letter from you but if you write to Miriam Goodall, my best friend at Claypoole, she will pass on whatever you say.*

Then I wrote, *Please forward if necessary*, on the envelope.

The next afternoon, as I washed rhubarb, I kept a careful eye on Cook. Half-a-dozen times a day, when she was sure Mrs. Bryant wasn't around, she would nip out for a cigarette. So when I saw her put down a colander and head for the door, I followed. I found her standing near the flowering currant, puffing smoke towards the nest. I held out the letter in both hands.

For a few seconds she studied my offering with the same expression she wore when a sauce curdled. She was going to refuse me, report me. Then she smiled. "Aren't you a sly one?" The next thing I knew she had slipped the envelope beneath her apron. "I'll make sure this sees the inside of a pillar-box tonight."

I bowed my thanks. Then I pointed out the nest with the bright-eyed bird. Cook stepped forward to look more closely. "So this is what you and Ross are in such a state about. I shouldn't be blowing smoke at the poor thing. Hard enough being a mother without that. How many blackbirds does it take to make a pie?"

I held up my hands and flashed two tens and a four.

Cook sighed. "I suppose you'll talk when you're ready. Well, back to the salt mines."

·   ·   ·

PUBLICLY, LIKE THE OTHER working girls, Ross ignored me, but when we were alone, she pelted me with uneasy questions. Did people who couldn't talk hear better? Was I cross? Had something happened in the infirmary? I shook my head, or shrugged, and eventually she too was lured into speech by my silence. As we were carrying slops to the pigs she told me what had happened the night of the ambush.

"One minute you were screaming bloody murder, then suddenly you passed out cold. Even when I pinched you, you didn't move."

So that was the bruise on my forearm, I thought, stepping around a thistle.

"I was scared you'd kicked the bucket," she went on, swinging the actual bucket she was carrying. "In our street once a bloke fell over, digging a hole. He never got up again. So I lugged you down the stairs and fetched Matron."

Of course Matron wouldn't have found me on her own; she never left her domain after lights-out. To hide my confusion—I didn't want Ross to be my saviour—I ran ahead to the pigsty. As I tipped the scraps into the trough, Thumbelina shoved Heidi aside. If I'd been alone I would have told her to mind her manners.

A few days later, when we were on our way to clean the gym, Ross finally revealed why Montrose, my predecessor, had had to leave. They had pretended, just for a laugh, to throw her out of the window; she had struggled so hard she'd broken her wrist. "She told Miss Bryant it was our fault. Of course she couldn't stay after that. As soon as she was better, Miss Bryant fibbed about her age and got her a job in a hotel."

The afternoon was warm, and when Ross stopped to wipe her forehead her hand left a smear of grime. I took pleasure in seeing the dirt, pleasure in not telling her about it. At last she gave up waiting for me to answer and spoke again.

"I don't know what she'd have done if you'd tattled," she said. "I worried you might. You're such a Goody Two-shoes."

As I swept the gym, I daydreamed about a kingdom of girls, a place where there were only girls, where none of the girls were bullies or idiots, and everyone studied harmoniously. If only such a place existed, Miriam and I would go there tomorrow.

FOR SEVERAL DAYS AFTER I returned to the Elm Room I didn't see Miriam. Then one morning in assembly I spotted her, not standing with her class but sitting on a chair beside the teachers. At lunch, when I set her plate down, I noticed her inhaler on the table. That evening in the bathroom I wrote another note.

> *Dearest Miriam,*
>
> *Are you all right? Your face is the colour of paper and I can hear you breathing. Have you seen the doctor? I hope, hope, hope I can come and stay with you in the holidays. Tell your father I am a good nurse. I will read to you all day long and take good care of you. I miss you.*
>
> *Love, your best friend, Gemma*

I carried the note around in my sock, waiting for a chance to deliver it. Finally on Saturday, as Smith and I were polishing the hall outside the library, Miriam limped towards us. I dropped my mop and, bending to pick it up, slipped the note into her hand.

That afternoon in the kitchen, Ross tugged my apron. Outside, in the flowering currant, the mother blackbird was no longer sitting on the nest. Four tiny beaks were visible above the rim of moss and twigs.

"They hatched," she whispered. "Just like you said."

I felt her arms go around me, and before I knew what was happening, she had lifted me up. I stared in wonder at the barely feathered heads with their filmy eyes and yellow beaks. Then I wriggled until she set me down.

"We'll have to gather worms for them. Maybe after supper this evening."

I nodded.

"How long before they fly away?"

I wasn't sure but I held up four fingers.

"Four days?"

I shook my head, and moved my hands farther apart.

"Okay. So we have four weeks to teach them to be our friends."

As she spoke, the mother bird appeared with a shrill cry. We stepped back and she flew down into the bush. I remembered my uncle telling me that birds fed their young with regurgitated food, which was why it was so hard to rear a fledgling. Even if we liked chewing worms, he had said, we don't have the right saliva.

MIRIAM DID NOT REPLY to my note, and two mornings in a row she was missing from assembly. There were rumours that Dr. White had been called in the night, that she was worse. Chopping onions, I angled the knife into my finger. In the infirmary Matron greeted me warmly. "Oh, Hardy, how . . . ?"

I held out my notebook with the note I had written earlier.

"Poor Goodall." She dabbed something stinging on my cut. "She's very poorly."

I seized the notebook and wrote, *PLEASE tell me more.*

She shook her head and pressed a piece of cotton wool to my finger. "The doctor thinks . . . Hospital."

For the rest of the day thoughts flashed through my mind like scenery rushing past the window of a train. Miriam had told me there was no cure for asthma, although a warmer, drier climate helped. That was why people used to go to the Mediterranean. "Your inhaler makes you better," I had said. I was dusting the piano in the music room.

"It makes me feel better," she corrected. "The asthma stays the same. And Dr. White says I mustn't use it too often. You need stronger and stronger doses."

"But people don't die of asthma," I had said. "Not like drowning, or the plague."

Standing beside me, Miriam played a scale, first with her left hand, then her right. She had promised she would teach me some songs soon. "Most people don't die," she agreed, "but when I can't breathe it feels as if I'm about to. Sometimes"—she played the scale with both hands— "I even want to. The only hope is that it will get better as I get older, and my lungs grow bigger."

"So you have to eat lots," I had said, "and grow quickly." But as she limped across the hall, Miriam had seemed not bigger but smaller, only an inch or two taller than me, and as thin as my mop.

THAT NIGHT I STOLE out of bed and down the stairs. I was tiptoeing past the bathroom when a figure in striped pyjamas loomed over me. "You're not sneaking around, are you?" said Ross.

I gasped and swerved into the bathroom. She stood in the doorway. "We wouldn't want you trying to see your fancy friend."

I managed to pee, washed my hands, and pushed past her, up the narrow stairs. Back in bed I listened as hard as I could. Although I knew how Findlayson whimpered, doglike, in her sleep, and how Gilchrist cried out as if she were being attacked, I could not identify Ross's night sounds. Her bed was on the far side of the room, and I was never sure if that grunting snore was hers. Or that melancholy sigh? How was it, I wondered, that night after night I sent messages to Miriam and was never sure they reached her but that Ross seemed to read my mind effortlessly? Or perhaps, I thought, she was simply paying attention. A few weeks ago, before the girls attacked me, she had remarked that Mr. Milne always parked squint after having a beer. "You'd make a good policeman," I had said. Her face had lit up. "That would be grand," she exclaimed. "Do you think they'd have me?" "No," I'd said. "You have to be good at sums."

Now I counted a hundred sheep, then two hundred. Just as I was about to try again, someone moaned, "No. No cabbage." Reluctantly I lay back down. I pictured the bodies piling on top of me, and Ross urging them on.

THE FOLLOWING AFTERNOON I was dusting the window-sills in the front hall when the door flew open and a man in an old-fashioned brown suit strode in, bringing with him a faint, familiar smell I couldn't name. His momentum carried him halfway across the hall before he remembered the door and turned back to close it, leaving a double trail of muddy footprints. As he retraced his steps, I recognised the tang of manure. Near the sofa he stopped to remove his hat and looked around. His hair receded in an emphatic W and his eyes were shadowed. After his noisy entrance he seemed uncertain what to do next. Then he spotted me.

"Girl," he boomed, "fetch Miss Bryant."

I dropped my duster and hurried to the corridor where Ross was wielding the floor polisher. I stood in front of her, pointing at the hall, until she turned off the machine and followed me.

"Fetch Miss Bryant," the man repeated. "I'm here to see my daughter."

Ross hurried away. While I returned to my dusting, he stationed himself in front of the empty fireplace and surveyed the room, not

with the appreciative gaze of most parents but rather as if he were measuring it for a carpet. Between one flick of the duster and the next, it
came to me that this was Miriam's father: the stern man with no use
for children. I longed to approach and explain that I was his daughter's
best friend. If only he'd let me come home with her I could nurse her
back to health. But even as I moved towards him, the door on the stairs
opened.

"Mr. Goodall," said Miss Bryant. "You got my message."

Hoping to escape attention, I ran my duster over the wainscoting.

"Yes," said Mr. Goodall. "I had a bull to see in Hawick. How is she?"
His voice, like Mr. Waugh's, was effortlessly loud. It was easy to imagine him calling out prices to crowds of men.

Miss Bryant raised her voice to match. "Your daughter has never
been a hypochondriac, but for the last week she's been so breathless she
can't get out of bed. Matron and Dr. White both think she'd be better
off in hospital."

"I don't hold with hospitals."

Their footsteps moved across the hall, and whatever came next was
inaudible. When I risked a glance over my shoulder, I saw that there
had been another witness to the conversation. Ross had followed Miss
Bryant into the hall and stood by the standard lamp, watching me. I
moved on to the next stretch of wainscoting. Don't speak, I shouted
in my head. Don't say a word. I dusted, I polished, I straightened the
magazines on the table by the armchairs. At last she walked away. Only
then did I feel free to send my message: Miriam, I'll come tonight. I
promise.

IN BED WHILE I waited for everyone to fall asleep, I had the awful
thought that Miriam's grey, smelly father had already taken her away.
But, however faulty my message-sending, I was convinced I would

know if she were gone. She was still here, but tomorrow, unless she improved dramatically, she would be sent to the hospital. Around me girls snored and sighed. Findlayson got up to use the bathroom; so did Drummond. I tried to decide if it was better to leave during one of the surges of noise that periodically passed through the room or while all was still. Suddenly I sensed someone beside my bed. I opened my eyes, ready to scream. In the gloom I made out a young man wearing a white shirt and dark trousers.

"Miriam needs you," he said. "Go to her now."

I did not hesitate. I rearranged my pillow to look like a body, placed my rolled-up cardigan where my head ought to be, and tiptoed to the door. Without stopping, I made my way to the sickroom. The bedside light was on; there was no sign of Matron. Miriam was propped up in bed, her face pale and gleaming. At the sight of me she started to smile. Suddenly her mouth wrenched open, and her eyes flared. The giant hand was holding her tight.

I ran to the bed. "Miriam, what can I do? Do you have your inhaler?"

She glanced down and I saw it lying beside her. "Can't talk," she whispered.

"What can I do?" I repeated. Her forehead was beaded with sweat. Gently I patted it with the sleeve of my pyjamas. I remembered a scene from *Anne of Green Gables* when someone with croup was put in a tent of steam. I looked around the room, hoping for a kettle. Meanwhile Miriam gathered her strength to push back the hand one more time. And one more. I had never thought of breathing as something that required willpower. What would happen if she fell asleep?

"Story," she whispered, her voice even smaller than before.

I began a tale about two brothers, both fishermen; the good brother likes the seals and shares his catch with them; the bad brother hates them. Suddenly I realised Miriam hadn't taken the next breath. Her eyes were glaring, her body arching, her hand fumbling with the inhaler. Quickly I took it from her, raised it to her mouth, and pushed the button as I had seen her do. She lay back, eyes closed. "Go on," she murmured.

"And then the bad brother . . ."

After only a few more sentences her breathing jammed again. I ran to the doorway of the room. "Matron," I called. "Help. Help."

I had barely time to hide behind the curtains before Matron, in a dark dressing-gown, was bending over Miriam, saying, "There, there, Goodall."

Soon she had Miriam settled in a tent of steam just like I had read about. She left the room and I heard her dialing the phone, begging the doctor to come at once, saying "ambulance" and "hospital." Then I heard her hurrying down the corridor and guessed she had gone to fetch Miss Bryant. I slipped out of my hiding place and knelt beside Miriam.

"I'm sorry I didn't come sooner," I said. "I tried, but Ross stopped me. Tonight the man from the library fetched me, the one you talked to about convoys and ice cream. He's watching over you. They'll make you better in hospital and when you come back I'll show you the baby blackbirds."

Beneath the towel Miriam made a gasping sound.

THE NEXT MORNING, AS we washed the silverware, Smith remarked that an ambulance had come in the night and taken Goodall to the hospital in Hawick. "One of the prefects said she nearly died," she added cheerfully.

The handful of knives I was drying fell to the floor.

"Dropping a knife is bad luck," said Smith, nudging one with her foot. "You've enough here to last a year."

She can't die, I thought. Adults were the ones who had accidents, or fell ill and died, not children. Yet even as I argued, I remembered the small graves in my uncle's churchyard: beloved sons and daughters gone to join their Redeemer. Somehow I survived my morning classes. Serving lunch, I deliberately touched a roasting pan. "Clumsy," said Cook and sent me to the infirmary. Once again I offered Matron my notebook: *Please tell me how Goodall is.*

"She's very . . . I'm afraid all we can . . ."

All we can what? I wrote.

"Pray," Matron said, holding up her hands.

The following morning in assembly Miss Bryant said the same thing. "Girls, today I ask you to pray for Miriam Goodall, who is very ill in Hawick Hospital."

I squeezed my eyes shut and prayed partly to God, partly to the young man. I promised to be good, to tidy my drawers, never to lie, not to hate anyone—even Mr. Milne, even Miss Bryant—if only they would make Miriam better. I pictured her lungs, bean-shaped like the picture I'd seen in a biology book, growing and growing.

In class Mrs. Harris reprimanded me for not getting out my books. In the kitchen Cook chivvied me to finish the potatoes. Meanwhile the rest of the school, the rest of the world, seemed oblivious to Miriam's fate. The weather had turned warm, and on the terraces the roses were in bloom; the regular pupils wore pretty green and white gingham dresses. My only solace was visiting the blackbirds. My guess of four weeks was proving surprisingly accurate. Even as I watched, one of the fledglings struggled to sit on the rim of the nest.

"Little buggers are growing up fast," said Ross. She had sneaked up behind me.

I started back to the kitchen but she grabbed my arm.

"I'll bet you a shilling," she said, "you never see her again."

chapter twelve

THE NIGHT WAS MUCH milder than the one on which I had taken my box to Mr. Donaldson, but gone were the high white clouds that had lit my journey from Yew House to the village; instead the sky pressed down, indistinguishable from the land. At the top of the stairs I stood counting, waiting for my eyes to adjust. When, at fifty, I could still barely see the driveway I almost gave up. To walk so far, alone, in such darkness, seemed impossible. Then I remembered Ross's taunt and set out across the grass. Hawick was only seven miles away. The Romans had marched through Britain at four miles an hour; I could be there in two hours. Perhaps even less, since running, I soon realised, was the best way to stay ahead of fear.

I slipped on the damp grass and fell once, then again. As soon as I passed the bend and was out of sight of the school I kept to the road. In the lodge all the lights were off. Nevertheless I tiptoed by on the far side, giving a wide berth to Mr. Milne's van. If he came after me I planned to take to the fields, where my speed was an advantage. Then I was safely past and heading downhill on a road I had not travelled since my first day at Claypoole. The animals in the fields were strangers; the trees had no names.

At the bottom I turned left and followed the line of willows. Soon I was crossing the river and entering the village of Denholm. Only a few houses still showed lights, but someone could easily look out of an unlit house and see me. I ran from one pool of shadow to the next, dreading to hear a voice shout, "Stop," but no one called after me; no dog barked. About half a mile beyond the village I heard my first vehicle. I climbed into the ditch and stayed there until the lorry was safely past. It left the silence even more absolute, the darkness even denser. Breathe, I kept saying over and over. I'm coming. Wait for me.

I had given no thought as to how I would find the hospital. In my mind all I had to do was get to Hawick and there it would be. But as I got closer I began to worry that I would have to search the town, street by street. I had no map, and even if anyone were around—a milkman, say—I would not dare ask for directions. Just past the first houses, though, a sign saying HOSPITAL pointed straight ahead. A few streets later, a second sign pointed to the right. I saw a low stone building with two wings.

Cautiously I approached the front door and, after peering through the lowest pane of glass, stepped into the empty hallway. I had been to a hospital only once before, when my aunt had had her mysterious operation, and I recognised the same mixture of smells that did not go together. Faintly, I was not sure from what direction, I heard women's voices. At the end of the hall one arrow pointed to GERIATRIC, MATERNITY, and WOMEN, another to ORTHOPAEDIC, MEN, and CHILDREN. I headed towards CHILDREN, stopping every few yards to listen until I reached an opaque glass door. Holding my breath, I gently pushed it open.

Four doors lined the broad hall; one, ajar, spilled a wedge of light. Beyond I glimpsed the ward, with two rows of beds stretching into darkness. I tiptoed past the lit door and approached the nearest bed; the curtains were drawn around it. When I peered between them I saw Miriam by the glow of the bedside light, propped up against several pillows. She wore a faded pink nightdress, unbuttoned at the neck; her pale face seemed even larger. At the sight of me her eyes showed pleasure but no surprise. Perhaps my messages had reached her. I stepped inside the curtains, longing to hear her exclaim over my presence. After my dangerous journey I could feel the blood running through my veins, my lungs effortlessly filling and emptying. It took me a moment to fit myself back inside my skin, to sit down calmly on the edge of the bed and reach for her hand.

"You're cold," I whispered. I slipped off my shoes, and taking care not to jostle her, I climbed under the covers. My first thought was that she smelled different; her flowery fragrance had been banished by something medicinal. In a low voice I told her how worried I had been, that I had walked through the night to take care of her.

"I saw your father yesterday," I said. "Is the hospital making you better?"

"They're trying. Daddy came and yelled at them this afternoon."

"Ross said you were going to die."

Miriam sighed. "I might. My head feels very strange."

"You can't," I said. "I need you." Even as I spoke, the awful truth came to me: everyone I had ever loved had died.

"Well, if I can't, I won't," she said. "Tell me a selkie story."

Whispering so quietly that it was almost like talking to myself, I began, "Once upon a time in a village by the sea a woman named Margaret lived in a house covered with shells. Her parents were dead but she loved her shells and she loved the sea. She was old enough to be married but . . ."

Despite the urgency, and the danger of discovery, I found myself growing drowsy. I yawned, I buried my head against Miriam's shoulder. I had not spoken for several minutes when she patted my arm.

"I have to tell you something," she said, her voice a tiny thread. "Make friends with Miss Seftain. She'll teach you Latin. You'll like that. And when you get older she'll help you to stop being a working girl. Keep telling the story. I'm going to try to sleep."

"So Angus followed Margaret into the shell house," I went on, "and the parlour was full of people he had never seen before. They all had beautiful brown eyes, like yours, and they all wore beautiful long dark coats . . ."

As the intervals between Miriam's breaths grew longer, so did the intervals between my words until we were both silent.

chapter thirteen

I WOKE TO A PAIR of blue eyes a few inches from mine. Above the eyes perched a white hat slightly askew; below, plump lips parted to reveal a few crumbs of toast. When she saw I was awake, the nurse jumped back and disappeared between the curtains. I heard a voice crying, "Sister."

I knew where I was—in bed with Miriam, in the hospital—and I tried not to know that one side of my body, wrapped in the blanket, was warm, the other, pressed against her, cold. Please, Miriam, I thought, wherever you are, take good care of yourself. Don't worry about getting sums wrong, or being untidy. Maybe your mother's there too, and you can grow beautiful blue flowers together and play with Spencer and never have to see your father. I hope your leg is better. I hope you don't have asthma.

A hand touched my shoulder. The uniform of the woman standing over me was the same lustrous blue as the flowers I had just imagined Miriam tending. She was older than the first nurse, but her fair hair, beneath her white hat, was as short as a boy's. I had never seen a woman with such short hair before.

"Hello," she said quietly. "Who are you?"

"I'm Gemma Hardy, Miriam's best friend. I knew she was ill and I walked from Claypoole to see her last night. I didn't want her to be alone. Please don't be cross."

"I'm not cross," she said, holding out her hand. "You're a very brave girl but you have to say goodbye to Miriam and get out of bed."

Like Miss Bryant, this woman was used to being obeyed. I climbed out of the bed and went around to the other side. Miriam was still propped against the pillows, slumped slightly to one side, her chin resting on her chest. Hesitantly I reached for her hand. It felt mysteriously different: heavier, denser. I kissed her pale cheek but I could not bear to say the word *goodbye*.

The woman stood beside me. "Do you know that poem by Robert Louis Stevenson?" she said. "'Home is the sailor, home from the sea, / And the hunter home from the hill'? Miriam didn't sail or hunt, but we hope in some sense she's gone home. We're just sorry that home is so far away."

"We used to say his poem about the shadow when it was sunny," I said. "He was ill as a boy and he got better. My uncle showed me his house in Edinburgh."

I was still telling her what I knew about Stevenson as she led me between the curtains, across the shiny linoleum, and into the hallway beyond the beds. In the bathroom, she started the bath, and handed me a towel. "Call if you need anything," she said.

As the youngest working girl I was last in line for our weekly bath and by the time my turn came the tepid water was filmed with scum; I would leap in and wash at top speed, flailing madly to keep the grime of the other girls at bay. Now the water was hot and clear and the bath so long that I could make swimming motions and move myself from end to end. My hair floated around me and my mind became liquid and dreamy. I remembered swimming one summer day with my uncle and cousins in the pool above the weir; I had towed Veronica around in a rubber ring. Through the window I saw a seagull arc by, followed by a dozen grey pigeons. It was still early. Six o'clock perhaps. No more than seven. I shampooed my hair and rinsed it, first at one end of the bath, then the other.

A voice at the door called, "Breakfast in five minutes." Reluctantly I climbed out, dried myself, and dressed in my mud-smeared blouse and trousers. For the first time since my train journey, I studied my reflection without fear of interruption. Beneath my wet hair, my eyes were still grey, my features still plain, but my cheeks were thinner, my forehead higher; my months at Claypoole had aged me beyond my years.

In the corridor the woman in blue was waiting. "I forgot to tell you my name. I'm Sister Barbara Cullen. Breakfast is served in my office."

Few meals, no matter how lavish, have given me as much satisfaction as that breakfast: two fried eggs, two sausages, bacon, grilled tomato, and white toast. I ate in ravenous silence. Meanwhile Sister Cullen worked at her desk. Only when my plate was empty save for a few tomato seeds did I raise my head to take in my surroundings: the broad desk, the filing cabinet, the cupboard with a key in the lock, and, most intriguingly, a poster, taller than I was, depicting a naked person with bones and muscles and organs.

"You were hungry," said Sister Cullen. "Now I'd like to ask you a few questions. It's still too early to phone the school."

As she spoke I realised that Miriam's death had propelled me back into the world of ordinary speech. Gently Sister Cullen asked me my age and circumstances, and I told her about being an orphan, about getting a scholarship to Claypoole only to spend most of my time cooking and cleaning. I told her how Miss Bryant had put me in Primary 7 not as a reward for my scholastic accomplishments but to conceal the age of her youngest working girl. I told her how Miriam had befriended me.

"And you her," said the sister.

I had never thought to wonder why Miriam had approached me. Now, as I gazed at Sister Cullen's pristine hat, I understood for the first time that Miriam, even with all the advantages of being a regular pupil, had, like me, no friends.

"So," Sister Cullen said, leaning forward, "you can't go back to your aunt's. And, I'm no expert on these matters, but I doubt there are many boarding schools that would take you for free. I fear your only option is to make the best of Claypoole. Perhaps Dr. White will have some ideas."

"He might be angry with me," I said and confessed my refusal to speak.

Sister Cullen shook her head. "You're a very determined person, aren't you?"

I had not thought of myself that way, but I stored up the idea to examine later. "Why did Miriam die?" I said. "I thought no one died of asthma."

"Believe me, I would have done anything I could to prevent it. Asthma is very hard to cure." She stood up from her desk and, approaching the poster, pointed to the lungs. When someone has asthma, she explained, the tubes that go from the face to the lungs and the smaller ones, actually inside the lungs, become inflamed and constricted. "Perhaps if Miriam had been in a sanatorium when she first developed asthma; if someone had made sure that she had the best possible diet, plenty of rest, and cheerful company . . . Well, who knows? But Dr. White took good care of her, and here at the hospital we did everything we could. When I went off duty yesterday, we thought her condition had stabilised. No one had any idea she would die in the night."

I stared at the dark red lungs as I asked the crucial question. "Do you think it was my fault?"

"Your fault?"

I meant, was I a monster? Did I hurt everyone I loved? Instead I repeated Miriam's remark that being upset made her asthma worse.

"You're asking did the shock of your visit trigger an attack? No, that would have happened anyway. I'm sure your presence made it easier. Didn't you see her face when you said goodbye? She looked as if she'd been smiling, and that was because of you. It would have been awful for her to be alone, or with strangers."

Then she announced that for today she was going to keep me at the hospital. I could make myself useful by reading to some of the younger children on the ward. One of her nurses, she added, had a daughter my size and would lend me some clean clothes.

I DID NOT HEAR what Sister Cullen said to Miss Bryant, but I pictured a glacier meeting a rock; the rock stands firm but the glacier just keeps going. Nor did I hear what must have been a wrenching phone call to Mr. Goodall. I was helping a little girl eat her porridge when he strode into the ward, still wearing his brown suit, and, ignoring the nurse hurrying towards him, pushed his way between the curtains surrounding the now empty bed. A second later he emerged and lurched towards Sister Cullen's office.

"You told me she was getting better. How could you let this happen? First you kill her mother, now her."

There was a pause—presumably Sister Cullen replied—then a single word rang through the ward.

"Murderers!"

Half an hour later I saw Sister Cullen, her hand resting on his arm, ushering him down the corridor.

That afternoon I was reading *Peter Rabbit* to a boy with a broken leg when another man in a suit appeared. At the sight of Dr. White, my voice faltered. After my weeks of silence, here I was, talking nineteen to the dozen. He listened for a moment, then told the boy he was sorry to interrupt but could he borrow me for a few minutes.

In the office he sat down in Sister's chair and urged me to take the other. To avoid his scrutiny I started counting the legs in the room: two for Dr. White, four for his chair, four for the table, two for me, four for my chair, two for the person in the poster. When there were no more to count I cautiously raised my head. Dr. White was regarding me with an expression that reminded me of the portrait of Lord Minto in the library at Claypoole.

"'If a lion could talk,'" he said, "'we could not understand him.' A philosopher named Ludwig Wittgenstein said that, and I think the same might apply to children. Sister Cullen is a very stubborn woman, almost as stubborn as you are, and she has persuaded Miss Bryant that you will not be punished for this—"

He paused, and I wondered if suddenly, like Matron, he was unable to finish his sentences.

"For this valiant deed," he concluded. "She has also made me promise that I will see you when I visit the school. I will be treating you for a chronic condition; that means something that can't be cured. This will be your chance to let me know if there are problems. If you don't plan to continue talking you can always write me a note. Is there anything you'd like to tell or ask me?"

For a few seconds more I clung to my silence, hugging it close as I had used to hug the green velvet curtain in my uncle's study. Then I asked the question I had not dared to ask Sister. "Can a person be cursed?"

Dr. White's mouth opened in surprise. "I suppose you are asking whether you might be cursed?"

I nodded, picturing my aunt, Will, Mr. Donaldson, Ross, Mrs. Harris, Miss Bryant, Mr. Milne lining up to write curse tablets and throw them into the source of the river Teviot.

"There are people," he said, "who would say yes. I am not one of them. After a decade of practising medicine, I do think that some people attract good luck. And some do not. You've been in the second category for the last six months, but that will change. You must take advantage of Claypoole to get the best education you can."

"But what will I do without Miriam? The other girls hate me. The teachers don't care whether I study or not. Only Cook likes me, and Matron a little bit."

"You'll find other—" Then he saw my face. "Forgive me, Hardy. You don't need platitudes. If you can't have a friend, is there anything else that would make your life at Claypoole easier? Something Miss Bryant might agree to."

I pictured having my own room, but no girl had that. Spending more time with the pigs, but that seemed a stupid thing to ask for. Learning to play the piano, but many of the regular pupils did not have this privilege. "If I could use the library," I said, "that would help. Next term, if I pass the exams, I'll be in Miss Seftain's class. Miriam said she was nice. I'd like to learn Latin."

"I'll ask about the library. Now go and finish *Peter Rabbit*."

THE FOLLOWING DAY AFTER breakfast, Sister Cullen announced that my lift back to the school had arrived. She led me briskly down the corridors I had tiptoed along two nights before. "Thank you for all your hard work yesterday," she said. "I hope for your sake we don't meet again. Or if we do that it's under very different circumstances."

I was about to fling my arms around her when I saw her outstretched hand.

In the car park the van was waiting. At the sight of Mr. Milne standing by the open door, his dungarees stretched tight over his belly, I almost ran back to the ward. But behind me I felt Sister Cullen willing me on, reminding me that I had no choice. I marched across the tarmac, and climbed into the back seat.

As we drove down the high street Mr. Milne commented on the weather, and then, when we had passed beyond the town, the sheep, but as I gazed stonily out of the window he too lapsed into silence. I recognised nothing from my nocturnal walk until we reached Denholm with its neat, white houses. Some surely held weak-minded wrong-doers, like Mr. Milne, and others strong-minded do-gooders, like Sister Cullen. In the field on the far side of the river half-a-dozen horses were circling. One of them, Mr. Milne said, had won the Grand National a few years ago. "That beast is worth twenty times what I earn in a year."

I glared at the horses. A member of their species had helped to kill Miriam. I hope you all fall at the first fence, I thought, and break your stupid legs.

"I know you're angry with me," he went on, "but why should I risk my job and my home for a lassie I don't even know? Would you do that for me?"

I wanted to say he could have refused to take the letter, but I sensed that he felt bad and that my not answering made him feel worse. Halfway up the hill, without warning, he pulled into the gateway of a field of corn. I reached for the door handle, ready to run if he turned towards me, but he stared straight ahead.

"Children are so bloody uncompromising," he said quietly. "You think everything's black and white, that I'm on one side and you're on the other, but, Hardy, you're more like me than you know. One day you'll see something you want—money, or someone else's husband, or a beautiful vase—and you'll think you'll die if you can't have it. You'll be ready to risk your whole future for a few hours, a few days with whatever it is. When that happens think of me: working out my sentence."

I did not understand his words—why would I want a vase or someone else's husband?—but the hair rose on my arms. Briefly Mr. Milne had removed the armour of everyday life and was allowing me to see his naked self. Since my uncle's death I had clung to the belief that I was making my way through the rough country of childhood to the safe, fertile land of adulthood. Now I glimpsed that what Miriam had said was true. The years ahead would change not only my circumstances but also my self more than I could imagine, and not necessarily in the ways I hoped.

We drove on in silence, but it was the silence of truce, not of battle. As we slowed down to pass the lodge, I saw a woman in the garden. Grey-haired and almost as stout as her husband, Mrs. Milne looked up from a row of peas. I felt a beam of unmistakable hatred streaming towards me.

The bell for morning break was ringing as I stepped through the back door. I went directly to the classroom and sat down at my desk, waiting for Mrs. Harris and the next lesson. Alone in the room where Miriam had first smiled at me, the realisation that she was never, ever, coming back rolled over me. I stood up and approached the map of Scotland. The word *Galashiels* was just as sturdy as the last time I looked. I pressed my finger to the black circle of the town.

chapter fourteen

THE DAY AFTER I returned to Claypoole Miss Bryant called out my name in assembly. "You're in for it," Balfour whispered, and I thought so too, but for once I didn't care. I knocked on the white door and made my way across the blue carpet. Performing her usual trick of looking and not looking at me, Miss Bryant said how sorry she was about Goodall. She did not want to know any details of what had happened—perhaps my visit to the hospital was connected to the sleepwalking that had led to my stay in the infirmary?—but she hoped I would settle down into being a diligent working girl.

"I fear we're stuck with each other, Hardy," she said, unwittingly echoing Sister Cullen. "Let us do our best to achieve a modus vivendi. Do you know what that means?"

"Way of life."

"Or way of living. There's a story you'll learn in Latin next year, a fable about the Republic of Rome. Picture the Republic as a large, able-bodied man. One day the limbs get exasperated with constantly feeding the stomach. They decide they won't bother to gather food; they'll just enjoy themselves. But quite soon they begin to feel dizzy and can no longer take pleasure in anything. 'See,' said the stomach, 'we are all related. If you don't feed me, you suffer too.' Claypoole is the same. All the parts of the school are related, and all the parts need to work together."

"Yes, Miss Bryant." I already knew the story. My uncle had used it in one of his sermons and afterwards, at lunch, we had joked that my aunt was the stomach and the rest of us were the limbs, busy serving her. My aunt had laughed and said that in that case she was going to have a second helping of roast beef. Now I wanted to tell Miss Bryant that the story didn't apply to Claypoole. If I stopped work no one would get dizzy, and when she had stopped feeding me, only Cook had cared. Instead I asked if I could go to Miriam's funeral.

"I'm afraid not," she said. "Mr. Goodall doesn't want anyone from the school present. But Mr. Waugh will say something in church next Sunday. And we will all remember Miriam in our prayers." As I headed towards the door she added, a seeming afterthought, that I might use the library when I was not working.

Two days later I was summoned to Dr. White's weekly surgery. Beneath Matron's absent-minded gaze our conversation lasted barely a minute. He asked if I was all right. I said I was. How was the library? Fine. Over the next several years our meetings followed this pattern except for the few occasions—measles, a sprained wrist—when I actually needed his care. I had the consoling sense that he and Sister Cullen were watching over me.

The week after Miriam died we had exams every day. The following week Miss Bryant read out the results in assembly, enunciating the names of the girls who had failed with special clarity. I came fourth or fifth in every subject except scripture, where I came last. In arithmetic, I suspected, I had done better than fourth, but it was not part of Miss Bryant's educational experiment for a working girl to be top of her class. As for the other working girls, they were always last, until the day when the results for French were read out and Findlayson had come fourth. Later, over the washing-up, Smith told me that Findlayson believed her father was a French sailor. When she was old enough, she planned to go to France and find him.

That summer there were no regular pupils at the school and only eight working girls. I had been dreading the long, lonely days, but on the first morning of the holidays Miss Bryant announced that we would be picking raspberries for the farmer who owned the pigs. For three weeks Ross marched us along the drive, down the hill, and past the crossroads to the fields of canes. The farmer handed out stacks of punnets—several boys and girls from Denholm were also picking— and left us to get on with it. We were paid by weight, so he had no need to chivvy us.

The leafy canes were much taller than me, taller even than Ross, and stepping between them I felt as if a lyre-bird might appear at any moment; for hours I picked in solitude save for the clouds of gnats. One afternoon I came upon Ross kissing a boy, her mouth gobbling up his. The next day I almost stumbled over Drummond and the same boy, lying on the ground. Hidden in the canes, I watched the boy rocking back and forth above her, grimacing. Below him Drummond, her red hair spread on the dark soil, kept her eyes tightly closed; once again I glimpsed her bra.

At the end of the afternoon the farmer returned to weigh our fruit and note our pay for the day. Then the raspberries were tipped into a barrel of acid, which bleached them instantly. Later, at the jam factory, dye would restore the colour. On the day I saw Drummond with the boy, the farmer remarked on her picking. "Only seven pounds, lassie. Were you taking a nap?"

She said nothing; the boy snickered. He had somehow managed to pick fifteen pounds. I saw Ross watching him, her lips parted over her chipped tooth. She and Drummond were good friends, but she too, I thought, would have been happy to lie down with him. I was glad there was something she wanted and couldn't have.

The week after Miriam's death, she had tried, as we walked to the gym, to apologise. "I'm sorry about your pal," she had said. "That was a shame."

"So why did you stop me seeing her when she was ill?" I demanded. "If I'd been able to take care of her maybe she wouldn't have died."

"I'm sorry," she said again. "Miss Bryant comes down on me hard when things go wrong."

For her these unadorned sentences were the height of eloquence, but like Mr. Waugh's insipid remarks in church—our dearly beloved pupil is at peace—and Miss Bryant's prayers, they made me furious. "You're a coward," I had said. "All you want to do is bully other people." Since then she had ignored me, except to give orders.

On Friday afternoon the farmer brought his cash-box and we lined up to be paid; as usual I was last. "Not bad for a wee 'un," he said, handing me two pound notes and two half-crowns.

I clutched the notes in wonder. It was the first time I'd touched money, almost the first time I'd seen it since I left Yew House, and I'd forgotten how a bank-note was different from other kinds of paper, and the feeling of possibility that went with it. Then I remembered my circumstances. "Can you keep it for me?" I said.

The farmer's face twisted in bewilderment. "Would you not like to buy yourself some sweeties? Or one of those new comics? My daughter is always after the comics."

With a wary glance over my shoulder—the other girls were collecting their jackets and bags—I said I had no purse.

"Och, I see," he said, following my gaze. "The next rainy day, when I give you girls a lift to the school, I'll bring what I owe you. You can be thinking of a safe place to keep your loot."

As we walked back up the hill, I braced myself for an attack, but the other girls were discussing a programme they'd heard on Matron's wireless; gradually I forgot my fears. I was daydreaming about what to buy with my money—a skipping rope, a bag of gobstoppers—when Ross and Drummond appeared beside me. We were just inside the school gates. Silently they plunged their hands into my pockets and then ordered me to take off my shoes and socks.

"I ate my pay," I said as I sat by the side of the drive, pulling off first one empty sock and then the other. "The half-crowns were delicious. The farmer's keeping my money. He thinks I'm too young to be trusted."

"Stupid moron," said Ross, but she seemed to believe me. While Drummond went to join the other girls she sat down on the grass beside me. "It's a pity you're not older," she went on. "I asked Miss Bryant if I could take my O-levels again next year. If I had someone to help me, like you and Goodall, I'm sure I could pass."

As I pulled on my shoes, I watched her fingers, pink with raspberry juice, pluck the petals of a daisy. Was she asking about love, I wondered, or something else? Gemma will help me. Gemma won't. For a moment I longed to say I would. Even though I was only eleven, I could still drill her in subjects, teach her grammar and reading, help her get into the police. Then I remembered how she had stopped me, over and over, from going to Miriam. I tied my laces, jumped to my feet, and stalked off.

On the next rainy day the farmer was as good as his word. As I climbed out of the Land Rover, he slipped me an envelope with my money. I had racked my brains as to a hiding place. The Elm Room was out of the question; so was my desk. An obscure volume in the library seemed like a good idea, but what if a teacher made a surprising choice? Finally, remembering the story of the third servant, I stole a polythene bag from the kitchen and, borrowing a trowel, dug a hole near a corner of the pigsty. By the end of the raspberry season, I had buried nearly nine pounds.

·   ·   ·

In August I moved up to Miss Seftain's class. I immediately liked two things about her: her excitement about Latin—she would pace the classroom, arms widespread as she described some neat construction— and her enthusiasm for space travel. She read us a poem she'd written in Latin about Laika, the mongrel stray who died travelling to the stars. A year later, when Strelka and Belka survived eighteen orbits and re-entry, we all wrote them letters. And when Yuri Gagarin made his famous orbit she led the entire school outside after supper to toast the night sky. Coincidentally her nickname was Birdy, after her crestlike hair and beaky nose, and at moments of passion it did seem as if she too might take flight.

From my first day of conjugating *amare—amo, amas, amat—*I loved Latin. When I told her that I had been a friend of Miriam's— *sum amica* Miriam—she persuaded Miss Bryant what a good advertisement for the school it would be if a working girl went to university: a triumph for her philanthropic experiment. Our tutorials became the high point of my week. We had been meeting for nearly two months when I confided what had happened with Mr. Donaldson.

"Poor man," said Miss Seftain. "Teachers are so vulnerable to rumours."

She wrote to various friends, asking if anyone knew his present whereabouts. No one did, but an Edinburgh friend revealed what had brought him to the village in the first place. He had been teaching at a famous boys' school, and one night had taken two of his pupils to a pub and then on a joyride around Arthur's Seat. It seemed unlikely that he was still teaching. "Although," Miss Seftain added, "there are places, like Claypoole, that are off the radar."

But despite my tutorials I was still a working girl, and my days were still ruled by Ross. She made no more overtures. I saw her laughing with Findlayson, playing cards with Gilchrist, but her muddy brown eyes ignored me as she told me to wash a floor, or hurry up with the carrots. To my surprise I missed our odd moments of friendliness. Perhaps during the holidays, I thought, I could find a way to make amends. Then one evening in early December I came into the Elm Room to discover her and Drummond packing. They were going to be chambermaids at a hotel in Kelso. When I went over to say good-bye Ross picked me up and swung me round. "Live up to your name, Hardy," she said, and planted a smacking kiss on my cheek. The next day she and Drummond were gone. Gilchrist became head of the working girls, and I began to understand that Ross had been a skillful manager. She knew how to divide the tasks so that everyone pulled her weight. Now, even with Mrs. Bryant's vigilance, the school grew dirtier; crises in the kitchen were more frequent. The next summer one of Cook's sisters left and was not replaced.

As for me, I was marking time in Form I. Miss Seftain kept me back for one year, and then a second. "You're not Mozart, Hardy," she said. "You need to be in a class with girls your own age. You'll just be miserable if you try to go to university at fifteen, and I doubt you'd get a place." Grateful for her protection, knowing I had no choice, I relinquished the superiority of always being the youngest in the class.

By the time I at last moved up to Form II, there were only eight working girls, and the number of regular pupils was also dwindling. At assembly the library was no longer filled; one table in the dining-room stood empty; a year later another was only half full. The gym teacher left to get married, and Mrs. Bryant took over the gym classes. The following year Mrs. Harris left to nurse her mother, and Primary 6 and 7 were combined under Miss Grey.

In Form IV, thanks to Miss Seftain, I sat eight O-level exams. The exams were set and marked by a national board, and I threw myself into preparation, knowing that, for once, I would not be judged as a working girl. The gym became an examination hall, and I loved the ritual of everyone filling pens and sharpening pencils, turning over the questions at the same moment, the teacher walking up and down between the rows of desks, calling out the time.

In August Miss Seftain invited me to celebrate my seven As and one B (scripture). She lived in a flat in the converted stables, and I hoped, at last, to be invited inside, but she answered my knock by saying she'd be out in five minutes. I perched on the wall, watching a yellow snail nudge along. Whenever I offered it a piece of grass it drew in its horns, only to unfurl them again a few seconds later. Like Miss Seftain, I thought, it was being cautious. However much she wanted to help me, she was determined not to follow in Mr. Donaldson's footsteps. She appeared, carrying a tea tray, and joined me on the wall.

"Well done, Hardy," she said, raising her cup to my lemonade. "I can see the headlines already: WORKING GIRL GOES TO UNIVERSITY."

We discussed the next set of exams, called Highers, which I would sit next year, and possible universities. I liked the idea of Edinburgh, but Miss Seftain urged me to consider Scotland's newest university: Strathclyde. "You want to be in the vanguard, Hardy," she said, "like Marcus Aurelius."

For all her talk of the vanguard, however, Miss Seftain too was slow to realise that Claypoole was changing. The regular girls now had a record player on which, after homework, they played catchy songs; on weekends, they wore pleated skirts and turtlenecks, or pinafore dresses. The Labour Party had been elected. Fewer parents worked abroad and more wanted their children to live at home. In the working girls' bathroom there were enough basins to go round. As the days grew shorter and colder the school seemed larger and emptier. One January morning, only a week after the start of the new term, Miss

Bryant looked out at us from the dais and asked us to sit down in our rows. With some scuffling, we knelt, or sat cross-legged, on the parquet floor.

"As you must have noticed," she said, "we are not as many as we used to be. Like a number of sister and brother schools, Claypoole has been losing pupils. There are several reasons for this, too complicated to go into, but the sad truth is that you cannot run a good school without a certain number of pupils because you cannot employ sufficient excellent teachers. A letter went out to your parents yesterday informing them that, due to circumstances beyond my control, Claypoole will close its doors at the end of this term. I have already spoken to several headmistresses who are eager to offer places to Claypoole girls."

A few girls had begun to cry; even a couple of teachers took out handkerchiefs. I gazed at the floor, trying to contain my jubilation. My life as a working girl was coming to an end. Not until lunchtime, when Cook asked what I would do in April, did I understand that within three months I would be homeless. When I said I'd no idea, her face puckered, as if the pastry she was rolling had stuck.

"Can you not go back to your old home?" she said.

"My aunt would sooner take in one of the pigs."

"Maybe"—she pressed down on the rolling pin—"you should ask Miss Bryant to find another school for you. You're a bright little thing."

There was no point in saying that any other boarding school would involve fees. Instead I asked about her plans.

"I'll see if there's an opening in Hawick. Sue"—she nodded towards the sister who still worked at Claypoole—"is getting married. Daft, I tell her, cooking for one ungrateful sod for free, as opposed to a hundred for good money."

I laughed, but for the rest of the day, while I studied and served supper and did the washing-up and got the dining-room ready for breakfast, I pondered Cook's question. None of the other working girls faced my dilemma; two had homes, of a sort, to go to; the other five had already begun to talk with excitement about the jobs in hotels Miss Bryant would find for them. But I was still only five foot three (an inch taller than Yuri Gagarin, Miss Seftain reminded me); I had no money, save for what I had earned picking raspberries, and, as far as I knew, no marketable skills other than cooking and cleaning, both of which I disliked. I wanted to go to university, but how would I study for my Highers, now only a few months away, and where would I live?

The day after Miss Bryant's announcement two girls were late for class—judging by their eyes they'd been crying—and our form teacher said nothing. Later Smith didn't show up to serve lunch; again no reprimand was forthcoming. Without a word, everyone understood that the rules were changing. Even the teachers started to be late for classes, and one or two skipped assembly.

That Saturday, a cold, frosty day, I left my broom in a downstairs classroom and walked over the playing fields to knock again at Miss Seftain's door. She answered, wearing a faded pink dressing-gown. "Oh, Hardy," she said, stifling a yawn. "Were we meeting this morning?" It was the first time I had seen her without glasses, or lipstick, and she looked oddly younger.

"No, but I need to talk to you."

"Give me five minutes—no, ten—and I'm all yours."

She closed the door in my face; some rules had not changed. Again I sat on the wall. This time I watched a thrush sampling the berries on a nearby holly-bush, spitting out some, eating others. My lack of a watch had turned me into a good judge of time. Just when I thought ten minutes has passed, Miss Seftain reappeared wearing, to my amazement, trousers. No teacher, to my knowledge, had ever worn them within the school grounds. She suggested we walk around the terraces. Mr. Milne still kept the lawns immaculate, but the flower-beds year by year had grown more rampant and now, in the dead of winter, were choked with stiff brown stalks. Only the snowdrops, with their tender white flowers, were in bloom. Miss Seftain nodded vaguely when I pointed them out. A tree was real when Ovid described it, not when it grew outside her window.

"So talk to me," she said, and I needed no further invitation to pour out my fears.

When at last I stopped she said, "I'd like to help you, Hardy, but I'm in difficult waters myself. Claypoole has been my home for fifteen years, and finding a job in the middle of the school year is tricky at the best of times. It looks as if I'll be moving in with my sister and her husband, neither of whom is thrilled at the prospect. I doubt many people will leap to employ a sixty-one-year-old classics teacher with an extremely poor record of university acceptances."

"You're a super teacher."

She produced her lipstick and, between applying it first to her upper lip, then her lower, said that she was a good teacher for girls like me but that she had little talent for stupid girls. "It's like trying to plough very hard earth. I just can't get the information into their brains."

Thinking of Cook's sister, I suggested she might get married.

"Married?" She threw back her head and laughed merrily. "Do you know who would marry me? Some man of eighty who had lost his wife and wanted a housekeeper. And do you know who a man my age would marry? Some woman of thirty-eight who was tired of working. Nearly fifty years after we got the vote that's still the way the world works. If anyone's going to get married it should be you."

"Me?" It was as if the frozen grass had turned suddenly red.

She hummed a few bars of "Here Comes the Bride," and then, seeing my face, laughed. "I'm teasing, Hardy. I hope you'll fend off suitors until after university. So do you have any idea what you might do?"

When I explained my utter lack of a plan, she asked if I liked children. "Child-care often comes with board and lodging."

"I don't know," I said. "I hate most of the girls here. I used to like my cousin Veronica before she became daft about fashion. Isn't there something else I could do? I want to go to university."

"Someday," said Miss Seftain. "Right now you need a job that will give you shelter, food, and clothing. If you don't want to work in a hotel then, I think, looking after children is your best bet. A nice, honourable family," she mused, "could be the making of you. Of course a horrible one could make your life misery."

"In which case I'd leave." A jackdaw had joined us and was walking on the grass nearby, taking its own constitutional.

"May you always be so redoubtable, Hardy. Have you noticed a magazine on the table in the front hall called *The Lady*? It has advertisements for au pairs and nannies, even the odd governess, though they're out of fashion. Is that a crow?"

"No, a jackdaw. See how it's partly grey and partly black? People say they're very intelligent. You can tame them."

"Not me," said Miss Seftain.

As if it understood, the jackdaw took wing.

I HAD NEVER, DURING all my years of dusting, felt tempted to open *The Lady*—both the name and the decorous covers promised tedium—but that night instead of doing homework I went to the hall and carried off the two copies to the Primary 7 classroom. Sitting at my old desk, I turned to the advertisements. Several were for assistants to elderly people, or domestic staff. The rest, as Miss Seftain had said, were for nannies. Each threw open a door.

> Nanny wanted for three well-behaved boys, 7, 9 and
> 13. Some housework and cooking. Self-contained flat.
> Central London.

My own flat in London! I saw myself walking down the streets whose names I knew from Monopoly, going to bookshops and museums. Then I imagined being alone in a house, day after day, with Will and his loutish friends. I must look for a situation with only one child, I thought, a younger, smaller child.

An advertisement for a governess for a nine-year-old girl in Geneva, Switzerland, seemed promising—I pictured Heidi and her goats—until I came to the phrase "passport essential." Cleaning the dormitories, I had several times come across a passport and studied the little booklet with fascination.

After reading the advertisements in both issues, looking for jobs in Britain that involved one younger child and no special skills, I had circled four possibilities.

> Experienced, live-in au pair sought for seven-year-
> old girl. Must be reliable, nonsmoker, able to assist
> with homework and deal with occasional tantrums.
> References. Suffolk.

> Nanny for four-year-old boy. Mother invalid. Father
> travels. Capable of supervising domestic staff and
> making decisions. Room with basin, c.h. References.
> Brighton.

> Widower, 42, seeks companion for eleven-year-old
> daughter. Cosy cottage, use of car and good salary for

right person prepared to make long-term commitment.
References. Cornwall.

And in the last column of the second magazine:

Nanny desperately needed in north of Scotland for
eight-year-old girl. No housekeeping or cooking. Must
be prepared to supervise lessons, read, play, and go for
walks. References. Mainland. The Orkneys.

At the sight of the address, Mrs. Marsden's stories of soldiers and
seals came flooding back. It was as if fate had tapped me on the
shoulder.

I had had no occasion to write a letter since my attempt to reach Mr.
Donaldson. The next day, using his stationery and borrowing fresh
envelopes from Miss Seftain, I wrote to all four advertisements, saying
what a good teacher I was and how fond of children. At the end of each
letter I put, as Miss Seftain had instructed, "References on request."
The following afternoon I queued up behind three regular pupils outside Miss Bryant's study. No working girl, to my knowledge, had ever
visited her voluntarily, but she did not seem surprised to see me walking across the blue carpet. I described my applications and asked if she
would act as a reference.

"For once, Hardy, I'm glad you're showing initiative. I think I can
truthfully say you are a conscientious worker and mature for your
age."

"And maybe," I suggested, "you don't need to say exactly how old I
am. I'll be eighteen in a couple of months."

"Let's pretend"—she made a quick note on a pad of paper—"that
your birthday is next week."

· · ·

A WEEK AFTER I dispatched my letters a heavy cream envelope, bearing my name, lay on the hall table. The widower in Cornwall wrote that I sounded delightful and that, if I lived nearby, he would have invited me to tea. "I very much regret," he continued, "that, while both I and my daughter would enjoy the company of a school-leaver, we really need someone older to provide stability to our household." The fact that my letter had summoned a response, even a refusal, seemed almost miraculous. I read the half-dozen lines over and over. Miss Seftain, however, was less impressed. " 'Enjoy the company of a school-leaver' indeed. You're well out of that one."

Another week passed and I began to worry that I had received my only reply. Even the desperate person on the Orkneys had found someone closer to home. A new copy of *The Lady* arrived and I sent off three more enquiries: one to Edinburgh, two to London. The next day, while I was polishing the corridor, Miss Bryant stepped out of her study to ask if I had news. I confessed my single refusal.

"Well, if you apply for more jobs, come to me. I can include a brief reference. By the way," she added, and I guessed that this was the real reason she had emerged, "I wrote to your aunt when I wrote to the other parents. She has not replied. I've never"—her bony forehead quivered—"known a guardian to show less interest in a ward."

She walked off down the shining corridor, leaving me to stare after her. Everyone was changing before my eyes.

That night I dreamed I was back in my room at Yew House, listening, as I had on so many evenings, to the noises from below. Then, suddenly, I was downstairs, peering around the sitting-room door. My aunt lay sprawled on the chintz-covered sofa, in the arms of Mr. Carruthers. Around them pranced Louise and Veronica, wearing party clothes. I crossed the corridor to my uncle's study. He was at his desk, writing.

"Why, Gemma"—he smiled—"you're just in time to help with my sermon."

"But my aunt, do you know what she's doing?"

"With Mr. Carruthers? Of course. She never much cared for either of us. And it's worse now that you're growing up and I'm dead. Tell me what to say after islands and stepping-stones?"

I suggested life belts. "Yes," he said, "we can rescue each other." While I stood beside him, he wrote down everything I said. Then the door burst open and Will was standing over us, his neck bulging.

"You're not my father," he shouted. "You're not my father."

And I was shouting back, until Findlayson shook my shoulder.

THE NEXT DAY A blue envelope addressed in neat, rounded hand-writing lay on the hall table. Once again ignoring my duties, I carried it over to the pigs. Even while I held it in my hand, I whispered, "Let someone want me. Let someone want me," as if the contents could still change. At the sight of me the pigs, several generations on from the original Heidi and Thumbelina, rushed to the trough, only to fall back when they realised I had no food. I sat on the fence to read.

> *Blackbird Hall*
> *Near Tingwall*
> *The Mainland*
> *The Orkneys*
> *Tel. Tingwall 235*
> *28 January 1966*

Dear Miss Hardy,
> *Sorry for the late reply. Let me tell you the situation. We live in the northeast part of the main island (though you may*

not know the islands—your letter doesn't say). Besides the
house and the farm we, my brother and I, have in our care
an eight-year-old girl. Nell's mother died last year, and since
then she's been running wild. There's no father in the picture.
I don't have time to keep her company or supervise her les-
sons. If you are still free, I offer you a tomboy for a pupil and
more weather than any person should have to deal with. This
is a lonely place—except for the birds!—and whoever comes
here needs to be forewarned. You are obviously very young but
perhaps Nell will like that. She ran away from the nice woman
we found to mind her in the autumn.

I propose a three-month trial. If you can, please telephone
to make the arrangements. Of course we will advance your
fare for the train and the ferry. I am authorised to pay you five
pounds a week plus board and lodging.

Kind regards,
Vicky Sinclair

Surely, I thought, it was another good omen that the house was
called after one of my favourite birds. But who did the wild girl belong
to, I wondered, and who had done the authorising? From behind me
came a grunt. I put the letter in my pocket and stood up to scratch
Thumbelina the Second. "I'm going away soon," I told her. She put her
trotters on the edge of the trough and reached her wet snout towards
me. If pigs could talk, I thought, we could not understand them.

No one was enthusiastic about my job. Miss Seftain called the
Orkneys a godforsaken place. Matron said Nell sounded like a troubled
child. Cook said, "For heaven's sake, Hardy, why would you want to

mind some brat in the back of beyond?" Dr. White still hoped I could take my Highers and apply for university. But no one could deny—I had had two more polite rejections—that I had no alternative. Miss Bryant told me to come to her study after six, when the rates went down, to telephone Miss Sinclair.

I had never made a phone call before. It was, I understood, a reliable way of doing what I had attempted with Miriam—talking to a person at a distance—but nothing had prepared me for the experience of holding a piece of black plastic to my ear and hearing a woman, nearly three hundred miles away, say in a light sing-song voice, "Good evening. Blackbird Hall."

"This is Gemma Hardy," I said. Across the room Miss Bryant frowned and mouthed something I couldn't decipher. "I'd like the job, please. I'm used to loneliness and I know about birds. I can teach Nell sums and writing, and Latin when she's older."

"You can teach her if you can catch her," said Miss Sinclair. "She led her last teacher a merry dance."

She promised to mail a postal order for my fare the next day and asked if I could come the following week. If I left Hawick on Monday, she explained, I could catch the Tuesday ferry. She would book me a room at a bed-and-breakfast near the station in Thurso. "My brother will meet the ferry," she said. "See you soon."

I replaced the receiver and reported the conversation to Miss Bryant. She shook her head. "I hope we've made the right choice, Hardy," she said. "I've never sent a girl so far away. I can't help wondering why they didn't get someone local. There are two good-sized towns on the Orkneys."

I had not thought of this before and I did not care to think of it now; no local girl, I was sure, knew Latin as well as I did. I curtseyed and left the room. Two days later a postal order for twenty pounds arrived. As she handed me four five-pound notes Miss Bryant said she had asked Matron to help me sort out my wardrobe.

For nearly seven years I had sported more or less ill-fitting versions of the school uniform. In the holidays I had worn cast-off skirts and blouses and then, as fashions changed, pullovers and trousers. Now, with Matron's help, I went through the overflowing lost-property box and chose various garments, which we laundered and repaired: a nice blue skirt, and a plaid one, several blouses and T-shirts, a cardigan, four pullovers, three pairs of trousers, and a blue pinafore that made me feel awkward but that she claimed was becoming. She insisted that I take the warmest coat that fitted me, an almost new anorak, and several pairs of shoes. To carry all this she presented me with a second suitcase and then, her parting gift, a green paisley dress that had belonged to one of the prefects. Matron was the only other person who was unequivocally happy about Claypoole closing. She showed me a photograph of a woman and three windswept children on a mountaintop.

"My daughter," she said. "In the Lake District."

When I wasn't organising my clothes I made my modest round of farewells. Miss Seftain gave me a copy of Ovid's *Metamorphoses* and a cardigan. Dr. White shook my hand and gave me a watch. "So you'll be able to scold your pupil when she's late. Sister Cullen wishes you godspeed." On Sunday Miss Bryant invited me to sit in the dining-room for my last meal, but I declined. After years of eating perched on an upturned milk crate, I had no desire to sit at a table and be ignored. That night's pudding was the detested tapioca, but in the kitchen, Cook produced a trifle in my honour. Ignoring the washing-up, we clustered around the table to devour the sweet fruit and custard.

"So why the special pud?" said Findlayson. She and I were the last of the original working girls.

"Hardy's leaving," said Cook. "We're wishing her bon voyage."

"But not," said Findlayson smugly, "au revoir."

An hour later, as I was about to climb into bed, I felt her watching me from across the room. Peeling back the sheets, I found two slices of bread and jam. I set them on the floor for the mice to enjoy and resigned myself to sleeping between the blankets. But the incident had cast me into a wakeful state; my mind travelled back to my last night at Yew House. As soon as I had saved enough money, I vowed, I would search for Mr. Donaldson. Meanwhile it came to me that I wanted a souvenir of Miriam. Not caring who heard me, I got out of bed and made my way to the library. Inside the almost full moon was spilling its silvery radiance through the windows. I walked unhesitatingly to the shelves where novels were kept. I was peering at the titles when a slight noise made me turn.

The young man, wearing his white shirt and dark trousers, was sitting at the piano. He played the first notes of "Auld Lang Syne," then swung around to face me. "I spent a year in the Orkneys," he said, "based at Scapa Flow. When we had time off we went fishing among the shipwrecks. For some reason fish are partial to wrecks; maybe they like having a house under the water."

"Will you visit me there?"

"I think my visiting days are over," he said quietly, "but you never know. Be careful of the causeway."

Before I could ask what causeway, he stood up, walked to the far door—his footsteps were as audible as his playing—and, with a brief wave, left the room. Alone I took down the slim red volume of *Kim*. Then I sat down at the piano and played the one tune Miriam had managed to teach me: "Auld Lang Syne."

PART
III

chapter fifteen

THE NEXT MORNING MISS BRYANT was waiting in the hall. She was beautifully dressed—I had never seen her otherwise—but the invisible shield that had made it hard to look at her directly was gone. I saw deep shadows beneath her eyes, a soft droop of flesh beneath her chin. Her subjects were leaving, her empire was vanishing; she was unlikely to find another.

"Goodbye, Hardy," she said. "Here is the address where I can be reached in the foreseeable future. I hope at some point—ten years from now, perhaps twenty—you will realise that you learned some valuable lessons at Claypoole." As if we were at a school prize-giving, she handed me an envelope and shook my hand.

"Goodbye, Miss Bryant," I said cheerfully. "Don't let your sister-in-law clean you out of house and home."

My new shoes squeaking with every step, I walked across the floor I had polished so often and, for the first time in seven years, used the front door. Outside the inevitable minivan was waiting, with the inevitable Mr. Milne at the wheel. But in the van, there was a surprise. In the corner, toadlike in her brown coat, squatted his wife. She did not look at me as I slid onto the other end of the seat, but she was not ignoring me, as Miss Bryant and the other girls so often had. I could feel the hatred pouring out of her.

"Good morning, Mrs. Milne," I said.

Her eyes slid round to glare at me.

"It looks like it might be a nice day," I responded, nodding towards the leaden clouds.

On the damp grass several blackbirds, descendants perhaps of the fledglings Ross and I had watched over, were searching for worms. At last I was the one leaving and the birds were staying. We drove through the school grounds in silence. Then, as we passed the lodge, Mrs. Milne began to speak. Her words, at first, were barely audible above the engine; yard by yard they grew clearer.

"—old geezer. Thought he could be Galahad forever. Those girls seemed to think so too. They didn't see my nightly treat: an old man with a belly and prickly balls. No, they scampered around with their bare knees and their little—"

The hair on my arms rose. This was not like Mr. Milne's outburst when he drove me back from Hawick, an attempt by one person to reach another. Rather Mrs. Milne was releasing the voice inside her head that most people learn, even when they're very young, not to let out.

"My mother used to talk about working her fingers to the bone. I'd squeeze her hand, and say these aren't bones. Now . . ."

Meanwhile her husband drove steadily, seemingly oblivious, but beneath his grey hair his ears had turned scarlet. When we pulled up in front of the station, I turned to Mrs. Milne and offered the least appropriate farewell I could think of: Veronica's to me, years ago. "Goodbye, Mrs. Milne. I hope you have a happy life."

On the pavement, as Mr. Milne lifted out my suitcases, I noticed that his dungarees no longer struggled to contain his belly; his flesh, along with his job, was disappearing. I was about to offer my hand—I had no wish to part enemies—when he too fired a parting shot.

"It seems right, your leaving early. You were never really a Claypoole girl, not even a Claypoole working girl. For some reason—Christ knows why—you think you're so much better than the rest of us. After that business with the cripple, Miss Bryant tried to get rid of you, but no one else would have you. We're all glad to see the back of you."

While he continued to list my shortcomings, I gathered my thoughts. When at last he spluttered to a close, I drew myself up to my full height. "May no one ever give you a job," I said. "And may you have to take care of your wife for a hundred years."

Before he could respond I picked up the larger of the suitcases and dragged it into the station. By the time I returned for the second case, the van was gone. Standing in the queue at the ticket office, I found myself gulping cold air. My mouth burned as if each word I'd spoken had been a fiery nugget. My curse wasn't written on a lead tablet and offered to Sulis, but I hoped it would nonetheless prove effective. When I reached the window, I asked for a second-class single to Thurso.

"Second class, single, child," corrected the clerk.

"No, adult. I'm eighteen. I could get married."

"You could indeed, ducky"—the clerk's bald head bobbed in the overhead light—"but why not save yourself six pounds? You can still get married at sixteen or seventeen."

Reluctantly I agreed to be a child one last time.

I had been looking forward to the journey north: the prospect of new landscapes, and new people. What I had not anticipated was the sense, even as I headed into the future, of revisiting my life so far. The first station we came to was Galashiels, and I studied the sullen, grey houses. Perhaps one of them had sheltered Miriam. Our friendship was still the only evidence I had, since my uncle died, that I could be loved. And what about Mr. Goodall? Was he still living there, even greyer and grubbier? Beyond Galashiels the countryside grew desolate, populated only by scruffy sheep and dark twisted trees. I thought of Ross's story of running away, and sleeping in a sheepfold. How lonely she must have been. Then houses began to appear, at first singly, soon in streets; the train slowed. We had reached Edinburgh. One by one I lifted down my suitcases. As I stood waiting for the crowd to disperse, I saw that the platform where I had embarked, years ago, was just across the forecourt. I dragged my suitcases over. Two boys in jeans and jackets were sitting on the bench, sharing a cigarette.

"Would you mind standing up for a moment?" I asked.

"What's this?" said the nearest boy. "Station inspection?" He leaned back, blowing smoke in my direction.

"Please," I said. "Just for a second."

"Come on, Brian," said the other, getting to his feet. "Do what she says."

As he spoke, his lips stretched over slightly prominent teeth; I had a flash of recognition. "Did you once want to work in a fish shop?"

"I don't know if I wanted to, but I do, down in Leith. How did you guess?" He cocked his head. "Do I look like a fish?"

"Not really. Seven years ago on this platform you carried my suitcase."

"It's possible," he said. "I get this train most days."

He tugged the other boy to his feet, and there, I pointed them out, were the words—FLY AWAY—carved into the wood. The boys peered, nonplussed. I thanked them and started to walk away, dragging my cases.

"If I used to carry your luggage," said the fish boy, coming up beside me, "I'd better not stop now." He took the cases out of my hands and asked where I was going. When I told him, he remarked that he had never been that far north. "You'll have to come back in seven years and tell me what it's like."

"I will."

"Okay. Same place, same time." He smiled down at me and then, as a train whistled nearby, turned and loped away.

But not everything had remained the same. The train to Thurso was a modern one with seats in rows instead of compartments, and when we reached the Forth Rail Bridge I saw that, after seventy years of solitude, it had a companion: not far away a slender suspension bridge now carried cars high above the water. Once we were back on land, passing fields and farms, I reached for my book and came upon Miss Bryant's envelope. Inside, folded in a sheet of paper, was a ten-pound note. I must have made some sound because the woman across the aisle looked over. "Someone's fond of you," she said.

"Actually I think someone's glad to see the back of me."

"Well, with enemies like that who needs friends?"

While she returned to her magazine, I examined the sheet of paper, wondering if it contained a final blessing, or curse, but there was only an address in Coldstream with a phone number. Once again I glimpsed the way in which departure ripped the veil from ordinary life, revealing things that were normally kept hidden. Why else had the young man appeared last night, and Mrs. Milne this morning? We passed through Perth, and a few minutes later I saw the familiar line of hills and the circular wood above the village. For a moment I longed to be back at Yew House, climbing the fort with my uncle, walking by the river. Then the hills were gone and I was travelling, untrammelled, towards the future. I opened my book.

BY THE TIME WE reached Thurso, it was past seven in the evening and the train was almost empty. One of the few remaining passengers, a bearlike man who worked for the forestry commission, helped me carry my suitcases to the bed-and-breakfast. An unsmiling landlady showed me to a surprisingly cosy room and said she had my supper waiting. I had had grand thoughts of how I would spend my first night of freedom—a pub, a conversation with a tall, dark stranger—but after a watery steak and kidney pie, bed seemed the only possibility. I fell asleep amazed at how silent the night was without my fellow working girls.

In the morning I explored the town, stopping often to gaze in the shop windows that lined the main street. After my years of privation the most ordinary goods—a rake, a tea-cup, a pork chop—were like the relics of a lost civilisation. At noon I retrieved my luggage and took a taxi to the ferry terminal. The *St. Ola* was waiting; the man who sold the tickets carried my suitcases up the gangway. I joined the other passengers on deck to watch the cars being winched aboard one by one; they looked oddly small and helpless, dangling above the water. Then the foghorn sounded, and in a swirl of engine fumes, beneath windy skies, we pulled away from the dock. The other passengers retired below; I clung to my place at the rail. Never again, I vowed, would I live in a place where I couldn't see the sea. Or at least bicycle to it. As we rounded the harbour wall a shaft of light broke through the clouds, pointing the way to my destination.

I have no idea how long I stood there before a voice said, "So what brings you to the Orkneys?"

I turned to discover a man in a duffle coat, leaning against the rail a few yards away. "How do you know I don't live there?" I said.

"I've lived in Kirkwall all my life. No native would stand out here, getting blown to bits, when they could be downstairs having a nice cup of tea."

"You are."

"Och, well"—his eyebrows disappeared beneath his woolen hat—"I'm a freak. I lost my boat last year. I miss the water."

His slight build gave him a boyish look, but from the dark shadow on his jaw and the lines around his mouth, I guessed him to be thirty at least, perhaps even forty. A pair of binoculars hung from his neck and a small, clear drip from the end of his nose. "How?" I said. "Were you shipwrecked?"

"No, God forbid. It's a long story. The short version is money and sibling rivalry."

"Like Cain and Abel?"

"Maybe." He sounded doubtful. "It's a wee while since I was in the Sunday school." He buried his face, briefly, in a capacious white handkerchief and then said it was my turn to answer his questions. I told him I was going to Blackbird Hall.

"Ah, you're looking after Mr. Sinclair's niece." His face brightened as he understood how I fitted into his world. "She's a little rascal, by all accounts."

"Who's Mr. Sinclair? The woman I spoke to, Vicky Sinclair, didn't use the word 'niece.'"

"Mr. Sinclair is the owner of Blackbird Hall. Nowadays he mostly lives in London, making money hand over fist. Vicky is his housekeeper. They're distant cousins."

So this was who had done the authorising, I thought. "Does he ever come here?"

"In the summer. You'll like Vicky. She's a grand lass. Did she mention her brother?"

"Just that they work on the farm together."

My companion's eyes darkened. "He's good with the cattle, Seamus, I'll grant him that, but hard as a horseshoe. I ran into him last month, walking around the Stones. He couldn't even be bothered to raise his hat. They say he never got over being a Bevin Boy, but plenty of people were in the war and didn't lose their manners."

What were the Stones, I wondered, and what was a Bevin Boy? I asked about the former, and the man said could he buy me a cup of tea. I told him I'd prefer ginger beer and followed him into the cabin.

When we were settled with our drinks by the window, he said that the main island of the Orkneys had several remarkable Stone Age sites, including a chambered tomb and a ring of standing stones. There was even a Stone Age village, which had been buried for centuries and emerged after a tremendous storm.

"Like Pompeii." I had loved translating Pliny's account of the eruption.

Again he seemed doubtful. "But I'm forgetting my manners," he said. "I'm Alec Johnson."

I gave my name and asked if I could borrow his binoculars. At first, as I fiddled with the focus, I saw only a blur of water. Then a cormorant flew by and I could count each dull brown feather. As dusk came on, Mr. Johnson drank his tea and read the newspaper; I alternated between gazing directly at the sea and gazing through the lenses. Almost too soon the lights of Stromness appeared, stretching along the harbour and up the hill.

"You must come back in daylight to see the town," said Mr. Johnson. "It's a pretty place. People here aren't fussy about appearances," he added, "but I'm going to run a comb through my hair. Good luck, Miss Hardy."

You're wearing a hat, I wanted to say. Then I understood that I was the one who needed to use a comb. I had left my Alice band at Claypoole, and the mirror in the ladies' room showed my hair wild as a scarecrow's. By the time I emerged and manoeuvred my suitcases down the gangway, the last car was being winched ashore and most of the other passengers had disappeared. No one stepped forward to greet me, and surveying the poorly lit harbour, I saw no one waiting. I had not thought to ask Miss Sinclair what I should do if her brother wasn't there. I set my luggage beside a stack of lobster traps and circled the nearest streetlight, trying to keep warm, trying not to worry that I had misunderstood the arrangements. Opposite the harbour I spotted a hotel. I was about to start lugging my suitcases over—surely it would have a telephone—when I saw headlights approaching. The vehicle, a Land Rover, came to an abrupt halt; a man climbed out. Even in the darkness his scowl was unmistakable.

"Gemma Hardy," he said flatly, each syllable a stone dropped into a deep well.

I admitted that I was.

"You're nothing but a wean."

"I'm eighteen," I said. "You're confusing size and age."

"No. I'm not." His scowl sharpened, and for a moment I thought he might simply turn and walk away. "Well, this is Vicky's mess," he said at last. "Come on."

"What's your name?" I asked, but he had already seized my suit-cases. Without a word he shoved them into the back, got into the driver's seat, and started the engine. I was still closing the passenger door when the vehicle jerked forward. We drove past a row of houses. Soon the last streetlight was gone. Wind whistled through chinks in the floor and around the ill-fitting door. I sat on my hands for warmth.

"How far is it?" I asked.

Nothing.

Remembering my conversation with Mr. Johnson, I tried again. "What's a Bevin Boy?"

"For God's sake, shut your trap."

Hard as a horseshoe, I thought.

Later I would learn that the drive took less than an hour, but on that first evening it seemed longer than all the rest of my journey put together. Bitterly I recalled Miss Seftain's comment about how depen-dent an au pair was on her employers. I was marooned, as surely as Robinson Crusoe. We passed the lights of a few isolated cottages, one or two other cars, but mostly dark fields. With no warning, Seamus turned off the narrow road onto a narrow track. We bumped along until a metal gate barred our way.

"What are you waiting for?" he demanded. "Open the gate."

I got out to do his bidding. As I struggled with the bolt, I felt his scornful glare, stronger than the headlights. I was small, I was useless, I was not what they had paid for. Finally the bolt relented and, stumbling in the mud, aware that my new shoes would never be the same, I pushed open the gate. The Land Rover roared through, drenching me.

I stood there, wiping ineffectually at the damp patches on my coat. Then I walked towards the passenger door with deliberate slowness. I was almost there when Seamus's door flung open. "For God's sake," he yelled, "close the gate."

"Close it yourself," I said.

He did.

When we were once again jolting along, the night seemed even darker. At last we pulled onto a gravel drive. A house loomed white in the headlights. We stopped. I climbed out, walked over to the only door I could see, and rang the bell. I just wanted to get the whole thing over with. Let Miss Sinclair dismiss me. I would return to Stromness, sleep on a bench in the harbour, and take the first ferry back to Thurso. The door opened. A woman, almost as tall as Seamus, was looking down at me.

"Gemma," she said. "I was beginning to worry something had happened."

"Are you Miss Sinclair?"

"Vicky. Why do you have mud all over you?"

"Your brother, if that's who he is, splashed me when I was opening the gate."

Vicky spread her hands and I saw that they were covered with flour. As I was to learn, she seldom apologised for Seamus—it would have been an endless task—but she did apologise for not coming to meet me. "One of us has to be here for Nell, even when she's hiding in her room. Come in." She stepped back, and I crossed the threshold of Blackbird Hall.

On that first evening I barely noticed the hall, with its grand piano and comfortable armchairs; what caught my attention were the trousers, very like my own, that Vicky wore beneath her flowery apron. As she led the way to the kitchen she asked, How was the crossing? Was I hungry? Had I seen the Old Man of Hoy? Oh, no, of course it was dark. Would I like a bath? Supper? She was as talkative as her brother was taciturn, and her voice was as warm as it had been on the phone.

"Let me just wash my hands," she said, "and I'll show you your room."

In the kitchen I smelled a fragrance I had not encountered since Yew House. "You're making bread," I said. The weight of my despair rose an inch.

"In your honour." She smiled, and I saw that I was guilty of what I had accused Seamus of: confusing size and age. She was much younger than her brother. Indeed that evening, with her glowing cheeks and thick brown hair falling to her shoulders, she looked barely older than the prefects at Claypoole. Later she told me she was twenty-seven.

Like Mr. Johnson, she offered tea, and this time I accepted. I didn't care for the bitter liquid but I knew that enjoying it was a badge of adulthood. Under Vicky's direction I moved the kettle to the centre of the hob, warmed the pot, and measured out the tea-leaves. With two spoonfuls of sugar, the result was drinkable. Meanwhile she punched down the dough and asked what the Borders were like. I told her about the soft, rounded hills, the remains of volcanoes—volcanoes in Scotland, she exclaimed—and the green fields. I described the abbeys the regular girls had visited on school trips, and Sir Walter Scott's house.

"We have all his novels in the library," she said. "I've never read a sentence. Maybe because our English teacher was always going on about *Ivanhoe*."

"You have a library?"

"Next to the dining-room. There's a good collection of history books—that was what old Mr. Sinclair liked—and almost every Victorian novel you can think of. Let me show you your room."

We climbed a broad carpeted stair, each stair rod gleaming. I was still determined to leave in the morning, but at the sight of my corner room, my despair rose another inch. A fire glowed in the grate, and the curtains were drawn snug across the four windows. Against one wall stood a large bed with a flowered quilt. Vicky turned on the lamp on the bedside table and another on the desk. Looking around, I caught sight of myself in the mirror on the wardrobe, and then of my suitcases next to the chest of drawers. In front of the fire were two armchairs and a low table.

"The bathroom is next door," said Vicky. "I hope you'll be comfortable."

"It's the most beautiful room I've ever seen."

"I'm glad you like it." But the little crease that appeared between her eyebrows suggested something other than gladness. Worrying that, once again, I had betrayed my age, I asked where Nell slept.

"Next door, but she's been hiding all day." Vicky wandered over to the dressing-table and fidgeted with the lace mat. "I should tell you that she's not over the moon about your arrival."

Why did that phrase "should tell" always herald unpleasantness? Was there no imperative towards happiness? "On the phone," I said, "you described her as leading her last teacher a merry dance."

"If only it had been an eightsome reel or a Gay Gordons." Vicky shook her head. "Poor Miss Cameron. She taught school in Thurso for thirty years before she came here. Seamus said she was husband-hunting, but who would come to the Orkneys to do that?" She described Miss Cameron's efficiency and Nell's awfulness: spilling things on her books, running away. Then in December the two were out for a walk when they spotted a fern they'd been looking for, for their scrapbook, on a ledge beside the sea. Nell climbed down to pick it and claimed to be stuck. Miss Cameron, despite her fear of heights, went to rescue her. As soon as she reached the ledge, Nell scarpered. Fortunately Seamus had heard Miss Cameron's cries. She left the next day.

"And since then," Vicky said, "Nell's been running wild. I'm too busy with the farm and the house to mind her. It was obvious you were just a slip of a girl—Mr. Sinclair laughed when I read him your letter over the phone—but he thought you'd be a friend for Nell. For all her naughtiness she's lonely."

"I'm eighteen," I said for the third time that day. "I'm just small for my age."

"You must be tired, after your long journey."

She spoke soothingly, as if my lie were irrelevant, and suddenly I felt exhausted all over again. I said I would take a bath, and she offered to bring up supper on a tray. In the doorway she paused. "Maybe keep your door locked. It's more than twenty years since Seamus came back from the war but he still sometimes sleepwalks."

"How far away is the sea?"

"Ten minutes across the fields. I'll show you tomorrow, if the rain stays off."

In the bathroom I filled the bath half full, added a handful of lavender bath salts from a jar on the window-sill, and sank down into the hot, fragrant water. Not since the hospital had I experienced such luxury. Back in my beautiful room I found a tray with a plate of macaroni and cheese and a little dish of canned peaches set before the glowing fire. As I sat down to eat I heard the distant roaring of my long-missed friend, the waves rolling all the way from Iceland, reaching land.

Unless Vicky asked me to leave I would keep my side of our three-months bargain. I was not afraid of heights.

chapter sixteen

After years of narrow beds fit for nuns and prisoners, I slept in my double bed with a sense of ease and woke to the knowledge that the wind had fallen and the day was fine. Vicky had told me to sleep as long as I wanted, another unknown luxury, and during the half-hour that I lay there, enjoying the warm expanse, the only sounds were those of a rooster crowing in the distance and, nearby, the cawing of rooks. When at last I pushed back the blankets, my feet landed not on the frigid linoleum of the Elm Room but on soft carpet.

Following Vicky's example, I dressed in trousers and a sweater. Then, eager for my first glimpse of the island by daylight, I drew the curtains at my four windows. On one side I had a view across the lawn to two beech trees, the bare branches crowded with the rooks I had heard. A swing hung from the taller tree and a bench stood between them. The other windows gave a view over the vegetable garden to the farm buildings and, beyond them, the fields. The whole of the garden was surrounded by a wall twice my height. Of the sea there was no sign.

Downstairs my cautious "Hello" was met by silence. Vicky had pointed out the dining-room the previous evening. The long table had been laid for two; a plate with several crusts marked, I guessed, the passage of my pupil. As I ate cornflakes and toast, I scanned the island newspaper. I was reading about the number of stray dogs found in the last week—six—and the number of licences issued to move pigs—seventeen—when I had the sudden sensation of being observed. I looked up, but the windows were empty. From nearby came a muffled giggle. In almost noticing Nell, I thought, I was doing exactly what she wanted. I decided then, as I ate a second slice of toast, on my strategy. I would not pursue her. I would explore the house and the farm, I would visit the sea, I would help Vicky and do whatever was asked of me. Eventually, I thought, like a hedgehog or a fox, my charge would emerge from her hiding place.

Just as I finished eating, Vicky appeared. She asked how I had slept, seemed pleased by my answer, and offered to show me around. Downstairs, besides the dining-room and the kitchen, were a library, a drawing-room, a billiard room, and a study. These last three were closed for the winter, but I was welcome to use the library. Seamus—she waved vaguely—occupied a room beyond the cloakroom, where he could have his dogs. I did not think to question how he could sleep-walk the length of the house. As for Vicky, she'd been using my room in order to be close to Nell but had now returned to her quarters beside the kitchen.

Upstairs we could hear music from behind Nell's door—she had her own radio and record player, Vicky explained—but she did not answer our knock. With a little shrug Vicky moved on to the schoolroom. The bright, spacious room was stocked with books, maps, notebooks, paint boxes, and crayons; there were even a blackboard and an easel. "This is perfect," I exclaimed. The rest of the corridor housed the guest rooms, each with its bed neatly made. At the far end, a tall oak door led to Mr. Sinclair's quarters.

"I keep it locked so Nell won't go poking around," Vicky said lightly, and I understood that I was not to poke around either.

We put on Wellington boots and jackets and headed outside. Vicky led the way around the cream-coloured house and across the lawn to a fountain. "It used to make a lovely sound," she said, "but it hasn't worked in years." The bowl was half full of murky water, and the dolphin in the centre was covered with lichen. We continued to the farmyard. She pointed out several barns, a granary, three henhouses, a duck house, a stable, a shed where tractors and machinery were stored, a byre for milking, and a dairy. As I followed her, I asked questions. Why were some of the hens so small? They were bantams. Why were there fragments of seashells everywhere? The hens ate them to harden the shells of their eggs. Why didn't they have pigs? Seamus couldn't be bothered, and she got too fond of them. How many cats were there? One for each rat.

In the dusty henhouse she showed me how to slip my hand under a hen to retrieve the eggs. "Do it quickly," she said, "so they don't have time to peck."

On my second attempt I retrieved two warm eggs from a drowsy red hen.

Then she told me that lunch was served in the kitchen at twelve-thirty and pointed out the path across the fields to the sea. There weren't many beaches on this side of the island, but the Sinclairs had their own cove. Beyond the farmyard not a single tree broke the horizon. In one field several black cows ignored me; in another a flock of curlews, pecking at the stubble with their curved beaks, took wing at my approach. Within ten minutes I was standing on a small beach between two headlands. The grey waves were flecked with white, and the wind was so cold it made me blink. My only companions were two gulls marching along the tide line. As I followed them, the larger one stopped to peck at something pink and fleshy: the remains of a skate. At the far end of the cove I knelt to examine the shell-covered rocks. I had a sudden image of myself, years ago, kneeling beside a rock, pulling off a limpet. Someone was beside me, a grown-up, but however hard I tried I saw only the limpet's frill of muscle, not the person's face. Perhaps more memories would return, I thought, carried back by the sea.

At lunch I met the other people who worked at Blackbird Hall. Besides Vicky and Seamus, there was Syd, the cowman, and his wife, who lived in a cottage behind the steading, a girl from the village, Nora, who came in to help Vicky, and her brother, Angus, who worked with Seamus. We were all in the employ of Mr. Sinclair, who, as Mr. Johnson had said, was a businessman in London. Although he lived more than five hundred miles away, he had strong views about his niece's upbringing, which was why no one ever laid a finger on her. "Spare the rod," Vicky said. "Thank heavens."

She was in charge of the house while Seamus ruled the farm. I was glad to know he had no authority over me. At lunch on that first day I studied him across the table, curious to see what darkness had hidden the night before. His fine brown hair fell over his forehead and his skin was weather-beaten to the colour of Mr. Waugh's pigskin gloves; beneath fair eyebrows, his eyes were the blue of a newly scoured knife. He must have sensed my scrutiny. Just for a moment, he looked up from his shepherd's pie and those steely eyes fell upon me. Quickly I turned back to my own plate. From then on, whenever I saw him coming, I ducked into a henhouse, or chose a different path across the fields.

BLACKBIRD HALL WAS, AS Vicky had warned, a lonely place. Kirkwall, the main town on the island, was an hour's drive; the neighbouring farms, to the north and south, were several miles away, and the village was a good half-hour's walk. I went there on my second day and found a few dozen houses, a church, a small school, and a post office that sold milk, bread, and other necessities. I bought a postcard of Kirkwall to send to Miss Seftain. I was retracing my steps when I heard a horse whinnying. In the nearby field a boy was riding a pony round half-a-dozen homemade tents. He waved and I waved back. Later Vicky told me this was the Gypsies' encampment.

For years, as I peeled potatoes and mopped floors, I had daydreamed about being free, but now the delight of my long, empty hours soon faded. I volunteered to feed the hens and gather the eggs, and I spent hours organising the schoolroom. Still the hands of my new watch circled slowly. I had told Vicky my strategy of letting Nell come to me, and she had agreed that it made as much sense as anything else.

"Miss Cameron behaved as if she were still in school, where all she had to do was ring the bell and the pupils ran to their desks. That certainly didn't work. But I'm no expert on Nell. At her age I would have flown around the treetops before I went against my parents. I'm afraid Alison let her get away with murder."

"Alison was Nell's mother?" I asked, just to be sure, and Vicky nodded.

ON MY THIRD DAY on the island I drew the curtains to discover rain scribbling across the windows. The rooks had vanished and the two beech trees stood like grey ghosts. After breakfast I trudged round the henhouses. Then I retreated to the library and lit the peat fire. A shelf in one of the bookcases held games and jigsaw puzzles. I cleared the largest of the tables, chose a puzzle of Edinburgh Castle, and began to sort the edges. I had last visited the castle with my uncle the Christmas I was eight. As we stood on the ramparts, looking out across Princes Street Gardens, he had claimed that every Scottish monarch since the fifteenth century had stood in just this spot. "A view fit for kings," he had said, spreading his arms. "And Mary, Queen of Scots," I had added.

Now one section of the Castle Rock eluded me. I tried piece after piece to no avail. "Oh, fiddlesticks," I said and flung myself down in an armchair.

"Miss Cameron said *fiddlesticks* is swearing," said a voice.

"I thought *fiddlesticks* was the opposite of swearing. That it meant you were trying not to swear." I was careful not to turn towards the door.

"Why did you say it?"

"Because I can't find a piece of the jigsaw."

"Jigsaws are stupid."

"Is that like saying ducks are stupid because they can't add? Or do you mean doing them is stupid?"

Suddenly she was standing in front of me, wearing a ragged blue pullover and dark brown trousers. "I'm Nell. And this"—she pointed to the black and white collie shadowing her heels—"is Tinker."

The dog growled and its hackles rose in one smooth motion.

"I'm Miss Hardy, but you can call me Gemma. Maybe you'd like to help with the puzzle? If I can get the edge sorted I'll be on my way."

Hands on hips, Nell narrowed her eyes. "Okay," she said. "Just for a minute."

Tinker settled down before the fire and I showed her the picture of the castle on the lid of the box and what I'd done so far. She seized an unlikely-looking piece of edge, and slipped it into place. "There."

"Well done. Now if we can do the corner by the battlements. Have you ever been to Edinburgh Castle?"

"My mum has." She reached for another piece, and I saw that her nails were ragged and filthy.

At Claypoole visiting parents had sometimes brought their younger children, and I had watched, bewildered, while the teachers exclaimed over them. Why was being small and inept considered praiseworthy? Size was simply an accident of inheritance, or age. As for being help-less, that was something to fix as soon as possible. The first tenuous strand of sympathy between Nell and me was my recognition that she was not the kind of child people exclaim over. She was thin, all elbows and knees, and she walked in an ungainly way with one foot sticking out. Her skin was sallow and her brown eyes were a little small. Her hair straggled to her waist. She was completely aware that in her case being a child carried few advantages; if she could have grown up tomorrow she would have. She reminded me of my younger self.

We worked on the puzzle for half an hour, during which she fired questions at me. I told her about Claypoole, and that I preferred seals to dogs.

"Seals," she said. "What is the point of seals?"

"They have beautiful whiskers and there are wonderful stories about them, rescuing sailors and helping people. What is the point of Tinker?"

"He protects me." She bit her thumb. "He herds sheep."

"Why do you need protection?"

"The blue piece goes here."

Presently I announced that I was going to get elevenses. Would she like some?

"No, thanks." She curled up in one of the armchairs by the fire. "I'm only here because of the rain."

Five minutes later, when I returned from the kitchen, carrying a tray with two glasses of squash and a plate of biscuits, the puzzle was scattered across the floor.

THE FOLLOWING DAY WAS equally stormy. In the library I lit the fire and tried to settle down with *Ivanhoe*, but I was too discouraged to read. Remembering Nell's small, skeptical eyes, I could easily imagine her continuing to shun me. In which case, I thought, Vicky would have no choice but to let me go, and I would have no choice but to seek another job. What could I do to lure her into my company? I thought of slipping a note under her door—*Come out. Let's make a truce*—but I doubted she could read. She seemed immune to the appeal of the farmyard and to the smells of Vicky's cooking. She had yet to appear at a meal, though often when I came down to breakfast it was clear she had been there first. Lunch she skipped, and in the evening, like me, she fended for herself. Vicky had said I was welcome to join her and Seamus for high tea, but I preferred to carry my plate to the library.

Now I set *Ivanhoe* aside, put on my outdoor clothes, and headed to the farmyard in search of Vicky. I found her in the dairy. "What a day," she said. "At least we don't have to worry about the milk going off."

Her nose and cheeks were red with cold and her breath hung in clouds over the milk she was skimming. When I offered to help, she said I could rinse the churn. With my back to her, running the tap, I described what had happened the day before. "Do you have any idea how I can get Nell to come to lessons? Is there anything she likes?"

"Besides being a hooligan and listening to pop music? I couldn't entirely say. She is curious about you. Last night I caught her raiding the larder, and she said she likes that you're small and wear trousers. Shall I ask Mr. Sinclair the next time he phones?"

"No. Please don't." In my alarm the churn clattered against the sink. I set it on the floor and turned to face her. "What will he think of a teacher who hasn't given a single lesson?"

"You can never guess what Mr. Sinclair will think." She poured a ladle of cream slowly into the butter maker. "I won't say a word, but if he asks, I can't lie. I expect he'll visit when the weather gets warmer. He often appears out of the blue."

As I retraced my steps across the rainy farmyard, I understood that the snowdrops in the hall, the gleaming grand piano, the rooms with their beds made and fireplaces stacked with peat, were all just in case Mr. Sinclair decided to visit. The house was always waiting for him. In the library my book lay on the table; the fire burned evenly. I went over to one of the windows and pressed my hand to the cold glass. My uncle had told me that the Romans made glass out of sand. The next day I had lit a fire in the sandpit, hoping to produce a pane, or even a few droplets, and ended up with a mess of blackened sand. Now, watching the rain smash down, I wondered if I would ever have a home again.

As if my thoughts had summoned him, my uncle appeared—not, of course, on the windswept grass but in my brain. He had faced the same problem of an intractable child when he came to Iceland. I pictured him, whether from my memories or his stories I couldn't say, rolling coloured balls over the rough ground. I had knelt behind a wall, watching, and then I had come over to roll a ball too. And he had talked, telling stories in a language that I didn't understand but in which the underlying message was clear: this man wished me well.

The library was, as Vicky had said, mostly stocked with histories and old novels, but upstairs in the schoolroom I found what I needed: *Pippi Longstocking*. When I was Nell's age I had loved the story of the adventurous girl who slept with her feet on the pillow and could lift a horse over her head. I carried it down to the library, left the door ajar, and began to read aloud. I stopped after twenty minutes, when Pippi was making pancakes.

"Go on."

"Only if you come and sit down."

"And Tinker?"

"And Tinker."

Nell sauntered in and perched on the chair opposite. Tinker took up his position on the floor beside her. "You didn't say *please*," she said. Her trousers were splattered with mud.

"I forgot," I said. "Please. Can you read?"

"None of your beeswax." She drummed her heels on the rug; Tinker flicked open one yellow eye and closed it again. "Go on. What happens next?"

"I'll make a bargain with you," I said slowly, improvising. "I'll read to you for an hour every afternoon, anything you want. In exchange you'll do lessons every morning."

"Except Sunday. How do I know you'll keep your word?"

"How do I know you'll keep yours? I'll swear on Tinker's head. If I don't read to you one afternoon then you don't have to do lessons the next day."

She leaned forwards so that her hair swept the rug. I watched uncertainly, wondering if I should offer further bribes. Then a small hand emerged through the curtain of hair to rest on Tinker's head. "I swear," she said. "Now you."

"You have to tell him not to bite me," I said, standing up.

"Maybe." She giggled. "Be a good dog, Tink."

I knelt down and cautiously reached out my hand. "By Tinker's head," I said, "I swear to read for an hour a day if Nell will do her lessons every morning, except Sunday."

Then I announced we would begin that day. As I read, Tinker slept and Nell listened, her face mirroring whatever was happening to Pippi. When the clock struck, I closed the book, fetched us both elevenses, and led the way to the schoolroom. The next day Nell knocked on my door and asked what she should wear to church.

chapter seventeen

ONE DAY, ONE BARGAIN, did not, of course, resolve all difficulties. Nell had never learned to concentrate, and sitting still, even for twenty minutes, was a struggle. She knew the alphabet but could read only a few words haltingly; when she wrote her own name the *l*s threatened to topple; her arithmetic depended on her fingers. Her table manners were terrible. She was cheeky and thoughtless. She hated to take baths or wash her hair. Some days we had trouble getting through ten minutes of lessons, and the weather raged inside and out. But over the next weeks and months she gradually became a better pupil and I became a better teacher. Together we tackled sums, reading, writing, grammar, tracing, nature, history, geography. Sewing I left to Vicky. Scripture I ignored.

By late March the grass was greening, and along the garden wall the jasmine and crocuses were in bloom. Leaves began to unfurl on the beech trees; one was copper, one green. Robins, blue tits, sparrows, chaffinches, wagtails, and thrushes came and went in the garden but no blackbirds. When I asked Vicky, she said a few years ago a pair had nested in the copper beech, but they weren't common. "The first Mr. Sinclair named the house on a whim. I doubt he knew a blackbird from a crow." Lambs started to appear, and Seamus had Tinker working in the fields with the other two collies. I had long given up locking my door, and in the mornings Nell would climb into my bed to turn the pages of one of her books and invent a story. We got up at seven-thirty, had breakfast, fed the hens, and collected the eggs. She was surprisingly fearless about slipping her hand under a broody hen. I followed Miss Seftain's advice—we exchanged letters once a fortnight—and made sure to start lessons at nine every morning and keep to the timetable I had pinned on the wall beneath the schoolroom clock. Like Miriam, Nell gave up easily in the face of difficulties, but when properly praised, she redoubled her efforts.

In the garden shed I discovered a brand-new child's bicycle: a Christmas gift from Mr. Sinclair. When I asked why she never used it, Nell said she couldn't be bothered, which I guessed meant she didn't know how. In the course of an afternoon, with me running back and forth across the grass holding the saddle, she mastered the skill and was thrilled. Another bike, for guests, Vicky said, was only a little too large for me. I lowered the saddle, and we started going on expeditions.

I took pleasure in all this, and in Vicky's praise: "Mr. Sinclair won't believe his eyes." I began to long for a visit from our mysterious employer. Several photographs hung in the library, and Nell had pointed out her uncle to me. In one picture he was playing badminton; in another he was walking on a beach with two men and a woman; in a third he was sitting on the bench under the beech trees, a book in his lap. The pictures were small, and all I could see with certainty was that Mr. Sinclair had dark hair, square shoulders, and good taste in white shirts. Nell said that he always beat her at Monopoly and, she added with a sly glance, he often let her stay up late. Besides regular lessons I had introduced a regular bedtime.

In the evenings, after Nell was asleep, I sometimes kept Vicky company while she made her shell flowers. The pink and white shells came not from the cove but by mail from Glasgow, and she sold the resulting bouquets in a shop in Kirkwall. She offered to teach me the skill, but after I broke three shells in a row, she put me in charge of the green raffia that covered the stalks. While she worked, making little holes in the shells and attaching wires and stamens, she told me she had lived all her life on the island with only two brief visits to the mainland. Her parents, both deceased, had worked for the Sinclairs. Seamus and her two older brothers had grown up with Mr. Sinclair and his older brother, Roy, who had died in 1953.

During one of these conversations I finally learned the meaning of the phrase Bevin Boy. In 1943, Vicky explained, Lord Bevin had declared that more coal was needed to fight the war; one in every ten men who enlisted was chosen by lottery to go down the mines. "Seamus wanted to be in the RAF, like Mr. Sinclair," she said, "but he ended up a Bevin Boy. At least it kept him safe."

No wonder he had cursed my innocent question. I was still shuddering at the idea of spending hour after hour underground as she described how her parents had spent the war in dread of a telegram. "If someone was wounded, or worse"—she reached for a clump of stamens—"that was how the news came. We'd see a motorbike coming down the road and we'd hide behind the curtains, hoping it wouldn't stop at our house." She had been too young to understand the first time the bike stopped, in June 1943, but not the second time, in April 1944. "My poor mother," she said. "Still I hardly knew my brothers, and the war was exciting. When a convoy was coming into Scapa Flow, you could feel the air buzzing even in our wee village."

I recognised another strange phrase, this one spoken by the young man in the library at Claypoole. What was Scapa Flow? I asked, and Vicky said it was the harbour below the south island. The German fleet had been held there in 1919, until they sank their own ships. Then in 1939, just before she was born, a German submarine stole into the harbour and torpedoed the HMS *Royal Oak*. Afterwards the Italian prisoners had built a barrier to protect Scapa Flow.

"Oh, I know about the prisoners," I said. "The person who first told me about the Orkneys said one of the prisoners had a beautiful voice and married an island girl."

"Who was that?" said Vicky.

I could easily have said something vague—a neighbour, a friend—but for some reason I answered with Audrey's full name.

"Audrey Marsden!" Vicky dropped her little hammer. "Where on earth did you run into her?"

"She used to cook for a neighbour, near Perth."

"I always wondered what had happened to her. She was one of those girls who had to leave the island suddenly. I see her mother sometimes in Kirkwall."

"Suddenly?" She had given the word special weight.

"She was expecting."

"You mean"—I hesitated—"she had a baby? We always called her Mrs. Marsden, but she never mentioned a husband, or children."

"Well, her husband wouldn't have the same surname, would he?" said Vicky. "It's not many women who can make Alison's choice and have a child on their own." She held up the flower, the four pink shells glowing on the end of their green stalk.

Later that night, lying in bed, I pictured Mrs. Marsden's neat bun and respectable clothes. Could someone who looked like that secretly have a baby? I remembered her saying that orphanages were dreadful places. Then I found myself thinking about Drummond and Ross. For the first time it occurred to me that perhaps their sudden departure from Claypoole was connected to Drummond lying down with the boy, between the raspberry canes.

I SPENT MANY HOURS in Vicky's company, but we did not exactly become friends; her duties as housekeeper set her apart, and we both had our areas of reserve. While I dodged questions about my past, she was reluctant to talk about Nell's mother, although the first time I asked, she did give a brief biography. Alison was one of those girls who can ride almost as soon as they can walk; she got her first pony when she was four years old and later, at boarding school near St. Andrews, she competed in gymkhanas. When she came back to the island, her parents had bought her a stallion named Mercury. One evening, Vicky said, she'd been taking a shortcut across the fields when this huge grey horse loomed out of the mist. She had screamed, and Mercury had nearly thrown Alison.

Which was what finally happened. One day the horse came home alone; Alison was found hours later. At first they had thought she would spend the rest of her life in a wheelchair, but after nearly a year and several operations, she could walk with a stick. Without her horse, though, she couldn't stand the island. She had moved to Glasgow and started leading a different sort of life, singing in pubs, who knew what else. After Nell was born, her parents wouldn't speak to her.

I would have liked to ask about Nell's father, the man who wasn't in the picture, but Vicky was already hurrying to the end of her story, describing Alison's death. "They said it was heart failure, that the pain-killers had weakened her heart. Nell was alone with her at the time. A neighbour spotted the milk on the doorstep."

I was still saying how awful as Vicky stood up to check on her scones. A few days later, when I asked why Alison hadn't sent Nell to school, she said she didn't know, and that was her answer to the next question, and the next.

ON EVENINGS WHEN I did not sit with Vicky or plot my lessons or take refuge in the library, I sometimes cycled into the village to visit Nora. A skinny girl of eighteen, Nora had been working at Blackbird

Hall for two years and still sang as she mopped the floors. She often talked proudly about her older brother Todd, who was at university in Aberdeen, but when I asked if she had any plans to leave the island, she shook her head. "Why would I want to do that? Besides," she added, "I'm engaged." Jock worked at the smithy and they were, Nora smiled, in no rush. Her first invitation to me was, I knew, prompted by Vicky, but soon it was understood that most Saturdays, if the weather wasn't too ferocious, I would bicycle to the village to play cards or dominoes with her and Angus and their parents.

Still, despite my success with Nell, my small social life, the solace of being near the sea and earning money, I sometimes found myself restless. My life was infinitely happier than it had been at Claypoole, but except for the odd trip to Kirkwall, I was mostly confined to a large house and a small village. I was on an island on an island. At Claypoole I had been sustained by the hope that once I left the school and became an adult, everything would change. Now what could I hope for? I would pace up and down the corridor with its empty bedrooms and the locked door at the end and wonder if I would ever be able to take my exams and go to university. Once again I envied the birds. A shearwater, according to my bird book, could fly to Iceland and back and scarcely notice.

EASTER BROUGHT A LAVISH chocolate egg for Nell but no sign of Mr. Sinclair. My eighteenth birthday passed unmarked, even by me; I recalled the date only the following day. Primroses and violets appeared beside the road and the lambs grew sturdier and butted heads in the fields. A few of the hens were left to sit on their eggs, and soon downy chicks darted around the farmyard. Then, in mid-May, the ferry went on strike. Seamus and Vicky complained furiously. The eggs and cheese, destined for mainland markets, piled up in the dairy. "And if the dispute isn't settled soon," Vicky said, "we won't get summer visitors." Or at least not many, she added. The planes were still flying. Playing in the garden with Nell and walking to the village, I found myself scanning the sky.

As the days lengthened, Nora organised a group of boys and girls from the village to play rounders in a field near the church. Thanks to the holidays at Claypoole, I was better than most of the girls; I couldn't hit the ball far, but I was a fast runner and a good fielder. One evening in early June, a Tuesday, I showed up to find that Todd had arrived home from Aberdeen. The ferries were still on strike, but he had talked his way onto a fishing boat. He was, like Nora, tall and thin, and everything he wore—his shirt, his jeans, his shoes—had a hole in it. I was on his team, and when we won, he said it was all due to my fielding. Then he produced his accordion, and everyone gathered to sing and drink tea or homemade beer. I didn't know most of the songs but I liked sitting there, being part of the group, laughing and joking about stupid things.

When I got up to leave, Todd followed me outside. While he rolled a cigarette, I asked him about university. What was it like? Was everyone very brainy? Did he spend every minute studying? Fine, no, no. As I launched into my fourth question, Todd said, "Shut up," and, leaning forward, pressed his mouth against mine. After a moment, several moments, he stepped back. "Watch yourself," he said, and disappeared inside. Dazed, delighted, I retrieved my bike and set off towards home. Perhaps it was to make those feelings last a little longer that I did not turn on my light but relied on the faint glimmer of the sky to reveal the strip of macadam that led back to Blackbird Hall.

Until his kiss Todd had simply been Nora's older brother, nice enough looking, good on the accordion, refilling his glass with home brew once too often. His main virtue had been his attendance at university. Now I remembered his occasional glances, his soulful singing. I longed to see him again, to ask more questions; my life had suddenly expanded. I rounded a corner to find the road blocked by a car. Beside it knelt a figure, a man. I stopped and dismounted.

"Hello," I said. "Can I help?"

Something clattered to the road. "Damn. I didn't see you."

He had the island accent mixed with something else. "I'm sorry," I said. "Bicycles are very stealthy. I need to get a bell."

"Stealthy." He snorted. "You need a light."

"You mean I need to use it." I had bought a new battery for my light in Kirkwall the week before. Now, pleased by my foresight, I unclipped it and knelt beside him, aiming the beam while he wound up the jack and struggled with the nuts and then lowered the jack and struggled some more.

"You're kind not to comment that I clearly have no idea what I'm doing," he said. "I haven't changed a tyre in years."

"I've never changed one, though I did manage to mend my first puncture the other day." From the safety of the darkness beyond the torch, I glimpsed brown hair and a smear on one cheek, oil or mud perhaps. I could tell by his voice that he was older—a man, not a boy.

"It isn't rocket science. Where are you heading on your stealthy bicycle?"

"Blackbird Hall. It's not far from here."

"I've heard of it. There's a farmer there who breeds cattle."

"Who has less manners than his cows."

"I see you have opinions," he said, slipping the wheel into place. "Are you part of the household?"

"I'm the au pair." Vicky had used the word *nanny* in her advertisement but that brought to mind someone with a bosom, stern and grey-haired.

"Au pair?"

"It means you're a member of the family with special duties. Here." I reached for the nut he'd dropped.

"Actually," he said, "it means a mutual exchange of services. *Au pair*—on the level."

"I don't teach French yet." I was explaining that my pupil was only eight when the wrench slipped and the man swore: "Bugger it!" I dropped the torch. The light shone upon two gleaming brown shoes, shoes so beautiful that I pictured them in a shop window in Edinburgh, costing more than I earned in a year. "Are you all right?" I said.

"I banged my hand."

I retrieved the torch and he stretched his left hand into the beam. In the light his index finger was already swelling, slightly crooked. "Broken," he pronounced.

"Oh, no. We should get a doctor."

"In this time and place I doubt that's an option. Don't worry. It's not fatal, just a useful reminder of stupidity." He finished the nuts and then held the light while he instructed me how to lower the jack and extricate it from the car. I could hear him trying to curb his impatience as I fumbled with the levers, but soon the jack and the punctured tyre were in the boot and he was assuring me that he was fine to drive.

"Farewell, stealthy cyclist," he said. "Thank you for your illumination."

He drove off into the darkness and I continued on my bike, pleased by my two adventures.

THE NEXT MORNING PASSED predictably, breakfast, hens, lessons, but the house seemed noisier than usual. The Hoover roared back and forth outside the schoolroom and the phone rang several times. It was only when I went to make our picnic—I had promised Nell we could go to the Sands of Evie—that I learned that Mr. Sinclair had arrived the night before.

"Imagine," said Vicky, "I was already asleep when I heard this commotion. I came out in my dressing-gown and there he was, saying he was starving."

I thought at once of the man I'd met the night before, but surely he would have said if he too were bound for Blackbird Hall. "Will he be at lunch?" I asked.

"He's off in Kirkwall. He wants to see you and Nell this evening. I told him how well you're doing with her. From now on you'll have your meals in the kitchen, unless, of course, he asks you to join him." Her tone suggested that this was unlikely.

The Sands of Evie was a long shallow beach overlooking Eynhallow Sound. Vicky had told me that sometimes on summer evenings you could hear the seals singing on the neighbouring islands; so far we had seen only the occasional dark head in the distance. On our last visit Nell and I had built a hut out of driftwood, but today all that remained of our efforts was a scattered pile of planks and branches. We sat on a rock, eating our sandwiches and discussing how to rebuild it. Then Nell began to speculate about what gifts her uncle might have brought. "I asked for roller skates," she said, "and some records and a new collar for Tinker." Since Nell had started lessons, Tinker spent his days with Seamus, but she still fed him every evening.

"A collar is nice," I said absently. I would braid her hair, I thought, and have her read a page from her favourite book, *Percy, the Bad Chick*. My excitement was tinged with apprehension. I had done well with Nell and I deserved praise, but praise might not be forthcoming. Mr. Sinclair, like Miss Bryant, controlled my world; what if he was equally tyrannical?

Nell said something else, which I missed. Then she announced she was going to pee and headed towards the long grass that bordered the beach. I wandered down to the water's edge and began to search the damp sand for cowries, the little curled pink shells that the Vikings had used as currency. I had found one on our last visit. When I gave it to Nell her small eyes had kindled. "I'll put it in a secret place," she had said, "and keep it forever." Now my search took me farther and farther along the beach. I was nearing the far end before I realised that Nell hadn't returned. Perhaps she had discovered a bird's nest, I thought, or a rare flower. I walked back, calling her name. Only the waves and the gulls answered me. What if something had happened: an accident, or something more sinister? I looked up and down the long line of grass and rushes that bounded the beach, but whatever footprints she'd left were mixed with the footprints we had made on our way down. My heart clamoured in my ears. I pictured men, dark cars. Running as best I could, the sand slipping under my feet, I retrieved our jackets and knapsack, and ran back to the field where we had left our bicycles. At once my fears vanished. Hers was gone; mine had two flat tyres.

As I pushed my bicycle back along the narrow, hilly road I understood that Nell was angry with me, but understanding did not stop me from getting hot and cross. By the time I reached Blackbird Hall all I wanted was to shake her and explain that I might lose my job if she didn't do me credit. Her bicycle was in the shed, but I knocked at the door of her room in vain. Vicky, shelling peas in the kitchen, hadn't seen her.

With less than half an hour until my meeting with Mr. Sinclair, I gave up on Nell and set to work on my own appearance. I had taken to wearing trousers most days, except Sundays. Now I put on black tights, my blue skirt, and a white blouse. I used the mascara I had bought in Kirkwall and brushed my hair until it shone. When I examined myself in the mirror, I was surprised by how serious I looked, and how grown-up. I could easily be nineteen, I thought. Even older.

I walked downstairs as if I were balancing a book on my head. The library door was ajar. I knocked and, when a voice called "Come in," stepped inside. A man was standing at the bay window, gazing out at the garden.

"The stealthy cyclist," he said, turning to greet me. "Otherwise known as Gemma Hardy."

"The inept tyre changer."

He did not move but stood looking at me across the length of the room, and I looked back at this man who controlled my future. Vicky had said he was handsome, but to my mind his forehead was a little too low, his eyebrows a little too heavy to deserve that adjective. His hair, longer than I'd ever seen a man's, almost touched the collar of his white shirt. He wore a blue pullover and dark corduroy trousers. His beautiful shoes were gone, replaced by soft suede ones.

"How do you do, Mr. Sinclair?" I said, advancing with outstretched hand.

"Forgive me," he said, raising his bandaged fingers. "Only a sprain. The doctor claims I'll be fine in a week or so. Meanwhile I must refrain from being polite, which isn't usually a hardship. I thought you were bringing Nell."

"I'm afraid she's done a disappearing act." I spoke lightly, trying to suggest that this was a trivial matter. "We went to the Sands of Evie for a picnic. She took her bike and came home early."

"In other words you did something that made her take umbrage. Well, she'll show up unless the mermaids steal her. She's a mercenary brat, and she knows me as a bringer of gifts. Tell me, how are her lessons going? Is she making progress?"

He went over to a trolley that had been empty the day before and which now held a dozen cut-glass decanters and bottles. While I registered the phrase "mercenary brat"—this was not the fond guardian of my imaginings—he poured himself a tumbler of amber-coloured liquid and sat down in the chair I had come to think of as mine.

"On the principle that I ought not to encourage underage drinking," he said, "I won't offer you anything. Sit down. Talk to me."

I said firmly that I wasn't underage, which was now true, and that I didn't drink.

"At least not often," Mr. Sinclair amended. "Last night, when you held the torch for me, I could swear I smelled beer on your breath."

To hide my confusion I went over and closed the door. Then I slid shut the window where he'd been standing. "Your niece," I said, "is an ardent eavesdropper."

I sat down in the opposite chair with my hands in my lap and my feet together, Claypoole fashion, and gave a brief report of how Nell had first shunned me and then capitulated. "We made a bargain. She does lessons every day and I read to her from whatever book she chooses. She's been poorly schooled, but she's bright. She's beginning to read. She knows her multiplication tables through times six. And we're studying nature and Scottish history. Until this afternoon things were going well."

He raised his glass and swirled the liquid, as if it were something to admire rather than drink. I saw how dark his eyelashes were and that if he grew a beard it too would be dark. His mouth was the same shape as Nell's. "Vicky says that too," he said, "and she says Nell likes you. But you're wrong about one thing. She hasn't been poorly schooled; she hasn't been schooled at all. Her mother had some romantic notion about teaching her at home, but she didn't have the patience." He shook his head and, at last, drank. "Enough of Nell. She will speak for herself when she shows up. Where did you come from? What are you doing here?"

I told him I had been at Claypoole School, and answered Vicky's advertisement. "Yes, yes," he said, waving away my answers. "I know all that—your youth, your flimsy credentials. I was asking a more existential question, if you know what that means."

"Concerned with existence." I gazed resolutely at the fireplace laid with kindling and blocks of peat. It was too warm to warrant lighting.

"How stiffly she gives the dictionary definition. Now you've taken umbrage. What I'm asking is, how do you come to be wandering this part of the planet?"

Still looking into the fireplace, I gave a clipped, three-sentence version of my life: dead parents, dead uncle, school.

"Thank you, Miss Hardy, for that generous, voluble—"

Before he could finish, the door was flung open and Nell hurled herself across the room. "Uncle Hugh, Uncle Hugh," she cried. Mr. Sinclair's drink went flying, the tumbler bouncing harmlessly on the hearthrug. He kissed her forehead, called her a ragamuffin, and set her down. Her hair was tangled, her shirt dirty, her jeans torn at one knee. She could scarcely have done me less credit.

"So what is this I hear about you running away and tormenting Gemma?"

"Did you remember my skates?"

"Has no one taught you your pleases and thank-yous? If you look in the hall you'll find a box with your name."

She was out of the room in a flash. "She reminds me so much of her mother," he said with a rueful smile.

While Nell carried in her box and knelt at her uncle's feet to unwrap its contents, I fetched a cloth and mopped up the whisky. She did get her skates and several records and two books, which she brought to show me: an illustrated encyclopedia and an atlas.

"These are beautiful," I exclaimed, and then, trying to sound more teacherly, added that they would be very useful.

"I always liked those kinds of books," Mr. Sinclair said. "Facts and pictures."

Nell was threading the laces of her skates when I stood up and announced that it was time for supper. "Where are you going?" said Mr. Sinclair. "Are you slipping off for a beer in the village? Oh, I'm sorry. We will not mention that again."

Trying to hide my embarrassment, I said it was lucky for him I had been in the village. "You might have hurt more than your finger, wielding spanners in the dark. Nell has supper at six-thirty and I need to prepare tomorrow's lessons."

"All right, all right." He raised his hands. "I bow to the disciplinarian."

To my relief Nell allowed me to lead her from the room. As she ate scrambled eggs she could not stop chattering about her gifts. I had last skated in the corridors of Yew House, but I promised to give her a lesson tomorrow. Surely, like bicycling, the skill would come back. Only when she was safely in bed and I was sitting beside her, reading a bedtime story, did I remark that it had been a long walk back from the beach. "Why didn't you tell me you were cross with me?"

"You wouldn't have listened." She studied the wallpaper next to her bed. Following her gaze, I saw several neatly drawn cats stalking among the forget-me-nots and daisies.

"You could have tried," I said. "Like you do in arithmetic when you try three times."

"Arithmetic is different," she said, still gazing at the flowers. "Six sevens are forty-two."

"Very good," I said and kissed her cheek.

In bed that night I listened not for the sea but for Mr. Sinclair's comings and goings. Even though the guest rooms still stood empty, the house felt different: inhabited in a new way, pulsing with life.

chapter eighteen

As I stepped out of my room the smell of bacon greeted me. At the kitchen table, Nell and I begged shamelessly for extra rashers. The doorbell, which had grown rusty since my arrival, rang just as we finished eating and then every hour or two for the rest of the day. Farmers and neighbours stopped by to greet Mr. Sinclair; members of the local council wanted to discuss a right of way; the golf course committee wanted to plan the summer tournament; the church needed repairs. The kettle was always on the stove, and Vicky was always making cups of tea and arranging plates of shortbread. The cowman's wife came over in the morning to assist her, and Nora stayed on in the evening to serve supper. Mr. Sinclair either had guests or was one. During the day, when he wasn't otherwise occupied, he worked with Seamus. One morning, glancing out of the schoolroom window, I saw the two of them, walking across the pasture. In their dark green jackets, dark trousers, and Wellingtons I couldn't tell them apart. Then the man on the left bent to examine something and I recognised Mr. Sinclair. Later, wandering in the field, I discovered the wild purple orchids common to the island.

I saw him only fleetingly until Sunday, when he occupied the front pew and read the first lesson: Samuel 1:17. I had last heard the story of David and Goliath when my uncle preached on how the small and weak can triumph over the large and strong. He had described David putting aside his borrowed sword and choosing five smooth stones from the brook. Now, seated next to Nell, I recalled how I had gone down to the river that afternoon, found five stones, and made a sling. But it had proved surprisingly hard to hit even a tree, let alone my cousin Will. "Come to me," read Mr. Sinclair, "and I will give thy flesh unto the fowls of the air, and to the beasts of the field." His voice was like a river: swift, bright, confident. As he turned a page of the Bible with his bandaged fingers, I thought, I was there when that happened; no one else was.

On Monday, when I bicycled into the village to post my letter to Miss Seftain, I heard a voice shouting, "Hello, hello." The Gypsy boy I sometimes saw riding the pony was running across the field towards me. I paused astride my bike.

"My mam says he's back," he said breathlessly. His cheeks shone like apples beneath his ginger hair.

"If you mean Mr. Sinclair, he arrived last week."

"My mam needs to talk to him."

"Ring the doorbell, like everyone else," I said, preparing to pedal away.

"But what should she bring him? A fish, nice and fat, wrapped in seaweed? Or honey from the moors?"

"Bring him a fish," I said impulsively. "He can have it for his supper."

Before I could add that I was no expert on Mr. Sinclair's tastes, he was thanking me and darting away across the field. At the post office the postmistress too asked about Mr. Sinclair. She'd heard, she said shyly, that he had a new job that involved meeting the Queen. "Has he said anything about Her Majesty?"

"Not in my hearing."

"If he does, could you ask how tall she is? My sister says she's her height and I say she's mine."

I promised to ask if I had a chance. As I bicycled home, I pictured

Mr. Sinclair bowing to a woman on a throne. She would confide her worries about the theft of the World Cup and the general election and he would give sage advice. But in the days that followed there was no opportunity to enquire about his relations with the monarch, or anything else. Once he emerged briefly from the library to admire Nell's roller-skating. Another time he came to the schoolroom, but only long enough to hear her six-times table. I knew from Vicky that he might leave at any moment—"I'll see his luggage in the hall one morning," she had said—and I began to devise lessons that required visits to the farmyard. I had Nell draw a map of the buildings, and we wrote a story about the rooster. One afternoon when we were playing with the ginger cat's kittens, Vicky appeared, a bottle of milk in each hand.

"Would you like to see the latest orphans?" she said.

She led us to a stall in the barn where two calves, both black and white, their heads much too large for their small bodies, wobbled on sticklike legs. Vicky gave Nell one bottle and then, seeing my face, offered me the other. The calf sucked intently, gazing at me with its dark eyes. When the milk was gone, it nuzzled my hand. That evening I suggested to Vicky that Nell and I take over their feeding.

"That would be grand," she said. "I'm so busy with all this company I'd lose my head if it wasn't screwed on."

Nell was delighted by our new project. She named the calves Petula and Herman and drew a portrait of each of them. We measured their height at the shoulder and, with much laughter, their girth and made a chart on which to plot their growth; at first the calves had to be fed four times a day. Still I glimpsed Mr. Sinclair only occasionally, talking to Seamus, or driving away in his sleek black car.

On Friday I bicycled to the village to see Nora. Her parents had gone to their weekly whist game, but Angus and Todd were both there, and so was Nora's fiancé. Jock was describing how he'd shoed a pony belonging to the Gypsies. "It was a clever wee thing," he said. "I asked how many shoes it wanted, and it tapped the ground four times."

Nora was still exclaiming as Todd said, "Did you ask it any other questions? How much it weighed? How often it rained this week?" His checked shirt was torn at both elbows.

Quickly—Jock had turned away, pink and frowning—I described my encounter with the Gypsy boy. "Do you know if his mother ever showed up with the fish?" I asked Nora.

"I don't," she said. "But he'd have enjoyed a nice fresh Gypsy fish." "He" nowadays was almost always Mr. Sinclair.

Then Angus, who seldom spoke, piped up that their father had been talking about the storm of '52, the one that swept away the henhouses. "A fisherman got into trouble off the cliffs. The waves were tall as haystacks, but Mr. Sinclair and his brother rowed out, and helped him get safely into the cove."

Todd groaned. "Every village on the island has a story like that. Either a mermaid or the feudal overlord saves someone from drowning. Do you know that three-quarters of this country's wealth is owned by less than ten percent of the population?"

"Mr. Sinclair isn't our feudal overlord," said Nora, swatting at her brother. "He's our boss, and we're always paid on time."

Before Todd could say more, she proposed a game of Scrabble, and the next thing I knew, he and I were partners, squabbling over our seven letters on their little shelf. At one point when we had an *x* he made *sex*; I changed it to *axe*, which got us a higher score. He made *later* on the shelf, and looked at me. The board changed, and it was *rattle* that fitted. Then we had a *y* and I unthinkingly made *yes*.

"Good one," he said, patting my arm.

We lost by twenty-three points and I said I'd better be going. "School tomorrow."

Outside I retrieved my bike from beside the garden gate. I was pedalling past the post office when Todd stepped into the road. The next thing I knew, my bike was on the ground and his face was buried in my neck. Axe, I thought.

"Come," he said, tugging at my wrist.

"No. I have to go home."

"Please. You're so pretty. Just for ten minutes." He found my mouth with his.

Was it the kiss, or the unexpected idea that I was pretty? "We have to move my bike," I said.

He was bending to retrieve it when we both heard the sound of an approaching engine. Headlights swept around the corner. A familiar car came to a stop a few yards away, and a familiar figure climbed out.

"What happened? Did you have an accident, Gemma?" Then he caught sight of Todd. "Or perhaps you're about to have one?"

"I hit a pothole," I said. "Todd was helping me straighten my front wheel. This is Todd McKay, Nora and Angus's brother. Todd, this is Mr. Sinclair."

"And is it straight now?"

"Yes, thank you. I'll be home shortly."

"Good. I wouldn't want Nell's lessons to suffer in the morning."

I was about to pedal off when, beside me, Todd spoke. "This isn't the nineteenth century," he said. "You employ Gemma; you don't own her. She can do whatever she likes in her time off."

"Todd," I protested. At the same moment Mr. Sinclair said, "Sir Launcelot speaks. Or should I say Mr. Marx? Thank you, Todd, for enlightening me as to which century we're in. It never occurred to me that I own Gemma, but I am responsible for my niece's welfare. I want to be sure that the person supervising her education is a good influence, and is keeping company with people of high moral character. Might I suggest that you kindly bugger off?"

"He was just helping me," I said. All desire to go with Todd had left me; still I could not hear him unfairly scolded. Without waiting for either my suitor or my employer to respond, I seized my bike, swung my leg over the saddle, and pedalled away. As soon as I was outside the village I stopped at a gateway into a field and crouched there until Mr. Sinclair's car drove slowly by. Only one road led to Blackbird Hall; he would, I thought, be wondering what had become of me. The idea was oddly pleasing.

THE NEXT DAY NELL was reading—"The little bear was cross"— when there came a knock at the schoolroom door. "Uncle Hugh," she exclaimed, dropping her book and jumping up from the table.

"Good morning, ladies. Don't let me disturb you." He sat down at the far end of the table, folded his arms, and, looking first at Nell, who was dancing around, offering to show him our eggshell collection, and then at me, said, "Pray continue."

"Nell, you can do that later. Please come and sit down. Let your uncle hear how well you can read." I squeezed my hands together so hard I could feel the bones bending. Had he come to tell me that I was dismissed? That I was not sufficiently upright to be Nell's teacher?

"Uncle Hugh, look, this is a starling's egg." She plucked an egg from the cotton-wool-lined box where we kept our finds and held it out to him.

"Nell. Please come and sit down."

"Gemma said this one might be a curlew's."

"I'm sorry," I said. "She's excited by your visit."

But even as I spoke, Nell gave a quick, mischievous glance over her shoulder; she knew exactly what she was doing. Furious, desperate,

I stood up and walked to the window. A bee, its legs knobbed with pollen, was buzzing against the glass. Come in and sting someone, I thought. I could feel Mr. Sinclair watching me as I reached to open the window wider.

"I'm sorry," I said again. "Nell seems to have forgotten her school-room manners."

Turning to face him, my right hand grazed the sill. "Oh," I gasped.

"What is it?" said Mr. Sinclair. He was suddenly by my side.

"The bee," I said. "It stung me. Poor thing."

"Why poor thing?" said Nell as Mr. Sinclair said, "Let me see."

"Because once a bee uses its sting it dies." I held out my hand and there, at the base of my thumb, was a red bump surmounted by the flimsy dark sting.

"We need tweezers and warm water and bicarbonate of soda," said Mr. Sinclair. "Nell, make yourself useful and go and fetch Vicky. Tell her what happened."

"It's just a bee," I murmured, but she was already gone. Mr. Sinclair brought over a chair and I sat down by the window. The beech trees swayed beneath my gaze and I had to keep blinking to steady them. He pulled over a second chair.

"Once, when I was Nell's age," he said, "my brother and I were out exploring near the Sands of Evie." He described how one of their dogs had chased a rabbit into the Broch of Gurness and stumbled into a wasps' nest. "We tried to brush them off, but there were so many and they were buried in her fur. Roy wrapped her in his jacket and carried her down to the sea. She died from shock, but at least the water calmed her. She always loved swimming."

As he spoke, the beech trees grew still and, because he was looking past me, I was able to steal a glance at him. His eyes were not, I saw, the deep blue I had thought, but only seemed so between his dark lashes.

Their colour was closer to the light blue of the Scottish flag. He was still talking as Vicky appeared, with a bowl of warm water, a pair of tweezers, and Nell. He stood up and surrendered his chair.

When Vicky had gone again, leaving me soaking my hand in the warm water, he said, "There, you look better. You were quite pale for a few minutes. Now that I've turned your morning head over heels, how about an educational outing. We could visit St. Magnus Cathedral, if you feel up to it."

"Oh, please," said Nell.

"Hush," he said sharply. "Let your elders and betters speak. What do you think, Gemma?"

I stood up and walked three times around the table. "I think I feel fine."

Mr. Sinclair gave an approving nod. "No vapours for you. We'll leave in ten minutes. Nell, bring your crayons and your sketchbook."

THE RED SANDSTONE CATHEDRAL was a familiar sight, standing as it did in the middle of Kirkwall, but on previous trips to the town I had always been too busy to go inside. Now I followed Mr. Sinclair and Nell up the steps to the beautiful arched doorway.

"This is part of your heritage," he said to her as he opened the door. "Your grandfather was christened here and your grandparents were married here. I want you to draw a picture of the inside. Several if you like."

"What's *christened*?" said Nell.

"Miss Hardy?"

"When a baby is christened she's given her name as a Christian and welcomed into the church. Sometimes she has godparents, parents in God, who promise to help her be good."

"Was I christened? Do I have godparents?"

"I don't think so," said Mr. Sinclair. "And I doubt it."

"So does that mean"—Nell stood completely still—"that I'm not welcome in the church?"

"No," I said quickly. "Everyone is welcome in the church, especially children. Godparents are just an extra. I don't have any either."

Inside the air smelled of cold stone, and, faintly, of snuffed candles. Sunlight shone through the many windows. "It's amazing," I said, gesturing down the aisle to the rose window at the far end, and up to the vaulted ceiling.

"It is," said Mr. Sinclair. Like many houses of worship, he explained, St. Magnus had begun in bad behaviour. Earl Rognvald of Norway had thought a cathedral would secure his claim to the Orkneys and get rid of the current earl. Since the twelfth century the building had been used as a prison, a market, a court, a seat of government, and a place to dry sails. "I can't help noticing," he added, "that scripture doesn't appear on your timetable. Are you neglecting Nell's moral education?"

Not waiting for an answer, he suggested to Nell that she sit down to draw her picture. Once she was settled on a chair, with her sketchbook, he said, "Come with me." We set off down the south nave. I could feel my muscles flexing in my calves and thighs, my lungs filling and emptying, my hand, still hot from the sting, throbbing quietly. Beside me Mr. Sinclair measured his step to mine. He was eight inches taller than me; the ceiling was many feet—fifty, a hundred—taller than either of us.

"You didn't answer my question," he said as we stopped beside a gravestone on the wall. "'August 1750,'" he read. "'Here was interred the corps of Mary Young . . . She lived regarded and dyed regretted.' I've always liked that."

"If you want me to teach scripture, I will."

"Actually," he said, still studying the stone, "I asked if you were neglecting Nell's moral education."

Scarcely knowing how to explain myself, I said that I didn't teach scripture because I didn't feel qualified, but I hoped Nell would go to Sunday school and that, as her reading improved, we could read the Gospels together.

"Let me ask another impertinent question," said Mr. Sinclair. "Do you believe in God?"

In Latin a question was phrased differently according to whether the answer yes or no was expected, but Mr. Sinclair's tone gave no clue to his expectations. "I don't know," I said. "I used to because of my uncle, but since he died I've met plenty of people who claim to be good Christians and wouldn't cross the road to help a starving child. If that's what it means to believe in God, then I'd rather not. What about you?"

"I'm afraid"—we started walking again—"I'd give the same answer, but I'm sorry to hear those words from you. When I was your age I would have answered yes and it made everything easier."

"Of course it's easier," I said, "if you have parents and plenty of money. God's in His heaven and all's right with the world."

"The war started when I was fourteen," he said quietly.

Before I could apologise we stopped at another stone. This one was to the memory of Thomas Smith, who had died on 12 September 1811. " 'He lived beloved and died regretted,' " I read. "Being beloved is better than being regarded."

"That just shows how young you are," said Mr. Sinclair. "Regard lasts longer than love and can lead to it, but love—"

Whatever pronouncement he was about to make was lost as Nell appeared around a pillar. We both admired her drawings. Then the three of us went to see the statue of Earl Rognvald holding a model of the cathedral; his tunic was shorter than my most daring skirt. From the chapel Mr. Sinclair led the way up a narrow stair. We passed the huge workings of the church clock and the three bells that chimed the hour before we emerged onto the roof, beside the spire. Kirkwall, the island, the harbour, and the sea lay before us.

"What an amazing view," I said.

"Can we see the rest of Scotland?" Nell asked.

"No," said Mr. Sinclair. "We're facing the wrong way, and it's too far."

"What about Glasgow?" she persisted. "Can we see Glasgow?"

"No," he said more gently, realising what she was asking, "Glasgow is part of Scotland. Even if the church tower were twice as high we couldn't see it." He was explaining that the cathedral had once been on the shore—much of Kirkwall was built on reclaimed land—when, almost beneath our feet, the bell began to strike. We stood there, counting, until it reached twelve.

Only on the way home, when Nell was safely asleep in the back of the car, did I have the chance to ask again if he wanted me to teach her scripture.

"Not unless you want to. What I want is for her to know the difference between right and wrong, not to be trapped, like her mother, in a single passion."

"Surely," I said shyly, "she must have had more than one, else Nell wouldn't be here."

He glanced over at me. "Clever but wrong. Sometimes Alison didn't care what she did, or was too drunk to mind who touched her."

"I thought people with money"—we were passing the only grove of trees I had seen on the island—"could solve these problems."

Mr. Sinclair laughed. "You haven't a clue what you're talking about. They can. But that would have meant Alison admitting that she was pregnant, and even at six months, she wouldn't. She was as stubborn as the wind. That helped her to walk again, but that didn't stop a baby coming."

"So no one wanted Nell." I turned to look at her where she leaned against the door, eyes closed, lips parted.

"Want, don't want, who cares. 'The world is everything that is the case.'"

"Who said that? You spoke as if you were quoting."

"A philosopher named Ludwig Wittgenstein. He was an Austrian Catholic who gave away all his money, fought against Britain during the First World War, and ended up with a chair at Cambridge University."

"'If a lion could talk,'" I said happily, "'we could not understand him.' But you're wrong. Children don't understand lots of things, but they know when they're not wanted. You wait to grow up, like a prisoner in a deep, dark dungeon."

"You obviously had an idyllic childhood." He patted my knee, once, firmly. "Just keep teaching Nell the way you are. Make her read and write and don't let her be too different from other people. One eccentric in the family is quite enough."

I knew he meant himself and I wondered, yet again, why he had never married. I had asked Vicky, and she had said she didn't know. He knew many people, he earned a pretty penny, he had a bonny tongue. Not long after Alison's accident, there had been rumours of an engagement but no fiancée had followed. We slowed down to turn onto the road to the house, and I asked if a Gypsy woman had brought him a fish.

"So you've been spying on me," he said lightly. "Yes, she did—two delicious sea trout. Unfortunately they were a bribe, not a gift."

"I don't need to spy on you," I said. "The whole island does that."

As I went to open the gate I thought that he and I were opposites in almost every respect: wealth, family, upbringing, position in society. He had been Hugh Sinclair all his life and had a hundred people to say so. Whereas I had scarcely a dozen who knew I was Gemma Hardy and no one who knew I had once been someone other than Gemma Hardy.

chapter nineteen

THE NEXT MORNING VICKY announced that five guests would be arriving that afternoon: three by plane from London and two by ferry from Edinburgh. She bustled around, airing the rooms and making beef Wellington. Nora picked a posy for each dressing-table. Angus cut the lawn ready for croquet and badminton. The prospect of company put Nell in a flutter. "Will we have dinner with them, Gemma?" she asked. "Should I practise my croquet?" Dinner was unlikely, I told her, but she would probably get to play croquet. I too had my hopes, although I did not voice them. We spent the afternoon hitting balls, awkwardly, through hoops.

On the stairs that evening a woman and a man, wearing matching white Aertex shirts, each gave me a hearty handshake and introduced themselves as Rosie and Dale Miller. The island was so peaceful after Edinburgh, they exclaimed. The other guests, two sisters and a colleague of Mr. Sinclair's, I did not see until church the following day. They arrived just as the bell fell silent. First came Jill, dark-haired and sturdy and wearing a pretty blue frock, then Coco, rearranging her blond hair even as she strolled down the aisle. Neither wore hats or gloves. As for the colleague, Colin, he was a pleasant-looking man in a suit. Rosie and Dale followed. Mr. Sinclair brought up the rear, frowning, irked, I thought, by their tardiness.

For the next few days the house was even busier than usual. The six of them explored the neighbouring islands and visited various golf courses. Coco, I gathered, was a keen golfer, and so were Rosie and Dale. Closer to home they played croquet and billiards. In the evenings the sounds of conversation and laughter rose from the library and the dining-room. Nell begged to sit on the stairs, just to listen to the merriment. I sat with her, gazing absently at a book, wishing I didn't feel like a servant, wondering why I minded.

Then Vicky announced that tomorrow, if the weather was fine, Mr. Sinclair planned an expedition to Skara Brae, the Stone Age village. Nell and I were to go too, and he had asked me to make sure that she understood what she was seeing. I had been in the library only twice since his return. Now, while the guests were out, I searched the shelves and found an island history. As Mr. Johnson had told me on the ferry, the village had been buried for thousands of years, only re-emerging in 1850 when a great storm blew the sand away.

On Thursday the skies were clear and the temperature so warm that both Nell and I wore summer blouses. After chores and an hour of lessons, we helped Vicky carry the food out to the car. I sat in the back, making sure the baskets of provisions didn't slide around. While she drove, Vicky reminisced about the time she had visited Skara Brae on a school trip with the history teacher.

"He kept calling it a village, so I expected a main street and houses, but there's just six or seven wee dwellings, half underground, with pathways between them. I remember thinking it would be a cosy place to spend the winter if everyone you liked was nearby. A boy called Tom and I sneaked off to one of the houses and pretended we were making supper. The teacher gave us an awful scolding."

"Why?" said Nell.

At Claypoole I had been surrounded by women who had no use for men, and I had assumed Vicky to be a member of that tribe. Now, as she winked at me in the rear-view mirror and explained the teacher's reaction—we were there to study, not play—it occurred to me that she too would rather be beloved than regarded.

The other cars were already parked. While Nell scampered over to join her uncle and his friends, I helped Vicky spread the rugs on a grassy knoll beside the village and set up a folding table for the food. She had made quiches and salads, sliced a ham, baked bread, and brought homemade cheese and butter. When everything was laid out to her satisfaction she dispatched me to tell Mr. Sinclair. He was standing looking down into one of the houses, pointing out the details to Coco.

"Those slabs on either side of the door were the beds," he said, "and the rectangle in the middle was the hearth. When I was a boy you could still find crofts on the island, with the fireplace in the centre of the room."

"But the bed is so small," Coco exclaimed. She was wearing a tight white T-shirt and a lavender-coloured skirt that fluttered around her bare legs. The heels of her white sandals kept sinking into the turf.

"People were smaller then, smaller even than Gemma. Picture it covered with sheepskins, a nice pillow of dry grass, your fire and your larder a few feet away, your family and your neighbours within hailing distance."

I announced that lunch was ready, and Mr. Sinclair clapped his hands. "Excellent. We'll eat now. Then take a nap on the Stone Age beds. Coco, this is Gemma. The au pair."

"How do you do?" I offered my hand.

"Hi." She raised her hand, the nails a brilliant scarlet, in a little wave of dismissal. Meanwhile Nell had run over and was tugging at her uncle's sleeve, asking if she could sit with him.

"Oh, please," Coco murmured.

I couldn't tell if Mr. Sinclair had heard, but he told Nell to sit with

Vicky and me. Children and servants, I thought. "After lunch," he added, "you can be our guide, tell us what you've learned about the village."

While everyone else praised the food and ate heartily, Coco, I noticed, drank two glasses of wine but barely touched her plate. When the platter of cheese was passed around, she made an excuse about watching her weight.

"Let me do that," said Mr. Sinclair, still holding out the platter. "Vicky made this one from our own milk, and the oatcakes are baked in Stromness."

"Vicky," she said, glancing in my direction and cutting the smallest possible wedge of cheese.

"The housekeeper," he corrected. "I showed you the dairy with the churns."

Coco tilted her head so that her fair hair slipped over her shoulder. "I had no idea you were such a farmer, Hugh. This is a whole new side of you, wandering around, studying the backsides of cows."

"I'm not a farmer," he said. "Not like my father; he was out in the fields rain or gale. He knew exactly how many head of cattle he had, how many bushels of oats. I remember he asked me once if I could point to one thing I had made in the last year. When I told him I'd helped to arrange a loan to Heathrow Airport, he laughed in my face."

I was curious to know how Coco would respond to this speech, but before she could answer Jill called over, "Guess what Colin's been telling me? His grandmother was a witch. She used to take part in ceremonies around the standing stones."

"Not a witch," protested Colin. "She had second sight. She foresaw her husband's death, and she always knew when a storm was coming. The fishermen used to consult her."

I had been too interested in the women to pay much attention to Colin. Now I understood that he was not just a London friend of Mr.

Sinclair's; he had grown up on the island. As for Jill, I'd discovered that she was training to be a vet. The day before, while I was feeding the calves, I had overheard her ask Seamus if she might accompany him on his rounds. "You couldn't keep up with me," he had said curtly. Undeterred, she had walked the fields with Colin, and later told Mr. Sinclair that the cattle were first rate, but the sheep might benefit from introducing some of the newer breeds, which produced more wool and had a lower mortality rate. All this was reported to me by Vicky. "Seamus will have kittens," she had said, "if he hears a girl saying his precious sheep aren't up to snuff."

Nell had dutifully perched between Vicky and me to eat, but as soon as her quiche was gone, she threw her crusts onto the grass and began to flit around, trying her charms on the guests. She talked to Jill and Colin for a few minutes, then moved on to Dale and Rosie. The night before, Rosie had won the badminton tournament, and today she was dressed for a country picnic in a neat blouse, slacks, and walking shoes. She asked Nell which beach she liked best and what other islands she had visited. To my relief Nell answered politely. Then she asked if Rosie liked Petula Clark.

"I don't really know her music," Rosie said apologetically. "Is she one of your favourites?"

I had never thought to wonder at Nell's choice of names for the calves, but now, as she listed several songs, I realised that even then she had been thinking of her mother. I pictured her at the top of St. Magnus, asking if she could see Glasgow. Perhaps when she was older we could go there for a visit. Vicky was gathering the food and I stood up to clear the plates. My years at Claypoole had made me acutely aware of people's leavings. I noted Rosie's and Dale's shining plates, Jill's and Colin's empty, save for a few shreds of lettuce, Coco's filled with food the pigs would have loved, and Mr. Sinclair's not spotless but close.

"Look at the little bird," Coco said. Several birds had discovered the crusts Nell had thrown on the grass.

"It's a pied wagtail," I said. "They eat all kinds of insects and in winter their faces get much whiter."

"A wagtail," Coco exclaimed. "What does it mean that all these birds associated with you-know-what are so small. Little willy wagtail? Little cock robin?"

I knew there was something behind her words that I didn't understand; still, I had to correct her. "Things are often different for birds," I said. "Look how beautiful the male peacock is with his huge tail, and the male mallard is gorgeous with his green head and white necklace. The females don't need to be flashy to attract attention."

But Coco had no interest in learning more about birds, or at least not from me; she was already turning back to the houses. "Perhaps we'll find a necklace," she said. "Or a chalice, whatever that is. Wouldn't that be super?"

I was about to explain that a chalice was a metal drinking cup, and also that any finds belonged to the government, but before I could speak, I felt Mr. Sinclair's gaze again. He gave me a little nod and allowed Coco to take his arm. She made a show of tottering over the short grass and then bent to remove her sandals. Her toenails were the same scarlet as her fingernails. While Nell and I sat with our sketchbooks to draw the village, she climbed down into one of the houses and insisted on trying a Stone Age bed. Knees to her chest she could barely fit on even the larger of the slabs.

"I feel like a sacrificial maiden," she said.

"Not exactly a maiden," called Jill from the next house. She was bending over the dresser, examining how the stones fitted together. It was easy to picture her in a white coat, splinting a dog's leg.

"Come and join me," called Coco, waving at Mr. Sinclair.

His shoulders gave a little twitch and he clambered down to perch on the stone shelf. "Maybe this was the seat reserved for the wise elders," he said, "which meant anyone over twenty-five. So tell me"—he turned to Nell—"what Gemma's taught you about the village."

"The houses are all the same," she said in her best explaining voice. "Each has two beds, and a fireplace and a dresser where people kept food and necklaces. In the book we read, it said that one of the houses had a place for limpets. Some of them have chairs. They think the village used to be farther from the sea. Gemma says they'll find out more when they dig more."

"And how old are the houses?"

"At first they said Iron Age but now they think neo . . . neo."

"Neolithic," I said. "New Stone Age."

A few feet away Coco was twisting and turning on her stone bed in a way that seemed designed to draw attention to her long tanned legs. Mr. Sinclair summoned Nell to show him her picture. She said she needed five more minutes. While I watched, she sketched in Coco and her uncle. She gave him a club and a beard, and Coco an off-the-shoulder bearskin and thick eyelashes. At their feet she drew a little tangled heap. "What's that?" I said.

"Coco's shoes," she whispered.

After Nell had shown her drawing to Mr. Sinclair and he had praised her depiction of him and the houses—"though you didn't do Coco justice"—I led her down to the beach. We played hopscotch on the damp sand until we heard Vicky calling.

On the drive home Nell said, "Does Coco want to marry Uncle Hugh?"

"She's certainly setting her cap at him," said Vicky.

"So then"—I couldn't see Nell's face but I could hear the pleasure in her voice—"I'd have an aunt as well as an uncle."

"Of a kind," said Vicky. We exchanged glances in the mirror.

That night, when Nell was at last asleep, and the sounds of revelry from the dining-room reminded me of a pack of hounds in full cry, I sneaked out of the house, retrieved my bicycle, and headed to the village. I had no plan other than to find Todd. I would be in his presence, and whatever happened would happen. Perhaps we would simply sit side by side, talking about university and his studies, perhaps . . . I knew only that the sight of Coco laughing and squirming on the stone bed had made me reluctant to climb quietly into mine. Would Mr. Sinclair be happy with someone who didn't know a pied wagtail from a mallard? The Iron Age from the Stone Age? And what would happen if she became the mistress of Blackbird Hall? I pictured Nell at a school like Claypoole. My lovely room, my job, gone in a flick of her scarlet nails.

"Au pair," Coco would say incredulously, shimmying her blond hair.

When I got to the village, Nora's house was dark. Perhaps, I thought, they were visiting a neighbour. I walked my bike down the road, studying the lit-up windows of the houses on either side, hoping to spot Nora, or Todd. I would tap on the window and Todd would look up with a smile. In one house I glimpsed the minister and his wife, in another the postmistress and her sister. If Nora and her family were visiting, it was farther afield. On impulse I stopped at the one place in the village I could legitimately enter at any hour. Leaning my bike against the wall, unclipping my light, I pushed through the gate into the churchyard. In all my weekly visits I had never before stopped to look at the graves. Now I began to walk up and down the rows, shining my torch on the stones, some new and upright, some old and perilously aslant. I came upon several Sinclairs, including Vicky's parents. At last I found Mr. Sinclair's brother.

"Roy Albert Sinclair, beloved son of Hamish and Elspeth. His Redeemer calleth. 1923–1953."

Next to him were their parents. Hamish had died in 1960, Elspeth less than two years ago, in August 1964. My torch caught a flash of scarlet. A vase of dahlias—the same colour as those blooming in the border at Blackbird Hall—stood beside the stone. I kept searching up and down the rows. No grave bore Alison's name.

Back at the hall the lights were still on downstairs. I put my bike in the shed and began to walk around the house, thinking to slip in through the back door. I had just turned the corner when the sound of voices stopped me.

"Can we go sailing tomorrow?" Coco said.

"If the wind drops, if the tide is right, and if Mr. Pirie will lend me his boat."

They were sitting on the bench beneath the beech trees; I could make out the glimmer of Coco's blouse and of Mr. Sinclair's white shirt. Grateful for my dark clothes, I edged closer to the fountain.

"Why don't you get your own boat? You could call it HMS *Coco*."

"Because it would pain my thrifty Scottish soul to spend money on something I used only two or three times a year. As a boy I had to gather driftwood and dig potatoes to earn my pocket money. My parents saved string and pieces of soap and the sticky edges of sheets of stamps. Buying a boat would be like burning money on their graves."

Rather than giving them red dahlias, I thought.

"So tell me, Madame Coco," he went on, "why did Giles decline my invitation to come here so vehemently? One week the two of you seemed to be heading to the altar. The next you'd prefer to be at opposite ends of the country."

"I don't want to talk about Giles. He's a philanderer." She said the word so lazily that at first I thought she was referring to some kind of shrub, a cousin of the rhododendron. She slipped off the bench and, stepping away from the trees, sat and then lay back on the grass.

"You have good stars here," she said. "My first boyfriend had a tele-scope. He taught me how to find the rings of Saturn, but we never had stars like this near Brighton."

"Giles might use an even harder word about you. Just when he lost his job you couldn't give him the time of day."

"Don't let's talk about Giles," Coco repeated. "Here we are in your Scottish stronghold. Colin told me today that there's a legend about your family: that only second sons will inherit. The oldest son is al-ways doomed. So that means you have to have at least two sons."

But Mr. Sinclair was not to be deterred. He began to give Giles's ver-sion of the break-up. He had uttered only a few sentences when Coco sat up.

"Do you know what Giles says about you? That you ruined the Mer-cer deal." I couldn't follow the story she poured out: something about one chain of shops buying another, and about how Mr. Sinclair, at the crucial moment, had revealed something that jeopardised the sale.

"You shouldn't believe everything Giles says," Mr. Sinclair said. He spoke softly, but I knew he was angry.

"I don't, and nor should you."

"Touché." He bent towards her.

Don't, I thought. Please don't.

I had never been able to send a message to anyone, not even Miriam, so surely it was only coincidence that at that moment Jill appeared in the doorway, calling her sister's name.

chapter twenty

THE NEXT DAY WAS a proper island day, the wind coming straight from the northeast, buffeting the rain against the windows. I was on my way to feed the calves when Jill appeared in the cloakroom to ask if she could accompany me; Nell had told her about our pets. They were old enough now to require feeding only twice a day, and we had moved them from the barn to the nearest field. As Jill and I trudged through the mud of the farmyard, I caught sight of Seamus coming out of the granary, a sack over his shoulder; since the arrival of the guests, he had been even more absent than usual. Now, without seeming to notice us, he headed towards the byre.

Petula and Herman were huddled in a corner of the field next to the drinking trough. At the sound of their names they began to struggle towards the gate, their slender legs sinking into the mud with each step.

"This is ridiculous," Jill said as we watched Herman pull a hind leg free. "They should be in the barn until the storm passes."

"Seamus won't like it." I wiped the rain from my face. "He already thinks I mollycoddle them."

"No farmer wants to lose his livestock. Besides, this isn't mollycoddling. Calves survive bad weather because they have their mothers to shelter them. Come on. You take one. I'll take the other."

In a moment she had opened the gate, ploughed through the mud, and looped her tartan scarf around Herman's neck. I managed to loop my own scarf around Petula. Together we led them back across the farmyard. Inside the barn Jill called out for Seamus and, when there was no answer, chose the nearest empty stall. We fed the calves and I asked if I should fetch a towel to dry them.

"They'll be fine," said Jill. "Just get them a bucket of water. What you need to watch out for in calves this age is scouring. If you see excrement on their hindquarters, call a vet at once."

She bent to stroke them one last time and joined me in the doorway. We both hesitated, daunted by the rain overhead and the puddles underfoot.

"Good grief," she said. "And this is July. I wouldn't like to be here in winter."

"I only arrived in February," I offered. "Vicky says in December it's dark by three."

"I'd hate that. At Skara Brae yesterday I kept thinking about the families who lived there—how bleak it must have been during a storm, the waves pounding on the shore."

"But the sea was their main source of food," I said, quoting the island history book. "And maybe people then were more like bears and could hibernate."

"Bears hibernate because there's nothing to eat," Jill said thoughtfully. "Perhaps there did used to be a human equivalent, a way to slow down the body. Forgive my asking, but why aren't you at university? You seem very bright."

Briefly, trying to conceal my pleasure, I explained about Claypoole closing and how I had needed a job. I hoped to take my exams next year, I added.

"I'm glad to hear that," Jill said with an energetic nod. "You should be studying alongside Nell. Come on, let's make a dash for it."

Holding on to our hats, we waded out into the rain.

While Nell and I did lessons, the guests lounged away the morning: reading, chatting, playing billiards. The sounds of their conversation made Nell fidgety, and she kept making excuses—a glass of water, the bathroom, a cardigan—to leave the schoolroom. She returned from the last errand, skipping gleefully. We were giving a party tomorrow, she announced, and despite the short notice people were saying yes. When I went to fetch elevenses, Vicky confirmed the plan and told me that Coco was insisting on fancy dress. In the wardrobe of her room she had discovered several evening dresses that had belonged to Mrs. Sinclair. "She went right ahead and tried them on," Vicky said, shaking her head at the impertinence. Mr. Sinclair had agreed to say that fancy dress was encouraged.

Even the promise of future excitement, however, did not placate Coco. At lunch she announced she was bored, bored, bored. She had come to the Orkneys to play golf, and if there was to be no golf today, then she wanted to go to Kirkwall. The six of them could have dinner and stay in a hotel. "I'm fed up with all these fields," she said.

"Ridiculous," fumed Vicky as she carried the plates into the kitchen. "They'll spend a fortune to eat fish and chips and sleep in the Kirkwall Hotel. She just wants to show everyone that she's got Mr. Sinclair eating out of her hand."

But in preparing for the party she recovered her good spirits. The prospect of the house filled with people appealed to her sociable instincts. She asked apologetically if I would mind sharing Nell's room. Some old family friends, the Laidlaws, were coming from the south island and needed a bed for the night. She made a long list of groceries, enlisted the help of Nora and another girl, and organised music. Todd would bring his accordion, and a couple of lads from the village were grand fiddlers. I had been fantasising dancing a reel or two with some unknown guest, but now, remembering the evening when Todd and

Mr. Sinclair had met, I resolved to watch the festivities from a quiet corner.

The next day the wind was even stronger, the rain heavier. Whatever time I had free from kitchen duties I used to help Nell fashion her costume. After wavering between a cat and a witch, she had chosen the former. We found a pair of black trousers in her wardrobe. A black cardigan of mine, with some pinning, made a top. We cut ears out of cardboard, painted them, and attached them to an Alice band. A black sock served as the tail. I practised drawing whiskers on her cheeks with eyeliner until she was satisfied.

"What about your costume?" she said.

"I'm helping Vicky with the food. I'll be dressed as a waitress."

I was joking, but Nell pouted until I promised that, once the food was served, I would come down in my own pair of ears. Far preferable, I thought, to be a second cat than to look as if I had tried to compete.

The guests returned that afternoon. Coco and Jill ran back and forth, asking for thread and safety pins, and Jill asked if they could set up the ironing board in the corridor outside their rooms. As I helped Vicky in the kitchen, I recalled the last Christmas at Yew House, when I had been left to peel the chestnuts with Mrs. Marsden. But this was different, I told myself; I was being paid for my labour. I pictured Coco, the belle of the ball in some elegant gown, and Jill, more sedately dressed, happy with Colin. As for Mr. Sinclair, I imagined him in his old RAF uniform, his goggles on his forehead, a silk scarf around his neck.

The candles were lit; the party guests began to arrive. Syd, the cowman, organised the cars, Nora took the coats, and the musicians struck up. Nell ran in and out of the kitchen, flicking her tail and reporting on what was happening. Mr. Laidlaw was dressed as a raven, she said, and had pretended to be frightened when she meowed. Someone else was Robin Hood. The musicians, even Todd, were wearing kilts. During

"The Grand Old Duke of York" I accompanied her into the library and stood near the door, watching. Coco wore a backless turquoise gown with silver fins attached on each side and a streamer of seaweed pinned, fetchingly, to the bodice. Jill was dressed in a pretty flowered frock with a cap and an apron. Colin had put together a sailor's uniform. As for Mr. Sinclair, he was resplendent in a dinner jacket and cummerbund, which, either by chance or by design, matched Coco's dress.

I had not seen dancing since I left Yew House. Now I watched with pleasure the way the men and women swung unerringly from partner to partner and how the music made possible a kind of order absent from everyday life. One day, I thought, I would go to a party like this and dance the night away with people who treated me like an equal. I would be beloved and regarded. At eleven o'clock the buffet was served, and I ran in and out, carrying cups of tea. Suddenly—I was refilling a milk jug—I realised I had forgotten the calves.

I went at once to make up the bottles. Outside I discovered a fine drizzle was still falling. Following the beam of my torch, I made my way to the farmyard. A hen clucked as I passed the henhouse. In the barn something rustled: probably a rat, probably two rats. I pointed the torch straight ahead until I reached the stall by the door. That morning the calves had been asleep in the straw, but now, wherever I shone the light, the stall was empty. Furious, I strode from the barn across the farmyard. Once again Petula and Herman struggled through the mud towards me.

"I'm sorry," I said. "I'm sorry." Clumsily, leaning over the gate, I managed to give each a bottle.

I was in the cloakroom, levering off my Wellingtons, when Nell bounded in, nose pink with excitement, ears askew. While I was gone, she told me, a Gypsy woman had knocked at the door of the hall. She had walked over from the encampment by the village and offered to

read the ladies' hands. Only the ladies, she insisted. She had set herself up in the alcove off the hall. Mrs. Laidlaw had stoutly refused to
consult her, and Rosie had said that, as a married woman, she already
knew her fortune, but a woman named Frances had gone, and then
Coco urged Jill to go and, when her sister returned flushed and smiling, went herself. The girls at Claypoole had sometimes asked Cook
to read the tea-leaves, and, before crucial hockey matches, they had
plucked the petals off daisies. Neither strategy had struck me as re-
motely reliable, but a real fortune-teller might be different. That night
I would happily have given someone sixpence, even a shilling, to tell
me what the next year would bring. "Is she still here?" I said.

"No, she's very cross," Nell said, and I realised she was talking about
Coco. When she rejoined the party, she had asked the musicians for
an eightsome reel. Then, despite the rain, she had vanished into the
garden.

"And where is your uncle?"

"He disappeared," she said, which I took to mean he had followed
Coco.

Please don't, I thought again. "How about we go to bed," I suggested.
"It's nearly midnight."

Nell swished her tail at me. "Don't you be cross too. I asked Todd to
play a special song. We have to listen. Put your ears on."

The library was lit now only by candles and a standard lamp beside
the musicians. They were playing a song I had heard on Vicky's radio and sometimes coming from Nell's room: "Dedicated to the One
I Love." Many of the guests had left after the buffet and there were
only half-a-dozen couples. In the dim light I made out Jill and Colin
wrapped in each other's arms. Rosie and Dale were waltzing stylishly,
the Laidlaws awkwardly. Mr. Sinclair and Coco were still missing. I
took Nell's hands and we began to circle the room. As we came near

the musicians I felt Todd—almost handsome in his white shirt and kilt—watching me. I blew him a kiss.

"Look," said Nell, "there's Vicky."

And indeed Vicky was waltzing with a man. One of the guests, I thought, until they turned and I recognised Seamus. His hair had been trimmed, and his face, freshly shaved, shone. Brother and sister, they made a striking couple: tall and strong and matching each other step for step. Also striking was the expression on Seamus's face, some combination of melancholy and joy I had never seen before. I steered Nell away. We were at the far end of the room when the overhead lights went on.

"Stop, stop," Coco shouted. Both her hair and her turquoise gown were darkened by rain, and her fins hung limply by her sides.

First one couple, then another halted uncertainly. So did the musicians.

"Don't you know you're dancing on board the *Titanic*? Everything you see here belongs to the bank. You'll get a bill in the morning for your food." She wheeled around to address the musicians. "When you get paid—if you get paid—hold the notes up to the light."

I searched the room for Jill, but she and Colin must have slipped away during the song. Mr. Sinclair appeared beside me. He had been standing, unobserved, in the shadow of the curtains. "Take Nell to bed," he said quietly. "She doesn't need to see this."

But Nell had let go of my hand and was walking the length of the room, a small black figure. She stopped in front of Coco, a cat confronting a mermaid.

"You should take two aspirin," she said, "drink a big glass of water, and go to bed."

"Who the hell do you—"

I did not hear the rest of her sentence. All I saw was Coco's raised hand. Then I was running. Mr. Sinclair and I reached them at the same time. While he restrained Coco, I put my arms around Nell.

"Time to read *Horace Goes Hunting,*" I said. "After midnight cats turn into little girls." For once she followed without argument.

In bed Nell fell asleep almost instantly, but my mind was racing. Might Blackbird Hall, like Claypoole, be about to go bankrupt? Everything seemed safe and prosperous—we had meat for lunch six days a week; the peat fires were stoked high—but then that had been true at the school too. Except for the dwindling number of pupils everything had seemed the same. Perhaps Mr. Sinclair had confided in Coco, or perhaps the mysterious fortune-teller had told her something. What was it she had said in the garden the other night? Something about how he had muddled an investment? Nell sighed and shifted in her sleep. What would become of her, and of me, if we had to leave the island? From the corridor came a wild cry, followed by footsteps. A few minutes later a car drove away, and a few minutes after that the same car, or a different one, returned.

The next morning I came downstairs to find Nora and Vicky mopping the library floor. No one else was around. Mr. Sinclair had driven Colin, Jill, and Coco to the airport. The Laidlaws had gone home, taking Rosie and Dale, whom they knew from Edinburgh, with them. "The house is so quiet," Nell said, and I agreed. I forced myself to go through our timetable: reading, spelling, copying, sums, nature. Nell drew portraits of various guests, and we labelled them and put them up around the schoolroom. But all the time I was listening for a car, a footstep, a voice that didn't come. What if he had decided to take a plane too and was already gone? But why should that matter when in a few days, a few weeks at most, he would be anyway? He had never, as an adult, lived at Blackbird Hall. I had pretended to be a good teacher, entirely dedicated to my pupil; now I would have every opportunity to make real on the pretence.

chapter twenty-one

ALL DAY THE SILENCE persisted. Only Seamus's Land Rover and the greengrocer's van used the track. Even the sheep and cows seemed subdued, and the swallows, nesting under the eaves, twittered faintly as they came and went. At last, when I could no longer stand it, I went to the kitchen on the pretext of making Nell a bedtime treat of hot chocolate. Vicky was at the table, sorting eggs. Now that the ferry strike had ended we were again sending them to the mainland twice a week. As I set a saucepan of milk on the stove, I said that Nell had been asking after her uncle's whereabouts.

"I've not an inkling," said Vicky. "He drove off this morning without a word."

"Did he take his things?" I had turned from the stove to watch her, as if her face might tell me what her words wouldn't.

"No. With the girls' suitcases there wasn't an inch of space."

"So he'll be back," I said. "I can tell Nell she'll see him again."

"Maybe." Vicky held up two eggs, one brown, one white, and put both in the carton to her right. "Last August he left almost everything. I packed his case and sent it to London."

"He'd leave without saying goodbye to his only relative?"

"I couldn't rightly—the milk."

Before I could seize the pan, milk gushed over the sides; the kitchen filled with a burning smell. "Oh, I'm sorry," I said.

"Not to worry," said Vicky. "There's plenty more in the larder. Mr.

Sinclair's business is Mr. Sinclair's business. He pays you and me to be companions to Nell so he won't have to think about her."

She was warning me, I knew, from further questions, but as I poured fresh milk, I could not help asking, "Is it true he might go bankrupt?"

A little cracking sound meant one less egg to market. "Heavens," said Vicky, setting the broken egg aside. "I hope not. I do know that the farm doesn't make a penny, even though the cattle bring a good price. But it didn't under old Mr. Sinclair either, and he knew the land like his own garden. Tell Nell she'll hear from her uncle soon. She can always talk to him on the phone."

"Of course," I said. "She'll like that."

Later, long after Nell and Vicky were both in bed, I walked down the track to the gate. In the west the sky was still light and the bats were out, uttering their high-pitched cries. From the fields came the lonely, fluting call of the curlews. The beauty of the evening only made me lonelier. And what was I lonely for? I asked as I climbed on the gate and gazed down the road along which any car must come. I was used to being alone and I had more friends here than I had had at any time since my uncle died. But I remembered how Mr. Sinclair had talked to me when the bee stung my hand, and how later he had asked my views about God, as if my answer mattered. In those moments I had felt seen by him, and I wanted, I thought as a bat swooped by, to go on being seen.

THE NEXT MORNING, WHEN I stepped out of my room, the familiar fragrance of bacon greeted me. Not daring to think what it might portend, I hurried down the stairs. There, in the kitchen, was Mr. Sinclair at the stove, wearing one of Vicky's flowery aprons.

"You're just in time," he declared. "What will it be? The full British breakfast? The more ladylike Orcadian?"

"What's the full British?"

"Bacon, eggs, mushrooms, toast. Oh, and fried tomatoes."

"Yes, please. Shall I make the toast? And one for Nell too."

"Two full British coming up." He waved the spatula for emphasis. "How would you feel about cancelling lessons today?"

"I'd want a good reason," I said, sawing at the loaf. "We already missed a day going to Skara Brae."

"What a Tartar you are. As your employer"—he began to crack eggs, one-handed, into the frying pan—"I am proposing that Vicky take Nell to Kirkwall to buy some clothes."

I said, truthfully, that I'd been meaning to ask about Nell's wardrobe. She'd grown in the last few months and almost everything she owned was too small. Then I remembered Coco's claim. If he was on the edge of financial ruin he shouldn't be squandering money on clothes, but it was not my place to say so. Instead I said that sometimes Nell and Vicky quarrelled. Maybe I should go along to arbitrate.

"No." He sliced a tomato and put the two halves facedown in the pan. "I have other plans for you. We'll explain to Nell."

At the sound of her name Nell appeared and was delighted at the unexpected treats of a cooked breakfast and her uncle's company. Watching her skipping around as she set the table, I scarcely recognised the cross, pinch-faced girl who, only a few months ago, had thrown the jigsaw puzzle to the floor. Her cheeks held some colour; her hair was neatly brushed. Even her eyes seemed larger and brighter. I buttered the toast and we sat down to eat. According to Mr. Sinclair, the eggs were a little overcooked, but Nell said they were perfect and I thought, but didn't say, that it was the best breakfast I'd eaten since the day of Miriam's death. We were mopping our plates when Vicky appeared, wearing one of her Sunday skirts. "Heavens," she said. "Look at my kitchen."

Mr. Sinclair told her to leave things be. "I don't promise to do the washing-up," he said, "but everything will be assembled in an orderly fashion." He handed her a sheaf of bank-notes and instructed her to buy Nell whatever clothes she needed and have a nice lunch. I detected no signs of anxiety as he put his wallet away.

"And what about Gemma?" said Nell, tugging playfully at the ravelled edge of my pullover. "She needs clothes too."

It was true—our expeditions and games had taken their toll—but I blushed to hear her draw attention to my shabby wardrobe. Happily Mr. Sinclair seemed not to notice; he and I, he explained, were going to plan her studies for the autumn. This seemed to satisfy Nell, but I could not help suspecting that something less pleasant was afoot. As I went to feed the hens and calves, a flock of speculations assailed me: Did he need to sell the house? Had he decided to send Nell to school? Was he going to hire a new au pair? The three-months trial had come and gone, unacknowledged, with no talk about the subsequent terms of my employment.

Back at the house I retreated to the schoolroom. Disconsolately I laid out books and began to make a list. Until I heard otherwise I would go through the motions. We needed a new copying book, and a geography book, and surely there must be a collection of poems and stories for a girl Nell's age, though what did any of it matter if I was being sent away? I was listlessly turning the pages of the arithmetic book—if Janet has two apples and Richard has three—when there was a knock at the door.

"Very diligent." He hadn't visited the schoolroom since the day I was stung. Now he glanced around the room, taking in Nell's drawings. "She has a good eye," he remarked, studying her picture of Petula and Herman. "I need you to advise me about lunch."

"Lunch for whom?" I said, closing the book.

"You and me. We're going on an outing."

I did not give him the satisfaction of asking where.

In the kitchen, while he made ham and cheese sandwiches, I gathered apples and chocolate biscuits and a bottle of lemonade. Twenty minutes later we were in his car, driving along the track. As we drew up to the gate I readied myself to climb out, but Mr. Sinclair was already walking towards it. What time had he returned last night? I wondered. If I had kept my vigil a little longer would we have met?

"I can close it," I said when he returned.

"Indeed you can," he said, driving through the gate, and nimbly climbing out again.

When we were once more bumping along, I said I wanted to ask about piano lessons for Nell. "She keeps trying to play. I'm sure she'd study hard."

"Maybe I should sell that piano. Look, there's Seamus's bull."

Black and massive, the bull was standing beside the gate of a field. As we slowed down, he raised his head and gave a sonorous bellow.

"He's calling to his concubines," said Mr. Sinclair. "What I don't understand is why he doesn't just charge the gate and hunt them down. You only have to look at him to know he easily could."

"He's domesticated," I said. "He's been taught not to charge gates."

"Is that what *domesticated* means? Knowing what you should and shouldn't do?"

"Not just knowing. Doing it. See, even the goldfinch isn't afraid of him." I pointed to the bird perched on the wall not far from the gate.

The bull let loose another bellow. Something about the mixture of desire and helplessness made me uneasy, and I was glad when Mr. Sinclair put the car in gear and drove on. As the bellowing faded he asked how I knew so much about birds.

"My uncle. He loved Roman remains and bird-watching."

"Digging and flying. And whereabouts did he do these things?"

Question by question he whittled away my determination not to talk about the past. I told him about my parents and Iceland, my uncle's untimely death, my aunt and Claypoole. He asked if I remembered my parents, and I said no but that I thought about my uncle almost every day.

"So," he declared, "you're an orphan twice over. Like Nell."

"Yes," I said. "What happened to her mother?"

"I'm still not sure I know." His knuckles whitened against the steering wheel; suddenly the fields were flying by. "At eighteen my sister seemed destined to lead a charmed life. She was clever, pretty, a wonderful horsewoman, and she had a lovely singing voice. But all she really cared about was riding, and the accident took that away."

His voice faltered as he described how determined his sister had been after her fall. "She learned to walk, to drive, to climb stairs. My father kept saying she had the Sinclair backbone. What we didn't realise was that all her efforts were aimed at riding again. She insisted they keep her horse. Seamus rode him for her, and she'd have him trot by the house so that she could watch. Then, when I was visiting at Easter, she asked me to saddle Mercury. We had a furious row."

He braked and I glimpsed the white flick of a rabbit's tail as it dashed across the road.

"The next day I happened to look out of the window, and there she was on Mercury. Seamus was holding the reins. Even from a distance I could see they were arguing. Suddenly Alison broke free and started cantering across the field. I dashed downstairs. By the time I got there Seamus was carrying her back to the house. A month later she moved to Glasgow."

He fell silent. When it seemed that he was not going to speak again, I reported what Vicky had said: Alison's heart had failed.

Mr. Sinclair let out a soft sigh. "My father had some old friends in Glasgow. The coroner was kind. She became addicted to painkillers, then to other things as well. A pretty girl with money, she could get whatever she wanted." He waved, as if the walls that lined the road were stocked with mysterious substances. "My disapproval just made her secretive. Nell was alone with her when she died. We don't really know what happened."

"What about Nell's father?"

"The birth certificate says father unknown. I suspect that was true, even for Alison."

"So you're Nell's only relative?"

"Yes, we're the last of the Sinclairs, though if you go back far enough Vicky and Seamus are distant cousins. Now perhaps you can understand why I'm not keen on piano lessons. I didn't care for Alison's musician friends, drinking too much and hoping to get lucky."

We passed a sign for the village of Birsay. Nearby stood a red sandstone ruin, several storeys high. "Not every pianist drinks," I said, though my only evidence was the music teacher at Claypoole, who had played even "For She's a Jolly Good Fellow" in a restrained fashion. "With winter coming," I persisted, "Nell needs indoor hobbies." He wasn't, I noted gladly, suggesting that either she or I leave Blackbird Hall.

"She can collect stamps. Make papier-mâché animals. Learn to cook. Practise cartwheels. Here we are. The Brough of Birsay."

He pulled onto the verge and pointed to an island a few hundred yards offshore. From this angle, with its sheer cliffs and smooth, grassy top, it resembled a lopsided cake with a single candle, a lighthouse just visible in the centre. At the side nearest Birsay the cliffs sloped down to the sea in a tumble of rocks and seaweed. A causeway, wide enough for a small cart, ran between the island and the mainland.

"We're going to see the puffins," Mr. Sinclair announced. "At least I hope so. Sometimes they're shy."

He slung the knapsack over his shoulder and led the way down the rocks and onto the causeway. I followed, trying to avoid trampling on the limpets and barnacles. Halfway across something caught my attention. A seal, drifting in the bay, was studying me with large dark eyes.

"Hello," I said, waving. "I hope you catch a hundred delicious fish."

"I don't think you need worry about that," said Mr. Sinclair. "I've never seen a thin seal."

As we continued walking, the seal dove and reappeared a few steps later. In this fashion it accompanied us across the causeway, finally disappearing only when we reached the shore. We climbed up the rocky beach and found ourselves standing amid low ruined walls. The island had been the site of a church and a monastery, Mr. Sinclair explained, and perhaps a farm.

"The Vikings had a settlement here," he said, "and then the Picts. Or was it the other way round? Sometimes I think about how calmly we speak about different colonizers when I hear people talking about the war. Maybe it wouldn't have been the worst thing for civilisation if the Germans had won in 1918. Hitler would never have come to power. Europe wouldn't have been torn to shreds. We'd all be listening to Wagner and reading Thomas Mann."

"Are you a pacifist?" We were walking around a ragged stone rectangle, the outline of a building. Inside the grass was thick with daisies.

"No. I'm too much of a coward. I used to come here as a boy. Once Roy and Seamus and I lost track of the time. We had to wade back across the causeway."

"If I knew about these things," I said, bending to examine the wall, "I'd be able to tell by the kind of mortar when this was built."

We left the ruins and walked up over the grass, following the south-ern rim of the cake as it gently rose. At its highest point, the cliffs fell uninterrupted to the rocks below. To the south, across the bay, Mr. Sinclair pointed out the tower of the Kitchener Memorial. Lord Kitch-ener had been on a mission to Russia in June 1916 when his boat sank off the island. We sat down in a sheltered spot a few yards from the crumbling cliff top to eat our picnic. At our backs wild thyme grew in clumps and a tiny four-petal yellow flower. Before us birds rose and fell, riding the air currents, scarcely moving their wings. A skua soared twenty or thirty feet and drifted down. Half-a-dozen fulmars circled and another, smaller bird with arched wings.

"They don't seem afraid of us," I said. "Do you think that's a kit-tiwake? The darker one." I wished I had brought Miriam's bird book.

"I'm afraid I wouldn't know a kittiwake from a corn-crake. A puffin is one of the few birds I can recognise. We'll have to look it up when we go home." He leaned back on his elbows, following the birds. "Did you ever read that passage in Milton where the bad angels are tumbling out of heaven like falling leaves? I had to memorise it at school. I can't remember half the boys in my class, but I can still remember those lines."

"We only did the sonnet about blindness." I was thinking how easily he had used the word *home*.

"Did your uncle, the archaeologist-minister, talk about souls?"

While his attention remained on the birds, I had the luxury of studying him unobserved. His head was tilted back so that his wavy hair touched his shoulders; I counted five silvery threads among the brown. His eyelashes were dark and surprisingly straight; his ear, the nearest one, was as neatly curved as a cowrie shell. "I don't think you can be a minister," I said, "and not mention souls, but he wasn't the kind of person who told people what to do."

Hearing my own words, an odd feeling came over me, not as if someone were walking on my grave but as if I were walking on someone else's. I was suddenly aware that I had been only a little older than Nell when my uncle died. How did I know what kind of person he was? A bird flew by so close that I could see the red rims around its eyes. "I'd love to come here with someone who knows about birds," I said.

"I am sorry," Mr. Sinclair said, "not to be that person. But you can watch them without knowing what they are. My father used to tell a story about a man who loses his soul and, after many travails, gets it back in the form of a seagull. Then, of course, he has to be careful of cats and hunters. I worry that with television people will forget the old tales."

"Nell and I are going to study island history this autumn. Perhaps we can write down some of the stories."

I followed the arc of a small white bird and hoped he would say something more definite about the future, but he was rummaging in the knapsack. "So," he said, "you really have no family. No long-lost cousins? No distant aunts, or geriatric great-uncles?"

"I do have cousins"—the white bird was gone, whether up or down I wasn't sure—"but I haven't seen them since I was ten, and even then they hated me." Daringly, like the birds, I flung myself on the air currents. "This is the first time I've had a home since my uncle died."

Mr. Sinclair held out a pair of binoculars. "And is that boy, Todd, part of what makes it home?"

"Thanks to you"—I took the binoculars—"I hardly know him. It's Nora who asks me to their house. Besides, he'll be going back to university soon." For a moment through the lenses I saw nothing but sky. Then a bird appeared, and another.

"How deftly she fails to answer my question. You should be a barrister."

"Why did Coco get so upset at the party? One minute she was busy being a mermaid, the next she was furious."

Suddenly the sky was gone; a navy blue shirt filled the lenses. Lowering the binoculars, I saw that Mr. Sinclair was on his feet, moving towards the edge of the cliff. "Do you know," he said, "that there are people who can't go near high places not because they're afraid of heights but because they feel such a lure to jump?"

"I'm not afraid of heights—at least not usually—but I don't want to jump either."

"Fearless Gemma."

I wanted to tell him all the things I was afraid of: forgetting my uncle, being confined in a small, dark place, leaving Blackbird Hall, not going to university, being cursed, his departure. Instead I said, "So do they believe they can fly, like Peter Pan?"

"I'm not a member of that particular tribe, but I'm guessing that it's about some kind of irresistible urge, the same one that draws people towards excess and ruin. Happily most of us never experience it. My sister did. Life didn't feel real unless she was on the edge and then— again I'm only guessing—being on the edge was almost too painful to bear."

As he spoke, Mr. Sinclair took another step towards the cliff top. "Please," I said. "Come and sit down."

"Do you wonder why I'm not married? Why I haven't produced an heir?"

"Servants always gossip about their masters, but it's none of my business. Mrs. Pirie, at the post office, thinks you know the Queen."

"Everyone in London knows the Queen."

A bird flew by so close that its wings seemed almost to brush his hair. "Would you like a sandwich?" I said.

"Spoken as if to a four-year-old. Yes, I'd like a sandwich."

To my relief he stepped back and sat down again. As I handed him the sandwich, I noticed little beads of sweat on his upper lip. I pointed out another skua and then what I thought might be a razorbill. The sight of the birds rising and falling and rising again was almost hypnotic.

"So that's what I am," said Mr. Sinclair. "Your master?"

"No, because that suggests you control every aspect of my destiny. You're my employer. You give me money. I provide a service."

"Like having lunch with me. Are you here now because I'm your employer?"

"I don't remember you giving me a choice."

He laughed. "And a good thing too. If I had, you'd have said something disparaging about how you'd seen puffins before. Or that you needed to prepare lessons."

"I've never seen a puffin. Where are they anyway?" I recalled the puffin pictured in *Birds of the World* with its burrow and its vivid beak.

"They're on the east side of the island, or they used to be." His mood had shifted again, like the day itself, and whatever darkness had drawn him to approach the cliff top was gone. We watched the birds and ate our sandwiches. I asked about being in the RAF: Had he felt like a bird?

"Not for a second, but I wasn't dashing around in a Spitfire. I was one of seven men crammed into a Lancaster bomber. It was cold and noisy and you could smell the engine. The best moments were coming back in the early morning, seeing the countryside laid out—fields and cows and little villages and church spires—and knowing exactly where the landing strip was. I felt supremely lucky. I doubt birds feel that way."

"Could you see people?" On the rare occasions when a plane flew over Blackbird Hall, Nell and I always stopped what we were doing to wave.

"When we came in to land."

He poured us both more lemonade and asked what countries I would like to visit. Iceland, I said, and he said, naturally, and after that? Remembering the long-ago lyre-bird, I said Australia for the fauna, and Italy for the history. Then I asked the question back.

"Russia for the culture," he said. "And Iceland, to see you."

He spoke lightly, but I felt myself blush. Muttering something about the lighthouse, I scrambled to my feet and set off towards it. Todd was right, I thought bitterly. Only a feudal overlord would joke about such matters. Away from the cliff top the ground was hummocky. Several sheep, scarcely pausing in their grazing, stepped out of my path. Gradually, as my cheeks cooled, so did my anger. It was just the way Mr. Sinclair talked, I thought. Without looking, I knew he was following me. The lighthouse, no taller than a two-storey house, was painted like a sailor suit in blue and white.

"It hasn't changed in thirty years," he said, coming up beside me. "And out there"—he waved towards the endless Atlantic—"is what our ancestors called the Far Islands: their version of Paradise. The place we sail to after death. They smell of apple blossom all year-round."

"I found a book of old Orkney maps in the library," I said. "One showed the last great auk on an island called Papa Westray. Another showed a man in a coracle, heading towards the edge of the world."

"Oh, I remember that. He looks quite cheerful, doesn't he?" Mr. Sinclair took off his jacket, spread it on the grass, and sat down. "The summer before the war our father took Roy and me on a tour of the lighthouses that Robert Louis Stevenson's father built on the west coast of Scotland."

I too spread out my jacket and sat down. Overhead an invisible lark unspooled its thread of song. "*Dr. Jekyll and Mr. Hyde* was one of my uncle's favourite books," I said. "He thought everyone had to struggle between the good and bad parts of himself."

Mr. Sinclair lay back. I noticed again how dark his eyelashes were. "Coco got drunk at the party," he said, "because the Gypsy told her something she didn't want to hear."

"How do you know?"

"She came and asked me about it, and I told her it was true."

"You lied to her. That makes you as bad as her."

"I agree, but anyone who believes that some random Gypsy holds the key to the future—especially a Gypsy who bears me a grudge because I wouldn't give her family more winter grazing—is an idiot. If there were a way to find out the future, wouldn't we all know it?"

I was about to say that nothing justified a lie—truth beareth away the victory, my uncle used to say—but even as I formed the words I remembered that I too had wanted to be one of those idiots who consulted the Gypsy. To cover my confusion I lay back and closed my eyes. Nearby I could hear the bees buzzing in the little yellow flowers; farther away the sea pounded on the cliffs below. I pictured us as the lark must see us: a man and a girl, lying on the grass a few feet apart, on an island shaped like a cake.

"You're cross," he said. "You think I behaved despicably."

A shadow crossed my face. I felt his breath on my skin but still I did not open my eyes. "It was despicable—deceiving Coco—but mostly I'm embarrassed because I wanted to have my fortune told."

"You're brave to admit it, Gemma, when I'm ranting away. Do you know why I misled her?"

Behind closed lids I considered the question. "You wanted to find out something about her," I ventured.

"What a veritable Sherlock Holmes you are. And do you have any theories as to what that something might be?"

An idea appeared in some distant corner of my brain, but I couldn't, or wouldn't, bring it into focus. "No. You'll have to tell me."

"At the risk of sounding vain," he said, "I had begun to notice that Coco seemed very enamoured of me on very brief acquaintance. I was flattered—lovely golfer worships curmudgeonly banker—but I couldn't help wondering if her attentions were entirely to do with my charms. So when she asked me if what the Gypsy told her was true— that Blackbird Hall was about to be seized by bailiffs—I said yes. What you saw, what I'm afraid everyone saw, was the effect of that information. Coco was a gold digger. I'm not proud of my deception, but I was in danger of committing a stupid male mistake."

Something touched my forehead, fleetingly. Then he lay back down beside me.

In a minute or two I heard his breathing change. I do not know how long I lay there, thinking over what he had said, before I too drifted away. When I woke, a sheep was grazing nearby. Mr. Sinclair was still asleep. As I watched him, his eyelids twitched restlessly; perhaps he was dreaming of flying. I stood up and circled the lighthouse. A few yards ahead a lapwing, with its unmistakable little crest, ran across the grass, dragging its wing. It was too late for chicks, but I followed anyway and then, remembering that birds often feigned injury to lead predators away from their nests, walked in the opposite direction. I soon found a depression in the grass. The nearby eggshell was intact save for an opening the size of a match head; the chick must have extricated itself, like Houdini. One more for my collection with Nell.

"Gemma, Gemma."

Cradling the eggshell in my palm, I hurried back around the light-house. Mr. Sinclair was on his feet, holding my jacket. "Why didn't you wake me? We'll be caught by the tide."

Almost running, we headed over the grass towards the ruins. The egg slipped from my grasp. Soon we had a clear view of the causeway.

At either shore it was still above water, but in the middle, for a distance of about fifty feet, it was already submerged. I stopped in dismay.

"We'll be fine," Mr. Sinclair said. "It can't be more than knee-deep."

"No. Let's wait until the tide turns. We've got water, food, warm clothes. Please. We'll go and see the puffins. It'll only be a few hours."

He put his hands on my shoulders and bent down so that his eyes were looking directly into mine. "Last time," he said, "the water was much higher and I was only a boy and we made it safely across. Do you think I'd suggest we do this if there were any danger?"

I wanted to say that I loved the sea but that water had taken first my father, and then my uncle. They hadn't been able to breathe water, and Miriam hadn't been able to breathe air. That the young man in the library had warned me against causeways. That I had heard of people falling into the sea and dying instantly of shock, even in summer. I blurted out only this last.

"You won't even get wet," he said. "I'll carry you."

He reached out his hand. Slowly I took it, surrendering to his warm grasp. No longer running, we moved through the ruins hand in hand and climbed down over the rocks to the shore and the causeway. My heart began to thrum.

"Come on," said Mr. Sinclair.

We reached the first lapping of water, and before I knew what was happening, he bent down and picked me up. I had no choice but to put my arms around his neck, and then, not wanting to see the rising tide, I buried my face against his chest. I could feel him walking slowly and steadily. Only once did the water splash my legs.

Then he was no longer walking. Were we sinking? Drowning? His arms tightened around me, I felt his breath in my hair and, at last, his face seeking mine.

chapter twenty-two

THERE WAS NO BACON the next morning, nor anything else. The house had, once again, deflated. Even before Vicky spoke, I knew that Mr. Sinclair was gone. Soon after she and Nell returned from Kirkwall someone had telephoned, asking to speak to him, and later he had spent nearly an hour on the phone. "Heaven knows how much that cost," she remarked. She had kept his supper in the oven, and when he came to retrieve it, he had said there was no help for it: he must leave on the morning plane.

"He said to tell Nell he'll be back for the harvest," she said.

Under cover of pouring cornflakes, I asked if she thought he really would return.

"Who knows?" She was making her list for the greengrocer's van and I saw her write the word *lard*. "Last week he said he was daft to live in London but then he goes back and forgets all about us. Maybe things will be different now Nell is older."

"Maybe," I said, trying to match her casual tone. I ate enough not to draw her attention and then, not waiting for Nell, went out to the farmyard. How could he have left? I demanded as I fetched the bucket for gathering the eggs. How could he have left without a message? So much—I ignored two Plymouth Rocks clucking for food—for his hand holding mine, his lips finding mine. And now all Vicky could say was "who knows," as if his return were a matter of no more importance than whether she should buy flour this week or next. I swiftly filled one bucket with eggs, then a second. The hens sensed my turmoil. Two of them pecked at me; several squawked.

I was still in a state of furious confusion when I reached the schoolroom. The sight of a single silver grey feather lying on the table stopped me. I picked it up, wonderingly; the barbs and barbules were perfectly aligned, as if the seagull had dropped it there five minutes before. Surely it was a message, but what did it mean—I have flown? I will return? My soul is here?

I was still holding it when Nell pranced in, wearing her new green pullover. "Pretty," she said. "Where did you get it?"

"I don't know. Maybe the fairies brought it?"

"Can I keep it?"

"Let's put it in our collection," I said and placed it with the various shells and rocks we'd gathered on the mantelpiece. As we settled to copying sentences I found myself thinking again of all the stories about women turning into trees, gods into swans. Perhaps the Brough of Birsay had transformed Mr. Sinclair and me not into, say, a skua and a kittiwake, but into two people who could embrace each other. Now, back on the mainland, we had resumed our habitual forms: employer and au pair.

In the days that followed I kept diligently to my tasks and my teaching but the hours limped by, especially after Nell had gone to bed. I often stayed up late, reading in the library. Sometimes I prowled the garden, or walked down to the cove. I would come back to find the house dark save for two lights, one outside Nell's room, the other shining from Seamus's quarters. What kind of farmer stayed up late? I wondered. On several occasions, searching the library shelves, I had noticed a book in a different place, or gone. I doubted Nora's dusting was the cause, and Vicky, like Matron, read romantic novels about lairds and nursemaids. That left only Seamus, but I couldn't picture him reading *Childe Harold* or *The Moonstone*.

One night I rediscovered the history book I had consulted about Skara Brae. Examining the illustrations, I came across a photograph of a group of standing stones named the Ring of Brogdar. "Legend has it," read the caption, "that the Ring can grant wishes and cure minor ailments." The next day I borrowed a map and, leaving Nell with Vicky, bicycled the eleven miles to the Ring. It stood on a narrow strip of moorland between two lochs. I walked the sheep path that circled the stones until I came to the tallest one, grey and patterned with lichen. I laid my hand on the stone—it was surprisingly warm—and made my wish. Please, please, please, let Mr. Sinclair return.

The next morning I awoke to a frenzy of bleating. When I stepped outside, the farmyard and surrounding fields were filled with sheep, crying anxiously as they waited to be sheared and dipped. Seamus was doing the shearing. He stood astride each sheep, bending down so that his checked shirt fell open almost to the waist, and ran the clippers over the animal, skillfully circling the legs, neck, and tail. The dirty grey wool fell, like a discarded garment, to the ground and the sheep emerged, half the size and pristine white. Before it could recover, the boys seized it and shoved it down a chute into a trough of pungent, murky dip. For a few seconds every part of it was submerged. Then it surfaced, blinking, the dip streaming off it. The last part of the ordeal, the branding, happily involved not an iron but a dab of red paint on the rump.

I stood watching, dumbstruck at the spectacle. I knew that the sheep were not permanently injured, indeed perhaps they were glad to be rid of the smelly coats they had worn all winter long, but the way Seamus seized each animal and forced it to do his bidding made it seem as if some primal struggle were being fought. I thought of the story of Jove and Callisto that I had translated for Miss Seftain. I would have watched all day if Vicky had not come out with mugs of tea.

On several occasions during those weeks I caught her eyeing me, and once when we met, taking each other by surprise outside the hay barn, I thought she might say something. Quickly I made a joke about the rooster sounding hoarse that morning. At the slightest prompting, I worried I would spill out my feelings for Mr. Sinclair. Then surely she would repeat the obvious facts, which I repeated to myself over and over as I brushed my hair and taught Nell the eight-times table and rode my bicycle with her down to the sea. I had written them out on a piece of paper, which I hid among my socks.

Mr. Sinclair	Me
Twice my age	*Only 18*
Banker	*Au pair*
Regarded & Beloved (many)	*Regarded (Vicky) & Beloved (Nell)*
Two homes	*A room in one of them*
Wealthy	*Forty pounds of savings*
Plenty of friends	*Few friends, no family*
Beautiful shoes	*Cast-off clothes*
Handsome, to some people	*Plain to most*
University	*Exams still to sit*

And in addition to all these was the item that I could not bear to write down, namely, that his life was full of women like Coco or, better still, like Jill, kind and talented and hard-working.

That Saturday at Vicky's urging—"You've been dull this week"—I bicycled to see Nora. The house was lit and everyone was sitting around the table, playing Monopoly. I squeezed in beside Todd, and he joked with me as usual, but something had changed. I no longer studied his unlined face with interest, or teased him about the holes in his sweater, and he no longer tried to get me on my own. The feeling that had no name was gone. How had that happened? But I added it to my litany of stern reminders: a single kiss, a single embrace meant nothing.

Day by day the fields of corn and barley grew more golden. If he was coming, then he must come soon. But the phone was silent. When Nell asked her, Vicky said only that the island was a long way from London. That night I sat in the library reading *Kidnapped* until the print swam into long dark snakes and all understanding of David Balfour's adventures fled. Abandoning the book, I stepped into the garden. The dew had fallen, and as I circled the house, I could smell the sweet, dense fragrance of the night stock blooming in the borders. A quarter-moon hung over the beech trees. As I passed the corner by the kitchen, I saw a square of light on the grass; I edged closer.

I had often glimpsed Seamus's room as Nell and I played in the garden, but I had never seen him there. Now he stood beside the fireplace, his elbows on the mantelpiece, his head buried in his hands. As I watched, I saw that his shoulders were shaking, almost—although this seemed impossible—as if he were crying. How odd, I thought, that we two, who had been enemies since our first minute together, should be the only ones awake for miles around, and each of us in the grip of despair. Somewhere nearby an owl screamed, the cry of the hunter.

THE NEXT DAY AT lunch, as she ladled out soup, Vicky announced that Mr. Sinclair would be arriving that evening. Nell jumped to her feet, knocking over her water glass, and in the bustle of mopping-up and mild scolding, I was able to hide my own delight. The talk turned to the harvesting, which would begin tomorrow; several boys had been enlisted from the village. They would start on the oats to the west, Seamus said. All signs of his nocturnal gloom were gone and he joked with Angus and Syd about sharpening their scythes, though nowadays most of the work was done by tractor. When I asked about gleaning— my uncle had loved the story of Ruth and Naomi among the alien corn—he laughed and said, "Bring your basket, lassie."

But that afternoon, when I walked to the cove with Nell, my delight dimmed. I had made no provision for my prayers being answered. The awkward questions that absence had allowed me to ignore began to surface. Mr. Sinclair was back, but for how long? His was the prerogative to come and go as he pleased without warning. He had the money, the freedom of a broad stage, the power to change my life from one day to the next. And I, what did I have to set against these assets? As Nell and I skipped stones, each bounce carried the answer: nothing, nothing. I resolved to keep my distance, a resolve that seemed in no way incompatible with pondering what to wear that evening.

It was Nell who spotted him as we let ourselves into the garden. He was sitting on the bench beneath the beech trees, dressed in a blue shirt and white trousers. In one hand he held a glass, in the other a London newspaper. She ran to greet him. When he had hugged and kissed her, he looked over at where I lingered beside the fountain.

"Gemma. Aren't you going to come and say hello?"

"How do you do?" I said in my best Claypoole voice. "I hope you had a pleasant journey."

One arm still around Nell, he studied me carefully. "Did you not get my message?"

Had there been a note that had gone astray? "What message?"

"From the wing of one of the few birds I know, a seagull."

So only the stupid ambiguous feather, no words committed to paper. "Yes, but it told me nothing. Nell, come and wash your hands before tea."

Mr. Sinclair half rose, as if he might follow her, then he sank down again. And, although it was the last thing I wanted to do, I walked away.

THAT NIGHT I STOOD at the window of my room, hoping to see him in the garden, waiting for me, but nothing moved across the dewy lawn. I did not have the courage to tiptoe downstairs and investigate the library. Enough, I said sternly to myself. I had my job, I was earning a living, saving money: What more could I hope for? Next summer, I vowed, whatever happened, I would look for a position in Edinburgh where I could study for my exams.

The harvesting began, and Mr. Sinclair, when he had no other engagements, joined Seamus and the other men. Vicky carried lunch to wherever they were working, and Nell and I went too, to picnic on the edge of the field among the poppies and thistles. After they'd eaten their sandwiches, the boys from the village sometimes played pig in the middle or leapfrog and allowed Nell to join in. While these games were in progress I could not help glancing occasionally at Mr. Sinclair where he sat beside the tractor with the other men. His skin had turned almost as dark as Seamus's and often he forgot to shave. Never once did I catch him looking my way.

Since my first week on the island there had seldom been two days together without rain. Now everyone remarked on the glorious weather, at first doubtfully—it couldn't last—and then, as day followed sunlit day, with the sense that perhaps we had earned it. By the end of Saturday one last field of barley, the largest and most golden, remained to be cut. On Sunday I drew my curtains to find the sky once again cloudless, but the blue had shifted slightly, from cerulean to azure, as if, far away, a veil had fallen. When I came down to breakfast, Seamus was in the kitchen, wearing his work clothes, haranguing Vicky.

"We need to get the barley in," he was saying. "The storm will be here by suppertime."

"Seamus, it's the Sabbath. We're not heathens." She stood facing him, holding the kettle, her cheeks bright with reproach.

"I'll work alone. No one need know. The Lord gives us fine weather so we can grow crops and harvest them." He swung round. "Ask Miss Hardy. She knows southern ways, people who work on Sunday and are none the worse for it."

Here was my chance, finally, to get in his good books, but I hesitated to cross Vicky. "Maybe you should ask Mr. Sinclair," I offered. "It's his barley."

"Your precious Mr. Sinclair," said Seamus. He stormed off towards the dining-room.

Why did he say *your*, I wondered, and had Vicky noticed? Quickly I asked if she needed help, and when she said no, headed out to tend the hens and calves.

I did not hear what transpired between the two men, but Seamus was in church, glowering in the pew nearest the door. He did not join in the hymn singing, and the minister was still saying the final amen as he clattered down the aisle. By the time we came out to the church-yard, he was gone. Meanwhile Mr. Sinclair, with not even a nod in our direction, drove off to visit the Laidlaws on the south island. Vicky, Nell, and I had lunch in the garden. Afterwards we bicycled down to the Sands of Evie. The whole sweep of water, out to the island of Rou-say, was a brilliant turquoise, and the three of us took off our shoes and waded into the sea, shrieking at the cold. When we had finished paddling we played statues.

The ride back was mostly uphill, and by the time we reached the house we were plucking at our shirts and flailing our arms to keep the midges at bay. As I put the bikes away, I was struck by the stillness. Save for the insects nothing moved.

"The weather's about to break," said Vicky, and the lowering sky did look as if it might rupture at any moment.

Indoors Nell could not settle to reading, or drawing, or draughts. Finally I suggested she play the piano in the hall. I had shown her the few scales Miriam had taught me and she enjoyed practising them and trying to figure out her favourite songs. She was working on "Mrs. Brown, You've Got a Lovely Daughter," and I was urging her to play more slowly when the first fat raindrops fell. Within minutes the wind rushed in like a pack of wild animals. We both jumped up to stand by the window. I stared into the swirling rain and said silently, I will forget Mr. Sinclair. I will forget Mr. Sinclair. A man who would lie about his finances to test a woman was not worth a moment's thought or affection.

"I love storms," sighed Nell. "When I grow up I'd like to be a weatherman."

"Weatherwoman," I was saying when a loud crack made us both jump.

"What was that?" said Nell. "What happened?"

But all we could see was rain and more rain.

In half an hour the storm had passed, sweeping on to the Brough of Birsay, and out to sea. On my way to feed the calves, I made a detour through the garden. The gnats were gone, and everything smelled sweetly of damp earth. Beneath the beech trees lay a dark mass: the branch from which the swing had hung. The white ropes were tangled among the copper leaves, and as I approached it looked, in the gathering dusk, as if the branch were being kept prisoner. Raising my eyes to the grey trunk, I discovered a gleaming scar.

The calves were once again barely able to pick their way through the mud, and when I tried to feed Herman the nipple kept slipping from his mouth. Petula refused even to take the bottle. Remembering Jill's advice, I fetched a rope from the granary and led them one by one to an empty stall in the barn. Still they refused to eat. I tucked them into the warm straw and promised extra milk in the morning. Back at the house Vicky and Nell were playing racing demon. They begged me to join their game and, in the flurry of slapping down cards, and then chivvying Nell to bed, I forgot to mention either the calves, or the tree.

THE NEXT MORNING VICKY told me that Seamus had gone to the barley straight from church and cut as much as he could with his scythe, but even that was probably ruined. "He's beside himself," she said, raising a hand to hide a yawn. I wondered if Seamus had kept her up late, venting his rage.

"I'm sorry," I said. "I don't think anyone could work harder than Seamus." It was the one good thing I could say about him.

"Just stay out of his way. Do you want some porridge?"

I had every intention of following her advice, but when I went to feed the calves, the stall was once again empty. Seamus had returned them to the field. Herman stood near the gate, his head hanging low, shuddering every few seconds. Petula had lain down in the mud. Both, I saw, were suffering from the scouring Jill had warned me of, their hindquarters caked in excrement. I ran to fetch Vicky and we dragged them back to the stall. While she tried to coax them to eat, I spread straw and filled the water bucket. They sank down, trembling, refusing the bottle.

"We need to get the vet," I said.

"Gemma, Seamus is the one who calls the vet."

I asked if she knew where he was, and she said he was stacking the hay. "But wait until lunch," she added. "I told you he's in a foul mood."

"Look at them." Petula's eyes were watering and Herman was making a low sound. "This can't wait."

Vicky tried once more to remonstrate but the calves were ill and my old fears were back. Everyone, everything, I touched was doomed. If only Mr. Sinclair were here, but he had spent the night at the Laidlaws'. As I hurried past the byre towards the hay barn I could already hear Seamus barking commands: "Over there." "Higher, lad." When I stepped inside he was standing next to the trailer, supervising Angus and another boy as they unloaded and stacked the bales. I knew that he knew I was there—I was always on his radar—but he didn't, for a second, glance in my direction.

"Seamus," I said, "I'm sorry to interrupt but the calves are ill. We need to call the vet. If you give me the number I can telephone."

"Leave a wee space," he called to the boys. "We'll stack them tight when they're dry."

I went and stood a few yards in front of him. The air was thick with dust from the bales and the only light came from behind him, through the open doors. "Please," I said, "they're very poorly. Can you tell me the vet's phone number?"

At last his pale eyes were glinting down at me. "What the hell do you think you're doing? If those calves are poorly it's because you haven't weaned them soon enough. Giving them names, treating them like pets, it's no wonder they're ruined. Don't you know vets cost money?" The last question landed at my feet in a glob of spittle.

"They're ill because you put them out in the storm," I said. "Jill's a vet and she told me that in bad weather calves need their mother for shelter. Please give me the phone number." The air felt as it had the previous evening before the rain, but now it was Seamus who was making everything hot and still.

"Are you telling me how to do my job? Get out of here before I make you."

I glared back at him, wishing, like David, I had five smooth stones. "What kind of farmer are you that you want to kill your cows? I've been saving my wages. I'll pay for the vet. Just give me the phone number."

Seamus took a step towards me and I took a step towards him. I had not fought anyone since my first year at Claypoole, but I knew now that the best way to hurt a man was to aim below his belt; my height made that easy. I clenched my fists in readiness.

"Gemma, go back to the house. I'll deal with this."

I turned, and there, standing on top of the bales of hay, twenty feet above the floor of the barn, was Mr. Sinclair.

Seamus stopped moving. Like the sky the day before, his eyes seemed suddenly veiled. All expression left his face. Even in my fury, I felt a flash of sympathy. I knew, only too well, what it was like to have one's life controlled by other people. He worked seven days a week taking care of the land and the livestock and yet, like me, he remained at the mercy of Mr. Sinclair's whims.

An hour later Nell was tracing a map of Scotland, struggling with the jagged west coast, when we heard a car pull up. From the schoolroom window I saw a man climb out of a Land Rover and Mr. Sinclair stepping around the house to meet him. When I went to fetch lunch for Nell and me—I couldn't sit at the same table as Seamus—Vicky handed me a note:

Calves will recover. Vet says feed twice a day this week & keep warm & dry. Next week start to wean.

I had never before seen his handwriting, and I studied the brief sentences as if there might be words hiding beneath the words, a volume of feeling coiled in the casual ampersands. I would never have let Nell get away with the poorly formed *r*s, the hastily looped *y*s.

THAT NIGHT AS I lay in bed, trying to read myself to sleep, I heard a knock at my door. "Come in," I called, moving over to make room for Nell.

The door opened a crack. "Gemma, get up. Put on your dressing-gown and slippers."

In the hall Mr. Sinclair waited, fully dressed. He motioned to me to follow. We went down the corridor and through the door to his part of the house. He closed it behind us and, I could not help noticing, turned the key. We stepped through another doorway. Later, when I saw the room by daylight, I realised that the furnishings were, by the standards of the house, quite ordinary, but on that first evening the Indian rugs, the books, the armchairs, and the sofa glowed with a golden light. Mr. Sinclair stood before me, holding out his hands; his finger, the one he had sprained changing the tyre, was still a little crooked. Then I understood that he was waiting for me to place my hands in his. I did.

"How old are you?" he said.

"Eighteen."

"Eighteen." He shook his head. "People will call me a cradle snatcher."

"Is that worse than being a gold digger?"

"Yes, because I should be old enough to know better. I would not want anyone, especially you, to say that I had taken advantage of you."

I felt as if I were back on the Brough of Birsay, standing on the edge of the cliff, the wind at my back, the birds, silver and black, soaring, and, just for a moment, everything in my life, even the losses, made sense because everything had been bringing me to this room.

"People will say things whatever we do," I said. "As long as we don't."

"Little sphinx. Don't you wonder if what the fortune-teller told Coco is true?"

I said that I did. "Claypoole seemed fine and then, from one day to the next, it was bankrupt. Now Blackbird Hall is my home, so if you're going to sell the house I need to know."

"And what will you do then?"

He was looking at me searchingly. Suddenly I understood that he had not brought me here to tell me that he had heard my secret messages, that he wanted nothing more than to spend his days at Blackbird Hall with me, going on expeditions. How stupid I was to have granted that notion a moment's purchase. No, he was trying to break the news that the house, and its occupants, were about to disappear.

"I'll have to find another job," I said, "one where I get board and lodging. Vicky will give me a good reference. But nowhere will be as nice as here." I spoke these last words so softly that I was not sure he heard them.

"And won't you be angry with me, Gemma, if I evict you from your home, like a cuckoo?"

"Cuckoos can't help it and I suppose you can't either. What will happen to Nell? I hate to think of her lost in some school, being bullied and scolded. She needs someone to be patient with her."

"As you have valiantly been. You've done wonders with her, and I will make sure that no one undoes your good work."

Years ago Dr. White had described my walking to the hospital as valiant, and that too had ended in disaster. Why did I always need to be valiant? Why couldn't I have a home, like other people? If only my uncle hadn't gone skating on that February day. If only Miriam hadn't forgotten to breathe. If only Miss Bryant hadn't run out of money before I could take my exams. And now, added to all those other losses, was the loss of Mr. Sinclair. I had cherished the hope that, despite our many inequalities, he had understood me: the stealthy cyclist. Quite gently, he had taken that away. Save for his hands holding mine I would have run back to my room.

"And what about me?" he said. "What should I do if I lose my home and my job?"

"You? What do you have to worry about with all your posh friends? Even if you can't be a banker, you can bale hay and give advice. You'll have to have fewer parties, and Nell won't have as many new clothes, but you won't starve."

He laughed, a little unsteadily. "That's what I love about you, Gemma. You're so dauntless, you go directly from A to B. Whereas all my life I've gone from A to B by way of G." He kissed me and pulled me down beside him into an armchair. "Why have you been ignoring me? Ever since I came back you've behaved like I was a leper. What did I do to deserve such treatment? I haven't dared speak to you."

"You went away." It was true but it sounded like something Nell would say. I made another attempt. "You're older than me, you have a fancy job, a wardrobe full of suits, but that day we went to the Brough of Birsay you spoke to me as if we were equals—not employer and employee. Then the moment we got back you became all-important and busy. You couldn't take five minutes to tell me you were leaving, like any friend." I felt him shift in the seat beside me, about to speak, but there was no stopping now. "And then you just show up again, with no warning, and you expect me to be thrilled. I have a life too. It doesn't begin and end with your comings and goings. How would you feel waiting day after day for someone who seems to have forgotten you exist? I may be your employee but I have opinions, thoughts, feelings."

Before I could say more his arms were around me. I could feel him shaking with what, after a few seconds, I recognised as laughter. "So you waited for me," he said, "day after day. And day after day I was working as hard as I could, struggling to get back to you."

The house was not in any danger, he told me. He'd let everything go before he sold the estate, but it wouldn't come to that. "I didn't mean to tease you, but I didn't know if you cared for me, if you would care for me even if I weren't your employer. To you it probably seems like the natural order of things that I own Blackbird Hall, but this house, everything, was always going to be Roy's. At school he won the same prizes our father had; in the war he won the medals. Then he drove his car off the road and my parents were left with me, the second-rate son. No prizes, no medals, not even a good degree. I only got a two: two."

He laughed again, giddily, as if he were opening presents very fast. "Nobody gives a damn about these things—two: one, two: two—but my father behaved as if the heavens had fallen. Being an orphan, Gemma, you don't know what it's like to have someone looking over your shoulder, judging everything you do. And when they're not there, you do the job for them: tell yourself, over and over, that you're not good enough. I left university determined to prove myself, and I did, but in a world my parents didn't understand, or give a ha'penny for. Once I sailed into Stromness on a friend's yacht. The first thing my father said to me was that the Sinclairs weren't show-offs. For a decade I only came here for funerals. By the time I realised what was happening to Alison it was much too late."

"Whatever you did or didn't do for Alison," I said, "you have a second chance with her daughter. Nell can be happy, she can do the things she wants to do."

"She can," he said gently. "All I'm saying, Gemma, is please don't put me on a pedestal. I'll have farther to fall. I own Blackbird Hall and you work here, but it could easily be the other way round. When I saw you this morning, standing up to Seamus, not caring that he was twice your size, I knew you were braver than I could ever be."

I started to protest—I hadn't been brave; I'd been angry—but he interrupted. "I'm sorry I didn't tell you that I had to go back to London. I'm forty-one years old and I've got used to doing what I please, not consulting anyone, but I never meant to take you for granted."

"I forgive you," I said and, miraculously, I did. The hard rock of anger that had stood between us since I saw him sitting on the bench under the trees rolled away.

He kissed me and slipped his hand down the front of my nightdress. I still had limbs, organs, feet, eyes, but the only part of my body I could feel was the few square inches where his hand pressed against my skin. I willed him to go on but suddenly he grew still; his hand was gone.

"No," he said. "This is going to be different, totally different."

He lifted me off his lap to one side of the chair, stood up, and walked to the fireplace, the window, the door, the window again. "I feel," he said, "like I'm about to jump out of a plane."

He stopped walking and stood before me. "Sweet girl. How I wish I was your age and knew what I know now. You must go back to bed. I promise there'll be no more coming and going without consulting you."

"And no more lies?" I said. "About money, or what you're doing, or anything else."

"And no more lies," he agreed. "Cross my heart and hope to die."

As I made my way down the corridor I saw a light on in the downstairs hall. From the kitchen came the faint clink of metal and china. Some other nocturnal wanderer—Vicky? Seamus?—was making a cup of tea.

chapter twenty-three

THE NEXT MORNING THE calves ate and stood without trembling. We had lessons as usual, and again I carried our lunch to the schoolroom; Seamus needed not to see me for a few days. After we ate, I was reading to Nell from *Anne of Green Gables* when Mr. Sinclair put his head round the door. Might he have the honour of our company? We could go to Stromness to explore the harbour and find a tearoom.

"Yes, yes, yes," said Nell.

"Does that suit you, Miss Hardy?" He made a little bow.

"I'd be delighted, Mr. Sinclair." I bowed in turn. "And if I could steal ten minutes to do some shopping that would be super."

And that was the pattern of the days that followed. Mr. Sinclair did whatever he did in the morning, the afternoons were devoted to Nell, and in the evenings, after dinner, we went for a walk or I tiptoed down the corridor to his sitting-room. Several times I caught Vicky looking at me askance, and I longed to explain, but I had no words for what was happening, for those long nightly conversations in which I told him about my aunt and Miriam and life at Claypoole and he told me about studying at Oxford; the three years he had worked in Paris; his life in London. Our conversations included many other topics, momentous and trivial: Were those stout leather buttons on men's cardigans attractive? Did animals have souls? What was the perfect picnic? Were men and women essentially different? Who invented the fork? Which was better: a reef knot or a bowline? I told him about Miss

Seftain's interest in space travel and the names and fates of the various dogs, mostly mongrels, who had orbited the earth: Belka, the squirrel, Strelka, the arrow. He told me about diving among the wrecks at Scapa Flow and seeing the stateroom of one of the German ships. We talked, it seemed, about everything. And night after night these conversations ended in passionate kisses from which, eventually, we separated. Then one evening as Vicky left for her choir practise she announced that Mr. Sinclair had spent most of the day on the phone.

"He'll be off again soon," she said. "Mark my words."

That night when I knocked on the door to his rooms there was no answer. He was not in the library, nor the billiard room, nor his study, nor the garden. I had never known him to go to the farm so late. And surely, I thought, he would not have gone down to the sea without me. At last I returned to his door and knocked again, a brisk, bold rap that belied my feelings. As I stood staring at the swirling grain of the wood, I remembered standing outside Miss Bryant's study, watching my tiny self in the brass doorknob, waiting to cross the blue carpet and be chastised. Then the door opened and Mr. Sinclair was looking down at me, his eyebrows drawn, his forehead furrowed. Behind him, from his sitting-room, came a burst of furious music.

"Gemma, what's the matter?"

"Where were you? You disappeared."

"No, I didn't. Here I am." He drew me inside. In the sitting-room, he turned down the record player and poured me a glass of red wine. First a drink, he said. Then I must tell him what was wrong. I had only tried wine a few times and did not care for the taste. Now I drank it as if it were medicine and blurted out Vicky's claim.

Mr. Sinclair nodded. "She's right," he said, his voice as calm as if we were discussing his choice of shirt. "I can't do all my work by mail and phone."

"But"—I stared at the beautiful red and blue rug, trying to keep the fleur-de-lys pattern in focus—"what about me?" If I was about to lose everything, then what did I have to lose by asking the ultimate question?

"Gemma, I need to earn a living. I can't stay here and I can't take you to London as things are now."

"So what can we do? Is there nothing to be done?" The fleur-de-lys blurred. Everyone, I thought, slips through my fingers.

I could feel Mr. Sinclair's eyes searching my face. Neither of us spoke for what seemed like a long time. "There is one thing we can do," he said slowly. Then he uttered a four-word question that I had read in dozens of books but which neither of us, in all our conversations, had ever mentioned. The words scattered to the corners of the glowing room. Once again I pictured the two of us from the point of view of a lark, standing in this room, in this house, surrounded by the farm, the island, the incessant sea.

He knelt at my feet. "Will you?" he said again. His eyes, looking up at me rather than down, were boat-shaped. I allowed myself to sail in them towards the edge of the known world.

I set down the empty wine-glass. "On one condition," I said. "Actually two."

"Two!" His teeth gleamed in the light. "She drives a hard bargain."

I held up my fingers. "One, I get to go to university. I have to pass the exams, but if I pass, then I get to go."

"I'll even help you study, but no going off to a hall of residence. You have to live with me." His dark eyelashes fluttered. "And what is two on this dreadful list?"

"Nell won't be sent away to boarding school, unless she wants to go."

"Gemma. How could your parents have known that you would turn out to be like your name?"

"They didn't. Gemma was my uncle's choice. My parents gave me another name." I reached down to help him to his feet.

"What is it?"

The name was there, waiting, but everyone who had ever known it was dead. "I'll tell you," I said, "the night we're married."

I expected him to argue, but an expression akin to relief came over his face. "I'll tell you my secrets then too. I have done things I'm not proud of, that might make you like me less."

I thought of Coco and of all the women who had surely come before her; he had told me about some of them: a secretary named Lydia, a debutante named Henrietta. I thought of what Nora had said about how he used to be a hellion, of the ways he had failed his sister and his parents. And I offered the words Miriam had drilled into me that first Easter when she was helping me catch up with my lessons.

"'Love is not love,'" I repeated, "'which alters when it alteration finds, or bends . . .'" But the next line was gone; even conjuring up Mrs. Harris's beady gaze did not bring it back.

"Something about tempests, I think," said Mr. Sinclair. "So there is nothing that could change your feelings for me? Swear to me that is so, Gemma."

Looking at the face I had first glimpsed by the light of a torch and was now licenced to look at freely, I saw emotions that I couldn't name. Just for a moment I pictured the boy in the raspberry canes, bending over Drummond with a tortured expression. But the boy was a stranger; why should I understand his feelings? Now I had to believe that what drew Mr. Sinclair's mouth tight, what darkened his eyes, was some mysterious aspect of adult affection that I would soon understand.

"I swear," I said, "but you must swear too. I've done things which I regret."

"Sweet girl, what on earth could you have done that you regret?"

"Don't treat me like a child. I may be younger than you, but that doesn't mean I don't have a past, haven't made mistakes."

He began to promise that he would never again treat me like a child but I interrupted. "You'll break your promise a hundred times. Please swear the one thing I want. That you won't allow anything, any secret, to change your feelings for me."

"I will," he said, "be constant as the northern star."

It was the most felicitous of oaths. I told him then about my parents and how they had survived their long engagement by looking at the North Star, the one thing, despite the eight hundred miles between Scotland and Iceland, that they reliably had in common. When I finished, he told me about a day during his boyhood when he and Alison had been playing on the beach. Suddenly half-a-dozen rocks had come whistling out of the sky.

"We thought the Germans were coming, but we carried home a couple of the smaller pieces and our father explained that what we'd seen was a meteorite falling." From the mantelpiece he retrieved a piece of dull black rock the size of his thumb. When he laid it in my palm it turned out to be unexpectedly heavy. "A token of my affection," he said, "until I can give you a ring."

Then he asked if there was anyone whose permission he should ask. Briefly I thought of Miss Seftain and how she had teased me about marriage as we walked across the frozen grass. "No," I said.

"So there are no obstacles," he said jubilantly.

He picked me up and kissed me and I stopped thinking about rugs, or stars, or larks, or anything except my body measured by his.

SAVE FOR THE STRANGELY heavy rock under my pillow, the next day everything seemed just the same: breakfast, hens, calves, lessons, lunch, a walk, reading. After tea, however, when I was labelling her drawings, Nell skipped into the schoolroom and said Uncle Hugh wanted us in the library. I brought a book, thinking he might ask her to read. But as soon as I saw Vicky, seated in an armchair, knitting, I knew that once again we were standing on the cliff top. It had not occurred to me that our nocturnal conversation would bring changes so soon. Don't say anything, I wanted to say.

Was it my thoughts or his own doubts that made Mr. Sinclair move his feet awkwardly, lean one way and then the other, push back his hair and look out of the window before turning to face three women whose combined ages totaled a little more than fifty? Just for an instant, I cherished the hope that he was about to propose an outing to Kirkwall or agree that Nell could, at last, have piano lessons.

"I want you both to know, to be the first to know"—his eyes flickered towards one bookshelf, then another—"that Gemma and I are going to be married."

Nell flung her arms around me. "Hurrah. I'll have an aunt."

As we embraced, I saw Vicky's ball of red wool rolling away across the floor. She was looking at me wide-eyed, one hand pressed to her chest, as if to still the inner turmoil, but by the time Nell had stopped jumping up and down she was on her feet, ready to shake hands with Mr. Sinclair and kiss my cheek. "I do congratulate you both," she said. He too, I saw, had registered her coolness; indeed, he had expected it. How could his twenty-seven-year-old housekeeper be expected to welcome the news that he was marrying his eighteen-year-old au pair?

"When are you getting married?" clamoured Nell. "Can I be a bridesmaid?"

"No—there won't be any bridesmaids."

"What about a cake? A white cake with a bride and groom on top."

"No," Mr. Sinclair said again. "We're not going to make a fuss."

Vicky stood up and announced that she had a pie in the oven. I stood too and told Nell we must tidy the schoolroom before supper.

"Wait," said Mr. Sinclair. "We have to talk."

"We can talk later, after Nell's in bed. Or you can help tidy the schoolroom." I held out my hand to Nell.

"But you'll have dinner with me?"

"Nell has supper in half an hour. I eat with her."

"We're engaged," he said. "Surely that makes a difference?"

"As little as possible, if I have any say, which the last ten minutes suggest I don't."

"Oh, bloody hell," he said, pushing a hand through his hair. "We're having our first quarrel. I'm sorry. I should have asked you before I told Vicky and Nell."

"You should have." Hand in hand with Nell, I left the room.

Later that night, after she was asleep, we sat together in the library. Now that our relationship was public, there was no reason to hide away in his room. Vicky, I knew, was safely visiting friends, and Seamus was out wandering the fields, or bowed over his mantelpiece, but I left the door ajar, a signal that everything was above-board. Mr. Sinclair apologised again.

"I'm sorry. I'm just so used to being in charge." Then he added that he had applied for a wedding licence. We would be married in the registry office in Kirkwall next week.

"Next week?" I exclaimed. "Besides, I thought we'd be married in a church."

"I'm sorry, Gemma. If your uncle were alive that would be different, but I don't want to lose one more day. If you like we can be married again in a church. People quite often have two ceremonies."

His eyes were glowing and I said yes to everything, agreed to everything, even though a part of me still wanted nothing to change, or to change more slowly. But it was too late for that. We had jumped off one cliff, and when we were married, there would be another cliff to fall over, farther, faster.

THE NEXT MORNING VICKY behaved as if the previous day's conversation had never occurred—the weather was awful; would I be sure to give the hens more shells—but I caught her studying my waistline. Before I came to lunch, I took off my pullover and tightened the belt on my trousers. I was not one of those sudden girls, like Mrs. Marsden.

For all her silence to me, I soon discovered that Vicky had spread the word. When I ran into Nora, polishing the piano in the hall, she dropped the duster and seized my hands.

"I can't believe it, I can't believe it," she said. "You and Mr. Sinclair getting married. What a slyboots you are. Who'd have thought of him marrying one of us? It's like something out of a fairy tale. Todd will be on the floor when I tell him."

"Thank you," I said, uncertainly.

"Oh, I'm forgetting myself." She swung our hands, smiling. "Congratulations. I hope you'll be very happy and not forget your old friends."

"Of course I won't." But even as I spoke, I knew that my days of playing games in Nora's living-room were over.

Her smile fading, she released my hands. "The thing I can't help wondering, Gemma, is do you really love him? Money isn't everything, and he's so much older. Won't you miss having fun?"

How could so few sentences contain so many insults? Last week I would have told her it was none of her business; did she really love her gullible fiancé? Now, as the future Mrs. Sinclair, I did my best to conceal my anger. "I think we'll suit each other fine," I said, handing her the fallen duster and hurrying away.

After lunch I sat down and wrote to Miss Seftain, telling her that, much to my surprise, I was going to be married next week. "It'll be a small ceremony in Kirkwall," I wrote, "just in the registry office. Later I hope we'll have a proper church wedding and you can come. Don't worry! I still plan to go to university. Mr. Sinclair says he'll help me take the exams and apply." Before I could change my mind, I addressed the envelope and fetched Nell. Together we bicycled to the village and she slipped the letter into the pillar-box. I heard the soft sound of it landing, already as far from me as if it had travelled a hundred miles.

THAT EVENING, SITTING ON the bench under the beech trees, Mr. Sinclair told me we would be married at the registry office at 11 A.M. the following Monday. We would catch the afternoon flight to Edinburgh.

"Why would we go to Edinburgh?" I asked. Above our heads the white scar left by the broken branch shone, and all around us the wind was shaking the plants and trees.

"For our honeymoon, Gemma. People don't just come back to the house where they've been living as though nothing has changed. Wouldn't that feel odd to you? Vicky and Nell wondering what we were up to?"

"Everything feels odd. How long will we be away? I have to make plans for Nell."

Then he explained, as if it had been understood all along, that we wouldn't be coming back. We would go directly on to London. His house was in a neighbourhood called Holland Park. It had four bedrooms, a garden; there were shops and restaurants nearby. Of course I knew he was needed at his office, but I had pictured us spending a few more days on the island. And then my visiting him in London, getting my bearings, before Nell and I moved there, irrevocably.

"But I won't know anyone," I said. "And what about Nell?"

"I have to work. All this"—he gestured towards the house in front of us, the fields behind—"costs a pretty penny. It's not Seamus's fault, but every year the farm loses money. As for Nell, she can come too, if that's what you want."

"Isn't it what you want? Your sister's child, your only relative. And don't"—I raised my hand—"say I'm too young to understand."

"Touché. I was going to say I'm too old to understand." He planted a kiss near my ear. "You've done wonders with her, but she should go to school, have friends her own age. And if you want to go to university you'll have to study. You won't be lonely, I promise. I have lots of friends. You already know Colin and Jill."

But they don't see me as a friend, I wanted to say; they see me as the au pair. All the items on my list were still true—I was a girl with no money or obvious talents; he was a middle-aged man with both—and in London there would be new entries.

As we spoke, the rustling in the branches overhead had been growing louder; the leaves too were having a conversation. Now Mr. Sinclair looked up. "My great-grandfather planted these trees on his wedding day," he said. "Heaven knows the secrets they could tell. Come, let's walk." Arm in arm we began to circle the house, dodging the croquet hoops that still dotted the lawn.

"I know you love this place," he said. "It's one of the many bonds between us. And we'll come here often. But if we stayed now it would be hard for our friends and neighbours. By going away we give them time to get used to our new situation, and you and I get a chance to practise being in the world together."

"Vicky thinks we have to get married," I said.

"We do, but not for the usual reason."

We passed the fountain, and I caught the musty smell of the basin full of water after the recent rain. Tonight Seamus's window was dark. Was he lurking in there? Or walking the cliff tops towards some secret tryst? I could not imagine any possible world in which he would welcome the news that I was the future mistress of Blackbird Hall. The wind was still rising, rushing past the house, rushing past us and the flowers in the garden, the grass in the fields. I heard a sheep bleating and, for a few seconds, the sound of Vicky's radio. Around the corner came a small white figure, moving over the lawn towards us. Even as I gasped I recognised Nell.

"What are you doing here?" I said, letting go of Mr. Sinclair and hurrying to meet her.

"I couldn't sleep." She threw her arms around me. "I couldn't find you."

"I went for a walk with Uncle Hugh. Vicky was nearby."

She pushed her head against me. "Mummy went for walks," she said in a muffled voice. "She went for a walk the night she died."

I felt Mr. Sinclair beside me, his hand on my arm, squeezing.

"Did she?" I said gently. "Do you know where she went?"

"She said she was going to the river, but sometimes she said that and changed her mind. Sometimes she came back smelling of smoke from the pub. But she didn't smell smoky that night."

The wind tangled my hair across my face. Mr. Sinclair's grip tightened. There was another question, something else he wanted me to ask. "Did she go alone?" I suggested.

"She wouldn't let me come." Nell spoke more loudly as if rehearsing an old argument. "He said the same when he brought her home. Not the same," she corrected, "but that she'd said the same to him."

I felt Mr. Sinclair's breath hot against my ear. "Ask her who 'he' is."

I did.

"You know," Nell said. "We see him all the time, with the cows."

For a moment I had no inkling who she meant. Then, even as I heard Mr. Sinclair whisper, "Seamus," I understood.

chapter twenty-four

I TOOK NELL BACK TO bed with me, and in the morning she was propped up beside me, reading. "You slept in, lazybones," she said. As we washed and dressed, she chattered away. She could hold her breath for forty-nine seconds; she was going to give her doll, Cilla, a new name. What did I think of Lulu? Or Dusty? When I asked if she remembered coming out to the garden the night before, she said yes, it was so windy she had wanted to pretend to be a pony. "I wanted to trot around," she said, "and toss my mane." Before I could ask further questions, she added that she'd been thinking about what to wear at the wedding and she'd decided on the pink dress with smocking that Vicky had made her for Easter. What was I going to wear?

In all my daydreaming about the future I had, oddly, given this question no thought; now it drove out everything else. Even for a simple ceremony my Sunday skirts and blouses were too ordinary. Indeed every garment in my wardrobe seemed limp and unappealing. I recalled the turquoise dress Coco had worn to the dance, and ruined in the rain. Might one of the guest room wardrobes contain a dress that would serve? But I was much smaller than Coco, and I shrank from wearing a dress whose history I didn't know. What if, unwittingly, I chose something Alison had worn right before her accident? Then I remembered the dress Matron had given me as a farewell gift. It had belonged to a prefect, one of the most elegant girls at Claypoole. I had never so much as tried it on, but I pictured the lustrous paisley fabric transforming me into a forest bride.

As soon as lessons and lunch were over I went to my room. The dress, when I lifted it down from the back of the wardrobe, was as pretty as I recalled, the delicate pattern of leaves and flowers conjuring up a lush jungle where a lyre-bird might sing. But when I pulled it over my head I could tell at once it was too large, and the mirror revealed a lost cause. The bodice gaped, the sleeves dangled, the hem drooped. Worst of all, the green gave my skin an olive tinge. I looked exactly like what I was: an orphan in a borrowed dress.

Silence greeted my knock at Mr. Sinclair's door. He must, I thought, be out in the fields, or meeting with a neighbour. I was almost back at the far end of the corridor when the lock clicked. I turned to see him standing in the doorway. He was wearing the clothes he had worn the night before, his shirt crumpled, his trousers creased.

"Are you all right?" I said.

"I'm fine," he said abruptly and then, as if remembering our relationship, came forward to kiss me. His eyes, I noticed, were red-rimmed and bloodshot.

"Hugh," I said. "May I call you Hugh?"

"What else would you call me? Now out with it. You're bursting with something."

I repeated Nell's question. "I know the dress is meant to be a secret from the groom but I can't ask Vicky for help."

His forehead grew smooth. "I'm an idiot," he said. "Of course you must have a dress. We'll go and buy one this afternoon."

"But you can't see it, not until our wedding day. That's bad luck." My uncle had officiated at many weddings, and I remembered the lore.

"I will drive you to the best shop in Kirkwall, hand you my wallet, and then take myself off to read the paper at the pub. I'll be ready in five minutes."

Startled by his alacrity, I hurried to my room to change—even to buy a dress I needed to look respectable—and then to the kitchen to ask Vicky to mind Nell. She looked up from the shell she was carefully threading with wire. "Of course," she said. "She can help me sort the stamens. You'll be needing new outfits now."

Again I glimpsed a hidden meaning. "I don't need new outfits in general," I said. "I haven't grown in three years, but I do want to look nice on Monday."

Vicky's expression softened. "I suppose you do. Will you pick me up a pair of tights, medium, not too light?"

Between morning lessons and my sartorial distraction, there had been no opportunity to ask Mr. Sinclair—Hugh—about our encounter with Nell the night before. Now, once we were safely through the gate, I said I didn't understand why he had wanted me to question her. "And what did she mean about Seamus? Was she saying he was there when Alison died?"

"That's what it sounded like, but I've asked her about that night over and over and she's never mentioned Seamus before."

I had always assumed Nell was afraid of Seamus—like me she tended to avoid him—but perhaps her avoidance signalled a more complicated relationship. "So were Seamus and Alison friends?" I said.

"Not really. Remember our bargain, Gemma. On our wedding night we'll tell each other our secrets."

For the rest of the journey he beguiled me with talk about the farm, and a client in Edinburgh he was hoping to meet on our way south. I remembered the lapwing on the Brough of Birsay, feigning injury to lead me away from the nest, but I followed uncomplainingly. Our conversations, which I had thought so free and far-ranging, had, I'd begun to notice, certain boundaries. Hugh did not care to talk about his sister, or the war, or, save for odd stories, his childhood. He pulled up outside a shop near the cathedral—"the only place on the island to buy a dress"—handed me sixty pounds in crumpled notes, and told me he would be in the lounge bar of the Kirkwall Hotel.

As I stepped into the shop, a wave of perfume transported me back to that time when I had still accompanied my aunt on shopping expeditions. And there behind the counter, as if memory had conjured her, was a woman whose blond hair was coiled around her head in exactly the same style as my aunt's. She was talking to a customer in a neat shirtwaist dress. Neither of them noticed me and I ducked behind a rack of jackets. I was looking at the price tags—one was thirty pounds, the next thirty-five—when I spotted a girl cleaning a mirror. I made my way over.

"Excuse me," I said. "I'm looking for a nice dress."

In the mirror the girl studied my pleated skirt and flowery blouse. "Do you have a particular occasion in mind?" she said.

"My wedding."

"Your wedding?"

Was no one but Nell pleased about my marriage? I turned to leave, thinking perhaps Vicky could alter the green dress; if not, I would wear my church clothes. Hugh wouldn't mind. Over and over he had said there would be no fuss. But the girl was still speaking.

"Congratulations," she said. "Do you have a favourite colour? A favourite style? You're either a small or a petite. Let me show you some possibilities."

For the next hour Deirdre brought a stream of dresses to the changing room and praised or rejected them as I tried them on. She had never met Mr. Sinclair but, being Kirkwall born and bred, she knew the name. Finally we settled on a dress the colour of the sea on a sunny day with tiny pink rosebuds around the neck, cuffs, and hem. Then she urged new underwear, new tights and shoes. I refused to buy a handbag but succumbed to a nightdress. When everything was packed in boxes and bags, including Vicky's tights, the bill came to fifty-three pounds. Deirdre walked me to the door of the shop.

"I hope you get the good weather," she said. "And I hope you'll be very, very happy."

As I walked down the winding street, people kept smiling at me—first two middle-aged women, then a woman with a baby, then a grizzled man in a tweed cap and anorak, then two girls my own age. When a boy on a tricycle beamed at me, I finally understood it was because of my own broad smile.

THE LAST DAYS OF my unmarried life passed as slowly as a snail creeping along a wall, as swiftly as a gannet diving into the sea. Every morning I gave Nell lessons; in the afternoons, when it was fine, we visited our favourite haunts. With Vicky's help I drew up a timetable for the week of my honeymoon: piano lessons were arranged, visits to two families with children Nell's age. Meanwhile Hugh worked long hours at his desk and paid several visits to Kirkwall. In the evenings we sat in the library or sometimes walked across the fields down to the cove. In moving to London I was breaking my vow to always live beside the sea, and I tried to store up the sights and sounds and smells of the ocean. One evening as we walked along the shore, I asked why he kept his door locked. Months ago Vicky had confessed that she'd cautioned me about locking mine, not out of the fear of Seamus sleepwalking but because Nell had ransacked Miss Cameron's room.

Hugh bent to examine a starfish, its pale pink arms curled stiffly in a strand of seaweed, and I thought perhaps he would dodge my question. But when he had put it back in the water he said, "I'm afraid you have an anxious husband."

"Fiancé," I corrected. I had only a few days to use the word.

"Fiancé," he said, kissing my hand. Then he told me he'd been looking into finding a tutor to help me prepare for my exams—"you'll have to decide what subjects you want to study"—and, in the excitement of discussing my choices, I forgot to ask what he could possibly be anxious about.

From the weddings at my uncle's church I had memories of flowers and organ music, white dresses and throngs of guests. My own wedding promised to have none of these, although Vicky had presented me with a shell brooch she'd made to match my dress. She and Nell would attend, and Hugh, I assumed, would invite the Laidlaws and some of his island friends, but I was content to leave the arrangements to him. In a few days I would be his next of kin and he would be mine. Later I would go to university and later still, much later, we would have children who would play on the Sands of Evie as Nell and I had done. An enormous sun dwarfed the few dark stars of worry. My dress hung in the wardrobe, my new underwear waited. I packed my smaller suitcase with clothes for Edinburgh. On top I put my precious photographs of my uncle and my mother, and my bird book. Everything else I packed for Vicky to bring when she brought Nell to London. Already my room was beginning to look as if no one lived there.

On my last evening at Blackbird Hall I went over Nell's lessons one more time, laying out the books and marking the tasks for each day. Then—Hugh was busy in his study; Nell was in bed; Vicky was at her choir meeting—I wandered outside. I had already said goodbye to the calves but I decided to visit them one more time. They loped over at the sight of me, and I offered my hand to each in turn. Herman rasped my hand with his long purple tongue and Petula nuzzled me with her whole head. "Be good," I admonished. "Don't bully the other cows."

As I turned to leave, the clouds in the west shifted and the windows of Blackbird Hall gave back the last flare of the sun. For a moment it looked as if the house were on fire, each window scarlet and dazzling. Red sky at night, I thought, shepherd's delight. Then a lamb bleated in the next field. Not shepherd, I thought, sailor. Maybe we would get the fine day Deirdre had wished us. I pictured us walking arm in arm down the main street in Kirkwall, then on a plane, seeing the island spread out below.

I was crossing the farmyard on my way back to the house when I heard voices coming from one of the buildings. Keeping to the shadow of the granary, I crept closer. With each step, the conversation grew louder not only with proximity but with anger. At last I edged around the corner and there, standing in the wide doorway of the hay barn, facing each other like boxers between rounds, were Seamus and Hugh.

"I'm telling you once and for all," said Seamus, "if you go ahead with this charade I'll no longer—"

"No longer what?" I said, stepping forward. "Why are you threatening Hugh?"

Seamus did not even glance in my direction. "Damn and blast you both," he said and strode off towards the tractor shed. A few seconds later we heard the growl of the Land Rover.

"Gemma, I've been looking for you." Hugh hurried over, breathing hard, his colour high.

"What's wrong with Seamus? Why is he so upset?"

"He wants a new bull, and I had to tell him we can't afford it this year. Let's go and have a drink in the library." He took a step towards the house, but I stood firm.

"What's 'this charade'?" I said. "Surely he was talking about us?"

His eyes darted towards the shed, as if to make sure that Seamus really was gone; then once again he met my gaze. "I'm sorry you had to hear that," he said. "He's got it into his head that I chose our wedding over his bull. I was trying to tell him that the former has nothing to do with the latter. The farm hasn't had a good year, what with the ferry strike and the storm ruining the barley. Come." Again he motioned towards the house.

"You don't think you should try to find him? Make another attempt to explain?"

"No, he'll drink and be furious for a few hours. Then he'll come round. He knows the economics as well as I do. Are you all packed and ready?"

Not waiting for an answer, he tucked my hand firmly into the crook of his arm and led the way indoors. From the trolley of bottles and decanters in the library he poured me a modest glass of wine, and for himself what he called a wee goldie, and we raised our glasses.

"Here's to a hundred years of happiness," he said fiercely. "We won't let anyone spoil our life together."

"A hundred years," I echoed.

He caught my grimace—wine still tasted bitter—and teased me about preferring Ribena. I was telling him what I remembered of Edinburgh, asking if we could visit the castle tomorrow, when we heard the first distant rumble of thunder. And then, even as we were exclaiming, came a flash and another peal much closer. A heavy-footed giant was stalking the heavens.

"It's a celestial celebration of our nuptials," I said. "Like in Shakespeare. Let's go outside."

"Gemma, the storm is almost overhead. We could be struck by lightning. When you're as old as I am, you can go out in thunderstorms."

I was laughing, pulling him towards the window, when the room filled with dazzling light and, almost simultaneously, a huge bang shook the house. For a few seconds the shelves of books shone on the inside of my eyelids. I couldn't move or think. The storm was suddenly not just a brilliant spectacle but a terrifying threat. Then Hugh drew me down behind a chair.

"We're quite safe," he said. "It struck something, but not the house."

The thunder growled, circling the chimney pots, but his arms were around me, and neither god nor electrical storm could separate us. Briefly I wondered if the storm had woken Nell; if so, I knew she would lie there, counting the intervals between lightning and thunder with keen satisfaction. The next peal was farther away, and the next still farther. At last we stood up and went over to the window.

"What's that?" said Hugh.

The flames I had seen earlier, reflected in the windows of the house, were flickering high up in the garden. After a few seconds we both understood. The green beech tree, the one that had survived the gale unscathed, had been struck.

"We have to save it," I said, heading for the door.

But Hugh stopped me. "Gemma, there's nothing to be done. The fire is too high up. If the tree is damaged we'll plant another. In fact, whatever happens, we should plant a tree to mark our marriage."

"A silver birch," I suggested, and he agreed.

THE NEXT MORNING I did not open the curtains on that side of my room; I preferred not to see the wounded tree, the second wounded tree, on my wedding day. I had breakfast with Nell in the kitchen, a hasty bowl of cornflakes, and then took her upstairs to braid her hair and help her dress. Once she was ready she sat cross-legged on my bed to watch my own preparations. When I pulled on the dress, she gasped and said I looked like a princess. It was true; in the mirror I barely recognised myself. The dress made me seem taller, and more graceful. I remembered how my uncle had described my mother on her wedding day: radiant. I put on my raincoat. Downstairs Vicky, in a purple tweed suit, was waiting for Nell, and Hugh, in a pinstriped suit, for me. He had a white rose in his buttonhole, and I wished I had thought to pick some flowers to carry, but it was too late now. The red sky of the previous evening had lied; rain was streaming down. Hugh held an umbrella over me as we walked to the car. Seamus's Land Rover was, as usual, parked alongside the tractor shed.

On the way to Kirkwall, above the beat of the windscreen wipers, and the noise of the engine, I asked what would happen at the registry office. I was suddenly worried that we should have rehearsed.

"It can't be too complicated," said Hugh. He was driving fast, leaning forward occasionally to wipe the windscreen. "Look at all the people who are married. I thought we'd have lobster for supper. Do you like lobster? And of course champagne?"

"I've never tried either."

"Oh, Gemma, there are so many things I want to introduce you to. Tonight we'll have a bottle of the best champagne."

The registry office was in an old building off the high street, behind a jeweller's shop. The vestibule smelled of the electric fire that glowed beside the secretary's desk. She greeted us pleasantly and said she would let Mr. Muir, the registrar, know we were here. A moment later a man of about Hugh's age emerged from the inner office. His upright bearing and triangular moustache made me wonder if he too had fought in the war. He wished us good morning and shook Hugh's hand, then mine.

"Do you have any witnesses?" he asked. "Guests?"

"Could you provide witnesses? In this weather our guests could be another half-hour."

"No," I exclaimed. "Nell would never forgive us if she missed our wedding." Turning to Mr. Muir, I asked if we could wait a few minutes.

"Of course," he said. "We've no one else coming, and it's a dreich day."

He retreated to his office, the secretary returned to her typing, and Hugh began to measure out the small hall with his impatient stride. "The old women of Hoy say it's bad luck to delay a wedding," he said. "Please, Gemma, let's go ahead."

For five more minutes I stood firm. Then, reluctantly, I took off my coat, and we summoned Mr. Muir; the secretary and a woman from the next office would be our witnesses. Mr. Muir had just begun to speak—"Good morning. We are gathered here"—when the door opened. Seamus barged into the room, followed by Vicky and Nell. I turned to give Nell a quick smile. When I turned back, Seamus, in his battered jacket and muddy trousers, was standing in front of us, beside Mr. Muir. Like Miriam's father years ago he carried with him the smell of the farmyard.

"If I can't have what I want," he said, his eyes fixed on Mr. Sinclair, "I don't see why you should have what you want."

I felt Mr. Sinclair—the name "Hugh" had fled—grip my hand. "Keep going," he said to Mr. Muir.

Seamus turned his metallic eyes on me. "Do you know who you're marrying?"

"Hugh Sinclair of Blackbird Hall."

Seamus put his hand on his chest and gave a little bow. "At your service. It suits him now to be laird of the manor, but there was a time when it didn't, and I was the one who answered to the name Hugh Sinclair."

I knew I shouldn't ask and also that not asking would make no difference. Seamus was the giant striding towards us now. "What do you mean?"

"Gemma, I'll explain everything later. Keep going."

He might not have spoken; Seamus stared at me steadily. Vicky cleared her throat. From her raised eyebrows and parted lips I guessed that she was not entirely surprised at the turn events had taken. All along she had harboured some secret dread about our marriage, beyond mere disapproval of the differences in age and class. I let go of Mr. Sinclair's arm and stepped back so that I could study the two men, him in his suit and Seamus in his farming clothes, side by side. I saw then what should have been obvious from my second meeting with Mr. Sinclair. Seamus was a little heavier, his hair was lighter and finer, but especially now that Mr. Sinclair was tanned from the harvesting, their colouring was very similar. They were of an age and a height, they had the same square shoulders, the same low foreheads; they were distant cousins, but they might have been brothers.

"Keep going," Mr. Sinclair said again to Mr. Muir.

But before the registrar could answer I spoke up. "If we can be married today," I said, "then we can be married tomorrow. Tell me what he means."

"This is most irregular," said Mr. Muir. "Mr. Sinclair, with all due respect, I think we should reschedule. Please consult me when you're ready."

Without further ado, he turned on his heel and retreated to his inner office. The secretary, who had come out from behind her desk to be our witness, returned to her seat and lit a cigarette.

"Are you married?" Nell asked. "Does this mean you're married?"

In the vestibule, awkwardly crowded by our little party, Seamus and Mr. Sinclair faced each other, each in the grip of emotions that had existed long before my arrival at Blackbird Hall but that my presence there had sharply exacerbated.

"Will you tell her," Seamus said, "or will I?"

Mr. Sinclair flung down his own gauntlet. "Where were you the night Alison died?"

At the end of weddings in my uncle's church the organist had played "Here Comes the Bride," and the church bells had pealed joyfully. Now from a nearby church came a single melancholy stroke. Mr. Sinclair kept tight hold of my hand.

Seamus closed his eyes. "I was waiting outside her flat," he said. "We'd quarrelled the night before, and I was hoping she'd step out to buy wine, or cigarettes. You know what she was like when she argued; she'd hurl any stone that came to hand. I'd hurled a few myself." He opened his eyes but not to look at us. "I was going to tell her I was ready to give up the farm, and move to Glasgow. I could work as a builder, or a joiner. The streetlights had just come on when at last she appeared, in her red jacket, and turned towards the river. We'd often walked that way together."

And now he turned to Mr. Sinclair, his gaze no longer fierce but stricken. "I've thought ten thousand times about what happened next. We were passing a pub and I stopped for a quick dram. I hoped the whisky would help me mind my tongue. I was less than five minutes, I swear, but by the time I reached the river she was already rolling down her sleeve—"

I pulled free of Mr. Sinclair, reached for Nell's hand and, before she could hear more about her mother, led her out into the rain. Neither of us had an umbrella, but at least she still had her coat. In an instant my new dress and shoes were soaked.

"Where are we going?" said Nell. "It's pouring."

I spotted a newsagent across the road and we ran towards it. Inside, the small shop smelled of paraffin. I bought us each a Mars bar and asked the woman behind the counter if we could wait there for the rain to pass.

"You'll be here all day," she said, "but be my guests."

"I didn't see you get married," Nell said.

"We decided to wait for a few days. Did you understand what Seamus was saying about your mum?"

She took a bite of her Mars bar and looked up at me with her small brown eyes. "Sort of."

"Your mother made a mistake—she took too much medicine—but she never meant to leave you."

Nell took another bite. In my haste that morning I had braided her hair too loosely; already one plait was unravelling. "You don't know what you're talking about," she said. "You can't even get married."

Her fist landed in my stomach with surprising force. I was doubled over when the shop bell clanged behind her.

By the time I had straightened up, retrieved her Mars bar from the floor, and told the shopkeeper I was fine, Nell had found Vicky on the other side of the road. From the doorway I watched the two of them hurrying along beneath a black umbrella.

Mr. Sinclair's car was still outside the registry office. I walked over, not bothering to hurry, opened the door, and got in. I sat Claypoole fashion with my hands folded in my lap, my feet, icy in my wet shoes, neatly together. Not everyone who was fond of me died, but everyone came to harm. The door opened. He handed me my coat, then he walked around the car, got in, and closed the door. Awkwardly, in the confined space, I pulled on the coat. We sat not talking, not looking at each other, while the windows misted up around us. I had no idea what he was thinking, or even what I was.

Finally he let out a deep sigh. "I want to show you something," he said. "Then we'll talk. Will you do this for me, Gemma?"

I must have said yes.

We drove north, the way we had come, and then turned onto the road to Stromness. Cursed, cursed, said the windscreen wipers. In the middle of nowhere, he pulled into a lay-by and turned off the engine. The rain pinged on the roof. He came around to my door with the umbrella. We followed a path across a field to a large grassy mound. He had brought me to Maes Howe, the chambered tomb that Mr. Johnson had mentioned on the ferry and that the island history described as a major Neolithic monument. A pathway led between the remains of the ramparts. At the foot of the mound a stone doorway, maybe four feet high, opened into a stone passage.

"Why are we here?" I said.

"To show you something."

"I don't like small spaces, especially small dark spaces."

"Nor do I." He guided my hand inside his jacket. Through his shirt I felt his heart knocking against his ribs. I had not looked at him directly since Seamus spoke; now I saw how pale he was beneath his harvest tan.

"Come," he said. "Let two scared people enter the tomb."

Slowly, stooping, he led the way along the passage. I followed, keeping my head down, counting each step until, at the twenty-fourth, the low roof disappeared and I straightened. I began to make out that I was in a room, roughly square, large enough to hold a couple of dozen people. Three of the walls had windowlike openings into further darkness. The only light came down the passage, and the ceiling rose, bowl-shaped. Mr. Sinclair led the way to a block of stone beside one of the openings. Not taking my eyes off the passageway, I sat down. He sat down a few yards away on another block of stone. If someone closed the door we would be buried alive.

"If there is any hope of your understanding what I am about to tell you," he said, "then it's in this place."

He did not ask if there was any hope, and I could not have answered.

"One day the autumn I was ten," he went on, "Seamus and another boy and I cycled here. My history teacher had asked me to copy the runes carved on the corner-stones"—he gestured in the gloom—"and while I was writing them in my notebook Seamus and Ted blocked the passage with hay bales. Afterwards they swore they'd only meant to leave me for five minutes, but a neighbour offered them a lift home on his tractor and they lost track of the time. I had no food or water; no way to budge the bales. I called for help until I was hoarse. I was sure I was going to die but that first I would go mad. Finally I passed out."

I had not thought of the sewing-room in years; now I saw the towering shelves of linen, the black gremlin of the sewing-machine. Had anyone come to him in the darkness? I wondered. Then sympathy was swept away by anger. What did this story of thirty years ago have to do with anything?

"Seamus and Ted were punished—they had to muck out the byre for a month—but for them it was just a joke gone awry. For me, it was the day that changed my life. I had discovered what I most feared. And my father had discovered I was a coward. He was the one to drag the bales away. When I came round he was standing over me saying, 'You've got no backbone, Hugh.'"

I heard his raincoat rustle, the fabric shifting as he moved.

"The war was my chance to prove him wrong. I spent the last four years of school imagining myself following Roy into the RAF, saving London, fighting off the Huns. At last I was eighteen. Seamus's birthday was the week before mine, and we went together to Kirkwall to enlist and have our medical exams. A fortnight later I met the postman in the village and he handed me an envelope. I'd been chosen by lottery to be a Bevin Boy."

"So you were both Bevin Boys?" Beneath my coat, in my wet dress, I shivered.

"No. Seamus was accepted by the RAF. I persuaded him to swap. What he said at the registry office was true. For nearly two years, everywhere but here, I was Seamus Sinclair and he was Hugh Sinclair."

While he explained how they had managed the exchange—letters, documents, blurred photographs—I stared down the passageway to where the rain was splashing on the grass. Behind his locked door he had been hiding not someone, or something, but himself. But how could he hide? I remembered all the friends and neighbours who had come to the house to greet his return. "I don't understand," I said. "When the war finished, weren't you always meeting people who knew you as Seamus?"

"Not often, and when I did I said I'd decided to go by my first name of Hugh."

"So how"—I pictured Seamus's steely gaze—"did you persuade him?"

"I offered him his heart's desire."

"Alison."

"Alison," he agreed.

"But," I burst out, "she wasn't yours to offer."

"That was the problem. I promised that if he took my place in the mines, I would do everything I could to persuade Alison to marry him, and to ensure that our father gave permission. And I gave him three thousand pounds I'd inherited from an uncle. I had no choice, Gemma. I knew if I was sent underground I would go stark, raving mad. When I was Nell's age there was a woman who used to push a wheelbarrow around the village, talking to herself. Once our football hit her house and she ran out screaming that a bomb had fallen. My mother said she'd been the best dancer on the island until her husband drowned."

My teeth were chattering so hard I cupped my cheeks to quiet them.

"And Alison," he continued, "liked Seamus. When you asked if they were friends I should have said they were more than friends. She was always following him around, trying to join in our games. I thought they'd be happy together. In '45, I came back, not covered with glory but free of shame, and Seamus came back, the farm-boy who had dug his way through the war. But he wasn't bitter; he was hopeful. He started working for my father, and in the holidays, when Alison was home from school, they were inseparable. I was off at university but whenever I wrote to her, I sang Seamus's praises, and I told my father, without explanation, that I owed him my life."

I did not look at Mr. Sinclair, I did not need to, but in my mind's eye he was changing, falling from that pedestal where, heedless of his warnings, I had placed him. "Is Seamus Nell's father?" I said.

"I wondered that—they were lovers on and off for years—but Alison was blue-eyed, like Seamus. As long as she was riding, she didn't want to marry him, or anyone. And he seemed happy to work on the farm and act as her groom. After her accident, though, he became a reminder of what she loved and couldn't have."

"Did Vicky know?"

Once again his coat rustled. "She knew Seamus was wild about Alison; everyone did. As for the rest, I think she guessed there was something amiss, but Seamus kept his word, until today. After you left he said he couldn't forgive himself for not taking Alison to the hospital that night. Of course he had no idea it was different from all the other times. Poor Seamus."

Gazing up at the dark ceiling, I remembered the evening I'd seen him leaning against his mantelpiece, shaking with grief. He too blamed himself for the loss of the person he most loved. "So he warned you yesterday, didn't he?" I said. "That was what he was telling you at the hay barn."

"I thought it was just drunken ranting. That he'd sleep it off and we'd be on the plane to Edinburgh by the time he woke up. I was an idiot."

I knew he was asking for forgiveness, but I was too busy redrawing my map of the last few months, marking the new shoreline. "Have you ever told anyone else about you and Seamus?"

"You're determined, aren't you, to get to the bottom of my box. I told Caroline, the woman I was engaged to."

"And she broke it off?"

"No." He gave a bitter laugh. "She could hardly wait for me to finish the story, to get back to talking about her wedding dress and where to have the reception. I was the one who couldn't stand it."

"So why didn't you tell me? You promised you wouldn't lie to me, but all you've done is tell me lies."

"Gemma, Gemma, you have everything back to front. It's because I admire you—your honesty, your boldness—that I couldn't bear to tell you. I did try to let you know that there were things in my past I wasn't proud of, but it was more than twenty years ago. I am still the same person who carried you over the causeway, who loves you, who wants to marry you. You swore nothing would change your feelings."

Mr. Sinclair kept talking, apologising, explaining. I stared down the passageway to where the rain fell on the grass.

"I'm freezing," I said.

At once he was standing over me, his hand outstretched. It was his hand I had seen first, before his face, as he struggled to change the tyre, and now, in the dim light, I saw his pale palm reaching towards me. I had only to put my hand there, surrender myself to his warm grasp, and everything would follow—a home, a family, university—but for how long? I recalled how easily my aunt had demoted me from beloved cousin to impoverished outsider. I stepped over to the passage and, lowering my head, walked towards the rainy light.

Mr. Sinclair stumbled behind me. As I crossed the field, he held the umbrella over me at an awkward angle. In the car he started the engine, the windscreen wipers, the heater. "Which way should we go?" he said in a low voice. "We can't go back to Blackbird Hall, and we've missed the plane. Besides, you need dry clothes."

"I have them in my suitcase. I want a room at the Kirkwall Hotel, where you stayed with Coco."

"Not with Coco," he corrected. "No, that would be horribly awkward."

"Somewhere else, then."

As we drove back to Kirkwall, I pulled my coat closer and tried to make a plan, but my brain, like my body, was frozen. The only future I could conjure involved immediate necessities: a hot bath, dry clothes, a bowl of soup. The rain was slackening, and in the fields the sheep and cows had begun to scatter. Periodically Mr. Sinclair said something. We would catch the plane tomorrow; we would be married in London. I did not bother to reply.

He stopped outside a small hotel on a side street near the harbour. I waited in the car. Presently he came out to report that he had got us two rooms, unfortunately on different floors. In the doorway of my room, he set down my suitcase and put his hands on my shoulders. "Please, Gemma," he said. "It's not as if I have another wife, or a mistress, or a child. I did something wrong when I was eighteen."

"And when you were forty-one. I need to take a bath."

"You poor darling, you mustn't catch cold. Take a bath, then come downstairs and we'll have lunch."

I hung up my limp dress, put on my dressing-gown and slippers and, locking the door behind me, went down the corridor to the bathroom. I ran the bath hot and, once I was in, made it still hotter until my skin flushed. I was almost sorry when the shivering stopped; it had been a distraction. Back in my room a sheet of paper lay beneath the door:

G, I'll be waiting downstairs in the bar. H.

As I dressed in trousers and a sweater, I saw that it was nearly two o'clock. I had expected by now to be married for three hours, to be on a plane approaching Edinburgh and a hotel room with a large, snowy bed. This room, with its single bed and single-bar electric fire, was barely larger than my attic room at Yew House. The only window overlooked a drab side street.

From our first meeting, when I had glimpsed his gorgeous shoes, I had known that Mr. Sinclair and I were unequal in the world's eyes, but I had allowed myself to believe that he regarded me as an equal. And the foundation of that belief was that he would never lie to me. Coco was prettier, more accomplished, wealthier, but he had lied to her; to me he told the truth. Truth beareth away the victory. In the street an old car clattered by. He had sworn to me on the northern star and at the same time he had told me that the stars were falling.

I went to my suitcase and took out the photograph of my uncle. He had helped me before in times of trouble, guiding my behaviour with Nell, soothing my anger. Silently I asked him what I should do. He eyed me steadily, kindly, unhelpfully. I wrote a note—*Mr. S., headache, taking a nap. G*—and slid it under the door into the hallway. Fully dressed, still holding the photograph, I climbed into bed. Nora had said our marriage was like something out of a fairy tale—a scullery maid marrying a prince—but now it was my feelings that seemed like a fairy tale.

I slept, or at least I left one level of consciousness, and returned not to Blackbird Hall but to the rooms and corridors of Claypoole. I had not been happy there. I had worked endlessly and led a severely restricted life, but I had had my alliances, I had grown, and, especially in the last years, I had been able to study. Now in my dream state I was, once again, bending over the polishing machine in the corridor outside Miss Seftain's classroom. Soon I would leave the sharp orange smell of the polish and go inside, and we would continue translating *The Metamorphoses*. Daphne would change into a laurel, Leda into a swan. Mr. Sinclair had changed from an eagle to a mole. Even in sleep I was aware of his knock at the door, his voice calling my name.

Miss Seftain had not replied to my letter announcing my marriage, there had not been time, but now in her classroom, as we bent over Ovid, she said, "Would you want to marry someone twenty years younger than yourself?"

And I said, "But that's absurd. Someone twenty years younger than me wouldn't even be born."

"Exactly."

Then, in the way of dreams, I was in another classroom—this one belonged to Mr. Donaldson—staring at a map of the British Isles. Each county was a different colour and Mr. Donaldson was standing behind me, clicking his yellow teeth. "Don't you want to know about yourself, Gemma," he said, "before you become somebody else?" Before I could summon the answer I slipped away into a deeper sleep.

I awoke to the sound of a car in the street, the dull light of late afternoon, and in my brain not a plan but an imperative.

PART
IV

PART
IV

chapter twenty-five

I STAYED IN THE LADIES' toilet until I felt the ferry gather speed and knew we had passed beyond the harbour wall and that Mr. Sinclair could no longer march up the gangplank, or row furiously after us. In the lounge I found a bench in a poorly lit corner, away from the few other passengers. But he would not need informants to guess my route. On the previous day I had continued to claim a headache and remained in bed. Now I calculated that he was unlikely to knock on my door before nine. I had got up while the sky was still dark and washed, dressed, and stolen out of the hotel at top speed. Only when I reached the main street had I allowed myself one swift backwards glance and there, in the dark facade of the hotel, was a single window glowing directly above mine. I had yearned then to run back, and hurl myself into his arms. Instead I had taken a firm grip on my suitcase and made my way to the taxi rank outside the Kirkwall Hotel. The taxi driver had told me that this was the only ferry from Stromness today. "Getting an early start," he had said, and I had nodded, speechless.

As soon as the ferry reached open water it began to pitch from side to side. I had not eaten since the day before, and now even my old friend became my enemy. I sat in the corner of the lounge, clutching my book, trying not to breathe in the smells of oil, cigarettes, wet wool, and rusty metal. Several times I almost ran back to the ladies'.

At last the noise of the engine slackened, the pitching subsided, the ferry docked. As soon as I stepped onto the pier—it was still wet from yesterday's rain—my stomach calmed. After five minutes I was ready to take my second taxi of the day, to Thurso. I asked the driver to let me off at a café. The windows were streaming with condensation, and inside several men in overalls were clustered around a table near the door; two women and a baby were seated in a corner. The waitress told me to sit wherever I liked.

"Good crossing?" called one of the workmen.

"A bit rough."

"Try a bacon roll," he urged.

Cautiously I ordered a cup of tea and, when I had drunk it without ill effect, followed his advice. The waitress brought the roll on a plate, the white china webbed with grey like those I had washed so often at Claypoole. As I began to eat I was struck by the notion that this roll was the only thing that gave me a place in the world. When the plate was empty, I would, once again, be homeless. I longed to order a second roll, and a third.

The men left in a noisy bustle and the women's conversation was suddenly audible. "A voice like a corn-crake," the one with her back to me declared.

"Three years in a row," said the other, "we've given her a retirement present and the next Sunday, there she is, back in her seat, belting out the hymns."

"Well, we all know Jean will be singing at her own funeral."

I looked at them, drinking their tea, complaining cheerfully while the baby dozed. Soon they would leave the café and go home to their houses with doors and beds and cookers. What would they say if I went over and said I was running away from my fiancé, and homeless? Did either of them need a maid? Or a nanny? I would work for bacon rolls and a place to lay my head. I pictured their smiles turning upside down, their nervous glances at their handbags, the baby.

When the waitress brought my bill I asked if there was a bus station in Thurso; buses, I'd heard, were cheaper than trains. "Indeed there is," she said. As she drew a map on a paper bag, she remarked that they didn't get many visitors this late in the year. Quickly I invented a fictitious cousin, a walking holiday in Inverness. "I hope it stays fine for you," she said. I thanked her and, with my handbag over my shoulder, my suitcase in hand, stepped into the street.

The bus station turned out to be nothing more than a large garage presently occupied by a man meticulously sweeping around the oil stains on the floor. He looked up long enough to tell me that the bus to Inverness left in an hour. I bought a newspaper and perched on the wall of a nearby house. After the ferry and two taxis, I had thirty-six pounds in my purse, a fortune to me, but until I found a job, I would need to pay for every night of sleep, every mouthful of food.

Holding the newspaper as a shield, I searched my life as if it were one of Nell's puzzles where the aim was to find the six parrots hidden in a tree. Was there someone I had overlooked who would take me in? To my surprise the first person that came into view was Miss Bryant. I pictured myself knocking on her door, then I pictured her dismay at the sight of me, followed by—and this was oddly distressing to contemplate—her helplessness. She no longer had jobs at her command, hotels asking for working girls. She would have no choice but to take me in herself, or send me away.

Who else? I thought. Dr. White had always been kind, but I was not sure he would smile if I appeared, unexpectedly, at his surgery. With Ross I had long lost contact. Matron, in the Lake District, was too far away. As for Miss Seftain, with her sister in Dunblane, she herself was a guest on sufferance. Besides, how could I explain, after my last letter, why I was fleeing my marriage? The secret was not mine to tell.

And even if I could, in veiled terms, hint at my reasons, I had only to remember Mr. Sinclair's voice as he talked on and on outside my door the night before—love, a mistake, years ago—to know that she would never understand. There was no obstacle to the marriage that had not, unbeknownst to me, been there all along.

"That's mine."

Two boys were playing hopscotch on the pavement. The lanky, dark-haired one reminded me of Nell. If she was following the timetable I had left she would—I checked my watch—be sitting at the kitchen table reading while Vicky made lunch. I had given her a story for each day we were apart. Today's was about a goat who lies to his master and gets his sons into trouble; I imagined Nell giggling at the goat's bad behaviour. Then I recalled our parting of the day before. I could not afford to think of Nell any more than of Mr. Sinclair. Quickly I returned to the newspaper. A blurry photograph of the Thurso school football team stared out at me. As I read down the list of matches—Inverness, Aberdeen, Wick, Ullapool—I remembered my dream of the previous afternoon. Mr. Donaldson, he was the hidden parrot. Years too late I could apologise for the wrong I had done him, and retrieve my box. At long last I could read the papers my parents had left me.

Other passengers began to seat themselves on the wall; the bus arrived. The conductor helped me lift my suitcase onto the rack behind the driver. As we drove out of town, I thought, just for a moment, of crying, "Stop! Stop!" I could still get off and go and wait by the ferry until Mr. Sinclair arrived the next day. But no, a man who would sell his sister, who would ask another man to go down a mine for him, who would lie and take advantage of his wealth—that was not the man I wanted to marry.

The bus was draughty and the seats hard, but in Inverness, I got out reluctantly; it too had become my home. The bus station was larger than the one in Thurso, with several buses lined up and groups of travellers waiting. Two men, their clothes ragged, their faces seamed with dirt, occupied a bench. I glimpsed sheets of newspaper sticking out between the buttons of the younger man's coat. "Want a seat?" he called. "Plenty of room for a bonnie lass." Hastily I turned away.

I had thought I might stay in Inverness, but now I decided to press on. There was still one bus going south that day, to Pitlochry. Hearing the woman in the ticket office say the name, I suddenly remembered I had been there once with my uncle and cousins to see the hydroelectric dam. We had visited the fish-ladder and watched the salmon swimming upstream to lay their eggs.

I bought a ham-and-cheese roll, a Kit Kat, and a bottle of Lucozade, and boarded another bus. It was almost full but I had two seats to myself. I set my bag beside me, drew my coat close, and, lulled by the motion and the bare moors of the Cairngorms, soon fell asleep. I woke when the bus stopped at a small village and a man smelling of onions stepped into the seat beside me. Silently he waited for me to move my handbag and sat down. In sidelong glances I saw that beneath his cap his glasses had been mended with black tape and his jacket was worn and patched. I fell back into an uneven doze.

I could not have said how many miles or minutes passed before I became aware that my new companion was leaning against me more than the lurching of the bus warranted. Something warm rested on my thigh. Opening my eyes, I discovered the man's threadbare cuff resting on the edge of my coat; his hand had slipped beneath. Meanwhile he was looking straight ahead, as if the hand and whatever it was doing had nothing to do with him.

"Excuse me," I said loudly, scrambling to my feet, "I think I'm going to be sick."

He had no choice but to let me step into the aisle. I moved forward to the only remaining empty seat, right behind the driver, where a chill draught kept me alert for the remainder of the journey. Dusk was falling as we entered Pitlochry, but I spotted bed-and-breakfast signs outside several houses. Surely one of them would have room for me. I would leave my suitcase, find something to eat, wash off the grime of the bus and the man's hand, sleep, and have a good breakfast. Then I could plan my journey to Oban. Perhaps the landlady would have an atlas.

The bus turned off the main road and pulled up beside the railway station. I climbed down and, not looking to see where the man went, I headed back to the main road towards the bed-and-breakfasts. I was walking past a row of shops when I caught, at first faintly, and within a few steps overwhelmingly, the smell of fish and chips. Suddenly I was so hungry that even a few minutes' delay seemed intolerable.

The man behind the counter wore a blue-and-white-striped apron; a white hat rested, comically, on his large ears. "What can I do for you?" he said. I asked for a large chips. Deftly he filled a grease-proof paper bag, wrapped the whole in newspaper leaving the top open, and held it towards me. "Salt and vinegar are on the counter. You're welcome to eat here." He was still speaking as I seized a chip. "You're hungry, aren't you?" he said approvingly.

"Starving. This is the best chip I've ever eaten."

"Och, it's not every day a customer says that. That'll be ninepence, please."

Still chewing, I reached into my handbag. My fingers found the newspaper I had bought in Inverness, a handkerchief, a brush and comb, a compact, a notebook and pen, the Kit Kat wrapper. Carefully I carried my bag over to the counter, and took out each article. My purse was here; it was just hiding, lost at the bottom. I had opened it half-a-dozen times that day as I paid for taxis, bought tickets and food. When the handbag was empty I shook it over the counter. A single hair clip fell out.

"Ninepence," the man repeated, his jolliness fading.

"I'm sorry. I can't find my purse."

"That's handy."

"I must have left it on the bus. I'll go and get it right now."

Leaving the chips, seizing my suitcase, I hurried back the way I had come. The bus was approaching and I stepped into the headlights, waving my free hand. It stopped. Beyond the glare of the lights, the driver pointed to the NOT IN SERVICE sign. I set down my case and put my hands together. Reluctantly he opened the door. "I'm going to the garage. There are no more buses tonight."

"Please," I said. "I lost my purse."

At once he pulled over and beckoned me aboard. I searched beneath what I thought was the seat where I had first sat. I searched behind and in front of the seat I had occupied for the rest of the journey. The driver fetched a torch and shone it back and forth over the dirty floor.

"It must be here," I kept saying as the beam caught matchsticks, sweet wrappers, a cigarette end, a pink comb.

He picked up the last. "Are you sure this is where you lost it?"

"I had it when I got on. I paid for my ticket. Then I got off, and it was gone."

But even as I spoke, I understood what must have happened. The man who had put his hand on my leg had put his hand somewhere else. Or perhaps the purse had fallen out when I jumped up, pretending to feel sick, and he had pocketed it. All day I had been careless about closing my handbag, behaving as if I were still on the Orkneys.

"Maybe you dropped it and someone picked it up?" the driver persisted. "You were the first one off. If you're lucky, they'll take it to the police station in the morning. Is there anything in it to prove it's yours?"

"The bus tickets," I said faintly.

"Well, off you go home now. Call at the station in the morning." He switched off the torch and returned to his seat.

At Claypoole I had seldom seen money, and at Blackbird Hall weeks had passed without my needing more than sixpence for the church collection. Now I was in the world where I was going to need money every day and I had none. I picked up my suitcase and climbed down into the street. The bus, my last link with my old life, drove away, and I forced myself to walk back to the fish-and-chips shop. There were still no other customers. The man was listening to the radio; I recognised one of Vicky's favourite programmes.

"I'm sorry," I said. "I lost my purse on the bus. I don't have any money."

His lips tightened and I braced myself for an outburst. Then he seemed to take in my raincoat, my suitcase, my bedraggled hair. He added a couple of chips to the bag and held it out. "Come back and pay when you can."

"I will," I promised fervently.

For a few minutes sitting at the counter, eating the chips one by one, I almost forgot my troubles but soon the bag was empty. I waved my thanks to the man, now occupied with other customers, and once more picked up my suitcase. At the street corner I set it down and stopped to think. It was nearly nine o'clock, dark and chilly. Where could I sleep? Recalling the men in Inverness, I thought I could look for a bench at the railway station, but that seemed too public; besides, there were laws against loitering. A park would be safer. I was wondering how to find one when, nearby, a bell chimed the hour. At once that seemed like the answer. My uncle had always left the door of his church open. In the sixteenth century, he'd told me, a person could seek sanctuary for thirty-seven days.

The town was not quite deserted—a few teenagers loitered on street corners, a couple of dog walkers were patrolling—but to ask directions to the nearest church at this hour seemed suspicious. Stopping periodically to switch my suitcase to the other hand, I followed the main road into town. I passed more shops and a large hotel. In the morning, I thought, I would apply there for a job. There was no question now of going to Oban. I needed food and shelter as soon as possible. Glancing up a side street, I glimpsed a second hotel. I walked over to take a closer look. Just beyond the hotel, across the street, was a church set back on a grassy mound.

A man with a walking stick and a small white dog was coming up the hill. I waited for him to tap by and headed towards the church. Please, I thought. I climbed the broad steps, set down my suitcase, and with both hands clasped the metal ring. The latch engaged; the door yielded. I picked up my case, and stepped inside.

In the darkness I stood, counting, waiting for my pupils to expand. By the time I reached seventy the arched outlines of the windows were faintly visible and, below, the rows of pews. I could still have drawn a detailed plan of my uncle's church, and leaving my case by the door, I walked down the nave towards the altar. Steps, I thought, and here they were: one, two, three. Arms outstretched, I circled the altar, searching for the vestry. My knee knocked against a chair; my hand met a doorframe and then a switch.

A few seconds of light showed me the familiar vestments hanging on a hook, also a counter, a small sink, and a kettle. A half-open door revealed a toilet. Once I was sure I was alone, I risked having the light on for five minutes, long enough to make use of the plumbing. In the dark I returned to my suitcase, chose a pew near the door, took off my shoes, and lay down.

·   ·   ·

I SLEPT POORLY. THE church was cold, the pew narrow and, even with cushions, hard. Sometime in the night I put on another pullover and wrapped the newspaper I had bought in Thurso around my legs. As I had years ago at Yew House, I parsed every sound into would-be kidnappers, thieves, rapists, murderers. Or if not two-legged assailants, then four-footed ones who would nibble my fingers and chew my nose. And if there were no sounds my brain whirled with thoughts of what I would do tomorrow without food, or shelter, or almost any money. I had found some coins in the pocket of my trousers—enough for a loaf of bread and a pint of milk. But all these difficulties were infinitely preferable to dwelling on the loss of Mr. Sinclair, and of Nell.

I woke to the sound of the clock chiming; my watch showed seven o'clock. In the vestry I washed and brushed my teeth. Using the mirror of my compact, I checked my face and hair and straightened my collar. It was important to look neat when I presented myself at the hotels. Beside the kettle, I discovered the makings for tea. I made myself a cup and added several spoonfuls of sugar and dried milk. I sat drinking it in the pew farthest from the door. If anyone came in, I could hide the cup and pretend to be an early worshipper. Then I read my book until the clock struck nine.

Not wanting the encumbrance, I left my suitcase tucked under a pew. Unless someone washed the floors, which looked to be a rare event, I was confident it would not be found. Outside the day was bright and mild. Behind the church the streets of the town stretched up towards the hills; in front were the rooftops of the buildings that lined the main street. In other circumstances, I thought, this would be a pretty place. I hurried down the steps and across the road to the hotel.

The hall was deserted, but the sounds of cutlery and conversation led me to the dining-room, where a dozen people were breakfasting. I gazed yearningly at their plates until the waitress, a girl around my age, asked if she could help me. When I said I was looking for the manager she sent me back to the hall with instructions to ring the bell.

I did and a woman appeared, her broad face shining, her spectacles resting on the wide shelf of her chest. "Good morning," she said. "Aren't we lucky with the weather?"

I said we were and that I was looking for a job. "I can clean, serve people. I've had a lot of experience preparing vegetables, washing-up, whatever you need."

She nodded approvingly. "I'm sure you're very well qualified, dear, but the tourist season is nearly over. We're letting people go, not taking them on. If you want to leave your name and address, I can let you know if we need someone at Christmas." As she spoke, she slipped on her spectacles to examine me more closely.

"I'll do anything. Wash windows, scrub floors. Feed the pigs."

The woman smiled. "We don't have pigs, more's the pity. Here." She produced a sheet of paper and a pen. "Write down your name and address. Do you have a phone?"

Hastily, mumbling that I would let her know, I turned to leave.

Back at the main road I headed away from the other hotel. Idiot. Even at Claypoole, when I had thought of myself as having almost nothing, I had had an address, and, I now recalled, I had offered references when I applied for jobs. I passed an electrical shop and a milk bar. Then a funeral director's and another church set back from the road. Just beyond the latter was a cul-de-sac of pebble-dashed bungalows: Newholme Avenue. I chose number seven because of the scarlet dahlias in the front garden. We were waiting for a phone. As for a reference, Miss Bryant would serve. Surely post was forwarded from Claypoole.

Fortified by my plan, I walked back to the other hotel I had seen the night before. The stout wooden door announced, as clearly as if it had spoken, that while Mr. Sinclair and his kind were welcome here, small insignificant people were not. I drew back my shoulders and turned the knob. The hall was larger and brighter but once again deserted. A murky picture of a stag at bay occupied one wall; next to it was a door labelled LADIES. Inside I washed my hands, relishing the soap and hot water. In the mirror I put on lipstick and combed my hair.

When I emerged a man in a suit was standing at the counter, thumbing pound notes out of his wallet. My heart jumped. His hands, his wallet, the slope of his shoulders were so much like those of Mr. Sinclair. Then his profile came into view, and the resemblance vanished. From behind the counter rose an unctuous voice. "Always a pleasure to see you, sir. We do hope you enjoyed your stay, sir. Haste ye back."

Turning from the counter, the man caught sight of me, waiting. "Good morning." He smiled. "Grand day."

I smiled back, and he strolled out into his comfortable, prosperous life.

"Yes, miss?" said the man behind the counter, his voice quite different.

"I'm sorry to bother you," I said. "I'm looking for a position as a chambermaid, or a cook's helper, or a waitress."

In so far as he could, given the counter between us, he looked me up and down. I must have passed some test, for he produced a clipboard with a form and told me to go and fill it out in the bar. The questions should have been easy—name, address, age, education, experience, references—but each was freighted with complications. In my neatest writing I wrote, "Jean Harvey," increased my age, claimed to have worked for two years at Claypoole, and listed Miss Bryant and Miss Seftain as references. Under DATE WHEN AVAILABLE I wrote, "Today."

Back at the counter the man was bent over a sheaf of papers. The only sounds were the scratch of his pen, the sifting of paper against paper. I pretended that I was playing statues with Nell and Vicky. If

I stood as still as possible then surely he would offer me a job. Three minutes passed, four, seven. Finally a woman in an apron bustled over.

"Harry, has number six left?" She held out an umbrella. "There's someone waiting to talk to you."

"They were on their way right after breakfast," he said, accepting the umbrella. "Thanks, Sheila. Yes, miss?"

"Miss Harvey. Jean Harvey. Here's the form. I hope I filled it out correctly."

He took the clipboard and, without looking at my answers, set it on a shelf and returned to his papers. "Excuse me, sir." I had not seen another hotel in town. "I was hoping for something starting immediately."

"We never hire without checking references." He turned a page.

I said that Miss Bryant of Claypoole School would vouch for me.

"Miss"—he reached for the clipboard—"Harvey, we're not taking on staff at the moment. We'll keep your application on file and notify you if we have a suitable position. Now, if you'll excuse me, I have work to do."

I felt myself shrinking into the carpet. I had been reduced, like Mr. Sinclair, to lying, and my lies had accomplished nothing. Suddenly the man spoke again, quietly and viciously. I caught only the word *police*. In my despair I had forgotten the bus driver's suggestion. "Thank you," I said. "Thank you very much."

But at the police station a man in uniform said that no one had handed in a purse. He leaned over the counter, frowning, and asked the same awkward questions—name, age, address—until I thought he was going to produce a pair of handcuffs. I said I would check back later and hurried away.

For the rest of the day, as I went from shop to shop asking for work, the word *no* rang in my ears. I even approached people in the street:

I asked a woman struggling with a pram if she needed a babysitter, a man with a border terrier if he needed someone to walk his dog, a window washer if he needed an assistant. But the answer was the same. At some point I went back to the co-op, where earlier a pleasant woman had said she'd hire me like a shot if it were up to her, and bought the biggest, cheapest loaf of bread, which left me with two shillings and threepence. Back at the church I counted the slices. Eighteen. If I had three now and three before bed it would last me until the day after tomorrow. I ate as slowly as possible.

I was finishing the third slice when the clock chimed; unthinkingly I checked my watch. Several times that day I had passed the jeweller's shop on the main street. Some of the watches in the window cost ten pounds, a few as much as twenty. Surely mine, which was almost new, would fetch five. That would be more than enough, I thought, to get to Oban if I hitchhiked and slept in churches. The shop was already closed for the day, but cheered by my plan, I decided to visit the fish-ladder. I had seen a sign for it beside the war memorial.

A ten-minute walk took me across the main road, past a park and a row of houses, to Loch Faskally. I had no memory of the placid loch nor of the massive dam, but as soon as I went down into the fish-ladder I recognised the series of ascending windows that lined one side, the water lit up behind them. A slim, freckled fish appeared in the lowest window, was swept back, and, a few minutes later, reappeared. Pressing my face to the glass, I said, "Swim harder."

My uncle had used the salmon in a sermon. Being a good Christian, he had said, often feels like swimming against the current. Sometimes it seems we are all alone, that no one cares what we do, but we aren't alone. God cares. That I could remember his words was a consolation, but the words themselves were not. The salmon swam upstream because it had no choice. Virtue was its own reward. As the fish reached the next window, a rustling sound made me look down. A rat was nosing along the floor. Quickly I ran for the stairs.

DESPITE COLD, HUNGER, AND the chiming of the church clock, I slept a little better on my second night. In the morning I went through my suitcase and chose a different blouse, a blue cardigan, and my black corduroy trousers. Thinking to lighten my load, I took my two precious photographs out of the frames I had bought for them in Kirkwall, and slipped them into my guide to Scottish birds. I set the frames on a shelf beside the hymnals, hoping someone else could use them. As for the meteorite, wrapped in a sock, I pretended that it did not exist. I stowed the suitcase under the pew. Then I took off my watch and polished it with the edge of my cardigan.

At the jewellery shop a girl stopped pushing a carpet sweeper. "Good morning," she said. "Can I help you?"

Her smile was so eager that I longed to pretend to be a normal customer, to look at half-a-dozen watches and say that I needed to think about it. But such play-acting would not fill my purse. I asked if I might speak to the manager.

"Owner," she said. "Mr. White's in the back. Let me fetch him."

Surely, I thought, it was a good omen that the jeweller had the same name as the giver of the watch. One wall of the shop was covered with clocks, and as I listened to the soft cacophony of their ticking, I remembered the gleaming cogs and levers of the clock in St. Magnus Cathedral. How rapt the three of us had been when it struck the hour. A man appeared from a doorway behind the counter. At the sight of Mr. White's narrow, dark face, nothing like that of the affable doctor, my heart began its own uneven ticking. I said that I had a watch for sale.

"Miss"—little slivers of metal were embedded in the word—"surely you can see that I deal only in new merchandise." He waved at the display cases.

"My watch is almost new. I've taken very good care of it." I held it out to him.

Reluctantly he dangled the watch by its strap. "This is one of the cheapest watches on the market. Brand-new it costs five pounds."

How foolish I had been to think that Dr. White would have bought me an expensive gift. "Can you give me half that?"

"I can't give you a penny. I don't deal in secondhand merchandise, except for antiques. Which this is not." He set the watch down with a precise tap on the counter.

"A pound," I pleaded.

Without another word he returned to his lair.

Throughout this exchange, the girl had been polishing a display case. Now she handed me the watch. "At least it tells the time," she said brightly.

Outside rain was falling, but I walked along too dazed to hurry, or even to stay beneath the awnings of the shops. What was I to do? Not one person in Pitlochry wished me well, or knew my true name, or cared whether I lived or died. It had been a mistake to be lured here by the memory of my uncle. He could not help me now. If only I had stayed in Inverness, I would never have lost my purse. I must leave this awful place at once. I would carry my suitcase and the remains of my loaf and stand beside the road south. I would get a lift to Perth and make my way west to Oban. People could live for weeks without food.

I had come and gone so often from the church that when the door didn't open, I thought the latch was sticking. I turned the ring again; again there was some obstacle. Only on the fourth attempt did I understand. The door was locked. I was on one side of it and my suitcase was on the other.

Not caring who saw me, I knocked on the door and, when there was no answer, pounded with the flat of my hand. A few flakes of faded red paint fell to the ground. A woman passing in the road below called out, "It's Friday. No service until Sunday."

"But a church ought to be open at all times. It's a place of sanctuary."

The woman turned off the road and, a shopping bag in one hand, a black umbrella in the other, approached the steps. She looked vaguely familiar, but after my day spent wandering the streets of the town many people did. It did not occur to me that I too, in my navy blue coat, might be a recognisable figure.

From beneath her umbrella the woman studied me. "You're the girl who was asking for work at the co-op," she said. "You gave your address as Seven Newholme Avenue. Are you Shona Ross's niece? Why are you trying to break into the church?"

"I left my scarf."

Before she could ask further questions, I hurried down the stairs and slipped past her back to the road. My only thought was to escape before she too threatened to call the police. Dodging a milk van, I darted across the main road and down under the railway bridge. My flight brought me to the park I had seen the day before. The grass was already sodden and in the distance a couple of football nets hung limply, but nearby a low building with a bench under the eaves offered refuge. I sat down. Was it possible that only a week ago I had woken in my luxurious bed, eaten a lavish breakfast, taught Nell her lessons, walked with her to the village, then Mr. Sinclair and I—

I stood up and did twelve jumping-jacks. As I turned to sit down again, I noticed in one corner of the bench a brown paper bag. Opening it, I discovered a roll filled with some kind of meat paste, only one bite taken. The bread was a little dry but the paste was still moist. I devoured it. Alert to new possibilities, I approached the rubbish bin at

the far end of the building. Two half-eaten bags of crisps and a chocolate biscuit rewarded my efforts. I rinsed my hands at the outdoor tap
and sat down to eat my booty. Then I took out one of my few remaining possessions: my notebook. On a clean page I wrote:

1. *Get back suitcase.*
2. *Leave Pitlochry.*
3. *Go to Oban.*
4. *Find Mr. Donaldson's sister.*

It was a short list but each item was Herculean. After my various
crimes—using a false name and address, sleeping in a place of worship—I did not dare go to the police again. As for the minister of the
church, all I could picture was Mr. Waugh towering over me, shaking
me with red-faced fury. I closed the notebook and put it carefully away
in my bag. Would I never see my beloved keepsakes again?

All at once I remembered that the vestry had a back door. I jumped
up and hurried back the way I had come. Rain had emptied the streets
and I saw no one as I trotted up the hill and around to the rear of
the church. Water spouted from a leaky gutter. Dodging the spray, I
reached for the doorknob. It turned in my hand.

For a moment I simply stood there.

Inside I tiptoed over to the vestry door and peered into the church.
When I was sure that nothing moved among the pews, I returned to
use the W.C., suddenly a matter of urgency, and fill the kettle. I let the
tea-bag steep for a little longer than usual and added an extra spoon
of sugar. As I sat in my pew, sipping the hot, sweet liquid, I pictured
the dry clothes I would put on: socks, jeans, my green sweater. Then
I would wait for the rain to ease before I started hitchhiking. I got
out my notebook and ticked off the first item on my list. And soon,

I thought, item two would be accomplished: leave Pitlochry. I set the cup on the shelf beside a hymnal and reached down.

My hand met emptiness.

I went up and down every pew—even the ones at the front, even the ones on the other side of the nave where I had never sat—but my suitcase was gone. I checked the piles of hymnals, the window-sills, the font, the pulpit, the organ. Suddenly I noticed—despair had blinded me—that the floor was damp in places. Someone had come, at last, to wash it. I sank down in the nearest pew and buried my head in my hands. How stupid I had been not to take the case to the jeweller's. And only to have Mr. White sneer at my watch. I pictured the stern policeman looking at my photographs.

Twenty minutes later I was standing beside a lay-by just south of the town, holding out my hand. I stopped counting after eighty-three cars. Some vehicles, I noticed, even sped up at the sight of me. Several came so close that I had to jump back to escape being splashed. I was of no more consequence to them, I thought, than the nearby litter bin. I wanted only to flee this awful place, and even that seemed impossible. Finally a red lorry pulled over a few yards ahead. The door opened and a man called out, "Where are you going?"

"Oban."

"I can get you started. I'm on my way to York."

I scrambled up into the warm fug of the cab and, exclaiming my thanks, settled into the threadbare seat. My companion smiled at me and I saw that, like Ross, he had a chipped tooth. He did not look like a kidnapper, or a rapist. We introduced ourselves; his name was Grant.

"Why are you going to Oban with no luggage?" he said. "You're not running away, are you? I don't want any trouble."

"I'm eighteen," I said. "I'm too old to run away."

"But Oban's not a day trip, even if you get a lift in a sports car."

"My suitcase was stolen."

"Stolen? Who would steal from a lassie like you? Did you tell the police? You should only take lifts from lorry drivers. That way you know who a person works for. We may not be the speediest vehicles on the road but we get there in the end."

"*Festina lente*," I murmured. "I'll talk to the police when I get to Oban. They're all connected nowadays."

"More's the pity." He embarked on a story about how he'd been pulled over in Aberdeen for carrying too much weight and later, when he'd been stopped in Glasgow, the police had known about it. I did my best to listen but, despite my wet clothes, I had begun to feel as if my face might burst into flames. I pressed my palm to the cold window and then my cheek. Something twisted in my stomach. The lie I had told the man on the bus was coming true.

"Och aye," said Grant. "The Glasgow police are—"

"I'm sorry. I'm going to be sick."

"Bloody hell. Hang on."

He pulled over. Still holding my bag, I scrambled out of the cab. I had taken only a couple of steps before I doubled over. Everything I had eaten at the recreation ground flew out of my mouth. Presently I heard Grant's voice.

"I need to be on my way. Are you well enough to come along?"

My body answered for me.

"You're in Ballinluig," he said. "You can maybe get a cup of tea at the garage. Here's a little something. Good luck, Jean." He handed me two coins and was gone.

When I was well enough to stand upright again, I put the half-crowns carefully away in my pocket. I was on the edge of a village of a few dozen houses. I saw signs for the garage Grant had mentioned, and a shop. At the former a man in greasy overalls told me that I couldn't shelter there. "Damned Gypsies," I heard him say under his breath. In the shop a woman kept her arms tightly folded. No, she didn't serve tea. No, I couldn't wait there. When I stepped back into the road the houses on the other side tilted alarmingly. I leaned on the window-sill and put my head between my knees.

Behind me the shop bell rang. "I told you, you can't stop here."

I felt too ill to get another lift and yet this village was the worst place to be stranded. There was no church, no library, not even a bus shelter where I could wait to recover my strength. The feeling of being on fire was gone; instead my teeth were chattering. One house had a rowan tree outside like the one at Yew House and I knocked on the door. The curtains at the window twitched but no one answered. At the next house a woman said she was sorry and closed the door before I had uttered a word.

Back in the road I leaned against a parked car and waited for someone else to shout at me. The rain had closed in and the hilltops were shrouded in mist. My mind was as grey and empty as the sky. Everything I wanted—love, a slice of toast, a warm bed, a job, my suitcase—was far, far out of reach. I was gazing vacantly in the direction of the main road when I noticed a flash of colour: a red telephone box. One evening at Blackbird Hall Vicky had reported that someone phoning Mr. Sinclair had reversed the charges; it was a way, she explained, to make a phone call with no money. I knew the number, I thought. I could phone. Explain that I was in this place called Ballinluig, ill, penniless. And then Mr. Sinclair would rescue me. One of the passing cars would suddenly be his. I would be warm, dry, safe. I bent over, wrapping my arms around myself, trying to stop shivering. I heard Mr. Sinclair repeating the number over and over, as if he knew my plight and was urging me to phone.

Suddenly there was a different voice, the voice that had led me to

Miriam years ago, that had warned me about the causeway. I had not heard the young man since I left Claypoole. Now he was saying something about cows.

"Go to the cows, Gemma. The cows will help you."

When the bout of shivering passed, I raised my head and looked around. On the far side of the main road was a field of brown and white cows and a smaller road winding away into the countryside. Perhaps the cows would have some kind of shelter where I could rest. My own species had proved hopeless. Why not try another?

chapter twenty-six

WHAT I SAW FIRST was not her face but three hollows, one at the base of her neck, one above each collarbone. Each could have held a small egg, a robin's perhaps.

"You're awake," she said. "Can you sit up and drink some lemon barley water?"

With her help I managed both. She turned my pillow and another part of her came into view: two hands, large for a woman, no rings. I sank back against the pillow, so relieved to be in a bed that I did not care where it was, or how I'd got there. But as the woman kept talking, I grasped that her name was Hannah. Her brother, a postman, had found me lying near the road. When he couldn't rouse me, he had brought me here, to the house she shared with her friend, Pauline, in the town of Aberfeldy. At the unfamiliar name I at last raised my eyes. Hannah's face was long and pale save for a smudge of colour high on each cheek. The grey-blue of her eyes matched her faded shirt. Her straight brown hair hung untidily down her back.

"We searched your bag," she said. "I'm sorry, but we were looking for a name and address. Is there someone I can telephone to let them know you're safe?"

"No. When did your brother find me?" I felt so weak that I would not have been surprised to hear that I had been in bed for a month, but Hannah said that Archie had shown up with me yesterday afternoon. They had called the doctor.

"He said you were suffering from exhaustion as much as anything else." Her forehead wrinkled. "Are you sure there's no one we can notify? Family? Friends? A teacher?"

Her anxious tone made me want to reel off the names of people to contact, but each, for different reasons, was forbidden. "I'm sorry if I'm being a nuisance," I said. "I'll leave as soon as I can." Even as I spoke, I sank lower in the bed.

"Goodness, you're not going anywhere at the moment. Pauline and I never use this room. We just don't want anyone worrying about you. Let's see if you can eat some toast."

Her footsteps descended four stairs, paused, descended more stairs. Alone, I took in that I was lying in a single bed in a modest room. A desk and a chair stood in one corner, an armchair in the other. On the pale blue walls hung several paintings. As I gazed at them, the bright swirls of colour became familiar flowers: sweet peas, delphiniums, nasturtiums. Nothing in the room was new but everything was well cared for. I was relieved to think I had found refuge with people who did not have much money; they seemed more likely to be kind, less likely to have any connection with Mr. Sinclair.

Footsteps ascended—already I was getting to know Hannah's heavy tread—the door opened and she reappeared, carrying a plate of toast and a glass of milk. "I forgot to ask your name," she said, setting them on the bedside table.

In the first moments of consciousness I might easily have forgotten my new identity. Now I announced myself as Jean Harvey. While I ate, taking the small bites Hannah urged, she sat in the armchair. She asked if I had been to Aberfeldy before and when I said no she told me that the town was on the river Tay, ten miles west of the main road between Perth and Pitlochry. After all my travels I had ended up less than thirty miles from Yew House.

"We moved here four years ago," she went on. "You could have knocked me down with a feather when I read the solicitor's letter. I'd never even spoken to my cousin, just Christmas cards, and here he was leaving me Honeysuckle Cottage. He thought it would be good for my work." She gestured towards the paintings. "And it is. We turned the garden shed into a pottery."

"I like the delphiniums," I offered shyly.

"Juvenilia," said Hannah, pushing back her hair. "But there is something that interests me about the blue. The nasturtiums look like they might be about to eat you."

I asked if Pauline was an artist too, and Hannah said no; she worked at the local chemist's. When the toast was gone, she helped me out of bed and across the landing to the bathroom. I stared in amazement at the circles round my eyes, my thin cheeks. I could have been twenty. Even thirty. What would Mr. Sinclair think if he could see me now? I turned on the hot tap and my face disappeared in a cloud of steam.

For the rest of the day I dozed and looked out of the window at a row of fir trees tossing in the wind. Soon after five I heard voices in the room below, then quick, light feet on the stairs and a tap at the door. If Hannah was an angular heron, the woman who entered was a plump wren. Her hair was curly, her cheeks pink, her figure a neat hour-glass.

"I'm Pauline. How are you feeling?"

"Better, as long as I don't try to do anything."

"That's your body's way of making sure you stay in bed. You were so ill that you lost consciousness. But you're young. You'll be up doing the Highland fling in no time. Can you tell me what happened? Can we telephone your family?" From behind spotless spectacles her green eyes studied me with concern.

I tried to come up with an answer and then gave the best possible one: tears.

"There, there," said Pauline. "I didn't mean to upset you. Would you like something to read?"

When I nodded, she disappeared and returned ten minutes later with a stack of books: an Agatha Christie, a Georgette Heyer, a book about Highland Perthshire, and Rider Haggard's *King Solomon's Mines*. I had read this last at Claypoole, and I seized it with delight. In the midst of so much turmoil Haggard's dramatic story remained unchanged.

The next morning I begged Hannah to let me get up. At first she said not without consulting Pauline, but when I persisted, she said what harm could it do so long as I promised to go back to bed the moment I felt poorly. She brought my clothes, which had been washed but not ironed. I dressed slowly—I was weaker than I had expected—and, keeping firm hold of the banister, descended the stairs.

"In here," Hannah called. I stepped through the nearest door and found myself in a smaller, cosier version of the kitchen at Blackbird Hall. Hannah was sitting at the table, reading the newspaper. "Sit, sit," she said as she stood. "How are you feeling?"

"Fine."

"The traditional invalid's reply." She aimed her chin at me. "Really?"

I confessed that I had counted the stairs, and that when I moved too quickly everything blurred. As I spoke something nudged my leg. A black Labrador was gazing up at me with soulful eyes. I stroked her glossy head.

"Emily, don't be a nuisance. She's called after Emmeline Pankhurst and, like her namesake, I'm afraid she can be pushy. You're light-headed. We'll ask Dr. Grady about that when he comes by. For now let's get you some breakfast."

"There's no need," I said, meaning the doctor. But Hannah was already at the stove. As she stirred the porridge, she said the town was lucky to have a doctor, a dentist, and almost everything else one might need: shops, a school, a cottage hospital, and a library. "And of course," she added, "our famous Birks."

"Birks?" At Claypoole the girls had often called each other a stupid birk.

"Birch trees," said Hannah, gesturing towards the window, although there were none in sight. But the Birks of Aberfeldy, she explained, was a gorge just outside the town where the Falls of Moness tumbled down the hill. Robert Burns had immortalised the place in a song. "When you're better," she concluded, "we'll walk up there. It's lovely at this time of year." She set a bowl of porridge on the table and again reminded me not to eat too fast.

I had worried that, now that I was upright, I would have to give an account of myself, but Hannah announced she was going to her pottery. "If you need anything, come and find me." Then she left me in the company of Emily and two cats, one calico, one grey. Under their combined gazes, I ate the porridge slowly, avoiding the lumps.

When I had finished, I washed the bowl and the saucepan and set out to explore. Downstairs, besides the kitchen, there was a small room with a cluttered desk and bookshelves and a living-room with a view over the garden to the hills. The stairs went up the middle of the house to a landing where they divided. To the left four more stairs led to my room and a bathroom; to the right were two more bedrooms, each with a double bed and a fireplace. The one with the carelessly made bed and hastily drawn curtains I guessed to be Hannah's. In the other room the books were stacked neatly on the bedside table, the clothes folded on a chair.

I fetched *King Solomon's Mines* and lay down on the sofa in the living-room. With the grey cat at my feet and Emily asleep on the hearthrug, I too soon drifted off. I woke to a hand on my forehead.

"Jean," said Hannah, "this is Dr. Grady."

"How do you do, young lady. You gave us quite a scare."

With his flyaway hair and prominent Adam's apple, Dr. Grady looked like a man in a hurry, but he set down his bag and, talking all the while to Hannah, examined me in a leisurely fashion. "I was in that pool just below the big willow tree—take a deep breath, good girl—when I felt a tug on my line. Bend forward."

His stethoscope, to my relief, revealed nothing untoward. All I needed was rest and food. "But if you rush around," he said, "you could end up with pneumonia. You must take it easy for the next week. If that's all right with you, Hannah," he added.

"Of course," she said. "Jean will just lounge around with the cats."

And that was what I did. I read and dozed and played with the animals. I gave little thought to the future. Whenever I told myself I must make a plan, I fell asleep. As for the past, I did my best to pretend that the events of the last few months had never occurred, but whenever the phone rang, I seized a book or played with a cat until the call was safely answered. Happily my hosts seemed to notice nothing. My strength began to return, and soon I was helping with household chores. On my fifth day I was making apple crumble, trying to peel the apples in a single sweep, when a man with the same long nose and chin as Hannah stepped into the kitchen without knocking.

"Hello," he said. "You look a hundred times better."

As he helped himself to tea, I did my best to thank Archie. "Don't thank me," he said. "If I'd given up smoking, like I vow to do every year, then I'd never have found you. I stopped to roll a cigarette, and there you were. I was afraid you were dead."

Cigarettes were Archie's sole vice, at least in his own eyes. Three years ago he had followed Hannah to Aberfeldy and taken rooms a few miles away in the village of Strathtay. He rose at six, winter or summer, took a cold shower every morning, and was a vegetarian. His postal route took him around the valley, to many small farms and hamlets. Last spring he had produced a pamphlet about the early road builders in this part of Scotland. At supper he asked if I'd seen Wade's Bridge. When Hannah said not yet, he explained that General Wade was an English general who had come to Scotland in the eighteenth century and built 240 miles of roads and forty bridges, including the one in Aberfeldy.

"Was that before or after Bonnie Prince Charlie?" I said. I could tell from the shift of Pauline's shoulders and the pointing of Hannah's chin that this was a familiar topic, but if Archie had held forth on the manufacture of toothbrushes I would have urged him on; I was so glad he was not asking difficult questions. While he and Hannah squabbled about Bonnie Prince Charlie, I looked from sister to brother. In Archie's case the bony nose and long chin combined to create a remarkable handsomeness.

As we ate the stew, his portion made with vegetables, the conversation turned to their neighbour Hamish, who, whenever a car backfired, dived for cover. "He thinks we're still fighting the war," said Pauline, and Archie said he'd stopped driving up to the house for fear of alarming him. After supper I excused myself to bed. I fell asleep to the sounds of their conversation, hoping I was not the subject, fearing I was.

The following morning Hannah was at the kitchen table. After the first day she had left my porridge on the stove and gone to her pottery. But today she was waiting. I moved to the stove, dumb with apprehension, and lifted the saucepan onto the hot burner. She was going to tell me to leave and I was going to have to pretend that that was fine. Once again I would sleep in a pew, or worse, and stand beside the road while cars sped by.

"Jean, forgive me, but I must ask you some questions. You're living in our home, but we know almost nothing about you. Obviously something happened that sent your life off the rails, and obviously you don't want to talk about whatever that was. You're not the kind of person who would normally be wandering, penniless, in the rain."

The heat of the stove beat against my face.

"Did you run away from home, or school?"

"No."

"Can you tell me how you came to be lying by the road near Ballinluig?"

"Not really. It involves too many other people."

"Is someone looking for you?"

"I don't know, but if they are, they don't deserve to find me."

"Did you commit some crime, or unkindness, that led to your present situation?"

Turning to face her, I dropped to my knees. "I swear I didn't. I did do things I'm not proud of, but nothing criminal. As for unkindness—" Mr. Sinclair's face appeared before me. "There are people who might claim I'd been unkind, but whatever I did, I believed was necessary." While I delivered my speech, the cats had sauntered over and were arching against me, purring. They forgave me, but did Hannah?

"For goodness sake, get up." She half-rose, as if to help me. "That's what we told Archie. Pauline and I both see how considerate you are. Whatever you've done, you're not a bad person."

On the stove the porridge began to bubble. I jumped to my feet and seized the saucepan.

"But our neighbours," Hannah continued, "are asking about the girl who nearly died in a ditch. Yesterday a woman came into the chemist's and said she'd heard that you'd lost your memory and didn't even know your own name. Someone else claimed you'd run away from school and asked if we'd notified the police. So you need to come up with a story about your origins and stick to it. You can try it out on us."

She went off to the pottery, her mind seemingly set at ease. My own was in disarray. Alone at the kitchen table I gave myself a lecture. Why on earth would Hannah and Pauline want to take me in? They had been more than kind, nursing me back to health, dressing me—Pauline was almost my size—and feeding me. I must make a plan, before they asked me to leave. But first I needed to invent a history that was plausible and not too interesting, something people would gossip about one day and forget the next. Oddly this did not feel like lying, any more than calling myself Jean Harvey did.

As I chopped vegetables for soup, I gave myself a dead mother and a father who lived in Edinburgh and had recently remarried. I would hint at a difficult stepmother, a second family. But how had I come to be wandering the roads of Perthshire with no possessions? Perhaps I'd been going to stay with an aunt in Pitlochry. Then I remembered the woman who had accosted me outside the church. Pitlochry was too close, too small. Questions might follow. Who was my aunt? Where did she live? Between one carrot and the next I moved her to Inverness.

So then what happened? I had been on the bus and something I'd eaten had disagreed with me. I had had to get off in a hurry at Ballinluig, and in my confusion had forgotten my luggage. I'd phoned the bus company but no one had seen my suitcase.

Over lunch, after Hannah had praised the soup, I rehearsed the story. "Not bad," she said. "But why aren't you going to see your aunt, now that you're fit again?"

"I can't bear to leave you and Pauline and Aberfeldy."

She shook her head. "You can do better than that."

"My aunt just lost her job—she's a hairdresser—and she's going to have to move into a smaller flat. She doesn't have room for me."

"That might work. Let's try it out on Pauline this evening."

I did.

"Your poor aunt," said Pauline. "And what does your father do?"

"A teacher?"

"No. And he's not a postman either." Pauline frowned. "I see him working in a big shop in Edinburgh. Maybe Jenners?"

That was the name of the department store, I recalled, that I had visited so long ago with my aunt and of which the shop in Kirkwall had reminded me. I had a sudden vision of myself in the middle of a lofty hall, transfixed by the sights and sounds and perfumes. Yes, that would be a perfect place for my imaginary father to work.

The following day I accompanied Hannah into town. She pointed out the library, the butcher's, the chemist's where Pauline worked, and the bank. In the main street she stopped every few yards to greet someone and introduce me. "This is Jean Harvey. She's staying with us while she finds her feet." Then I would smile and say that I was much better, thanks to Hannah's cooking.

When we got home I said, "No one asked me anything. Why did I need a story?"

"Jean, we live in a polite town. They're not going to pester you to your face, but they'll all be buying aspirin now, asking Pauline. And when I return my library books this afternoon they'll be round me like wasps to a glass of beer. The next time you go into town someone will mention Edinburgh. Or make a joke about Jenners. Or say what a shame your aunt lost her job."

That was exactly what happened. The following day the woman at the newsagent remarked that I must miss the big city. And the day after that the butcher said how lucky I was that Archie had found me. "A young lass couldn't ask to meet a nicer family than the Watsons."

·   ·   ·

IN THE DAYS THAT followed I gave up all thought of leaving. I took on more of the household duties: I filled and raked the stove, walked Emily up the hill, carried bags of clay to the pottery, cleaned and shopped. I even ventured to make supper, which Hannah, whose job this normally was, particularly appreciated. I still wanted to go to Oban, to find Mr. Donaldson, but the days were getting shorter and colder, and I dreaded travelling without money. If I could stay in my blue room through the winter and get a job, then I could save money for the spring. One day, when I was helping Hannah wedge the clay, I confided that I was keeping an eye on the help-wanted advertisements in the window of the newsagent.

"That's a good idea," said Hannah. "What are your skills?"

I pushed down on the cool, damp clay. "Mathematics, teaching small children, feeding hens and calves, cleaning. I can polish a floor until it shines like a skating rink. And my cooking is coming along."

"Indeed it is. And you forgot reading; you're a great reader. Pauline sees people all day long. She can ask around if anyone needs help."

Outside the window a female blackbird was fluttering disconsolately above the empty bird table. "That would be super," I said.

On Saturday, when I ran into Archie outside the greengrocer's, I explained that I was looking for a job. "If you hear of anything on your rounds," I said, "housework, babysitting, teaching, will you let me know?"

Archie took his cigarette out of his mouth. "I will," he said.

He was on his way to the library and I fell in beside him. As we crossed the square I asked how long he had been a postman.

"Six years."

"What were you before that?"

"How old do you think I am?" For a moment he almost smiled. "I was a student. I studied classics, not a subject that leads to a host of jobs."

"But why a postman? Wouldn't you rather work in a bookshop, or a library?"

"No. I like being out of doors, seeing the sky, having time to think. I'm not a great one for people, all that chitchat about weather and health and whose dog did his business in the street. I'd rather follow my own thoughts."

"You make it sound like they're something separate from you," I said.

"Don't you ever have that feeling? Some thoughts you know where they come from, but others could have come from Mars. Or Kirkwall."

At the mention of the familiar town I startled. Had I let something slip while I was unconscious? But no, Archie wore his usual intelligent frown; it was just the first example that came to mind. We had reached the library, and without waiting for an answer, he stubbed out his cigarette and swung through the door. I was tempted to follow him; to say yes, I did know what it was like to have uninvited thoughts show up in my brain. Did he have any suggestions as to how to get them to leave? But already he would be absorbed in his beloved books.

THE FOLLOWING THURSDAY I found myself, as I hardly ever did, having lunch alone with Pauline. She had come home unexpectedly, and Hannah had stayed out in the pottery to work on a set of bowls. After praising the Scotch broth, Pauline said that Archie had stopped in at the chemist's that morning. He'd heard of a job that might suit me. I sat up straight, ignoring my soup, while she explained that a woman who lived in the village of Weem needed help with her grandson.

"It sounds perfect," Pauline said. "Archie says she'll pay you twenty pounds a month and board and lodging."

But I don't need lodging, I wanted to say. "How far away is Weem?" I asked. "Do you know her?"

"Twenty minutes' walk? Half an hour? It's just across the river. You can ask Archie when he comes to supper. He knows Mrs. MacGillvary much better than I do. I'll take some tea out to Hannah." She got up quickly and I knew she was ducking my real questions: Did I have to take the job if I hated Mrs. MacGillvary? If I took the job, did I have to live there?

Leaving a note saying I'd gone for a walk, I headed up the hill with Emily. As soon as I closed the gate of the field she took off, zigzagging after rabbits, real and imaginary. I trudged behind her. So much for my good soup, for the shopping and cleaning I'd done that morning. And it was not just the housework. In the evenings the three of us read, or played cards, or watched television. Sometimes Pauline would play one of her records. "Listen to what happens to the violins here," she would say, and Hannah and I would lean forward, trying to catch her meaning. My thoughts of Mr. Sinclair, of Nell, of all that I had lost, were always present, but gradually I had allowed myself to believe that I was indispensable to their household. Now I knew I was wrong.

At the top of the field I leaned on the gate to look out across the valley. There, on the far side, was the forbidding ruin of Castle Menzies and above and behind it the crags known as Weem Rock. To the east of the castle I could see the rooftops of the village; perhaps even now I was looking at the MacGillvarys' house. I called to Emily and she bounded up, rabbitless but cheerful. We dropped down into the Birks.

That evening, over the nut loaf I had painstakingly made, Archie told us that the MacGillvarys had lived in the valley for thirty years. George was a surveyor. Marian gave piano lessons. Years ago they had adopted two children, both a disaster. The boy had been in and out of trouble with the police and had at last settled in Newcastle. As for Ginnie, the kindest thing people could say about her was that she was high-strung. Without telling her parents, she had married an Italian. Two years ago she had shown up with Robin and announced that she was moving to Rome.

"It was a lot to cope with," Archie said, "becoming parents again at their age. Then last April George had a stroke. He used to climb a hill in the morning, translate *The Odyssey* in the afternoon. Now going to the bathroom is a major expedition. I told Marian you'd come round tomorrow at four to see if you suit each other."

With each new detail my heart sank further, but Hannah and Pauline kept nodding eagerly. Only a few days ago Pauline had hugged me and said I was the little sister she'd never had. No, Hannah had said. She's my little sister. How stupid I had been to believe them. As soon as I could I retreated to bed.

THE NEXT MORNING, WHEN I took Hannah's coffee out to the pottery, she was at her wheel, a bowl rising between her hands. "If you can't stand Mrs. MacGillvary," she said, not taking her eyes off the clay, "you don't have to do this. And if it's awful, you can come back."

"I can?" I said, almost spilling the coffee. From one moment to the next the horror of the MacGillvarys faded. I didn't have to go; I could stay in my blue room and look for another job. But even as I set the coffee down, I remembered Pauline's claim that the job sounded perfect, and how pleased she and Hannah had both seemed the night before.

"Does Pauline think that too?" I said carefully. "I worry I've already trespassed on your hospitality long enough."

Hannah started to laugh, and the sides of the bowl trembled. "Sometimes you can be so Scottish, Jean. Just like Archie. You aren't a trespasser or, at this stage, even an honoured guest."

So what am I? I wanted to say, but Hannah's attention was once again focused on the wheel. Watching her hands shape the clay, I knew she would not give the answers I craved: a beloved family member, an almost sister, a dear friend. She was offering me a reprieve, I thought, not a home.

chapter twenty-seven

A<small>FTER LUNCH</small> I <small>CHANGED</small> into the blue cardigan and black corduroy trousers I had worn to visit the jeweller's shop. I wanted Mrs. MacGillvary to be talking to Gemma Hardy as well as Jean Harvey. As I crossed Wade's Bridge and walked along the road lined with poplars that led to the far side of the valley, I pictured the household: a drooling, walleyed child, a hatchet-faced woman who had driven both of her adopted children away, and, somewhere out of sight, a furious, motionless man. The house would be sepulchral and reek of cabbage and medicine. Archie had drawn me a map marking the two churches in Weem and the MacGillvarys' house behind them. It had, he explained, no name. "I used to tell George he didn't deserve to get his mail. He always said they'd managed fine without a name for a hundred and fifty years."

But when I turned up the track between the churches, the house looked neither gloomy nor nameless. The windows shone, and in the garden chrysanthemums and dahlias bloomed. My knock was answered by a woman with pale yellow hair and a gentle smile, so different from the woman of my imaginings that I asked for Mrs. MacGillvary.

"You must be Jean." She smiled again and held out her hand. "I'm Marian."

She ushered me into a sitting-room. "Robin just woke up," she said. "Make yourself at home. I'll be back in a minute."

At one end of the room, near the French windows, stood a grand piano, the gleaming lid ajar. I played middle C and then, as the note hung in the air, wondered if I should have asked permission. Quickly I moved over to the bookcase. I recognised a collected works of Shakespeare that had been in the library at Claypoole. Then my eyes fell on a novel titled *He Knew He Was Right*; I was examining the frontispiece when the door opened. Marian reappeared with a small boy in her arms, his face hidden in the crook of her neck.

"He'll be raring to go in a minute," she said. "Do you have much experience with children, Jean?"

I had been so busy with my gothic imaginings that I had failed to consider what questions Marian might ask. Now, with no time to invent, I said that my last position had been as an au pair to an eight-year-old girl. I could teach reading, writing, arithmetic, history, geography, Latin . . .

"Wonderful," said Marian. "You'll appreciate George's books. But Robin is not quite at that stage. What he needs is someone who'll play with him and teach him his letters and numbers. I want him to be ready for school next year. You'll find"—she smoothed his hair—"that he's very sensitive. He gets upset when he feels rushed, or when someone is cross."

She was assuming, I realised, that the job was mine. To my surprise, I felt a gust of relief at the prospect of clear duties, and a bed that depended on work, not favour. As Marian spoke, Robin at last raised his head. His eyes were as round and blue as one of Hannah's bowls.

"Hello, Robin," I said. "I'm Jean." I lifted my hand in a little wave. After a moment he waved back.

The following morning, when Hannah dropped me and my borrowed suitcase off, there was a note on the door: *Gone shopping. Make yourself at home.* On the kitchen table was a cup, a box of tea-bags, and a plate of biscuits. Why would anyone run away from a mother like this? I wondered. But Marian was not my mother, and as I sat at the table, surveying the geraniums on the window-sill, the cheerful plates on the settle, I could not help wondering what I was doing here, babysitting a little boy, with no chance to find Mr. Donaldson, or to study for university. My life had not merely come to a standstill; it was in reverse.

A dull thud interrupted my thoughts. I had forgotten about Mr. MacGillvary. Worried that he would suddenly lurch into the kitchen, I jumped to my feet. A second thud drove me out to the garden. Wanting to appear busy, I began to deadhead the roses. I was on the second flower-bed when a car drew up. Robin waved from the passenger seat, and Marian, as soon as she got out, apologised for not being home to welcome me. Together we carried in the groceries. She settled Robin with his toy cars on the kitchen floor and said she would show me around.

"I'm sure you've heard," she said as she led the way upstairs, "that George has been poorly. He's still convalescing."

"Archie told me."

I was bracing myself to confront a nightmare, but the man I saw when she opened the door might have been on his way to an office. He was seated in an upright armchair, dressed in a three-piece suit, a handkerchief folded in his breast pocket, his tie neatly knotted, his shoes polished. Only as I came closer did I take in his drooping mouth, his unfocused eyes. On the floor beside his chair lay two books: a paperback and a hardcover. The thuds.

"Dear, this is Archie's friend, Jean Harvey. She's going to help with Robin."

"Hello, Mr. MacGillvary. I'm looking forward to teaching your grandson."

He swayed slightly. Perhaps he was nodding.

In the hall Marian pointed out her bedroom. Robin had a little bed at the foot of hers. Then she showed me the bathroom and led me down the hall to her daughter's old room. She hadn't had time to get it ready, but she thought it would give me the most privacy. At first sight the clutter of boxes and furniture only compounded my despair, but by the time Marian called me to lunch a vase of late roses stood on the chest of drawers, the bed was made, the carpet clean, the bookshelves orderly. I had even dragged in a small desk and appropriated a couple of lamps. The result was not as pretty as my blue room, but as long as I took good care of Robin, it was mine.

MARIAN AND I HAD agreed that I would mind Robin every morning except Sunday, and on Tuesday and Thursday afternoons when she gave piano lessons. "Be sure to tell me if you need more time off," she had said. "I don't want to wear you out." On my first Thursday Robin and I were in the kitchen when Archie showed up to read to George; Robin scurried under the table with his colouring book.

"Hello, Jean. Hello, Robin," Archie said and set to making tea. He was as at home here as at his sister's. "How are things going?"

"Fine." Eager to change the subject, I asked if he and George discussed their reading.

"No, he won't talk to me, or to anyone but Marian. I think he's afraid of slurring his words. I'm not always sure how much he listens either."

"So why do you keep coming? If he doesn't speak or listen."

Kettle in one hand, teapot in the other, Archie said simply, "For Marian. I hope it's a small comfort that someone is still paying attention to the person named George. But these days I read whatever I want."

Before I could ask what that was, Robin emerged from beneath the table and flung his arms around my knees. "Garden," he implored.

．　　．　　．

THE NEXT DAY MARIAN returned from the shops pale and distraught. While Robin played with his cars, she confided that something awful had happened in Wales that morning: in a town called Aberfan a colliery tip had slid into a primary school. More than a hundred children had been buried alive. "It's just unbearable, Jean," she said. "Please try to make sure Robin doesn't hear about it."

"How dreadful," I said. In all my worst imaginings of prisons and tunnels I had never pictured the earth itself engulfing me.

Even as I tried not to think about children like Nell and Robin buried alive, a small part of me registered that Marian was treating me as an adult. But that night, after Robin was in bed, when I wanted to talk to her about the disaster, she was sequestered with George. And that was how it was night after night. When I wasn't looking after Robin I found myself lonely in a way that I had not been since Claypoole. I read, I went for walks, I made lists of birds. I tried not to complain on my visits to Honeysuckle Cottage, but those evenings were the only times I forgot my unhappiness. If I had had enough money I would have left for Oban immediately. One morning Robin kept asking to change his clothes. Finally—he was on his third sweater—I led him over to the mirror.

"What's wrong with what you're wearing?" I asked.

He pointed not at his reflection but at mine. "You look sad," he said.

He was changing his clothes, I understood, in the hope of changing my mood. I knelt down and explained that I was sad but it wasn't because of his sweater. "You can help me by eating porridge and playing with your letters."

"What's your favourite letter?"

"G."

"Why?"

"Because it's the first letter of the name of a little clam called a *Gemma gemma*. And it's a letter in your surname. And it's the first letter of *garage*."

"*Gemma gemma*," said Robin.

I was so pleased to hear my name that I picked him up and twirled him around.

That afternoon, when Archie arrived, Robin and I were kneeling beside the stove, playing tiddlywinks. For once Robin didn't retreat but kept playing while Archie put on the kettle. Was there cake?

"I made gingerbread yesterday. Can you play by yourself for five minutes?"

"Yes," said Robin, "but I'll probably win." He flipped a counter into the cup.

"Of course you should win if you play by yourself," said Archie. Usually he continued upstairs as soon as his tea was made, but today he set his books on the table and sat down. He was still wearing the dark trousers of his postman's uniform but had changed his jacket for a grey pullover.

"Who's that torturing the piano?" he said.

"Marian's bête noire, Frances Hunter. She never practises." I cut a generous slice of gingerbread for Archie, smaller ones for Robin and myself. "What are you reading today?"

"A history of Iceland. And maybe some pages from one of the sagas too."

"Iceland!"

Robin raised his head anxiously. I gave him a reassuring smile.

"Good gingerbread," said Archie. "It's an island, roughly the size of England, in the north Atlantic. It was first discovered by Irish monks in the eighth century and became an outpost of the Viking Empire."

"I know where it is," I said. "I was just wondering, why Iceland? I thought you were interested in Scottish history."

"I am. Iceland has a long connection with Scotland."

I handed him a second slice of cake and reached for one of the books. It opened to a map. While I stared at the jagged outline of the island, Archie said that the early settlers had had a law that a man could claim as much land as he could light bonfires around in a day. A woman could have as much land as a heifer could walk around in a day. I asked which was more, and he said he didn't know, but if I was interested he could loan me the books. "It would be grand," he said, "to have someone to discuss my reading with again."

That night I began to read about my native land, a country of hot springs, volcanoes, and earthquakes, where in summer the sun shone almost all night long and in winter the endless dark was lit by the aurora borealis shimmering across the sky.

ON FRIDAY HANNAH ASKED if I could come and help her wrap her latest batch of tableware. I arrived at the pottery to find her standing at her work-table, clipboard in hand, counting off the rows of plates, bowls, mugs, egg-cups, and candlesticks. "Look at you, Jean," she said, "your cheeks all rosy from walking. No one would recognise the half-dead girl Archie dragged home. I just finished checking the inventory. I'm hoping you'll help me to pack the boxes. We have to be sure not to make them too heavy."

As I reached for a sheet of newspaper and a plate, she said this was her last delivery of the year. "Pauline has agreed I can take three months to work on my sculpture. How are things at the MacGillvarys'?"

"Marian has two new pupils. And Robin drew a picture of a bird and wrote *Robin* underneath, though the *b* and the *n* were backwards. What do you mean, Pauline agreed? Don't you make what you want?"

Hannah set a bowl in the middle of the paper. "I have to pay my share of expenses. The plates and bowls bring in money—people will pay a little extra for something pretty, but no one wants the sculptures. At least not yet," she added, gesturing to a tall column in the corner. The Tower of Babel was covered with indentations modelled, she'd told me, on the ancient cup and ring marks found throughout Scotland.

It had never occurred to me that Hannah might need money, but of course houses came with bills and insurance. Pauline, despite her university degree, probably earned little more than a shop girl. Not knowing how to apologise for my myopia, I held up the bowl I was about to wrap—a lapis lazuli blue with golden leaves around the rim—and said, "This is so pretty."

"Thank you. I came across the leaves pressed between the pages of my dictionary and decided to use them as a mould. Next spring I want to do the same with flowers: daisies, daffodils, columbines. Archie said you're keeping him company in his reading." She looked up from her wrapping. "He was wondering why you aren't at university."

Before I could stop myself, I burst out that I was dying to go to university. I wanted to study mathematics, or classics. "I like both, but people say in pure maths you reach a point where you can't understand what the numbers are doing. Classics seem safer."

"Why should you suddenly not understand numbers? That sounds like something male teachers say to girls. But if you do decide on classics, I'm sure Archie would tutor you. Have you done your exams?"

"No. My school closed down before I could take them."

In all the weeks I'd known Hannah this was the most I'd told her about my past. I could see, by the way she carefully stopped watching me, that she had registered the fact. "Closed down?" she said. "I've never heard of such a thing. You can still do the exams."

"I don't see how."

"Don't wrap those." She pointed to two bowls. "I'm going to photograph them. Pauline knows the headmaster of the school. We'll get his advice."

While she went to the house to fetch her camera I turned to wrapping egg-cups. Through the window I could see Weem Rock and the hills beyond; above the tree line the sun shone on a white farmhouse. For the first time since I'd caught the ferry, I glimpsed a future that extended beyond Oban. I would never get my life with Mr. Sinclair back, but perhaps I could find a way forwards. When Hannah returned she photographed the bowl. Then, before I knew what was happening, she took a photograph of me. I was kneeling beside a box, holding a plate, gazing up at her.

THE NEXT TIME ARCHIE visited George he stayed to talk to me about our reading. The word *saga*, he explained, meant both history and story, and the authors, mostly writing in the thirteenth century, had made use of facts when it suited them. The saga we'd read was part of a group that featured skalds, or poets.

"They're not like our poets," Archie said. "They don't simply sit around composing. They go out and slay dragons and fight off rivals."

"Wordsworth and Coleridge didn't sit around," I said. "They were always tramping across the moors. And several poets fought in the First World War."

"You're right. But no dragons. Grant me that." He smiled.

In the opening pages of the saga, Thorstein, the father of the heroine, has a troubling dream. He is standing outside his house and a beautiful white swan is sitting on the ridge-pole. Somehow Thorstein knows that the swan is his daughter Helga. While he stands watching, an eagle, with black eyes and claws of iron, flies down from the mountains and perches beside her on the roof. The eagle is chattering happily to the swan when a second eagle arrives from the south. The two birds fight to the death and both fall off the roof. The swan remains alone and dejected until a third bird arrives from the west. He and the swan fly away together.

Archie commented on how effectively the dream foreshadowed the events that followed. I argued that it made it seem as if Helga had no choice; she was doomed not to marry the man she loved. "If everything's been foreseen," I said, "how can she act otherwise?"

"That's a very old question," said Archie. "Hannah would say that the problem is that Helga obeys her father. If it were up to her she would have stayed true to Gunnlaug and never have married Hrafna."

"But it's hard to overcome the customs of your country." At Claypoole, when all the girls turned on a single victim, no one had dared to intervene. "I think the real problem is Gunnlaug," I went on. "He promises to return in three years to marry Helga, but he's so taken up with his success at the English court that he can't be bothered. He's not worthy of her, yet he causes all this trouble."

"'Things learned young last longest,'" quoted Archie. "I hope not." A tremor passed over him, and I wondered again what lay behind his choice to be a rural postman.

"Me too," I said. We turned to other aspects of the story.

Later, as Archie was buttoning his jacket, he remarked that many Icelanders could trace their family back a thousand years. "Hannah and I don't even know the name of our great-grandfather." He presented me with our next reading project: *Njal's Saga.*

For the rest of the evening, I kept thinking about Archie's parting comment. My uncle had never mentioned my father's family, but perhaps there were still people in Iceland who were in some way related to me, and who knew it. Perhaps even now my grandparents were floating in a hot spring, wondering about their Scottish granddaughter.

.　　.　　.

HANNAH WAS AS GOOD as her word. She spoke to Pauline, and Pauline spoke to the headmaster. He agreed to let me sit the preliminary exams in February and the Highers in May, and to lend me the necessary textbooks for English, algebra, trigonometry, history, Latin, and French. Archie volunteered to coach me in Latin, and Pauline offered to lend me her Shakespeare. So my future, for the next few months, became clear. I would stay in Aberfeldy until May. Then I would go in search of Mr. Donaldson. Between Robin and my studies, my days were full. Only at Marian's urging—you've been cooped up for weeks—did I decide one bright, cold Sunday in December to walk up the hill to the white farmhouse I had seen from the pottery window. With a couple of sandwiches in a knapsack, I followed the path up through the beech trees to the little spring at the foot of Weem Rock. According to Hannah, St. David's Well had long been a resting place for travellers, perhaps a sacred site. I knelt down to dip my hand in the clear, cold water and watched the leaves at the bottom stir.

From the well the path traversed the hillside, climbing steadily. Soon the beeches gave way to conifers and birches. These too were beginning to thin when I caught sight of a stone house set back from the path. The roof had fallen in but the walls were intact. Who had lived in such a lonely place, I wondered, and why were all the windows barred? The house looked too grand to be a shepherd's cottage. Hoping to discover some relic of the occupants, I stepped inside, but there was only a rusty saucepan and a couple of empty tins buried in the nettles. On the hearthstone lay a small pile of mossy bones. Some animal—a sheep or a fox—had crawled in here to die. If I had found a ruined house near Ballinluig, I thought, that might have been me. I hurried back to the path.

Another hundred yards brought me out of the woods to a field of sheep. I sat on a fallen tree to eat my sandwiches. Nearby a crow was strutting back and forth. Tomorrow, I thought, I would take Robin to the library to look for a bird book. When the crow came close, I threw him a piece of bread. Mistaking my gesture, he took wing. As I followed his flight, I saw that on all sides leaden clouds were massing on the hilltops. Even as I took in that the day had changed, I heard a pattering sound, as if thousands of little feet were running over the hillside. The wind sprang up and pellets of hail the size of barley stung my face. I ran to shelter beneath the nearest pine tree. The air was a commotion of white. Suddenly, out of the whiteness, I heard a voice, shouting.

"Mr. Sinclair," I shouted back.

I stared at the driving hail, dumbfounded. All the miles, all the hours, all my efforts had not yet driven him out of my brain.

Within ten minutes the sky was clear and the hail was already melting into the grass, but I decided to give up on the farmhouse and go home. I was again on the path, passing the ruined house, when I heard the solid tramp of someone approaching at a good pace. Archie came into view, striding along with a shepherd's crook much like the one Seamus had carried. His dark green jacket hung open, and a red tartan scarf was wrapped jauntily around his neck. He could have been a Roman centurion, I thought, conquering Britain at four miles an hour. When he caught sight of me, he neither waved nor smiled but somehow it was clear he was pleased.

"Jean," he said. He stopped a few yards away and stubbed out his cigarette. "Did the hail get you?"

It was not his fault, I thought, that he didn't know my name. "I sheltered under a tree. One minute the sun was shining; the next I couldn't see across the field."

"Hill weather. You never know what it will do. Did you hear me shouting to Thor? Urging him on." He waved his crook with mock ferocity.

"I thought I heard something. There's a ruined house back there."

"It belonged to the Menzies family. The story goes that they built it for one of their daughters, who went mad. She lived up here with her minder. It was a nice house, quite civilised except for the bars at the windows."

"Did they visit her?"

"What would be the point of putting her halfway up a hill if they were going to visit? No, I think it was a case of out of sight out of mind. That was how they dealt with undesirable relatives in those days."

"Why did she go mad?"

He cocked his head. "She's caught your interest, has she, the mad-woman on the hillside? I'm afraid we know almost nothing more about her. This was well before the First World War. George claimed her fiancé jilted her at the altar, but that's just local gossip."

He began to ask about my Latin homework, but all I wanted was to be alone with my thoughts. "I have to go," I said. As I stepped forward, Archie's eyebrows rose. Did he think I was about to hit him? Embrace him? At the last moment he stepped aside and I hurried past.

The trees were still dripping from the hailstorm, and several times on the muddy path I almost fell. If anyone had done the jilting it was I. But Mr. Sinclair would not go mad. He had discovered, long ago, what would topple his sturdy mind. Not a woman but a small, dark space. From under my feet a pheasant started up with a whir of wings, barely clearing the bracken. Unlike Helga, I thought, I did have a choice. I could try to find Mr. Sinclair, and unless he had radically altered his life, that would not be hard. Or I could stop looking for him in phone calls and hailstorms. Why had I left if I was going to carry him with me every step of the way? When I reached St. David's Well again I knelt down and put my right hand in the water. Silently I vowed to forget him. And then, to make the oath more binding, I said the words aloud.

"By this sacred place I vow to forget Mr. Sinclair."

FOR CHRISTMAS, ARCHIE GAVE me a history of the Vikings and at midnight on New Year's Eve he kissed my cheek and announced that he really was giving up smoking. A few days later I was playing cards with Hannah and Pauline after our weekly supper when Pauline remarked that Archie seemed to spend all his time at the MacGillvarys' nowadays.

"And we know why," said Hannah with a nod in my direction.

"We're reading about Iceland," I protested. "And he helps with my Latin. It has nothing to do with me."

Hannah made a shushing motion and put down a jack and a queen. "We'd be glad if it did. I don't like to see Archie turning into a crusty old bachelor."

"Isn't this the pot calling the kettle black?" I said. "You're always complaining about people who think a woman can't manage without a man. Why should it be different the other way round?"

"Quite right," said Pauline. "Of course it isn't different, but the people we love are different. Archie is Hannah's beloved brother. We want him to have companionship."

I discarded a nine and ten of clubs. "Archie ought to have been a skald," I said lightly. "An Icelandic poet, travelling the world and making poems."

"It's funny the two of you being so interested in Iceland," said Hannah. "If I were going to study another country I'd want to go south, to the Mediterranean. Sunshine."

"And olives," added Pauline.

"In Iceland," I said, "the sun hardly sets in summer, and there are huge flocks of Arctic terns, and geysers, and hot springs. They're much more civilised than we are. They were writing the sagas when we were in the Dark Ages."

"You'll have to go there one of these days," said Hannah.

Fumbling my cards, I said I couldn't play.

The moon was out and I insisted that I did not need a lift back to Weem. I had made the journey so many times that often I scarcely noticed the landmarks, but tonight my footsteps echoed in the empty streets, and as I approached Wade's Bridge the river glinted in the moonlight. I had not thought of Archie, with his bachelor routines, as being susceptible to female company, and even if I had, I would not have thought of myself as that company. All those feelings had come to an end as I sat in the gloom of Maes Howe listening to Mr. Sinclair. Every month I was surprised when my body declared its secret life. And there was no evidence that Archie found me attractive. His kiss on New Year's Eve had been less warm than Hannah's, and when we talked it was mostly about our reading. I knew what passion was, and this was not passion. If he was interested in me it was only because he had confused my enthusiasm for Iceland with something else.

Beside the road the stiff-branched poplars stirred in the breeze. Avoiding Archie was not, given my friendship with Hannah and Pauline, and his with George, an option. What I must do, I thought, was tell the truth: that I needed to study for my exams. We would translate Latin in a businesslike way, but there would be no more lively discussions of romantic sagas.

I let myself into the house and climbed the stairs. In the upstairs hall a low murmur of voices stopped me. Perhaps Marian and Robin were discussing a dream. No, the voices came from George's room. He had never spoken to me or, as far as I knew, to Robin, but now, alongside Marian's light musical tones, I heard a darker, deeper voice.

chapter twenty-eight

ROBIN'S BIRTHDAY WAS THE last Saturday in January. Together we iced the cake I had baked and wrote *Happy Birthday Robin* on top. Cautiously he pushed five red candles into the icing. Marian had invited the neighbours with children close to his age, and while the grown-ups chatted, I organised Robin and his guests to play hunt the thimble and pin the tail on the donkey. The first he enjoyed, but at the sight of the blindfold for the second he fled under the nearest table and had to be coaxed out again. We had just sung "Happy Birthday" when Archie arrived. He apologised for being late and, with a small bow, handed Robin a package. Robin carried it over to where I sat near the window.

Nell had opened presents gleefully, flinging paper into the air, but Robin insisted that we peel back each piece of Sellotape and carefully unfold the brown paper. Inside was a slender, homemade book, the pages sewn together. On the cover was a drawing of Wade's Bridge with a boy standing on the parapet and the words *Robin's History of Aberfeldy and Weem*. Archie was talking to Marian, but I saw him glance over, waiting for Robin's reaction, and for mine.

"Archie made a book for you," I said. "Look. It's all about your home."

Inside the book each double page had a picture on one side—the Black Watch Memorial, the town square, the Birks, the inn where Bonnie Prince Charlie might have stayed—and on the other a little story.

"Pretty," said Robin, pointing to the picture of the Birks. Robert Burns sat beneath the trees, pen poised over a notebook.

"It is pretty," I said. "I'll read it to you before bed."

The other adults insisted on seeing, and the booklet was passed around, to much admiration. Archie explained that Hannah had helped him with the pictures. "That's you," he said to Robin, pointing to the boy on the bridge, "though of course you must never climb up on the parapet."

"I won't," Robin promised fervently.

Later, after the guests had gone and we were washing up, Marian remarked that the book must have taken Archie weeks. "Such a formal man," she added, "but he has a warm heart." I wondered if she too thought that Archie had designs on me.

That evening I drew up a plan of study for the next month. I had always felt superior to the girls at Claypoole who couldn't keep straight Iago and Othello, a hypotenuse and a diagonal. All the books I'd read, all the lessons I'd sat through, were still waiting, I was sure, in some unvisited corner of my brain. But the last few weeks had shown me how much I'd forgotten. I would have to practise writing essays, doing translations, memorising the complexities of nineteenth-century history. The only subjects that came back effortlessly were algebra and trigonometry. Looking over my list of dates and goals, it occurred to me, for the first time, that I might sit the exams and fail.

The next morning as I read about the three pigs, Robin protested that I was going too fast. I began again. Again he said, "Too fast, Jean."

"I'm sorry. I'm worried about my exams."

"What's an exam?" He placed a small hand on my knee.

"You have to answer questions about something, say, English history, in a certain period of time, and you only have one chance to give the right answer."

"Horrid," he said. "Let me help."

"I wish you could, but you're too young."

"No, we can read your books. I want to."

Beneath his wide-eyed gaze I considered his suggestion. Surely, I thought, it would do no harm if instead of reading about pigs and rabbits we read about Gladstone and Disraeli. If we made charts and pictures of historical events. If we made lists of vocabulary words for French and Latin. Marian, when I explained my plan, said fine but no violence. And so our mornings began to include my studies. While he understood almost nothing, Robin turned out to be unexpectedly helpful. "That's different from last time," he would say, when I recited the dates for the repeal of the Corn Laws or conjugated a verb, and he was almost always right.

At Pauline's suggestion I had asked the headmaster of the school if I could sit in on the Form V classes during my free afternoons, and so I became a pupil again. The other girls and boys, only a year or two younger than me, often seemed more childish than Robin, but I was glad to have the teachers' guidance. One Monday, after Latin, I was sheltering from a sudden shower with two of the girls: Joan and Margaret. As we lingered in the doorway, trying to decide if the rain was lessening, Joan said wasn't I the girl the postman had found half-dead in a ditch. I said I was and repeated, for only the second or third time, the story about my aunt in Inverness, and getting ill on the bus.

"And the lezzies took you in," said Margaret.

"I work for Mrs. MacGillvary." I scarcely knew what I was saying.

"The lesbians," said Joan, gleefully. "The dykes."

"My dad says Hannah ought to have been a bloke," said Margaret.

I walked blindly into the rain. It was none of my business. It made no difference. But once again I had failed to understand the people around me. At Claypoole there had been crushes between girls, but I hadn't thought of these feelings as having a place in the adult world. I had never said the word *lesbian*, seldom seen it written. Just down the road from Honeysuckle Cottage was a bungalow shared by two women; the flat above the chemist's was shared by two girls. Were all these women in love? A tractor was grinding towards me and I stepped onto the verge to avoid being splashed. As I started walking again, I recalled those evenings of television and music, when I had felt myself so much a part of their household, and all along they had been secretly wishing me gone so that they could get into one of those double beds and put their arms around each other.

The next day, going over my Virgil translation with Archie, I kept making mistakes. Finally he said, "Jean, you knew the subjunctive last week."

"I'm sorry. Could we take a break?"

He nodded and said why didn't he make us some hot chocolate. By the time he returned with two steaming mugs I had realised that I couldn't ignore my new knowledge. As he handed me a mug and sat back down, I asked how long Hannah and Pauline had been friends.

"I couldn't say. Eight years? Ten? They met at university. Did I put in enough sugar?"

"Just right. At school yesterday a couple of girls were talking about them."

Archie held his mug chest-high between both hands and regarded me steadily. "There's a story," he said, "about Queen Victoria that won't be on your exams. Her ministers wanted to make homosexuality illegal for both men and women, but no one knew how to explain to the queen that some women liked each other, and so the law was passed only against men. Most of our neighbours are probably like Queen Victoria. That doesn't stop them from being fond of Hannah and Pauline."

"But—" I stopped, not knowing what I wanted to say.

Archie raised his chin. "You're not going to tell me that, after all they've done for you, you disapprove of my sister and her beloved?"

"No. Of course not. I just feel so stupid. There I was, living in their house, trying to be the ideal guest, with no notion that they shared a room."

"Well, it's not my job to speak for two eloquent women. Three," he added with a nod at me. "But they had long debates. Hannah wanted to tell you. Pauline worried it would put you in a difficult situation."

"Did you ask Marian to give me a job?"

He inclined his head. "You were working so hard to make a home for yourself, and they didn't know how to tell you that they needed their privacy. Then you spoke to me in the square, and the next day, when I came to read to George, Robin was hiding under the table."

"So you saved my life twice."

"I wouldn't say that. Hannah will tell you I'm thick as a brick when it comes to humans. But that first day when I carried you to the van you kept begging me not to go to the police." He gestured around the room. "This seemed better."

"This is better." I looked at him in his armchair, his long legs stretched out before him, his long narrow feet in their thick green socks. "Do you think," I said, "one can ever know another person?"

I meant the question in a very particular sense, but Archie wriggled his toes at the opportunity to wax philosophical. "For the most part," he said, "I'm not bothered about whether I know other people. What worries me is do I know myself?" Two philosophers, he went on, one French, one Scottish, had pursued this question. René Descartes claimed that a person was a *res cogitans*, a thing that thinks. David Hume had a different view. When he went looking for a self he found nothing there, just a mass of sense impressions.

Finally I interrupted. "Please," I said, "don't tell Hannah and Pauline about the girls at the school. Can we say that I guessed and asked you?"

"We can," said Archie.

It seemed oddly fitting that, as he left, the first snow was falling. In the morning I woke to find the muddy fields and leafless trees white and pristine. Robin and I made a snowman in the garden with a carrot for a nose and currants for eyes. Later we went tobogganing by the river, and he proved surprisingly fearless. "Another turn, another turn," he kept saying. That evening, I made my way to Honeysuckle Cottage. As soon as the three of us sat down to supper, I said, looking from Pauline to Hannah, that I owed them an apology. "I'm sorry you felt you had to keep a secret in your own home."

"Thank you," said Pauline, bobbing her head.

"We appreciate your saying that, Jean," said Hannah.

I had thought they might talk about when they understood their feelings for each other, what it was like to live in a town with few hiding places. Instead Pauline launched into a story about a salesman who'd come into the chemist's that day, then Hannah commented on the kale we were eating; our conversation followed its usual orbits. But when Hannah got up to fetch dessert she placed her hand on Pauline's shoulder, a gesture I had seen her make dozens of times, and smiled at me.

THE SNOW STAYED FOR a week and melted the day the preliminary exams began. Marian had rearranged her pupils so that I had the necessary mornings and afternoons free, and she and Robin helped with last-minute studying. When the results came, and I turned out to have got five As, they both applauded. Under the headmaster's supervision, I wrote to Edinburgh, Glasgow, Aberdeen, and St. Andrews universities, asking to be considered for late admission in mathematics, and received provisional acceptances from Edinburgh and Aberdeen.

Snowdrops gave way to catkins, catkins to pussy willow; aconites sprang up in the garden, and crocuses, scilla, and forsythia soon followed. The geese began to fly north. On my walks I saw oystercatchers and lapwings. Soon the swallows would return. I studied. I took care of Robin. I visited Pauline and Hannah. I ignored the voices that came from George's room. When Archie invited me for a walk, or once a drink, I found a reason, usually Robin, to refuse.

I was doing a good job, I thought, of keeping everything on an even keel when one Saturday afternoon Hannah invited me to accompany her to Pitlochry. My dread of the town had receded, and I accepted with alacrity. We loaded the car with fruit bowls and drove out of Aberfeldy past the caravan site and the distillery. In the village of Strathtay, Hannah showed me the house where Archie had rooms. A few miles farther on, we had just passed a field of cows when she pointed to an oak tree beside the road. "That's where Archie found you."

The tree, with its broad trunk and still dead leaves, was gone in an instant, but I felt an odd twinge at seeing the place where I had almost died.

The shop that sold Hannah's pottery turned out to be opposite Newholme Avenue, the site of my false address. I helped her to carry in the bowls and said I'd go for a walk while she talked to the manager. As I passed the milk bar and the electrical shop, I was struck by the difference having money made. I could stroll into any one of these establishments and, even if I didn't make a purchase, be treated politely. I turned up the road to the church. I was gazing across the grassy knoll at the faded red door when I heard a tapping sound. The elderly man with the little white dog was approaching.

"Excuse me," I said. "Do you by any chance know where the minister lives?"

"Och, aye, lassie. See the house with the black gate." He raised his walking stick to clarify my destination.

Before I could reconsider, I walked over, opened the gate, and knocked on the door. Almost immediately it was flung open by a freckle-faced girl only a little older than Nell. When I asked for the minister, she called over her shoulder, "Dad. Someone wants you," and ran off down the corridor.

A man of about thirty, fair skinned, slender, the opposite of Mr. Waugh, appeared. His half-moon glasses were perched on the end of his nose and in one hand he held a pen. "Good afternoon," he said with a kindly smile. "Would you like to come in?"

"Last October I sought sanctuary in your church and someone took my suitcase."

"Oh," he said, removing his glasses altogether. "You're the girl who slept in the church. I'm sorry that you didn't knock on my door then."

"I didn't think of it. Or if I did, I was afraid you'd be angry."

His eyes crinkled. "My dear, almost everyone, including my wife, would tell you that my sermons are dull as ditch water, but I've never turned away anyone in need. I'm glad to meet you at last. Can I offer you a cup of tea?"

He reminded me so piercingly of my uncle that I could barely speak. "Someone's waiting for me," I managed.

"Well, let me get your suitcase. I have it tucked away in my study."

As he headed down the corridor, I thought how much of my suffering—the gloomy church, the hotel managers, the odious jeweller, the meat paste—had been unnecessary. All I had had to do was knock on this door.

In a couple of minutes he returned, carrying my case. "Here you are." He gazed at me earnestly. "I don't mean to pry, but the police have you listed as a missing person, which means that someone is suffering because of your absence. May I have your permission, Miss Hardy, to tell them that I've seen you and that you're all right?"

My brain seethed with thoughts I couldn't pursue. I had my possessions back. Mr. Sinclair was searching for me. My exams were only a few weeks away. This kind man would be disappointed if I refused him. Behind us the church bell began to chime.

"You can tell the police I'm all right," I said. "But they shouldn't waste their time looking for me."

"I understand." He held out his hand and, when I raised mine, clasped it briefly in both of his. "Good luck," he said. "Fight the good fight."

I hurried down the street, my suitcase, heavier than I remembered, banging against my legs. Hannah was leaning against the car, eating an apple. "Have you been shopping?" she said.

"A friend was keeping it for me."

"A friend? I thought you had no friends. Or none we're allowed to know about." She stood up and hurled the apple core in the direction of the railway line. "What's going on? Are you thinking of leaving?"

"No," I said. "Not really."

"I note the hint of qualification." She stepped forward and seized my shoulders. "Whatever you do, Jean"—she aimed her blue eyes and sharp chin at me—"don't disappear on us, like you did the last people you lived with." She gave me a little shake. "You owe us more than that. Promise."

"I promise."

As we drove south, effortlessly covering the distance I had travelled so painfully, Hannah told me that the manager of the shop had offered her twice as much display space as last summer. "I'll have to come up with more designs, but I might actually make some money."

I said great and wonderful. Then I remembered to ask about her sculptures, and she said she was working on a piece inspired by Mary, Queen of Scots. By the time we reached Weem, she seemed to have forgiven me.

At the MacGillvarys' I carried in my suitcase, braced for more questions, but the chorus of "Old MacDonald" was coming from the sitting-room. In my room I closed the door and lifted the case, green, scuffed, familiar, onto the bed. As I raised the lid, I held my breath. On top of my folded clothes lay a sheet of paper:

Dear Miss Hardy, we're here if you need us.

Followed by the minister's name, address, and phone number. Before I did anything else I copied the details into my notebook and folded the paper into my purse. Anything, I had learned, could be lost.

After all these months I had almost forgotten the contents of the case. Now each item came back to me freighted with memory. Here were my walking shoes, my new nightdress, the blouse I had been wearing the first evening I met Mr. Sinclair, the two skirts I'd worn to church so often. Safe between the pages of my guide to Scottish birds were my photographs: my uncle alone and with my mother at the Botanical Gardens. As I gazed at them, glad to be reunited, it occurred to me for the first time that I had no photograph of my father. Indeed I didn't even know his name.

I hung up my clothes and slipped the case under my bed, trying to ignore the heavy sock at the bottom. If I discovered the meteorite, I might have to throw it away.

THE EXAMS WERE FAST approaching, and I needed every spare hour to study, but the return of some of my possessions had awakened a passionate longing. I could not stop thinking about my last night at Yew

House and the box I'd barely glimpsed. One afternoon when Marian was giving lessons and Robin was taking a nap, I rang directory enquiries and asked for a Mr. Donaldson in Oban. When I said I had neither a first name nor an address, the operator gave me two numbers. I tried both and got two puzzled men; neither had ever been a teacher. Then I rang the operator again and asked for a Miss Donaldson. This time there was only one number. The woman who answered said she didn't think she had a brother.

The next day when I went into Aberfeldy the bus for Perth was standing outside the cinema. I went over and asked the driver how to get to Oban. He said I would have to go via Perth and wrote down the schedule. At supper that night I told Marian that I needed to visit a friend. Could she manage without me this weekend?

"Of course. You've been working so hard, Jean. Friday is no problem, and Robin can play quietly while I give lessons on Saturday."

The only other person I had to tell was Archie—we always studied after school on Friday—and for once I could see him struggling not to question me: Who was this mysterious friend? By way of reassurance I said I'd like to translate the Catullus on Monday.

I borrowed an overnight bag from Marian, packed my Latin and algebra textbooks, and caught the first bus to Perth, and then another bus to Oban. Mindful of my last journey, I put half my money in my pocket with Marian's phone number and safety-pinned it shut, and I kept my bag closed at all times. As we wound past hills and lochs, I tried to make a plan. Oban was not, I thought, much bigger than Aberfeldy. I could enquire at the library, if there was one. Shops. Pubs. Surely in an hour or two I could canvass the town. Then, of course, even if I found his sister—her name, I suddenly recalled, was Isobel— there was still the task of finding Mr. Donaldson. He might be living in Cornwall, or Timbuctoo.

When I got off the bus the first thing I noticed was the smell of the sea; the next that a building resembling the Colosseum overlooked the town. Could the Romans have come this far north and built something so splendid? But at the first shop I went into, a bakery, a woman told me that McCaig's Tower was a nineteenth-century folly. She herself was from Mallaig and didn't know an Isobel Donaldson. In the sixth shop I tried, a butcher's, the man behind the counter wiped his hands on his bloodstained apron and said, "That will be Isobel Bailey, will it not?"

"That's right," said the woman he'd just served. "She used to be a Donaldson."

Twenty minutes later their directions brought me to a modest bungalow. Standing at the gate, staring at the grape hyacinth that lined the path to the front door, I was aware of how much I had to gain or lose. In Nell's company I had gradually learned to forgive the two huge errors of my life: not going skating with my uncle; writing a letter to Mr. Donaldson. But there was no reason for Isobel Bailey to forgive me, if indeed she was even at home. At last I walked up the path and rang the bell. My luck held. The door opened to reveal a white-haired woman, ramrod straight in her tweed skirt and blue pullover. Yes, she acknowledged stiffly, she was Isobel Bailey.

I introduced myself as Jean Harvey, a former pupil of Mr. Donaldson's. I was passing through Oban and had remembered him saying he came from this part of the world. "He was so helpful to me. I'd like to thank him."

She neither smiled nor frowned but did something in between and asked if I had time for a cup of tea. She showed me to the living-room and went to put on the kettle. As I sat in one of the armchairs, I noticed an ashtray on the table. I pictured Mr. Donaldson clicking his yellow teeth.

Isobel returned with tea and shortbread. I accepted both and, in response to her questions, said I'd come from Aberfeldy and that the journey had been fine.

"Which of Henry's schools were you at?"

"Strathmuir. I left when I was ten. Does he live nearby?"

"In a sense." Isobel's teaspoon clinked against her cup.

"Is he dead?" I whispered. Now I could never apologise, except to a stone in a churchyard.

"Henry might say yes but no, he's in an old-age home. Most of the time he doesn't know me, or even the nurses he sees every day." She explained that he'd lived with her and her husband until, finally, they couldn't manage. "He didn't know the difference between day and night. We'd wake up at two in the morning and he'd be frying an egg, getting ready to go for a walk. They take good care of him at Bonnyview, and he doesn't seem to mind it. I'm sorry you've come all this way for nothing."

"But he was such a good teacher, and he wasn't old." Even as I spoke, I recalled how on some days Mr. Donaldson had been so vigilant, while on others he had simply stared out of the window.

"You're kind to say so," said Isobel. "A slip of a lass like you, everyone over twenty-five must seem old. Do you not know what happened?"

When I shook my head, she set her tea-cup down decisively. "Henry is the only brother I have, but it's no secret that he didn't always act in his own best interests. He was just a wee bit too fond of his dram. That was how he came to your school, which, not to be rude"—she gave me a little smile—"was a step down for him. But he was making the best of it. He'd joined the village curling club, found a foursome for bridge.

"Then there was some muddle about a girl. He never would say exactly what happened. He was dismissed with no references and moved in with Findlay and me. We were glad to have him, but the whole thing preyed on him, especially when he'd had a drop to drink. I used to come into the kitchen and find him chatting away to himself."

Isobel looked over at me, her eyes suddenly intent. "I'd swear on the graves of our parents that Henry was innocent. He regarded teaching as a sacred duty. He would never have laid a hand on one of his pupils. Or on any child. I used to hope that wretched girl would come to her senses and admit she'd made the whole thing up. Maybe he'd given her a bad mark and she wanted revenge? But whatever her reasons she ruined my brother's life. No one would give him a job. He picked up a bit of tutoring. Eventually even that was too much for him."

"What an awful story," I said. My voice came out high and squeaky.

"Yes," said Isobel, suddenly matter-of-fact again. She helped herself to another piece of shortbread. "I can't help thinking he'd still be fine if he'd been able to go on teaching, but the doctor says that's daft. His brain is deteriorating. It's not to do with jobs, or moods. Our dad was going that way when he died of pneumonia."

As she spoke, a black cat appeared around the corner of her arm-chair and came over to inspect me. "What beautiful eyes she has," I said, offering my hand.

"He. Alfred was Henry's cat. Sometimes I take him with me to Bonnyview. He seems to cheer Henry up."

"Could I visit him? For five minutes?"

"He won't have a clue who you are."

"I'd just like to say thank you. You know how it is when you're young. You never thank anyone." I tried not to sound desperate. Alfred, obligingly, offered his belly.

"Och, well, I suppose it can't do any harm. Visiting hours are from two to four. You've missed today, but you could pop in tomorrow. In fact, if I know you're going, Findlay and I might skip a Saturday and get caught up in the garden."

"I'll definitely go." With a final pat to Alfred, I stood up. "I don't suppose you have a picture of Mr. Donaldson. It's so long since I saw him."

"Even if you remembered him perfectly you might not recognise him." She left the room and returned with a framed photograph of herself, Mr. Donaldson, and a man I guessed was her husband, smartly dressed, standing in the sunlight beside an oak tree. "This was sports day at Henry's school in Edinburgh. His house won three cups, and all the parents were coming up to thank him. Remember this when you see him tomorrow."

I promised I would. She told me how to find Bonnyview and wrote down the name and address. On the doorstep she said, "Even if Henry doesn't know you from Adam I'm glad you came. Especially because you were at that school where everything went wrong. Did you know the girl who accused him?"

"No," I said, shaking my head, moving down the path. "She must have been in a different form."

I asked about rooms in three small hotels and took one in the third and cheapest. Sitting on the bed with its cheap slippery sheets, trying to focus on my Latin textbook, I went over and over the conversation with Isobel. I had longed to tell her that I was the wretched girl but that the real culprit was my aunt. But tomorrow I would have the chance to tell Mr. Donaldson. I pictured him saying he forgave me, leading me to a small room, pointing to my box tucked away on a shelf. And then, as I pored over its contents, I would know, beyond doubt, that I had once been someone's daughter.

BONNYVIEW WAS A LARGE red sandstone house that might, at first glance, have been mistaken for the home of a prosperous family. At second glance the bars at the windows, the lack of curtains, the high stone wall around the garden and the locked gate, all suggested an institution. I had arrived at one-thirty and, after peering through the gate and seeing no one, I resigned myself to leaning against the wall, holding the bunch of daffodils I had brought, my bag at my feet. No other visitors joined me, and I was still standing there alone when, at exactly two o'clock, a stout elderly man, wearing a uniform not unlike Archie's, opened the gate.

"You're very punctual," he said. "Those may not be allowed."

"The daffodils? Why not? I brought them for Mr. Donaldson."

"Some of the patients eat them. They'll tell you inside if they're okay."

As I walked up to the black door I felt as if I were ten years old again. On a small desk in the hall were a bell and a notice saying VISITORS RING BELL. It emitted a forlorn tinkle. While I waited I studied the pictures of boats that hung around the room. I was examining a schooner when I heard footsteps and turned to see a nurse with a broad, dimpled face approaching.

"Sorry to keep you waiting. Who are you here to see?"

"Henry Donaldson."

After ascertaining that I didn't know where the lounge was, she told me to follow her. As I did, down first one corridor, then another, I confessed that I wasn't sure I would recognise Mr. Donaldson.

"I'll introduce you," she said. "Are you one of his former pupils?"

"How did you know?"

"Nurse's intuition. When I was a girl he taught for a year at the high school. He had a reputation for being able to get anyone through their exams, until I came along. Here we are."

The large glassed-in room, an addition to the old house, looked onto the garden. Seated singly or in small groups, a couple of dozen elderly men and women were reading, knitting, talking, dozing. The nurse led me over to a man seated alone at a small table, laying out rows of cards.

"Henry," she said, "you have a visitor. Say hello."

"Hello." He did not look up from his cards.

"Good luck. Here, let me take those. Look, Henry," she said, raising her voice. "She brought you some lovely daffs. I'll put them in a vase in the dining-room."

"Couldn't they go in his room?"

She shook her head. "He'll see them at supper."

With a pat to my shoulder, she was gone. I was left alone with Mr. Donaldson. Still he did not raise his eyes from the cards. Watching his hands, I saw on the little finger of his left hand a gold ring. All at once I recalled how sometimes, when he was writing on the blackboard, the ring had sent a flash of light darting around the classroom.

"Mr. Donaldson," I said. "I'm sorry I've taken so long to come and see you. I couldn't get here before." He put a queen of hearts on a three of clubs, then added a seven of spades. "I'm terribly sorry that I got you in trouble."

Isobel was right. I would not have recognised him, not because he was stooped and gaunt but because his affect was so changed. Suddenly he spoke, and I saw that his yellow teeth were just the same. "Open your books to page fifty-three," he said. "We're going to practise long division."

I stared at him uncertainly. He had not even glanced at me and his hands were still moving over the cards, but it was the first hint that perhaps, dimly, he recognised me. I sat down opposite him, and took out my algebra book and my notebook. I found the chapter I'd been studying and set the open book on the table beside the cards.

"The first problem is about square roots," I said. "I don't understand it, sir."

His hands paused. He looked at the book, looked again, then gathered the cards into a deck and slipped them into his pocket. "Let me see." He read over the problem silently and began to explain it, step by step. I wrote in my notebook. At last he sounded like the man I remembered. "Well done," he said genially when we had completed the problem.

"Mr. Donaldson," I said, "I'm Gemma Hardy. I'm the girl who got you fired."

"Gemma Hardy." He had said the words "square root" with more interest.

I reached out and took his hand, the one with the gold ring. Behind his smudged glasses, I glimpsed his red-rimmed eyes. "I have to go soon," he volunteered. "I'm going to Fort William today."

I understood that the journey was imaginary but I saw my chance. "I'll help you get ready. Let's go to your room. You'll need a coat and scarf." Still holding his hand, I urged him to his feet. We began to make our way across the lounge. Mr. Donaldson spoke to no one and I followed his example, only apologising when he brushed someone's newspaper.

We were in the corridor when we met another nurse, a younger woman pushing a trolley. "Henry," she said, "where are you off to?"

"We're just fetching a book from his room," I offered. "He's been helping me with a couple of maths problems." I flourished my textbook.

"Oh, that's nice. He's in room eight, second corridor on the left."

Now that I knew where we were going, I urged Henry along more purposefully. The room would not be large. Surely if my box were there, I would find it. The door of number eight stood open. Inside, it looked heartbreakingly like a dormitory at Claypoole—three single beds, three bedside tables, three chests of drawers—but the bars at the windows spoke to a grimmer purpose. In one corner was a cupboard.

"Which is your bed?" I said.

Mr. Donaldson sank down on the one in the middle. He seemed suddenly tired by the prospect of his nonexistent journey. I bent down to check the bedside table, and then under the bed. "Which is your chest of drawers?" I asked, and he pointed to the one nearest the window. All along I had pictured the box just as it had been when I handed it over years ago. Now it occurred to me that he might have transferred the contents, perhaps to several large envelopes. I searched the drawers, hoping for the crackle of papers amid the neat stacks of underwear and socks, pullovers and shirts. Then I turned to the cupboard, which was divided into three sections.

While I was doing all this Mr. Donaldson sat vacantly on the bed. I returned at last from my fruitless search. His brain was the one place I couldn't open.

"Do you know who I am?" I said.

"The cleaner?"

"No, I'm Gemma Hardy, one of your pupils. Years ago I gave you a box to take care of. Do you know where it is?"

"You can plot square roots on a graph," he said. "The curve flattens as the numbers get higher. They get farther and farther apart."

"Please, this is very, very important." Like the nurse, I realised, I was raising my voice, as if volume might reach him when all else failed. I knelt down in front of him, putting my hands on his bony knees. After all these years I had found him, and yet almost every trace of the person I remembered was gone.

Mr. Donaldson looked down at me in a puzzled way. "Did you drop something?"

"I'm asking you a question."

"I used to ask a lot of questions. That's part of being a teacher."

"You were a very good teacher. You helped lots and lots of people. Now, please, can you answer just one question for me."

"You have to be patient," he said. "Sometimes it takes me a while to find the answers."

Slowly, clearly, I explained again who I was and about my box. Then I stayed kneeling, willing him to understand, to remember, to answer. At last, in a low voice, he began to speak.

"You were my downfall. Or to be exact that woman who claimed to be your aunt was. I was no match for her innuendoes. If you'd been a boy maybe it would have been different." He sighed. "Or maybe not. I kept your box and when I was booted out, I brought it with me. Not the box, the contents. I kept them in my room at my sister's, with my books." He glanced around. "They wouldn't let me bring my protractor and compass here, not even my slide rule."

"Do you remember what was in the box when you emptied it?"

"So many questions. You should be a teacher. There were some photographs, a recipe for fish pie—it sounded nice—a diary, bundles of letters, a couple of shells, a piece of rope tied in a knot, some dried flowers. I'm afraid that the shells may have got broken."

"That doesn't matter. Do you forgive me?"

"I do. None of this would have happened if I'd been a more competent adult. Even at—"

"Henry, what on earth is going on?"

A woman in a uniform I hadn't seen before stood in the doorway, her eyebrows pinched in a frown; a little gold watch was pinned to her chest. I scrambled to my feet.

"It's my fault," I said. "I was pestering Mr. Donaldson about an algebra problem—I have my exams next month—and he thought he had a book here that would help."

"Oh, dear." She made a clucking sound. "He does go off on wild-goose chases. All our books are in the library, just to the left of the lounge. That's the place to look. But I'm not sure if Henry can be of much help these days."

"We'll take a look," I said, "before I go and catch my bus."

I led him down the corridor to the room called the library. There were three bookcases full of tattered paperbacks, a table, and a couple of chairs. Mr. Donaldson sank into one of them. He got out his pack of cards and began to lay them out in orderly lines. I sat down opposite him and, before I could forget, wrote down the contents of the box that might or might not still exist.

chapter twenty-nine

By the time the bus pulled into Aberfeldy, the evening smoke was rising from the chimneys and the streetlights were glowing. I was glad that no one knew of my return and that I could walk alone back to Weem, past the poplars, silent on this windless night, and slip into the dark house. In the kitchen I stopped to eat a slice of toast. Then, avoiding the creaking boards that Robin and I had mapped one afternoon, I climbed the stairs. In my room I went at once to the chest of drawers and the photograph of my uncle and mother. After all my failures their laughing faces were unchanged. I was staring at them, wonderingly, when the door of my room opened.

"You came back." The legs of Robin's favourite red pyjamas pooled around his feet.

"I told you I was only going away for a couple of days. What are you doing up?"

"Everyone says that." He never spoke of his mother directly, but her absence, I guessed, had been presented as a matter of days and, with no explanation, commuted to years. He swung back and forth on the doorknob. "Did you find what you were looking for?"

I sat down on the bed to untie my shoes. "Yes and no," I said, tugging at the laces.

"Those are like up and down."

"I was looking for a person and I found him, so that's the yes." The knot loosened. "But he was keeping some things for me and he doesn't have them anymore."

"So they're lost." He let go of the doorknob and approached. "Can we look for them?"

On the bus I had asked myself this over and over. Of course Isobel might have already destroyed the contents of the box, but it was also possible that she had not yet looked through her brother's papers, or that if she had, she had not recognised the letters and dried flowers as mine. Why should Mr. Donaldson have anything that belonged to that wretched girl? The thought that my parents' final words might be so close and yet out of reach was tormenting. Was there a law that could compel someone to give you back your property when they didn't know they had it? As the bus drove over the hills and moors, I had pushed these questions round and round my brain.

Robin studied me anxiously. "Can we?" he repeated.

"I'm not sure. But I am sure that you must go back to bed. Granny will be upset if she finds you gone."

He patted my knee, hitched up his pyjamas, and padded away.

At breakfast the next morning Marian asked if I had had a nice time with my friend in a way that made it easy to say yes and change the subject. Did we need potatoes? As for Archie, he was unusually brisk when we went over Catullus. I shouldn't try to be too poetic, he scolded. Above all I must start timing myself. It was no good doing one brilliant translation when the exam required three. He made no mention of my trip.

The exams were now less than a month away and I had a strict timetable for studying, but whatever had begun with my visit to the minister was not answered by my meeting with Mr. Donaldson; indeed, it was growing at an alarming rate. If I couldn't have my box back—and the more I thought about approaching Isobel, the more that seemed impossible—then I needed to see the land from which it, and I, had come. As I played tiddlywinks, as I washed dishes or hung out laundry, as I worked on maths problems or memorised irregular verbs, I pictured a village of brightly coloured houses beside the sea with geysers and glaciers, puffins and whales. I pictured knocking on the door of a house and being welcomed as a long-lost granddaughter. I pictured meeting someone who resembled me the way Archie resembled Hannah—with the same hands, or hair, or little toes.

In making the journey I faced almost as many obstacles as the skalds in their small boats; the first was my lack of a passport. I asked Marian if, by any chance, she knew how to obtain one, and she said the post office had forms. She had got one for Robin last summer, just in case they suddenly had to go to Rome. The next day I bought some stamps I didn't need and, while the postmistress was counting my change, picked up a form. Later in my room I discovered that the questions, like those on the hotel application, were fraught with unexpected rocks and whirlpools. Besides money and a photograph, I needed a birth certificate. For the first time since leaving Yew House, I sat down and wrote to my aunt. The first version of the letter read:

> *Dear Mrs. Hardy,*
>
> *I wonder if you remember me, your late husband's niece. You sent me to the dreadful Claypoole School when I was ten. Even the hard-hearted headmistress said she'd never seen a guardian show less interest in her ward. I hope you will not be disappointed to learn that I am still alive and making my way in the world . . .*

I tore up the page and wrote, as politely as I knew how, begging her to send my birth certificate and enclosing a stamped envelope addressed to Miss Harvey, c/o MacGillvary. I did not dare to use my real name for fear Archie would notice, but I trusted that my aunt would not study the envelope. In the days following my trip, he had gradually forgiven me and, as if sensing the turn my thoughts had taken, had begun to speak of Iceland more often. Why not go there this summer? Two could travel more cheaply than one, he added, turning a page of Ovid. It would be a reward for my exams.

"I may not deserve a reward," I said, but I could feel the smile spreading across my face. I had never before coveted something so expensive. In Pitlochry I had learned that money could be turned into almost anything, but that clothes and books and watches were not so easily turned back into it. In all his wonderful stories Ovid had forgotten to write about the ultimate alchemical substance.

I knew that in talking about Iceland I was encouraging Archie, but not, I thought, in an inappropriate way. He was Hannah's brother, my tutor, we were friends. Then one evening, walking back from Aberfeldy, I glimpsed a couple on the grass beside the Black Watch Memorial. "Jamie, don't," the girl said, her voice signalling the opposite. "Come on," the boy said softly. "You know you want to." Their two shadows merged again.

As I crossed the bridge, I ran my hands along the parapet in order to feel something—anything—other than longing. If the self was a mass of sensations then I could be rough granite, soft moss, the smooth concrete seams between the stones. But what I was longing for was not Archie. I did not want to lie on the grass with him and let him put his hands inside my clothes. And he, I was convinced, did not want that either. When he touched me, to take a cup of tea or retrieve a book, his touch was no different from Marian's. But

I also remembered my journey from Kirkwall: how easily things could go awry, how quickly people became predators. It would be good to have a protector in that country, where I no longer spoke the language or knew the customs. I began to allow Archie to utter sentences like, "When we go to Reykjavik we must visit the cathedral." I began to make remarks about visiting Thingvellir, going to see the hot spring.

A WEEK PASSED WITH no word from my aunt. I was on the point of writing again, when one day during lunch the phone rang.

"Gemma?" I heard Marian say. "I'm afraid there's—"

"Wait," I called. Knocking over my chair, I ran to the hall.

"Hold on," said Marian into the receiver and then to me, "A woman is asking for Gemma."

As she retreated to the kitchen, I said, "Hello. Who is this?"

"Who is *this*?"

From the first syllable I recognised my aunt, her voice hoarse, as if she were about to cough. "Aunt," I said. "This is Gemma."

"That woman didn't seem to know who you are."

"Did you find my birth certificate?"

"I want to talk to you. I'll be expecting you this Saturday."

"I work," I said. "How would I even get to Yew House?"

"I'll send someone to fetch you. Be ready at two o'clock." And she was gone before I could protest, or ask if the same person would bring me back.

I stood in the hall until my heart slowed. In the kitchen Marian and Robin were finishing their tomato soup and debating what Robin should plant in his garden this year. Did he remember the nice big radishes he had grown last year? Yes, but he didn't like the taste of them. I ate my soup quietly until there was a lull in the conversation.

"That was my aunt," I said. "She always calls me Gemma after my mother. I'm going to visit her on Saturday afternoon."

"What a pretty name," said Marian.

For several months I had contrived not to notice that Aberfeldy was less than thirty miles from Yew House; they were long country miles, over the hills, and no one, in my hearing, had mentioned Strathmuir. Now every night my dreams carried me back there, and during the day stray memories ambushed me: my aunt, in her gown, sweeping off to the party on Christmas Eve, my aunt driving past as I walked to and from school, my aunt siding with Will when he hit me over the head with *Birds of the World*, my aunt at Perth station telling me to be good. But I was not, I reminded myself, returning to that life. No one could shut me in the sewing-room. Louise and Will had surely left home, and Veronica, if she was still there, was too self-absorbed to be anyone's enemy.

Still, adult reason could not entirely quell childhood fears. On Saturday morning I woke at six and wrote a note to Marian: *If I don't return this evening please tell Archie to contact Mrs. Hardy at Yew House, near Strathmuir, Perthshire. Tell him to come and get me at once.* Once again I safety-pinned money and Marian's phone number into my pocket. There was a phone box in the village, I remembered, not far from the school.

I was eating my cornflakes when Marian came into the kitchen, her hair unbrushed, her cardigan unbuttoned. "Jean," she said, "I hate to ask but I need a favour. George had a bad night. I just spoke to Dr. Grady and he's coming this afternoon. Is there any chance you could take Robin with you to see your aunt? He gets so upset on these occasions."

I started to refuse. Then I took in the shadows under her eyes, the lines bracketing her mouth, and suddenly it seemed like a good idea. Robin's presence would protect me not just from kidnapping but also from what I dreaded still more: being changed back into my younger self. "Of course," I said. "I hope he won't be bored."

"Thank you. Thank you so much." One line of worry disappeared from her forehead as she hurried from the room.

Robin, when I announced our plan, was less enthusiastic. "Must I?" he said. Grudgingly, he helped me gather up some cars and colouring books. At five to two we went outside to wait for the mysterious chauffeur, and at five past two a black car turned into the lane and came to a halt. A woman climbed out, wavy brown hair reaching to her shoulders, a blue sweater reaching to midthigh, jeans tucked into boots. As she started towards me, I recognised Louise, still carrying her Lares and Penates proudly before her.

"Gemma?"

"How do you do." I stepped forward with outstretched hand.

"Not too bad." She gave me a hearty shake, as if we were business acquaintances. "You've grown, and you're prettier than I expected. Remember how we used to tease you by singing, 'Skinny ma linka long legs, big banana feet'? You'd run to the toilet whenever we started up. Who is this?" She nodded at Robin, who was standing behind me, clutching the gate.

"This is Robin. I'm his nanny. Robin, this is Louise."

Louise gave a hoot of laughter. "Heavens, for a moment I thought he was yours."

Robin stared at her. Who was this large, loud woman? We climbed into the back of the car, leaving her alone in the front. As she drove through Aberfeldy, past the Birks, and up the hill, she told me that Veronica was spending a year in Paris. "She's meant to be working on her French but she's mostly studying fashion and flirtation."

"What about your brother?" Even now I did not care to say his name.

"Don't ask." She gave a theatrical groan. "He's in London, spending money like water. His big plan, you may remember, was to play football for Scotland, which he had a snowball's chance in hell of actually doing. Now he's an apprentice at an insurance company. Hopefully someone's around to fix his mistakes."

"And what about you? Are you still living at Yew House? How are your horses?"

"Gosh, I haven't ridden in years. I'm the assistant manager at a hotel in Edinburgh. It suits me. Lots of people coming and going, always something new."

I stared at her profile, my aunt's plump cheeks, my uncle's straight nose. It was easy to picture her behind the counter of a hotel, scowling at my application form.

"I've been coming home at weekends," she went on, "to deal with Mummy."

"Look," Robin exclaimed. Two Highland cows, with their curving horns and shaggy heads, were peering over a wall.

"You can draw me a cow later," I said. "What's there to deal with?"

"Cancer. But I'd give ten to one she'll see the decade out, and the next one too. Those doctors don't know how tough Mummy is."

Her tone was so jolly that it took me a moment to grasp that my aunt was gravely ill. Years before at Perth station I had cursed her. Now, like the rain that fell on the Welsh hills and bubbled up, eight thousand years later, in the hot springs of Sulis, my curse was finally coming true. But I felt little sense of victory.

"Will and I were always telling her not to smoke," Louise continued, "but she wouldn't listen. What's so strange is that she's had this bee in her bonnet about talking to you. She went on and on about it. I even contacted that school: Clayfield, Claymoor. When it turned out to be closed, I didn't know what to do. I was thinking of putting an ad in the *Scotsman* when your letter came. It's as if you knew we were looking for you."

"I had no idea. I thought your mother was going to marry Mr. Carruthers."

"Mr. Carruthers." Louise laughed. "I'd forgotten about him. No, she's never remarried, though not for lack of opportunity. She'd be all alone if it weren't for me and Audrey."

"Audrey? Audrey Marsden?" I felt Robin staring at me.

"Who else? When Veronica left last year, Mum did the sensible thing and invited her to move into the house. Now there's a nice young couple paying rent in the cottage, and Audrey has been a godsend, driving her to doctors, taking care of things. Heaven knows how much we'd be paying for taxis and nurses without her."

In my preoccupation with my aunt it had never occurred to me that Audrey might still be at Yew House. At the prospect of seeing the person who had first told me about the Orkneys, I was struck dumb. And surely, I thought, as we squeezed past a lorry, she would have known Mr. Sinclair.

Except for Robin's occasional exclamations—pheasants! sheep!—we drove in silence past moors and lonely farms down into the next valley. Presently I caught sight of the circular wood above the village. A few minutes later the hill with the Roman fort came into view. Driving through the village, I glimpsed the school, and my uncle's church. The field, where Celeste and Marie Antoinette once grazed, was filled with corn. Then we were turning through the familiar gateposts, driving up the familiar drive. As we stopped outside the house Louise said, "She looks a little different."

But I was too overwhelmed by my first sight of Yew House to pay attention. In a rush, I recognised the light over the front door, the rowan tree beside it, the antique boot scraper, the roses growing by the bay window. Whatever my attitude to the occupants of the house, these things had been my childhood friends. Louise opened the door; I crossed the threshold. The hall, which had always smelled of dogs and cigarettes and furniture polish, now smelled of nothing but cleanliness. I kept tight hold of Robin's hand.

"I'll tell her you're here," said Louise. "What do you want to do with him?"

"Robin will come too. He knows to be quiet when grown-ups are talking."

"As you wish." She marched off down the corridor. Once again it was easy to imagine her cajoling a difficult guest, reprimanding a sloppy workman.

While we waited in the hall I told Robin how I used to play on the stairs with Louise. I was describing how we had dared each other who could jump farther when she reappeared, beckoning. I bent down beside Robin. "My aunt is a bit scary," I said, "but there's nothing she can do to us." He nodded doubtfully.

The sitting-room had been transformed. Gone were the faded blue wallpaper and the chintz sofa. Now the walls sparkled with brightly floral paper; the sofa was the colour of sand; the rest of the furniture had also been replaced. Only the picture over the mantelpiece, showing a flock of adults and children skating on a village pond, was the same. My aunt was seated in an armchair by the fire, a tartan rug spread over her knees. After Louise's warning I had been braced to find her as altered as the room, but with her golden hair piled high, she looked much as she had at Perth station.

"Hello, Aunt," I said. "How are you? Robin, this is my aunt."

"Isn't it obvious? Who's that?"

"This is Robin, the boy I take care of. He's going to play while we talk." I led him over to the bay window and laid out his cars, his colouring books and crayons. "Is everything all right?" I asked.

"I'm thirsty," he whispered.

To my surprise my aunt heard. "Louise, get the child a drink. Gemma, sit down here where I can see you. I must say you've turned out better than I feared. You were such a plain little thing."

Now that I was seated a few feet away I could see other changes that suggested illness. Her eyes were duller and her hands, although beautifully manicured, were rivered with veins. "Do you have a copy of my birth certificate?" I said.

"Still the same bull in a china shop," she said, shaking her head with a faint smile. She stared into the fire, and I understood that she was waiting for the threat of interruption to be past. I got out my notebook and pen, wrote the place and date at the top of a page and sat waiting. It was possible, even likely, that I would never see my aunt again. Louise returned, expertly carrying a tray with a glass of orange squash, a cup of tea, and a plate of chocolate biscuits. While I thanked her, my aunt told her to go away and close the door. Then she told me to turn on the transistor radio that sat on the nearby table and place it near the door. When the radio was burbling away and I was back in my seat, she pulled her rug closer and began.

"To my surprise," she said, "you have recently been weighing on my conscience. It's like you to nag. You were always an annoying child."

Her thin fingers fretted the fringe of the rug. I waited. All of this had clearly been planned in advance, and needed no urging by me.

"Your uncle," she said at last, "had not only a sister but a younger brother."

"That's right. There was a photograph in his study of the three of them. Then it disappeared."

"I put it in my chest of drawers. Ian and I were courting when he died. He was driving home to Edinburgh from seeing me in North Berwick when his motorbike went off the road. I didn't hear about it until the following day. I always think I've had twenty-four hours' more happiness in my life because of that delay. People talk about premonitions, but I didn't have the slightest inkling. No cracked mirrors, no spilt salt, no voices on the wind." She shook her head and I caught the glint of earrings.

"The last night I saw Ian," she said, "I told him I was expecting."

Hearing the word Vicky had used about Audrey Marsden, used in the same way, I made a little sound.

"I was sure we'd get married, else I'd never have—" She made a vague gesture. "Still I was so nervous telling him I felt like I'd swallowed a goldfish. We were at the pub, and I remember Ian burst out laughing so loudly that people turned to look at us. 'How clever we are,' he said, 'we've made a baby.' We agreed, then and there, to get married the next week. Who knew when the army would give him leave again? Our parents would be shocked, but we didn't care. Ian was handsome and clever and I was confident he'd flourish after the war. And my grandfather had left money in trust for me that I'd get when I turned thirty or married. I hadn't mentioned this to Ian for fear it might seem like hinting. When I told him that night he just shook his head. 'Beauty, brains, and money,' he said. 'How did I get so lucky?'

"We stayed until last call. Later, of course, I blamed myself for the accident. If he'd left earlier, if he hadn't had one more drink. When I heard he was dead, I fainted and was in a fever for three days. My mother insisted it was a blessing I missed the funeral, but I think it made it even harder to accept what had happened. For years afterwards, whenever I heard a motorbike, I was sure it was Ian."

I had written: Ian, expecting, trust fund, accident. In the background the radio gave cricket scores. By the window Robin made faint "broom broom" noises as he trundled his cars back and forth. My aunt seemed unaware of any of this, or even of me, her audience. She was looking squarely into the past.

"When my fever abated," she went on, "I assumed I'd lost the baby. Gradually it dawned on me I hadn't. My mother guessed my condition. She started making plans to send me to Ireland; the story was I would help out on a horse farm. I would have the baby there, give it up for adoption, and come home. No one would know, and some other nice boy would come along and marry me. She had the good sense to say this last part only once. I had a ticket to sail from Glasgow to Belfast the following week when Charles came to call. We had met a couple of times, and he knew how Ian felt about me. It was a dreich afternoon but I dragged him out for a walk to get away from my mother. We headed up Berwick Law. We were at the top, standing in the rain, looking down on the Firth of Forth, when the word *baby* popped out of my mouth. Charles smiled and for a moment he was the spitting image of Ian. 'That's grand news,' he said.

"Then I blurted out everything, my last conversation with Ian, my belief that I'd caused his death, the whole Ireland plan. I remember watching a ship sail into the Forth, very, very slowly, and saying I didn't think I could bear to give him up. I was sure I was having a boy. But my parents would disown me if I didn't, and I would only get my inheritance if I married. All the way down the hill we talked about alternatives. Charles suggested I could stay in Ireland for a few years and come back with the baby, pretending to be a widow. But even two years somewhere cheap would take more money than either of us had.

"That night Charles phoned; he'd had an idea. 'Promise you'll think about it for twenty-four hours.' When he suggested we get married, I was furious. I remember shouting, 'Don't you have any respect for your brother's memory?' and hanging up. But after my parents left to play bridge I walked round and round the house, thinking. If I married Charles I could keep the baby. I could use my inheritance to buy us a house. Then, in a few years, we could get a divorce. I knew Charles would be a good father.

"At breakfast the next morning I told my parents. My mother asked if I was sure. My father just patted my shoulder and went off to the coal yard. We married in a registry office, and Will was born six months later. Soon afterwards Charles got this parish. We moved here and began to share a room. Louise and Veronica came along. When your uncle wanted you to live with us—he'd made a promise to his sister—I couldn't say no."

"So," I had to say it for myself, "Will is not my uncle's son." As I spoke I remembered the dream I had had at Claypoole, when Will had shouted, "You're not my father."

"You sound pleased." My aunt's dull eyes regarded me curiously. It was the first sign she'd given of being interested in my reaction.

There was no point in explaining how this new fact changed everything for the better. Suddenly her blind partiality for Will made a sad kind of sense. As did her and my uncle's unlikely union. Living at Yew House, I had taken their marriage for granted, but since meeting Mr. Sinclair, I couldn't help wondering why my uncle had chosen someone so cruel and vain. Even as I had this thought, I realised that my dislike for her had ebbed. Now that my aunt didn't control my life I could afford to forgive her.

"Not pleased," I said. "Relieved. And"—another idea rushed in— "that was why you had my uncle buried in Edinburgh, rather than here, in his parish."

"Charles always said you had brains. Yes, I wanted to be able to visit Ian, and having Charles there made it easier. With him and my parents dead, no one else knew. I've thought of telling Will, but he's already furious with me for being ill."

As if to demonstrate, she began to cough, a dry hacking that shook

the rug across her knees. Robin looked up; he had abandoned his cars
for his colouring book. I hovered over her, offering water. Finally she
managed a few sips and the cough subsided.

"Why did you tell me?" I said.

She spread her thin hands. "The doctor claims I'll be well by midsummer, which is balderdash. It began to weigh on me that I'd kick
the bucket and no one would know. With everyone else I have something to lose. But you can't possibly think worse of me than you already do."

It did not occur to me to contradict her.

"I'm sure you don't remember when you first came here," she went
on. "I would try to read to you and play with you. But you pushed me
aside and howled for your uncle. Eventually I stopped trying."

"I was three years old," I said. "I missed my father."

"I know, but your crying made me feel as if you knew that I had
never loved your uncle, as if you were determined to give him the love
I couldn't."

So Miriam was right; she had been jealous. "I thought you always
hated me."

"Not always," she said judiciously. "I did try to make you welcome.
Your uncle never betrayed for a second that Will wasn't his. But nothing I did made a difference, and after Charles's death, you turned into
a little monster, hitting your cousins, breaking their toys."

She yawned, as if the mere memory of my bad behaviour fatigued
her. I bit back my retort. Mindful that I might not have another chance,
I said I had something I wanted to tell her. Did she remember Mr.
Donaldson, the schoolteacher?

"From Edinburgh?" My aunt raised her eyebrows. "Poked his nose
in where he shouldn't have."

Briefly I described my visit to Oban, what I'd learned about Mr.

Donaldson's life after he left the village. "You ruined him. People believed whatever you said about him and he couldn't get a job again."

She gave an imperious sniff. "He ruined himself. If he'd been any kind of a decent teacher he'd have found work. I couldn't have you in the house, upsetting Will, quarrelling with Louise and Veronica, making us feel like bad people. That's the thing about you, Gemma. When you came in a few minutes ago I thought you'd grown up, but you're still the same. After all these years you can't accept you might not know the whole story."

Suddenly Robin was standing in front of my aunt, holding his colouring book. "You're calling Jean the wrong name, and your hair is funny."

Following his gaze, I saw that my aunt's abundant golden coils were no longer her own.

"Rude child," she said calmly and reached to straighten her wig.

She was nicer, I thought, than she used to be. I drew Robin to me and asked again about my birth certificate.

"I could have sworn Charles kept the papers to do with you in the bottom drawer of his desk, but Audrey said it was empty. When we finish talking, look for yourself. Perhaps you'll have better luck. But don't get your hopes up about anything else. After your father died, Charles tried to find out if there was any money from the house, the boat, but writing to people who barely had two words of English—well, it was hopeless. By any normal reckoning you owe me thousands of pounds for your board and keep."

"Just like Will owes my uncle thousands of pounds. Fathers aren't cheap."

"Rubbish," she said faintly.

I stared at her lips bright with lipstick, the rings rattling on her thin fingers. "Do you know anything about my parents? Where they lived? What my father's name was?"

"Gemma, I never liked you. I never liked your mother. I'm ill. Remembering your family history was not my favourite thing when—"

Before she could finish, Robin piped up again. "Don't speak to Jean that way. She came all this way to see you."

"Hush," I said. "May I go and look in the study now?"

"You may. Come back and tell me what you find. I'm going to close my eyes for a minute." She leaned back in her chair and did so.

I gathered up Robin's toys, moved the radio back to the table, and leading him by the hand, stepped out of the room and across the corridor to my uncle's study. Here, to my huge relief, nothing had changed. His desk, the bookcases, the thick green curtains, the armchair beside the fire, even the ashes in the grate looked exactly the same. I asked Robin if he would draw me a picture of the room. "It belonged to someone I was very fond of," I said.

I settled him in the window-seat and turned to search the desk for the second time. The sermon about no man being an island still lay on top, facedown. "We each begin as an island," I read, "but we soon build bridges." I slipped the pages into my notebook. I worked slowly down through the drawers of notes, sermons, and letters. If I had not discovered the box years before, it would be waiting for me now. Finally I had no choice but to open that last drawer. As Audrey had said, it was empty, or almost. In the bottom lay a faded magazine with a boat on the cover. I recognised the strange words as Icelandic. How had it come into my uncle's possession? I wondered as I turned the pages showing photographs of boats and ponies. And there, between a page of print and a picture of a box of herring, was a faded brown envelope addressed to Charles Hardy at Yew House. I drew out a piece of paper folded in three. My mother's name, my father's name, my Icelandic name, and the name of the hospital in Edinburgh where I had been born were written in meticulous black copperplate. A second piece of paper showed that my uncle had legally changed my name to Gemma Hardy.

"What happened?" said Robin, sliding off the window-seat and running to my side. "Did you get a splinter?"

"No," I said, though I did feel as if something had pierced me. "I found what I was looking for."

"Oh, good," he said comfortably. "Jean, I need to go to the loo."

When he agreed that he could wait for five minutes, I sat down in my uncle's chair, pressed my palms to the desk, and silently began to speak. I'm sorry, I said, that your life was so much harder than I knew and that there were so many things I didn't understand. I could never do what you did, marry someone I didn't love, but I admire you for paying your brother's debts. If there is an afterlife I hope you've met people who cherish you. Thank you for coming to Iceland and for taking me into your home.

Then I picked up his fountain pen, something he had used every day, and put that too into my bag, along with the magazine, the precious envelope, and the sermon. Hastily—Robin had repeated his request for the loo—I approached the bookshelves and retrieved *Birds of the World*.

When we emerged from the W.C., Audrey Marsden was waiting in the kitchen. So, unfortunately, was Louise. Beneath her watchful gaze, Audrey and I greeted each other. She looked younger than I remembered. Her hair, no longer pulled into a severe bun, fell in soft waves around her face, and instead of her pale twinsets and dowdy tweed skirts, she wore a vivid turquoise sweater and dark trousers. Vicky's theory about her sudden departure from the Orkneys seemed much more plausible. She offered cake and more tea and then asked what had become of me since I went away to school. "You were such a wee thing to send off alone on a long journey."

"You made me a nice lunch. All my favourite things. The school was awful. They treated the working girls—that's what they called us—worse than servants, but there were a couple of good teachers. Then the school closed down and I went to the Orkneys as an au pair. Now I look after Robin near Aberfeldy."

"The Orkneys," said Louise. "Isn't that where you come from, Audrey?" She and Audrey were sitting at opposite ends of the table; Robin and I were together on the long side. Audrey gave a faint nod.

"You used to tell me stories about the islands," I continued. "That was one reason I wanted to go there. I worked for someone who knew you at school, Vicky Sinclair. She said how much she admired you," I embellished.

Almost despite herself Audrey looked pleased. "I'm amazed she remembers me," she said. "I was eight or nine years older, and she lived in the back of beyond."

"She runs into your mother in Kirkwall sometimes."

"You have a mother?" said Louise. "I've never heard you mention her." She was looking on in a jocular fashion, her interest piqued at the notion that her mother's housekeeper of so many years had secrets.

"We're not on good terms," said Audrey. "More tea? How's the cake, young man?" Another lapwing, I thought, running broken-winged away from her nest.

"Nice," said Robin, and then, seeing me mouth the words, added, "Thank you."

"Vicky works for Mr. Sinclair of Blackbird Hall," I persisted. "Did you know him?" It was the first time I had said his name to another person since Maes Howe. Just this once, I bargained.

Audrey straightened the turquoise cuffs of her pullover. "By sight. I'd have thought Vicky would be married by now. She was a lively girl."

"You can never tell who's going to get married," said Louise.

"Mummy was convinced I was a hopeless case until Brian came along." She raised her hand and I noticed the ring. As she continued to bring the conversation back to what she regarded as its proper focus, I caught Audrey's glance. If Louise left the room, I thought, there might be more to say. But Louise kept talking, and it was Audrey who at last stood up, saying she must check on my aunt.

"I'd like to say goodbye to her," I said. "Robin and I need to go soon."

"At your service." Louise touched an imaginary cap.

But Audrey returned to report that my aunt was fast asleep. "Talking to you must have tired her," she said.

"Yes," said Louise. "What did she want to see you about?"

Her brown eyes quickened, and I was suddenly aware of my power. My aunt's story was like a smooth stone. If I threw it, it would break open the life of Yew House. "Just something about my parents," I said. "I'm going to university in the autumn and I needed to get a couple of facts straight."

"Are you talking about money?" Louise said sharply. "Because if so, you don't have any claim on Mummy. She did her best by you, but that's all past now."

"No, I'll get a grant. Still you'd be surprised how many forms ask about your parents."

Audrey started to say something about my present situation, but Louise was moving to pick up Robin's bag of toys. Quickly, not wanting her to see the book and the magazine, I stepped forward to retrieve it. Then on a page from my notebook I wrote down the MacGillvarys' address and phone number. "Here," I said to Audrey, "if you ever need to reach me. Please thank my aunt for me. I'm glad I saw her again."

We both hesitated, not knowing whether to shake hands or to embrace. Then I reached my arms around her. As I kissed her cheek, I smelled a familiar fragrance: my aunt's perfume. Looking again at her smart trousers and pullover, I wondered if those too came from my aunt. And why not? No one could possibly be paying her enough for all she was doing, and soon she would lose both her home and her job.

In the car Robin slumped against me, asleep before we reached the end of the drive. Louise remarked that Mummy was marvellous. Except for the occasional cough, you would never know she was ill, would you. No, I said, and then, it seemed a natural question, I asked if she remembered her father.

"Of course. It was awful when he died. One minute he was telling me to do my homework, the next he was gone. No one could believe it—a grown man going through the ice." She braked for a crow in the road. "Most of my memories are from when I was small. He would carry me on his shoulders, make up songs and stories. Then you came, and Mummy started teaching me to ride."

I was still thinking about this last sentence, and how it echoed my aunt's claim that my arrival had changed the household, as she began to talk about her wedding. "Veronica wants to design the dresses, make everything French, but I wrote to her last week that we might do things sooner. Just in case Mummy's cough gets worse. I don't need a French dress."

We had passed no houses for miles, but now on the left was a white-washed inn with a sign: TRAVELLERS WELCOME. Louise asked if I remembered going there for lunch. "It was the day we went to the fish-ladder in Pitlochry. You had a ginger beer and Will made you laugh so hard it came out of your nose."

A moment ago I would have sworn that I had never set foot in the inn. Now I recalled the five of us sitting around a table, Veronica and me perched on the edge of our chairs. We had eaten sandwiches and bags of crisps, each with a little screw of blue paper containing salt. My aunt was right, I thought; I did know only part of the story.

chapter thirty

As we walked up the lane, Robin kept stopping to pick the daisies that grew on the grassy verges. I was happy to wait for him. Watching him bend over the flowers, I wondered if he would remember any part of this outing in a few months, any part of me a year hence. Probably not. From his point of view the visit had been dull, save for my aunt's wig slipping and the cake, and although he was fond of me, someone else could easily take my place. Someone else would. Smoke was rising from our neighbours' chimneys and I heard the sound of the radio in Mrs. Lewis's kitchen. If Marian hadn't cooked, I would offer to make scrambled eggs and baked beans for supper. That had been Nell's favourite meal. What was she doing on this April evening? It was quite possible that I would never see her again either.

"For Granny," Robin said, brandishing a dishevelled posy, and began to run towards the house. Suddenly I remembered George. "Robin," I called, "wait." But after his long afternoon of being good, he kept running, impatient to see his beloved grandmother. The gate stood open and he trotted down the garden path. After a brief struggle with the doorknob, he was inside.

"Granny," I heard him call, "we're back."

I followed, picking up first one fallen daisy, then another. Perhaps after supper, I thought, I would do something outrageous, like go to the local pub and treat myself to a shandy. I was at the kitchen door when Robin started to scream. A few seconds later he barrelled into me, his cheeks scarlet. In one flailing hand he held a sheet of paper.

"I can't read," he cried.

I knelt to put my arms around him. "Robin, the note is for me. Let me read it." Finally—he hated to surrender any vestige of his grandmother—I pried the paper from his small fingers.

Saturday, 3:30

Jean,

  Dr. Young thinks George needs emergency surgery. Gone to Perth Infirmary. Can you take care of Robin? I'll phone.

  Marian

Robin cried for almost an hour. Marian, like his mother, was gone forever, and trying to persuade him to the contrary was like throwing a glass of water onto a burning building. Only when I had shown him her piano and her bed and her wardrobe full of clothes and her Wellington boots did he calm down enough to help me make supper. I opened a tin of baked beans; together we broke eggs into a bowl. I was fishing out fragments of shell when the phone rang. Robin raced to the hall. He stood beside the ringing instrument, mute and imploring.

"Hello," said a woman's voice. "Marian is phoning from Perth. Will you accept the charges?"

"What charges?" In my confusion I forgot Vicky's lesson about how to make a phone call without money.

"Do you want to talk to Marian MacGillvary?" said the operator.

"Yes, of course." The air on the line changed. Before Marian could say anything I said, "You have to talk to Robin. Tell him that you're all right and you'll be back soon." I knelt down and held the receiver to his ear. Faintly I heard Marian say she had gone to Perth to take care of his grandfather. She would see him tomorrow, or the day after. He must help me and be a good boy. Robin nodded, solemnly, not realising that she couldn't see him. "Say goodbye," I said, and he did.

I reclaimed the phone, and asked about George. Marian reported that he was still in surgery. They had had to call the doctor in from the golf course. She was staying in a bed-and-breakfast near the hospital. "I'm sorry to land you with Robin but I'm in no state to drive back and forth. I want to be here when George wakes up."

Her voice broke on the "when." She promised to call again tomorrow and was gone. As I replaced the phone, I recalled the Latin phrase *annus mirabilis*; today was my *dies mirabilis*, day of wonders. I had seen my aunt. I had learned that she too had a secret sorrow. I had two pieces of paper that proved I was Gemma Hardy. And as Jean Harvey I was in sole charge of a small boy and a large house.

Together Robin and I finished making supper and ate. He took a bath and I read to him about parliamentary reform. Then, using cushions from the sofa, I made a bed for him on the floor of my room. While he snored softly I sat at my desk, copying the details of my birth certificate into my notebook. Here was the time and place of my birth, 3:37 A.M. on 18 April 1948. My mother's maiden name: Agnes Hardy. My father's name: Einar Arinbjornsson; his occupation: fisherman. For their address they gave Yew House. The certificate was copied from the registry of births, marriages, and deaths in Edinburgh. The idea of these details, safe in some office, was profoundly reassuring. So too was the discovery, when I opened *Birds of the World*, that the lyre-bird and the puffin and the fairy-wren were still there, enjoying their habitat.

. . . .

THE NEXT MORNING MARIAN dialed directly. As she reported that George was awake and had said her name, I heard the soft click of coins dropping into the phone. She did not mention coming home but told me that I would find housekeeping money in the top drawer of her dresser. When I looked beneath her neatly folded underwear, there was more than two hundred pounds, mostly in the one- and five-pound notes her pupils paid her.

As the day progressed, I learned what Marian's life had been like before I arrived. My timetable for Sunday read:

9–10 Algebra + trigonometry

10–11 Latin

11–12:30 French

12:30–1:30 Walk + lunch

1:30–2:30 French

2:30–4:00 English

Tea

4:30–6:30 History

Supper

King Lear + *Great Tradition*

By the time I put Robin to bed I had managed a few algebra problems and twenty minutes of French, but when I opened *King Lear*, I was so tired that I could not keep Edgar and Edmund straight. After half an hour I closed the book in despair. I would never get the results I needed unless I studied hard this last week. On Monday afternoon, when I usually attended classes at the school, Robin and I walked into Aberfeldy to post my passport application. Then we went to Honey-suckle Cottage. At the sight of my face, Hannah fetched some clay and set Robin up on a sheet of plastic on the kitchen floor. Could he make us each a present? Under Emily's scrutiny, he set to work.

Hannah already knew about George. Now I told her that Marian was staying in Perth. My exams started next week, and these last days of study were crucial. And what if Marian was still away next week? How could I sit the exams and take care of Robin? At the sound of his name he shot me an anxious stare. Quickly I asked what he was making.

"A cat," he said, grinning at Emily.

"People will rally round," said Hannah. "Robin can help me in the pottery. And won't some of the neighbours mind him?"

"But what about the exams?" I repeated. Hannah still didn't seem to understand how demanding Robin was, how much I needed to study.

"Marian will be back. Here," she said to Robin, "let me show you how to make a vase out of snakes." Kneeling beside him, she began to roll out a coil of clay.

We had been back at the house for an hour when there was a knock at the door and a voice called, "Hello." Hannah must have telephoned Archie as soon as we left.

FOR THE NEXT FOUR days he came every afternoon after his deliveries. He played with Robin, helped me study, and, to my surprise, took over the cooking. This last he approached like a chemistry experiment, measuring ingredients and timing each stage precisely. "Is this finely chopped?" he would ask. "What does *thickened* mean?" After supper, when Robin was safely in bed, we sat at opposite ends of the kitchen table, both reading. Sometimes Archie quizzed me on that night's subject. His French was hopeless, but he read over the essays I had written in history and English and made suggestions. At nine-thirty he would close his book, get to his feet, and bid me good night. Once he praised my Horace translation, another time he wished me sweet dreams, but for the most part our conversation seldom strayed beyond the immediate demands: Robin, groceries, news of George, my studies.

On Friday evening the three of us were in the kitchen when a car drove up the lane. Often, at the sound of visitors, Robin still vanished beneath the table. Now he was running for the door. A minute later he reappeared in the arms of his grandmother.

I had not known that a few days could so greatly change a person who had money and a bed. Marian's skirt hung in folds, her hair, unwashed, clung to her head, and her cheeks had a bruised look. She greeted Archie and me quietly. Still carrying Robin, she went upstairs to unpack. Half an hour later they joined us for supper. While Robin told her about the wigwam he had built with the Lewis children, she toyed with Archie's vegetable pie.

Finally I said, "How is George?"

"This was delicious." She set down her knife and fork. "The doctor says he should be ready to come home in a fortnight, but he won't be able to manage stairs. I thought we could turn the dining-room into a bedroom for him? It's warm and near the loo. We usually eat in here anyway." She clasped her hands, looking from me to Archie.

"What does Dr. Grady think?" Archie said cautiously.

"He hasn't seen George since the operation, but I expect he'll say what he always says: that it's a lot for me to cope with. What he doesn't understand is that George hates being in hospital. The nurses are very nice but there's no privacy. And they only allow visitors for a couple of hours a day."

"Still," Archie persisted, "George is a big man. What if you need to lift him?"

"The district nurse will help with all that," said Marian firmly.

Soon afterwards she went upstairs with Robin and didn't return.

Over the washing-up, Archie talked about Ovid's exile to the Black Sea. While there he had written a curse poem called *The Ibis*. Who did he curse? I asked. Did it work? But Archie didn't know. When he put on his jacket and gathered up his books, I followed him outside. The night was clear and moonless, and I at once wished that I too had brought a jacket. As we leaned against his van, looking across the valley at the lights of Aberfeldy, I tried not to shiver.

"Marian looks awful," I said.

"Does she? I thought she was just a little tired."

"I'm worried she won't understand that I can't take care of Robin next week. All she can think about is George."

"No," said Archie, his stiff green jacket creaking. "She knows how important your exams are. Speak to her tomorrow, when she's had a good night's sleep."

Somewhere above us on Weem Rock a bird was crying, a lonely, ravenous sound. Just for a moment I thought of the madwoman at her barred window. "But whatever she says," I said, "if I'm in the house, then I can't just shut the door of my room and ignore Robin needing something."

"And," Archie said, creaking again, "you're a better person because of that. What about going to the library? They have tables."

"It's closed on Tuesdays and Thursdays." I did not list the other problems: the librarian's love of gossip, the lack of a bathroom.

He began to pace up and down the lane, receding into the darkness and reappearing; above us the bird continued to scream. After half-a-dozen turns he stopped a few yards away. "We need your fairy godmothers," he said. "I'll ask Hannah and Pauline if you can use their study. It's farther to walk than the library but you'd be safe from interruptions."

"That would be perfect," I said. "If you're sure they wouldn't mind."

"Hannah will phone. If I don't see you again, good luck on Monday."

"Thanks," I called over my shoulder. I was already hurrying down the path, longing to be warm again.

ARCHIE WAS RIGHT. WHEN I spoke to Marian the next day she got out the calendar on which she noted her pupils' lessons and made me write down the dates of my exams. "You must take whatever time you need," she said. "You've more than earned it." Then Hannah phoned and offered me refuge. The next two weeks flew by as I immersed myself in each subject and, as soon as those exams were past, moved on to the next. I saw Archie only once as I was walking to town, and he gave me a lift in his van. He asked me how English and algebra had gone and listened to my worries about French and history. "Thanks to you," I said, "Latin is under control."

He said nothing, but the muscles in front of his ears flexed in the way they did when he was pleased.

Latin was the last exam, and, when the teacher told us to turn over the questions, it was as if the sentences themselves were opening doors, inviting me in. I wrote without stopping until the final bell and put down my pen almost sadly. When would I get to translate Virgil again? Once I stepped out of the school, though, I felt elated. I called goodbye to Margaret and Joan, who were both complaining how hard the exam had been, and ran most of the way back to Weem.

Marian's car was gone and the house was empty. I wandered from room to room wanting something to happen, some outburst of merriment and pleasure. I turned on the radio. I played scales on the piano. I tried on Marian's perfume. I took a sip of the sherry she kept for company. But I could not settle to anything. Finally I decided to walk up the hill to St. David's Well. Perhaps the local deity would calm me.

Beneath the trees the light was green and sombre; last year's leaves crackled underfoot. Several times I thought I heard another footstep and halted, waiting to see who might appear, but there was only silence. At the well the water was lower than usual. As I dipped my hand in it and touched my forehead, I caught a glimpse of something shiny among the dead leaves on the bottom. Someone had thrown in a sixpence. I would have done the same, but as usual, my pockets were empty. Kneeling there, I realised that despite my vow, I was missing Mr. Sinclair. He would have insisted on a celebration, whether that meant singing to the seals or dancing around the library. I knew I had done well, except perhaps in French, and that my new friends would share my delight when the results came, but there was no one to whom I could confess my present satisfaction.

I was looking for some offering for the spring—a pretty pebble, or a few flowers—when again I heard footsteps and this time a voice saying, "No, bad dog." A tall woman with a crest of hair like Miss Seftain's and two brindled terriers, each straining at the lead, came into view. The dogs lunged towards me, but she held them in check.

"Good afternoon," she called. "They're quite friendly. Baxter, heel."

She walked past, still talking to the dogs, and headed down the far side of the rock towards Castle Menzies. I gathered some forget-me-nots and laid the small blue flowers on a rock by the well. Staring into the pool, I said, "Please let me find a way to go to Iceland."

I was turning to follow the woman—I had never been to Castle Menzies and the ruin was at least a destination—when I heard the sound of another approach. Archie appeared through the trees. He raised his crook in greeting. "Here you are," he said, not seeming at all surprised. I wondered if he had stopped by the house. "How was Latin?"

"All right. There was that passage from Virgil we did a few weeks ago, and then a short piece by Tacitus and one of Horace's poems about farmers and bees. I was glad you'd made me time myself."

"So you're done?"

"Yes." All I could not say made me curt. "Someone threw sixpence in the well."

"People have been doing that for years, though I've always wondered what a naiad would do with money. My theory is that Gypsies started the custom. Periodically they come along and clean it out."

I saw him notice the forget-me-nots but he did not comment. "In Bath," I volunteered, "people used to throw coins and jewellery into the hot spring."

"And votive statues, too," he said. He stabbed his crook into the mud and, leaving it, upright but listing, came forward to dip his hand in the water and touch his fingers to his forehead, the same gesture I had made.

"I'm glad to find you alone," he said. His eyes were very clear, and high on each cheek was a flush of colour; Hannah blushed in the same way. Hidden in one of the beech trees, a blackbird began to scold. "We share so many interests, Jean. The Everyman Library claims that books are the ideal companions, but you've taught me that the ideal is sharing books with a kindred spirit. I know you're younger than me, but I've seen how mature you are in your dealings with Marian and Robin. You don't shirk your responsibilities. I'd like to celebrate your exams results by inviting you to go to Iceland as—"

"Archie," I burst out, "I'd love to go to Iceland."

In my excitement I did not catch the end of the sentence. I was still debating whether to ask what he'd said when he stepped forward and kissed me on the forehead.

chapter thirty-one

As I followed Archie back to the village—the path was too narrow to walk side by side—I saw how white his neck was above his collar. I hadn't noticed at the well, but he must have been to the barber recently. Marian's car was parked outside the MacGillvarys' and I asked if he would come in for tea. He said he was sorry. He'd promised to help Hannah load the kiln. "Thank you, Jean," he said, smiling at me. "I'm so happy." Before I could thank him in turn, he headed down the lane. Watching him disappear, I thought that the naiad had answered my request with miraculous speed.

In the kitchen Robin was playing pirates; Marian was at the stove. "How did the exam go?" she said.

"All right. I really enjoyed translating the Virgil."

"That's a good sign. When I enjoy playing I always play better. George walked round the ward today."

The three of us ate bangers and mash as if nothing had changed. I was longing to talk about Iceland, to say that Archie and I were at last going to visit, but any mention of travel would only upset Robin. Afterwards, as I gave him his bath, I read to him from *The Little Mermaid*. It was the first time in months I'd read to him from one of his books rather than one of mine. The picture at the front showed a ship with white sails bobbing on a blue sea; nearby a mermaid was combing her hair. "Pretty," said Robin. He was sailing his own ship, pushing it up one side of the bath and down the other. But as I read about the little mermaid's willingness to sacrifice almost everything for her prince, to walk on knives and give up her underwater garden, Robin's ship sailed more and more slowly. Finally, with a decisive shove, he sank it.

"Stop," he said. "We'll have bad dreams." Ever since the morning we had both reported dreaming of foxes he had regarded our dreams as communal.

"I'm sorry," I said. "Finish your bath and I'll read you something else so we have good dreams."

In bed, after only a page of *The Wind in the Willows*, his eyes closed. I tiptoed away to brush my teeth. It was just past eight, not yet fully dark, but suddenly I could not wait for the day to be over. All I wanted was to think of Iceland, to imagine seeing the landscape my mother had loved, with its volcanoes and glaciers and wild ponies. And perhaps, in some small village, I would find my grandparents.

THE NEXT MORNING, WITHOUT an exam looming, was like a holiday. "No lessons today," I said to Robin. Instead we went out to the garden. With Marian spending most of her time at the hospital, it had been neglected. Now I showed him several common weeds, and we set to work. As Robin pulled out the groundsel and I dug up dandelions, I told him how at school I had had a friend, Miriam, who grew beautiful blue flowers. "What happened to her?" he said. I was trying to think how to answer when Marian appeared on the edge of the lawn.

"George is coming home," she announced jubilantly. "An ambulance will bring him after lunch. And Jean, Hannah phoned to ask you to supper. I said you'd let her know if you couldn't."

Exams had interrupted my weekly suppers with Hannah and Pauline and I was glad to think they'd noticed. They would understand my pleasure in going to Iceland—I pictured Pauline bobbing, Hannah's long smile—and advise me how to contribute to the trip. While

Marian went to buy groceries, I hoovered George's room and picked sweet peas for the bedside table. Remembering my own convalescence, I got Robin to help me clean the windows. We were polishing the last pane when Marian returned.

"Jean, you're a wonder," she said. "I don't know how I'd manage without you."

"Robin helped me," I said, storing up her words of praise against the blame I feared was coming.

PAULINE ANSWERED THE DOOR wearing a green dress I had never seen before. She was still kissing me on both cheeks when Hannah appeared; she too was smartly dressed in black trousers. "Congratulations," she exclaimed, hugging me so hard my feet left the ground. Was it possible that somehow, perhaps through the headmaster, they knew the results of my exams?

"We couldn't be happier," Pauline added.

By now they had whisked me into the kitchen, where the table was set with Hannah's plates and flowers and wine-glasses. I was taking all this in, and my hosts' greetings, as Hannah remarked that Archie would be here any minute. He had gone to get wine.

"But—" I stared down at my faded corduroy trousers, my scuffed shoes.

"I know," she said. "It's all wrong, the groom providing the wine at the celebratory dinner. Pauline thought I'd pick up a bottle and I thought she would. Your future sisters-in-law are enthusiastic hosts but inept."

Emily bounded over, and as I bent to bury my face in her warm fur, I knew, as clearly as if he were speaking them now, the words I had missed at the well. Archie's proposal to visit Iceland had been linked to another proposal; I had, unwittingly, accepted both. But to admit my error in the midst of Hannah and Pauline's festivities, to voluntarily cast myself out of this glowing circle, was more than I could manage. "Good dog," I murmured to Emily and asked how I could help.

"Light the candles," said Hannah, handing me a box of matches. "So tell us, did Archie propose on bended knee?"

Before I could answer, there was the sound of a van pulling up outside. The door opened and my second fiancé stepped into the room, a bottle of wine in each hand. He too was smartly dressed, in a grey suit with a pale blue shirt and a red tie.

"Jean," he said, "you're already here. I could have given you a lift."

"It's a lovely evening. I needed the walk." I bent to light the candles; the wicks caught at once. "They sent George home from the hospital today."

"Oh, I had no idea." Pauline bobbed. "How does he look?"

As Archie uncorked the wine, I described George's return. How his hair had turned from pewter to snow and how thin he'd grown but that he'd managed to walk from the garden gate to the house with two canes. "He's different," I said. "He stopped in the garden to admire the laburnum. And he said hello to Robin and me."

Archie started to say something, but Hannah interrupted with glasses of wine. "Here's to the two of you. Many congratulations. We couldn't be happier and we wish you all happiness."

"Congratulations," said Pauline.

We clinked glasses—"Hear our good crystal," said Hannah—and drank. Archie remarked that the custom of clinking was thought to have originated with the Greeks, a way of proving that the wine wasn't poisoned. Pauline asked if poisonous wine sounded different. Archie smiled and started to explain. Any kind of wine still tasted bitter to me, but I had eaten almost nothing that day and I could tell, after only one sip, that it would make everything easier. While Hannah remarked how romantic it was, Archie finding me by the side of the road, the two of us falling in love, I kept drinking. We sat down to salmon, fresh peas, and new potatoes. Seeing Archie and Hannah by candlelight, I was struck all over again by their matching blue eyes, their high cheekbones and long chins.

"The one thing I regret about getting married," Archie said, "is leaving here. I've applied for a transfer to Edinburgh so that I can keep Jean company at university."

"You've already applied?" My glass almost toppled to the table.

"Just today. Often transfers take months to come through."

"We'll miss you," said Hannah, "but it'll be nice to have an excuse to visit Edinburgh. Is it too soon to ask if you've set a date?"

"Yes," I blurted out. Surely that too hadn't been arranged when I wasn't looking.

"But not too soon to ask where we're going for our honeymoon," said Archie, smiling at what he took to be my modest confusion. "We're planning a trip to Iceland."

"Oh, yes," said Pauline, "you've both got a bee in your bonnet about that place."

Archie began to rhapsodise about the sagas. Meanwhile Hannah refilled everyone's glasses; Pauline offered more food. "Eat up, Jean," she urged. Looking down, I discovered my plate almost untouched. My long training at Claypoole triumphed over my turbulent feelings. I picked up my knife and fork and set to work.

Usually at Honeysuckle Cottage I helped to serve and clear, but tonight Hannah and Pauline waited on us, and it wasn't until the last morsel of pudding was gone, and Archie said well, we all had to work in the morning, that I pushed back my chair. As the meal progressed I had noticed the candles growing brighter, my companions wittier. Now my legs wobbled, as if I had just stepped from a boat to dry land.

"Oh," I said, clutching the back of my chair, "I've had too much to drink."

"Good for you," said Hannah.

"No harm in getting a little tipsy," Pauline added, and gave me the advice Nell had given Coco: a glass of water and two aspirin before bed.

"And you'll come next Wednesday, won't you?" said Hannah. "We have to make the most of your company."

At the MacGillvarys', Archie walked me to the door and asked if I could manage the stairs. "Of course," I said with dignity. I wondered if he would take advantage of my state to kiss me on the mouth or slip a hand under my sweater, but he kissed my cheek and told me to hold on to the banister. As I undressed, fumbling with buttons and bra hooks, I couldn't help giggling. Archie didn't fancy me, not one jot. And no wonder, I thought, when I caught sight of my flushed cheeks in the bathroom mirror. In bed, I watched the chest of drawers and the desk rise into the air. Then I took two aspirin and turned off the light.

ON FRIDAY, AS SOON as Marian left for the shops, I searched the telephone directory until I found the number for a travel agent in Perth. "Oh, we don't get many enquiries about Iceland," said the man who answered. "You can fly, or take a boat. Do you have a preference?"

"Whatever's cheapest," I said, trying to speak quietly. The phone was in the hall, outside George's room. The man promised to investigate and asked me to call back tomorrow. I put down the receiver with the sense that I had taken a small step towards sorting things out with Archie. Once I knew the cost, I could offer to contribute to my ticket, and explain that I did not want to get married. And I would at last reveal why I wanted to go to Iceland. Somehow, in my flight from the

Orkneys, my awful days in Pitlochry, I had lost sight of the fact that not everything about my past was a secret.

Robin and I were at the kitchen table, writing rows of *R*s, when we heard Marian's car. A moment later she came into the room, almost running, and embraced me. "Jean, I was at the chemist's, picking up George's prescriptions, and Pauline told me the wonderful news."

Even as I apologised for not telling her I could not help contrasting the response to my second engagement with that to my first.

"No, no," said Marian, "it's my fault. I said to Pauline I've been in such a state about George. You could have told me you were going to the moon and I'd have said, 'Can you buy some milk?' Many congratulations."

"What about?" said Robin. "What's happening?"

"Jean and Archie are getting married," said Marian. "Isn't that nice?"

He shook his head vehemently. "You'll drown."

"Robin, what are you talking about?"

"He's thinking of the Little Mermaid," I explained. "That was a made-up story. Mermaids don't exist. People thought they did because sometimes fishermen mistook seals for women. They both have long eyelashes. Look, I'll draw you a picture."

I did, carefully giving the seal whiskers and the mermaid a scaly tail. Robin protested that they didn't look at all alike. How could anyone confuse them? "Maybe," I said, "a seal got some seaweed stuck on its head and a sailor thought it was hair."

"Like your aunt." He giggled.

When I telephoned the travel agent again, he said I could fly from Glasgow to Reykjavik at the end of June for 195 pounds. Since coming to the MacGillvarys' I had saved 83 pounds.

·   ·   ·

DAY BY DAY MORE people learned that Archie and I were engaged, and day by day I felt more helpless to explain that we weren't. By virtue of his job he was a well-known and well-liked figure in the valley. Several elderly people claimed to owe him their lives. He had been the one to notice curtains still drawn, milk on the doorstep, and raise the alarm. Two women credited him with getting them to the midwife in time. Once he had interrupted a burglary. People were glad that he was getting married and glad that he was marrying the girl he'd rescued. It was, as Hannah had said, a romantic story, and gradually, I too became swept up in it. Archie was a kind, truthful, clever man. He would help me at university, encourage me to pursue my interests. I pictured evenings like the ones we had spent when George was in hospital—Archie cooking supper, both of us reading and studying. As a married woman, I told myself, I would have certain freedoms. I would never again have to sleep in a church. But at night I dreamed of barred windows and small, dark rooms.

On Saturday Archie suggested an outing to the village of Fortingall. It was a nice walk, and the hotel there did afternoon tea. We left his van parked in a lay-by and set off down the narrow road. In the fields on either side the cows and sheep drowsed in the heat. Nearby bees buzzed among the buttercups and scarlet campion. Archie remarked that he'd like to keep a hive or two, maybe after I finished university when we lived in the country again. He began to tell me his ideas for our honeymoon. A week, he thought, would give us a couple of days in Reykjavik and time to visit various sites in the western part of the island. Maybe we could go to Reykholt, where Snorri Sturluson, the author of several sagas, had lived. He was said to have received visitors in his bathing-pool.

"Archie," I said, bending to examine a clump of purple vetch, "couldn't we go to Iceland as friends? I've been saving. I can—"

"Friends?" he exclaimed. "But we're not friends. We're engaged to be married."

I picked a flower for courage and held it to my face. "I'm so grateful to you. But I'm not sure I have the right feelings. This trip will be a chance for us to make sure we're suited."

"Are you proposing"—he came to an abrupt halt—"that we travel together without being married? What would happen in hotels?" He gestured at a field of cows as if we were hotel guests and they were judging us. "I'm afraid you've lost me."

I kept walking, counting on him to follow. If I stopped, I would have to look at him, and if I looked at him, it would be even harder to say what I was trying to say. "But we've been talking about going to Iceland for weeks. You never said we could only go if we were married."

"Jean." My false name was both a rebuke and a summons, as Archie strode past me. Now I almost had to run to keep abreast. "Anyone with a passport and enough money can go to Iceland. I invited you to go as my wife. If for some reason you've changed your mind—Hannah did warn me how young you are—then we won't be taking a honeymoon. Surely you know"—his voice was almost muffled by his footfalls— "that I'm not the kind of man who goes to bed with a woman to whom he isn't married."

Of course you're not, I thought. You're not the kind of man to go to bed with anyone. To you *love* is just a Latin verb. The vetch was already wilting in my grasp; I let it fall. But if I succumbed to my anger . . . I pictured Hannah, Pauline, and Marian all frowning. I pictured Iceland vanishing across the ocean, the whole country sailing away. I would never get to retrace my journey. My grandparents, if they were still alive, might die. My cousins, if I had any, might forget my name.

"Everything's just happened so fast," I said. "I'm worried I won't be a good wife. I am young. And then there's Marian. She can't manage both George and Robin."

I stammered on in this vein for another minute or two and gradually Archie's pace slowed. I was right, he said approvingly, to be apprehensive. Marriage was a big step, but he wasn't looking for someone to wash his shirts and sweep the floor. What he needed was a comrade to share his interests, to remind him that being a postman was only part of his life. "I'll talk to Marian," he added. "Then we can set the date."

His good mood restored, Archie changed the subject. Did I know, he asked, that Fortingall was famous for its yew tree? People said it was planted when Pontius Pilate was governor of Jerusalem. "Imagine"—his eyes glowed—"someone who heard Jesus preach the Sermon on the Mount could have sat beside that tree."

On Monday while Marian was giving a lesson, and Robin was happily arranging his model farmyard, I once again went to use the phone. More than two months had passed since I retrieved my suitcase, but I was sure that the minister with his kindly smile would remember me. I would tell him everything and he would advise me how best to extricate myself. The phone rang only once before a woman said hello. I asked to speak to Mr. Duckworth.

"I'm afraid he's not here. Can I help?"

"When will he be back? I can phone later."

"The end of September. His parents were in an accident and he's taken a leave to look after them. My husband is minding the parish. Shall I fetch him? He'll be happy to talk to you."

Through the window above the front door a cloud was visible, so white and substantial that it looked as if I could set a ladder up against the trees and climb aboard. Suddenly I was back on the Brough of Birsay, lying on the grass near the lighthouse while the lark sang and Mr.

Sinclair slept. Then I was in Pauline and Hannah's kitchen, clinking my glass to theirs, and to Archie's. "Thank you," I said. "I'll wait until September."

I was still staring at the cloud when, from George's room, the sound of the hourly pips on the radio reminded me that I had promised to take him for his constitutional. He walked in the garden several times a day and Marian insisted that he be accompanied. "No jacket," he said when I knocked on his door. We headed out. As we walked across the lawn, he pointed to the faint path he had worn through the daisies.

"You must have walked to Edinburgh by now," I said.

"For Marian." He stopped and, still holding his stick, put one hand over his heart.

"She loves you," I said.

He gave a slight nod. We passed the laburnum with its cascade of golden flowers, once, twice. "Bad phone call," he said.

Such a simple phrase to contain my disappointment. I explained that the person I had hoped to talk to was away. "I really needed to ask him something," I said.

"Love," said George. After several steps, he added, "Not Archie's tea. Matter?"

A wagtail, one of the birds Coco had made fun of, was running along the edge of the flower-bed. "That's what I can't decide," I said. "Archie is kind and clever. We both like history. Maybe that's enough."

"For him."

It took me a moment to guess his meaning. "For him," I agreed. "He seems to have no interest in . . ." I followed the flight of the wagtail onto the wall. What words could convey that feeling of being connected with another person, and the way in which that feeling raised a curtain between oneself and the world so that everything—a slice of bacon, a beech tree, a pair of shoes, a snail, a standing stone—was more vivid? "Certain things," I ended feebly.

George nodded again. "Careful," he said. "Diff—, diff—"

He stopped walking and looked down at me, his mouth twisted. I looked back—he was, as always, perfectly shaved—searching for what he was trying to tell me. "Archie and I are different," I said slowly. His watery eyes agreed. "You're telling me," I continued, "that those differences won't be easy to ignore."

"Yes." He patted his heart again and then pointed to me. "Careful," he repeated.

How strange, I thought, that this man, whom I had known only during his illness, sensed what Marian and Hannah and Pauline seemed so ready to ignore. But at least I had one ally. Two, if I counted Robin.

When I announced after supper that I was going for a bicycle ride, Marian said it was a beautiful evening. I borrowed Mrs. Lewis's bike and, not bothering to phone in advance, set out. Better to risk Archie's absence than to arouse false expectations. Nor did I plan what to say. I simply gave myself over to the journey, following the road on the north side of the river. A few weeks ago the woods had been bright with bluebells; now the flowers were mostly gone. I pedalled along, enjoying the small rush of speed on the hills and the occasional glimpses of the river. All too soon I came to Archie's village. His red post office van was parked beside the house Hannah had pointed out. A woman in an apron, still holding a rolling pin, answered my knock.

"Archie," she said. "Top of the stairs, on the right."

When I knocked on that door Archie called, "Come in." Slowly I opened it and peered in. He was sitting in an armchair, holding a book.

"Jean! What are you doing here?"

"I was out for a bike ride. May I come in?"

"Welcome to my very humble abode. Here, have the armchair. Can I get you something? I can offer tea, Nescafé, lemon barley water, and gin."

"A glass of water, please."

Archie stepped out to fetch the water, and I surveyed the room. Besides the armchair it contained a table and chair, a bookcase, and an umbrella stand holding several golf clubs. On the bookcase was a photograph. When I went to look I saw that it was the one Hannah had taken of me in the pottery, smiling up at her. Quickly, hearing his footsteps, I sat down again. As he handed me the glass, I noticed that the door, closed when I arrived, was now ajar. He was worried, I thought, about what his landlords might think.

While I drank the tepid water, he told me about their three children, whom he occasionally helped with homework. "They'll miss me when we move," he said.

I set aside the glass, unbuttoned the top button of my blouse, and stood up. Archie was sitting on the hard chair at the table, still talking about the youngest boy's struggle with the alphabet as I approached.

"I don't have your patience," he said. "I'm glad you stopped by. I've been meaning to show you this book of early maps of Scotland."

I put my hand on his. If he kissed me, I thought, if he started to unbutton his own shirt, if he looked at me and said, "How lovely you are," if he put his hand down the neck of my blouse, then perhaps, still, everything would be all right. We could be married and go to Iceland and share a room in a way that mattered.

"This first map was done in stages. It shows the route of the Border riders."

"Archie," I said. "Do you like me?"

"Of course I like you. That's why we're getting married. See how the map-maker drew in a cross for each abbey and a little flag for each castle."

"But marriage isn't all about skalds and old maps." I moved my hand from his hand to his forearm. Through the cotton of his shirt I could feel the heat of his skin.

"I walked this path once." As if unaware of my touch, he lifted his hand to trace the route. "It took three days and each night I slept in an abbey. I was probably breaking the law, but it made me feel like a pilgrim."

I stroked his arm. "Archie." One of my Latin translations had been about Caesar hesitating on the banks of the Rubicon. To lead his troops across the small stream was to declare war with Rome. "Would you like to kiss me?"

"Jean. What's got into you?"

A blaze of colour appeared high on each cheek. Still holding the book, Archie was on his feet. Three steps carried him to the door. "My van's been making a strange noise," he said. "Mr. Stewart promised to take a look at it this evening. Can you let yourself out?"

His feet thudded on the stairs. Looking out of the window, I saw him hurry down the garden path and, still clutching the book, without a backward glance, climb into the postal van and drive away.

I pocketed the photograph and followed. I knew now exactly what I was going to do. Pedalling at top speed, I headed back along the narrow road, hoping to arrive home before Marian went to bed. My efforts were rewarded. As I stepped into the kitchen, I heard a low hum of conversation from George's room. I tiptoed up the stairs to her bedroom. The dim light filtering through the curtains revealed Robin, already asleep in his bed, and next to him the chest of drawers. Holding my breath, I glided across the room. The underwear drawer opened easily, the money made no noise, but as I closed the drawer, Robin asked drowsily what I was doing.

I knelt beside him. "Are you awake enough to remember something?"

"I think so."

"Tomorrow, very early, I have to go away to find my family, but I'll come back soon. Ten days or two weeks. So what you have to remember is that I haven't disappeared. I've gone away to do something that's very important. I'm going to write a letter to Granny and Grandpa."

"Okay," he said and rolled back into his pillow.

In my own room I packed my clothes and my precious photographs, and sat down to write to Marian and George. Of the few letters I had written in my life this was by far the hardest. As I laboured over the sentences, I kept thinking I should put the money back and ask for a loan. But what if they refused? I remembered Mr. Milne's words the day he had driven me back from the hospital. He had turned out to be right. I was prepared to go to almost any lengths to get what I wanted.

> Dear Marian and George,
>
> Forgive me for leaving without saying goodbye to anyone but Robin. Don't forgive me for taking all your money, Marian. It's a terrible thing to do and I promise to return it as soon as I can. I am no longer engaged to Archie—I never should have been. He mistook one feeling for another. Whatever he says about me is probably too kind.
>
> I took the money because I want to go to Iceland to find my grandparents, or any other members of my father's family. I don't think I can go forward until I know what lies behind me. I am sorry not to explain better. I will be back in two weeks, or less, if you still want me to work for you. I'll understand if you don't.

Thank you for giving me a home and for being so kind to me.

Love, Jean

P.S. My real (Scottish) name is Gemma Hardy.

Then I wrote a short note to Hannah and Pauline; I would post it in the morning on my way to the bus. I tried not to think of the irony that Archie would be the one to slide it through their letter-box. As for him, there was no need to write.

PART
V

chapter thirty-two

Since childhood I had waved whenever I saw a plane pass overhead, and while I waited at Glasgow airport, I had witnessed half-a-
dozen of the huge machines rush down the runway and rise into the
sky, but as I sat in my window-seat, and my plane hurtled over the tarmac, it seemed impossible that even the most vigourous engine could
lift all these people and seats and suitcases into the air. On and on we
bumped. Then, just as it began to seem that we would do nothing more
than circle the airport and return for a cup of tea, a giant force was
pushing me back in my seat; my arms and legs were suddenly twice
as heavy. The buildings and cars grew smaller with astonishing speed.
We passed through the clouds, which had looked so solid from the
ground, into dazzling sunlight.

The seat beside me was empty, and except when the air hostess
brought me a neatly quartered shrimp sandwich and a glass of water,
I gazed out of the window. Once or twice the clouds opened and I
caught a glimpse of the distant sea but no sign of the Far Islands with
their blossoming apple trees. Mr. Sinclair had been right. This kind of
flight was not at all like that of a bird; it was too noisy, too purposeful.
Sitting there, in my seat paid for with stolen money, looking out at the
endless sky, I allowed myself to picture him, just for a moment, standing on the tower of St. Magnus, pointing out the old shoreline to Nell
and me.

The skalds had taken months to sail from Iceland to Scotland, but after barely two hours the pilot announced our descent into Reykja-vik. I leaned forward to catch my first sight of the country where I had spent three years and about which almost everything I knew came from poems written seven hundred years ago. Grey sea, black rocks, and occasional clumps of reddish weeds or shrubs filled my gaze. Of the city there was no sign.

On the steps of the plane the wind lifted my hair. I breathed in the smell of hot engines and the perfume of the woman in front. Over her shoulder, beyond the airport building, I saw a line of bare, angular mountains. Then I was inside the building and a man in uniform was stamping my new passport. "Welcome to Iceland, Miss Hardy. Enjoy your holiday." My suitcase too had made the long journey. Again I followed my fellow passengers, this time into the customs area. The two men on duty waved me through without a glance. I found myself in a large hall with windows along one side, a row of desks on another. The travel agent in Edinburgh had advised me to change money at the airport, but looking around I saw nothing that resembled a bank. Behind one of the desks a woman in uniform was knitting something green. "Excuse me," I said. "Do you speak English?"

"You will tell me," she said, needles still clicking. "How may I help?"

"I have only Scottish money, pounds. And I don't know how to get into the city."

"See behind you—Change—they will change your money. The bus to Reykjavik goes outside. One hundred kronur. You buy ticket on the bus."

I thanked her and, encouraged by her friendliness, asked if she could recommend a cheap place to stay. I worried she might not understand *cheap*, but she nodded. "Change money, come back, I will phone."

When I returned a few minutes later with my kronur carefully tucked into my purse, she held out a piece of paper. "Get off when the bus stops. This is the house of my aunt. One night, seven hundred kro-nur. Her English is better than mine. She will aid you."

She had printed the address and drawn a map, beginning with the bus station and ending with a little house. I thanked her profusely.

"I am glad to help," she said. "My aunt asked why you visit."

It was absurd to think the first person I met would have the answers, but I got out my notebook and showed her the page on which I had written my father's name. "I'm looking for this person's family," I said.

She set aside her knitting—it was obviously a scarf—and studied the page. "No," she said. "I do not know Einar Arinbjornsson."

"Please, say that again." I had hoped that Icelandic, the language I had heard and spoken for several years, would sound familiar, but even at second hearing my father's name was only a rumble of syllables.

"Who is this person to you?" said the woman.

"My father. He died in 1951. I've never heard his name before."

"So you look for your family as well as his. But go. The bus is soon. Good luck. When you fly home, stop and tell me what happens."

I promised I would. Outside, the bus was waiting. I fumbled over my money until the driver plucked out a note and gave me a ticket.

Iceland, Iceland, Iceland, I kept thinking. Through the windows of the bus the landscape looked very old, but I knew from my reading that it was the other way round: geologically Iceland was a young country. The soft hills near Claypoole were old volcanoes; these jagged moun-tains were new ones. We passed mile after empty mile of the black rocks I had seen from the air. Lava, I guessed. Once I saw a herd of brown ponies. Was this the country my mother had fallen in love with? Then, almost suddenly, we were in a town, a city. An odd rippling church spire rose above the brightly coloured houses. At last there were trees.

When I got off the bus, the driver looked at my map and, after a brief consultation with another passenger, pointed me across the square. With two wrong turns I made my way to a quiet street lined with houses. Number eleven was much smaller than its neighbours; with its walls of green corrugated iron and its red corrugated roof, it reminded me of a garden shed. Lace curtains hung in the two front windows, and along one window-sill stood half-a-dozen cacti. The sight of these last gave me the courage to knock. Almost at once I heard firm footsteps. The door opened and a pair of bright brown eyes stared at me alertly. The owner of these eyes was an inch or two shorter than me and wore a black dress, with a cream-coloured cardigan over her shoulders. Around her neck hung a pendant with a bright red stone. She held out a hand with a ring on every finger.

"Welcome, Scottish girl. I am Hallie, short for Hallgerd." Her cheeks, when she smiled, pleated into many tiny lines.

I told her my name was Gemma.

She led me to a small plain room with five pieces of furniture: a narrow white bed, a chair, a bedside table with a lamp, and a low chest. The window was the one without the cacti, looking out onto the street.

"Don't worry," Hallie said. "You will sleep well." She waved her hand, as if casting a spell. "Rest now. Supper will be in one hour."

I had planned to begin my quest immediately, perhaps question a few people in the neighbouring streets, but at her words I realised how tired I was. I lay down, pressed my cheek to the plump pillow, and closed my eyes.

I woke to Hallie calling, "Supper. Five minutes." In the bathroom across the hall I studied my reflection as I washed my hands and brushed my hair. If I was on the other side of the mirror, then I must be on this side too, here, at last, in Iceland. When I stepped into the sitting-room, a table beside the window was laid for supper. Hallie insisted that I sit while she brought in some kind of meat, peas, and potatoes. "Simple food," she said.

For several minutes all I did was eat. Meanwhile she told me she had grown up in the village of Kirkjubaejarklaustur, a place famous for disaster. In 1783 a volcano had erupted nearby at Lakagigar. While the lava flowed towards their houses, the villagers had gathered in the church to listen to the minister deliver what came to be known as the Fire Sermon. Miraculously, the lava had stopped short of the village.

"But his preaching did not stop the volcano," said Hallie. "It erupted for eight months. Almost a quarter of the people in Iceland died and many, many animals. The sulphur turned their feet yellow, poor things. Even faraway places, like England and France, had clouds of ash. Iceland has many volcanoes. Did you see the lava on the way from the airport?"

"Yes," I said, pleased to have my guess confirmed.

When she grew up, Hallie continued, she had moved to Reykjavik to study, and there met her husband. He had worked in a hotel; that was how they both learned English. His heart had stopped five years ago and now she did the accounts for several local businesses. She had no children, and the woman at the airport was her favourite niece.

"Now tell me your story," she said. "Where you come from, why you are here."

She gazed at me steadily while I told her how the deaths of first my parents and then my uncle had severed me from the Icelandic side of my family. "I'm going to university in the autumn," I said. "I wanted to find out if I have any relatives—grandparents, perhaps an aunt or uncle."

"Did you know that Scotland is part of our sagas?" said Hallie. "Earl Thorfinn was greedy and ugly and ruled the Orkneys from a place called Birsay. Some say he was Shakespeare's Macbeth."

"Birsay?" I recalled the red sandstone ruins on the edge of the village.

Hallie nodded; her pendant flashed. "Yes, the gods were on his side for a while. How many days do you have to find these people?"

"A week. I'm worried it's not long enough to search an entire country."

"If there is any place this is possible," Hallie said, tapping the table, "it is here. We are a not large island with a not large population. People know each other and know each other's families. In one way or another many people here are related."

"In Scotland," I said, "we have a registry of births, marriages, and deaths."

"We have the same. Tomorrow morning I will take you and translate. What became of your parents' house?"

"My aunt said no one answered my uncle's letters about it."

"If the house belonged to your father," said Hallie meditatively, "then it should belong to you."

"But it's all so long ago. Sixteen years. Someone else must be living there now."

"Still, you are a daughter of Iceland. Tell me your father's name."

I fetched my notebook. Like her niece, Hallie said the name aloud: Einar Arinbjornsson. By the end of the week, I thought, I would be able to say it. "What about your name?" she said. "Did you always have a Scottish name?"

"No. But I'm not sure how to say my own name either." I turned the page and showed her.

"Fjola Einarsdottir," she said. "It is a good name. Fjola is a flower—white or purple—called a violet. And Einar—your father's name—means 'he who fights alone, a great warrior.' So your name has a soft part and a hard part."

"Fjola Einarsdottir," I repeated.

"I wonder why you were not called Violet in Scotland," said Hallie. "It is a name for girls, isn't it?"

"Yes, for flowers and girls. I don't know why. My uncle chose my name, and I never thought to ask."

"You can be Fjola here," said Hallie. She stood up from the table and announced that she was going for an evening stroll. "We will start to spread the word," she said. "I have neighbours who like to talk. Could you clean the plates? The door is open. Go for a walk if you like, or go to bed. We have breakfast at eight."

The sun was still high, and after I had washed the dishes and put them away as best I could, I went for a walk. In the nearby streets many of the houses, like Hallie's, were made of corrugated iron and had roofs of different colours; some were whitewashed or harled. Beyond the rooftops I saw the jagged mountains, and between the houses, from two different directions, I glimpsed the sea. Reykjavik, Hallie had told me, meant "smoky bay." While the houses looked different the trees were familiar—rowans, birches, firs—and so were the flowers—lupins, snapdragons, roses, daisies, marigolds, and pansies. As I walked, I recounted the momentous events of the last forty-eight hours. I had broken things off with Archie, who had saved my life; I had stolen from the MacGillvarys, who had been nothing but kind to me; I had ruined my friendship with Hannah and Pauline. How could I tell them that their beloved brother had refused to kiss me? Perhaps, I thought, his preferences followed Hannah's but he didn't know it yet. Or perhaps he was like Miss Seftain and didn't care about anyone in that way. And now I had flown to Iceland and was walking down a street in Reykjavik, the city where my parents had met. Only Marian and George, if they cared to think about it, knew I was here.

A man was approaching with a small white dog, similar to the one I had seen in Pitlochry. As we drew level, it tugged towards me. The man nodded and said something—Good evening, I imagined, or He's friendly—and I nodded back, delighted to be taken for an Icelander.

AT BREAKFAST OVER SLICES of bread and cheese and sweet, dark coffee, Hallie reported that she had called upon four of her neighbours and told them about my search. "It is like a saga," she said. "Scottish girl seeks lost family. Soon, you will hear, people will come knocking on my door."

"You're very kind. I should tell you that I don't have much money. You shouldn't give me so much to eat."

All the little lines in her cheeks bunched together. "Not kind," she said, shaking her head. "The truth is I am old and bored. This is an adventure, and Icelanders like adventures. That is how we got here in the first place. So today"—she clapped her hands and I heard the click of her rings—"we will go to the registry and see what we can find. At the central post they have books with telephone numbers for everyone in Iceland. We can look there too."

Ten minutes later Hallie and I were walking down the street. She pointed out the huge church spire I had noticed the day before. They had been building the Hallgrimskirkja since the end of the Second World War. "It is a homage to God and to a volcano," she said. "Here in Iceland we have many things that shoot up: geysers, volcanoes."

"And you have puffins."

"Yes, you ate last night." She saw my face and laughed. "You think we should not eat birds with their pretty beaks, but there are so many of them, millions, and they taste good."

In fact the meat had tasted of fish, but I said yes, it was good, and that I was glad I hadn't known sooner. As we walked, Hallie insisted on pointing out various sites. "I know you are not a tourist," she said, "but I must show you my city."

We passed a lake with swans and mallards, then an olive-coloured church: the Dominican cathedral. In the nearby square Hallie pointed out a statue of a man in a frock coat; I did not catch his name. A street lined with shops led us to a large white house—"the strongest house in Iceland," Hallie said. Once a prison, it was now used by the government. Slowly we climbed a hill towards another statue. This man wore a horned helmet and carried a shield. Ingólfur Arnarson was the first settler, Hallie told me. Like him, we stopped to gaze out over the harbour. My job was to admire the view while she got her breath back.

Two more streets brought us to an official-looking grey building. Inside Hallie waved me to a chair and, taking my notebook, approached the desk. I heard my father's name, and the woman behind the desk—she had the same broad cheeks as Hallie—turned to look at me. She disappeared and returned, disappeared and returned. Periodically Hallie asked me questions: The month and year of his death? Was I his only child? Did he have siblings? The woman consulted a large black book, then another. She took my notebook and dashed off a couple of lines.

"What's happening?" I asked Hallie. She told me to wait.

After nearly half an hour she came and sat beside me. "It is possible I will drop dead on the way home," she said, "so let me tell you what we know. Your father was born in June 1919 in the village of Stykkisholmur on the Snaefellsnes peninsula. His father was a fisherman. He had an older sister, Kristjana. His parents were both dead when he died. See"—she held out my notebook—"I have written down the names here."

"So I have an aunt," I said.

"If she still lives," said Hallie. "Why didn't she take you in?"

"My uncle promised my mother that if anything happened he would look after me."

"Perhaps she knew the future," Hallie said, turning the thinnest of her rings. "Iceland is famous for people who see trolls and elves. You must remember, not all relatives are good relatives. I myself have some cousins who are villainous and a sister who wishes me posthumous."

"I have some Scottish cousins who feel like that about me," I said. "So how can we find her?"

"We will go and look in the telephone book. But first I must sit for a few more minutes."

Since the previous evening I had revised my idea of Hallie's age several times. At first sight I had taken her for sixty or even seventy. Then, over supper, her kindness and energy had made her seem younger. But as we walked into the city she had placed her feet with the care of an older person. Now, seeing her sink back in the chair, I offered to find someone else to help me at the post office.

"No, no, now it is my quest too, and the post is on our way home."

Soon she gathered herself and led the way back down the hill, past the bronze warrior, to the post office. While she searched the telephone directory, I watched the Icelanders come and go. If I had an aunt, and if my aunt had children, then one of these oblivious people might be my cousin. Hallie found no listing for her in the directory, but she told me not to worry. Many people in Iceland did not have a phone. Someone would know someone in Stykkisholmur who had known my family.

As we walked back through another large square, she drew my attention to a building with a carved falcon perched on either end of the ridge-pole. Long ago, she said, it had been the King of Denmark's falconry. I told her the story from the saga of Helga's father's dream and the various bird suitors killing each other.

"I did not know that," she said, "but it sounds most Icelandic."

Back at her house, Hallie announced that, now that we had the name of the village, she was going to consult her neighbours again.

While she went to call on them, I ate some bread and cheese and paced my small room. I felt like running through the streets, calling my aunt's name until someone answered. Then I recalled Hallie's comment. "Please," I said uselessly, "let her be alive." Thoughts of my new aunt led to my old aunt, whom I had scarcely considered since my visit. Was she still sitting in her armchair, I wondered, or had she moved on to her final resting place? I tried to send my question into the universe, a long, slender wire snaking its way towards Yew House, but nothing came back.

At last I heard the front door open. I hurried to meet Hallie. Standing in the dim hall, smiling, she announced that one of her neighbours knew someone on the peninsula who knew my aunt Kristjana.

"She's alive," I said, clapping my hands.

"She was last week."

Messages had been relayed; replies were awaited.

That evening Hallie drew a family tree for my father's side of the family, with many question marks. Had my grandparents had siblings? Probably. Did my aunt have children? We would find out soon. I stared in wonder at my own name at the end of this tracery of branching lines. In one way or another I was connected to these people.

Hallie put a dash beside my name. "This is where your husband's name will go. Below will be your children, if you are so blessed."

"I'll never get married," I said.

"Forgive me," said Hallie. "Old women are presumptuous. We like to see trees grow."

THE NEXT MORNING I laid the table and put on water for coffee. Then I sat down to study the Icelandic-English dictionary I had discovered in Hallie's bookshelves the night before. I copied out the numbers from one to ten and the words for *yes, no, thank you, good morning, sorry,* and *bathroom.* I could not find a word for *please.* When Hallie at last appeared, I greeted her. "*Gooan daginn.*"

She laughed and corrected my pronunciation. "You made the table. *Takk fyrir.* Thank you. I am sorry to be late. This is the trouble with being old. Today my legs wanted to stay in bed. But soon"—she must have seen my anxious expression—"I will go and ask if there is news."

Over breakfast I entertained her with my efforts to pronounce various words. I was practising *left* and *right*—*vinstir, haegri*—when, in the hallway, the phone gave an odd monosyllabic ring. Hallie went to answer. I heard the rise and fall of her voice and twice my own name. After nearly ten minutes she returned.

"Fjola," she exclaimed. "Your aunt is found. She still lives in Stykkisholmur, where she and your father grew up."

Delight swept me out of my seat. "That's wonderful. That's fantastic. I have an aunt and you know where she lives. Can I go and see her?"

"Tomorrow. You have missed the bus today. She is eager to see you."

"That's wonderful," I repeated.

"Wonderful," agreed Hallie. "There are two things she asked me to tell you." She held up her hand with its gold rings, and I caught a note of warning. "First, she is blind; she lost her sight a number of years ago. Second, she speaks no English. Happily her daughter, Berglind, can translate. She will meet the bus."

For months, I had daydreamed about finding someone who would look at me and see my parents; who would find my mother in my ears, my father in the shape of my hands, both of them in my straight brown hair and grey eyes. But my aunt might never have seen my mother and had last seen my father many years ago. It would be I who had to study her features for evidence of kinship. I remembered a book I had read about Helen Keller and how, when she met someone new, she ran her fingers over the person's face. Perhaps my aunt would do that.

"She can talk," I said. "She knew my parents."

We agreed that I would return to stay with Hallie the night before my flight back to Glasgow. That way I could tell her what had happened and be at the airport in good time.

The remainder of the day passed in helping Hallie—I weeded her small garden and cleaned the windows—and in visiting the Hallgrimskirkja. "You can be sure," she said, "that your father went there at least once." As I walked up the road to the church, it got bigger and bigger, and when I stepped inside I could not help marvelling at how bright it was, and how empty. Like the landscapes I had passed through on my way from the airport, it was utterly bare.

DURING THE SIX-HOUR JOURNEY the bus-driver stopped more times than I could count for people to get on and off, or to be sick, or to go to the bathroom. Out of the window I saw the twisted black rocks, the pointed shapes of old volcanoes, herds of brown and black ponies, and small sheep grazing on the brown grass. The occasional field shone emerald green in contrast to the greys and blacks. The countryside was wilder and emptier than any I had ever seen—for miles we saw no other cars, no houses, no animals, no birds—and yet it was here that I'd come to find my family. One of our stops was beside a road running east into a broad valley.

"Reykholt," called the driver, and I recognised the name of the village Archie had mentioned where the saga writer lived. Would he, I wondered, ever come to Iceland?

Stykkisholmur was not like the Scottish villages I knew, houses standing shoulder to shoulder along neatly organised roads. Instead the brightly coloured houses were fitted into the landscape wherever the rocks permitted. Even on the main road there were wide gaps. The bus rounded one last corner and stopped beside a small grey church.

For several minutes I gave no thought to the fact that I was in my father's birthplace, my first home; I was glad simply to be on steady ground. I set my suitcase on the steps of the church and walked up and down, taking deep breaths. When I was able to look around, I saw that the harbour, filled with boats, was only a hundred yards away. I sat down and got out the lunch Hallie had made me.

I was finishing the last sandwich when I heard the sound of a horse's hooves. Round the corner came a young woman riding a brown pony, waving. "Hallo, hallo," she cried. "I am Berglind."

She rode over, slid off the pony, and held out her hand. "Hallo, Fjola."

For a moment I simply stared at her wide grey eyes, her fair, freckled skin. Mistaking my silence, she started to apologise. "I wanted to meet you like a hero, but Isolfur is lazy. He wouldn't trot." Her brown hair was almost the same colour as the pony's and she wore it in a single thick braid.

"No, it's fine," I said. "I was just surprised. I'm not used to being called Fjola."

She laughed. "We will have lessons to say your name. Do you remember me?"

I shook my head. "I don't remember you, or my aunt, or my parents. I hoped that coming here would bring back memories but it hasn't, so far."

"Perhaps you remember," said Berglind, "but not in your brain. Will you ride?"

I refused as politely as I could and she said we would all three walk. She picked up my suitcase and, calling to Isolfur, not bothering to hold his reins, set off. I have a cousin, I thought, who acts like Pippi Long-stocking. Loping along beside her, I asked how old she was. Twenty-six. Did she have brothers or sisters? Two brothers who worked in

Reykjavik. Did she remember my parents? Yes, she used to go sailing with them on calm days.

"Your mother had very blue eyes," she said, "and she could touch her nose with her tongue. Can you?"

"I don't think so. Do you remember other things about her?"

Berglind swung my suitcase. "Come on, Isolfur," she called over her shoulder. "She made English custard from a tin. I can smell it. She had a book of empty pages, and she drew birds and plants and fish. She had a blue dress she liked. Once I spilled juice on the skirt and she said it was all right. She and I taught you to walk—you walked from her to me, and back again. I see you have not forgotten your skill."

I laughed, delighted by both the fact and her phrasing. "You speak such good English."

"Your mother was my first teacher. Then I studied at school. Now I have the radio. I am happy to practise on you. We do not get many visitors in Stykkisholmur."

"I hope it's not rude to ask, but why is your mother blind? Was she in an accident?"

"No. It happened over a few months. Our neighbours say it is because she sees other things."

"What sort of things?"

"Weather. People. Last week she told me we would meet a new relative soon."

So, even before I had visited Archie and stolen the money, my aunt had known I was coming. I was still grappling with this news when Berglind pointed out a house. "Where we live. And those"—she indicated two brown ponies grazing nearby—"are Isolfur's brothers."

"Do you live here too?"

"My husband and I both." Then she looked over at me. "Sorry. I forget you have no parents to live with. Maybe that is why you are so small."

Inside the house a woman wearing a white blouse and faded blue trousers set aside her knitting and rose to meet me. "Welcome, Fjola," she said. "I am your aunt Kristjana."

She too wore her hair in a single braid that hung almost to her waist. She stepped forward, holding out her hand. I stared at her wonderingly. Beneath her unlined forehead, her pale blue eyes were very still. Ignoring her hand, I reached to hug her. She smelled of soap and of something that reminded me of the sea.

THE PHRASES SHE UTTERED when we met turned out to be Kristjana's entire stock of English; Berglind had taught them to her that morning. As for my uncle Ulfur—his name meant *wolf*—and Berglind's husband, Gisli, they both knew only *hallo*, which was the same in Icelandic. The men worked together, repairing boats. They came home at six, and we ate lamb stew at the kitchen table. When Berglind was not translating, I looked around and saw that the hems of the curtains were frayed, the table scarred, the plates and cutlery well used. My aunt and her family did not have much money.

After supper we went for a walk. Kristjana, arm in arm with Ulfur, gave directions as we made our way along the hilly, winding, unpaved roads. She pointed out the cottage where she and my father had grown up, the school they had attended, the mooring where their father—he fished for scallops and herring—had kept his boat. As we stood looking at the harbour, two eider ducks swam by. I was about to ask Berglind their Icelandic name when a dark head surfaced.

"Oh, you have seals," I said.

"We do," said Berglind. "People are cross—they eat many fish—but I don't care. Your mother used to say if I was a good girl I could ride a seal all the way to Scotland."

She waved to the seal, just as I had done months ago on the causeway, and, I guessed, translated our exchange for her family. As we started back up the hill a white-haired man carrying a basket came loping towards us. Kristjana stopped and introduced me. I heard the words *Fjola, Einar, dottir.* The man set down his basket and clasped my hand warmly. Dottir, I thought.

Back at the house we drank a kind of tea made, Berglind said, from stinging plants. Kristjana patted the seat next to hers and I sat down. Berglind pulled up a chair, ready to translate.

"It was a long time ago," Kristjana said. "You must forgive us if we have forgotten many things about your parents, or if the things we remember are small. But you have found us. You can come back again."

"Please," said Berglind.

"Tonight you will tell us what you have done since you left with your uncle. Tomorrow, when I have put my thoughts in order, Berglind will help me tell you what I can about your father and your mother. I think you will like to take notes. Perhaps—who knows?—you will remember something for yourself."

As best I could, not mentioning either of my fiancés, I described what had happened since I left Iceland. Both Kristjana and Berglind said they were sorry to hear about my uncle's death. "I only met him once," said Kristjana, "but he was a good man."

"And you are a wanderer," said Berglind. "That I cannot imagine. I was born in this house and I know the names of the spiders who make their webs in the windows. I like having adventures—Gisli and I travel every summer—but then we come home."

"I never meant," I said, "to be a wanderer."

．　　．　　．

THE STORIES KRISTJANA TOLD of my parents were, as she promised, quite ordinary. I had travelled eight hundred miles to learn that my mother liked custard, my father tied better knots than any other fisherman in the village, they had played backgammon and eaten smoked fish, one summer they had gone on an expedition to Blaa Ionid, the Blue Lagoon. "Agnes came back wishing that Stykkisholmur had a hot spring," said Kristjana.

"I wish that too," said Berglind.

Of course there were more stories about my father, whom Kristjana had known for so much longer. When he was a boy, she told me, he had a black and white dog called Smoke. He had begun to fish almost as soon as he could walk; like many fishermen, he had never learned to swim. Once he and Kristjana had played truant to climb Mount Helgafell. Ever since the sagas, Berglind explained, it had been a sacred place. If you climbed it from the west, in silence, and then descended to the east, without looking back, you would have three wishes granted. "They must be pure wishes, though," she said. "Not for yourself."

"But I tripped on a rock," said Kristjana, "and broke my silence, and Einar looked back to see what had happened, so neither of us got our wishes."

During the war Einar had moved to the city and become one of the hundreds of men employed in building the new docks for the British Navy. Then he had met Agnes. She didn't know how: At a dance? In the street? "*Ast*," she said, spreading her hands.

"*Ast* means *love*," added Berglind. "It happens at the most inconvenient moments. No wonder people invented Cupid, running around with his bow and arrow."

"They were soul mates," I said.

Kristjana pursed her lips in a way that made me wonder if Berglind had translated correctly. When she spoke again it was haltingly, and Berglind's English was slower too. "Maybe," she said. "Einar told me several times they both wanted to give up. He thought your mother was a coward because she would not leave her parents. And my parents and I were not happy. We thought Agnes would bring heartache to Einar. How could a girl from a city live in our little village? But we were wrong. Everything that was hard—the darkness, no shops, fish, fish, fish—Agnes embraced. Once in winter she came to our house long before it got light. She made scones and eggs. We ate by candlelight, all of us talking and laughing. She told me she had never cared for Edinburgh, so many people pressed together, ignoring each other. Her only doubt was when she was expecting you. She persuaded Einar to return to Scotland for a month so you could be born in a language she understood. She promised to be braver with her second child."

A ghost sister, or brother, touched my shoulder.

Patiently Kristjana and Berglind answered my questions. My mother had never learned to knit, she liked jokes, she waved her arms when she spoke Icelandic, once when she came across a dead fish she had stopped to draw it, she liked dancing, she played hide-and-seek with Berglind and her brothers, she wasn't shy but she could happily spend entire days alone, she was always interested in the sky.

"Did she believe in God?" I asked.

Kristjana's eyebrows rose. "I am not sure I know the answer. We all pretend to be Christians, go to church, say our prayers. My guess is she believed in some god or goddess who lived in waves and clouds and other people."

"Do you believe in God?" Berglind asked.

"I used to, until my uncle drowned."

"But don't you think"—Kristjana touched the table, the wall—"that there has to be a reason why there is something, rather than nothing?"

"No," I said. "I think some things just are, like puffins and volcanoes, and then humans invent other things." I told them the story I remembered from long ago about the snow being who visited people's houses when something bad was going to happen.

"So only in winter," said Kristjana thoughtfully. "I have never heard of that. Perhaps it was a story your father made only for you. Now Berglind will show you the photographs we have of Einar."

On the table Berglind spread out half-a-dozen photographs: my aunt and my father in my grandfather's boat, both wearing shorts; my grandparents and the two children on a picnic; my father playing with a black and white dog, standing beside a bus, in the prow of a boat; my father and my mother in the doorway of a small, white house, my mother holding an alert baby with wispy dark hair. I stared in wonder at this last, my father's boyish face, his arm around my mother, her arms around me.

As if she could see my expression Kristjana said, "You must have the one of your parents together but I would like to keep the younger ones. I know it's foolish but sometimes I hold them. I am glad to have Einar close at hand."

I thanked her as best I could. Then I went to my suitcase and took out the photograph I had taken from Archie's bookshelf. Here was its rightful place. Berglind described it to her mother—I heard her say Fjola several times—and they agreed that the Scottish cousin would have a place of honour on the mantelpiece.

WHEN ULFUR CAME HOME, Berglind borrowed his van. She drove her mother and me to the outskirts of the village and down a track to the cove where my parents had lived. The sky was overcast, and we parked above the small jetty. Nearby was a beach covered in small black stones. Not far away was another beach pink with scallop shells.

This was where my father had kept his boat in bad weather; this was where my parents had walked and I had played. Berglind led the way to a small white house with a red roof. I recognised it but only from the photograph they had shown me. The memory I had had of my uncle rolling balls across the grass must have come not from my own eyes but from his stories. By the front door were a clump of pansies and a tangled wild rose.

"My mother says," said Berglind, "that it looks much the same as when your parents lived here but sadder."

How did she know? I wondered. "Who lives here now?" I said.

"A stranger. The uncle of a woman who works at the fish market."

Remembering Hallie's question, I asked if my parents had owned the house.

"Ah," said Berglind, "you are thinking about money. Perhaps you are really an heiress." She smiled at me.

"No," I said crossly. "I didn't come here for money. My plane ticket cost more than I earn in six months. But I have nothing from my parents. Of course I wonder what became of their things."

Kristjana tugged her daughter's sleeve. Berglind translated and then turned back to me. "I am sorry. Blame the radio. What I said sounded rude but by mistake."

Her wide eyes regarded me with such candour that my anger melted. I said her English was excellent and that I forgave her. Then Kristjana said that we must discuss these matters later. For now she wondered if I would like to see inside the house. She knocked and we all three waited. But as the minutes passed, nothing stirred.

"What a pity," said Kristjana. "When you come back we will make arrangements. Now we will wait for you at the van."

Alone I circled the house. Then I tiptoed towards it and looked through each window in turn: a bedroom, a small sitting-room, a kitchen. The furniture was plain, like my aunt's. On the walls were several pictures of boats. Nothing was familiar until I looked in the kitchen window. Then I caught sight of the red and brown linoleum. I knew at once I had crawled and walked over it many, many times. Every seam, every spot and scar, was familiar. If I had been able to go inside I would have lain down and kissed that faded floor.

I had no idea how much time passed before I tore myself away. In my notebook I drew a picture of the cottage and a little map of where it stood in relation to the jetty and the two beaches. I scrambled down to each in turn and chose a black stone from one, some pink shells from the other. I might never find the contents of my box, but Mr. Donaldson had mentioned shells.

As we drove back past the harbour Berglind slowed. "See the blue boat," she said. "She is called after you."

In bold white letters there was my name, *Fjola*, on the bow of the boat.

AT SUPPER BERGLIND TOLD me she had to work the next day. Thinking she meant cleaning the house or making soup, I said I could help. She laughed her boisterous laugh. "Not unless you know how to dry fish. Today I didn't go because of you, but tomorrow I must be there at the big building near the harbour."

It had not occurred to me that she had a job. Abashed, I thanked her. "I don't think anyone's ever taken a day off work for me before," I said.

"It's not often I find a lost cousin. What will you do tomorrow?"

"Could you draw me a map of how to get to the mountain that grants wishes?"

"Helgafell? I can. It is about five or six kilometres south. I can lend you a bicycle. Although we call it a mountain it is only a few hundred metres high."

Gisli began to clear the plates from supper; I rose to help. Last night I had sat shyly while he and Berglind joked over the washing-up, but I knew enough of the household now to fetch and carry. As I scraped the plates into the bucket for the hens, Kristjana said something in which I caught my parents' names. Berglind took the plates out of my hands.

"Mother wonders," she said, "if you would like to visit the grave of your parents. We could take flowers from the garden. Is something wrong?"

I looked over at my aunt, who was smiling in my direction. "No, I'm just sorry I didn't think to ask. I must seem very thoughtless."

Berglind shook her head. "We both say you are very thoughtful, and my mother adds the grave is not the important thing but that you live far away and maybe it would be good to see."

In the garden we picked tall daisies. Berglind found a jam jar and filled it with water. Once again she borrowed the van. I had pictured a little cemetery romantically overlooking the harbour, but she told me no, it was on the outskirts of town; I had passed it, without noticing, on the bus. The cemetery was surrounded by a thick hedge and, as we stepped through the gate, the leaves rustled in the breeze. Small birds flew in and out of the branches. Many of the graves were marked by white wooden crosses, some by stones; they all faced in the same direction. My parents had two stones side by side.

"Here is your name," said Berglind, pointing to the second line. "'Agnes, beloved wife of Einar, and mother of Fjola.' I used to think they were quite old when they died. Now they seem young."

The idea that I had all along, without knowing it, been here in this cemetery, in Iceland, took my breath away. I reached out my hand and traced the letters: F-J-O-L-A.

THE NEXT MORNING I helped my aunt in ways that did not require words. I hung out laundry, I gathered the eggs from the dozen hens, I chopped onions and did the ironing. As we worked, I saw how deftly Kristjana weighed the kettle, how she felt the water to see when the clothes were rinsed, how she wrapped the cheese tightly. When the clock struck eleven she made me a sandwich, filled a bottle with water, and handed me an apple. Then she made a pushing gesture with her hands and opened the door.

I tucked my trouser legs into my socks and retrieved the bicycle. To get to the main road I had to go down to the harbour, then I pedalled back past the church and the scattered houses and the cemetery, out of the village. Last week at this time I had been walking with George and Robin in the garden. Next week . . . but I would not think about that. What I must think about were my three pure wishes. Could I wish for my aunt's eyesight, my uncle's resurrection? But no, I thought; I must wish for something both pure and possible. George's health? Archie's forgiveness? A chance to return to Stykkisholmur?

Beyond the village rough moorland stretched in all directions. Save for a few sheep and ponies I was utterly alone. Berglind had told me that before Iceland converted to Christianity, the god Thor had lived on Helgafell. Later it had been the home of Gunner, the heroine of one of the sagas. Icelanders hoped to be taken into the mountain when they died. I came round one more bend and there, to my left, rising out of the flat landscape, was Helgafell. A track led from the road past a small lake to the mountain. As I pedalled along I counted a dozen swans swimming on the windy water. Near the foot of the hill I leaned the bike against a fence. A sheep path zigzagged up through the long grass. Soon the grass gave way to rocks, large and small, and in the distance I could make out the colourful houses of the village and beyond the islands in the bay. A small stone ruin, the remains of a shepherd's hut or hermit's cell perhaps, marked the summit. The wind rushed in my ears as if it had come all the way from Scotland.

I was heading down the path to the east when I heard a soft cry. Two ravens were rising and falling in the wind—Thor and Gunner, I thought—but I was careful not to follow their flight too far. I must not look back. I started walking again, stooping now and then to pick ripe blueberries; they had a faint bitter taste.

"Gemma," called a voice. "Wait for me."

"Who is it?" I stopped to scan the empty hillside. "Where are you?" A sheep raised its head. The two ravens circled.

"Where are you?" I repeated. But only the birds and the wind answered.

Presently I began walking again. This was not like the muffled shout in the hailstorm. I had heard the words clearly and recognised their speaker instantly. Mr. Sinclair was looking for me, was still looking for me, and I could no longer deny that I was glad. Since I stole out of the hotel in Kirkwall, I had learned that I too was capable of lying to get what I wanted, or to avoid what I dreaded. I had betrayed my uncle's ideals. And perhaps, it came to me now, he felt that he had too: pretending to marriage and fatherhood. As I circled the base of the mountain back to where I had left the bicycle, I realised that, like my aunt and my father, I had lost my wishes.

WHEN BERGLIND RETURNED FROM work I told her and Kristjana that near the top of the mountain a sheep had startled me; I had looked back.

"Too bad," said Berglind.

"You are in the family tradition," said my aunt. She set aside her knitting and clasped her hands. "I have thought about this all day, and there are two things I must tell you. Berglind, you must translate without comment and you must, both of you, forgive me for not telling you sooner. The truth is, I am ashamed. I liked Agnes, but something unfortunate happened. The first time I met her I saw how she would die. I did not know what to do. I tried to warn her not to walk on the rocks; I tried to warn Einar. But rocks are everywhere. How could I warn her against them? So I could not be friends with your mother because I was always wondering if there was something I could do to save her.

"Then one day, soon after she became pregnant, I told her what I'd seen."

"What did she say?" I couldn't imagine the bewildering conversation.

"She was angry, and she was frightened." My aunt pressed her hands to her temples, as if the memory still pained her. "She made me promise not to tell Einar, but I think that was why she went back to Scotland for your birth, and why she made your uncle promise to take care of you if anything happened. What I described, her pleasure in Iceland, that was true, but her pleasure grew less after I spoke."

"What about my father?"

"Did I see his death? Happily, no. I was able to enjoy his company until the last day of his life. I never see things about my close family. I see nothing for Berglind or her brothers, or Ulfur."

"And," I had to ask, "what about for me?"

Kristjana lowered her hands and leaned slightly forward. "I do not need to see the future to know that you are a very determined person. Your determination will bear fruit. Now the second thing."

Gradually, as I heard her begin sentences, break them off, begin again, it dawned on me that my aunt was embarrassed. My parents, she said, had owned their house, and when my father died, I had inherited it. After many delays it had been sold, the mortgage had been paid off, and the rest of the money put in a bank account for me.

"But why didn't anyone tell me?" I thought of all the times when even a small amount of money would have made a large difference.

"Two reasons," said my aunt, "neither pretty. I wrote to your uncle with Berglind's help—it was more than four years later—and he wrote back saying it would be better to keep the money here for you until you were of age. He gave me your Scottish name for the bank. Any money, he said, might make war with your aunt. We wrote again when you became eighteen to the address we had, but no letter came back."

Yet another of my aunt's betrayals. Even as I opened my mouth to denounce her, Isolfur, or one of his brothers, neighed, and in the few seconds that followed I suddenly knew, as clearly as if I were standing in Edinburgh, the answer to the question I had pondered at Hallie's. My anger was too late; there was a new grave beside my uncle's and his brother's. "I'm sorry," I said. "And the second reason?"

Kristjana turned towards the window where the sun was still high above the rooftop of their nearest neighbour. "Our life here is not easy. One winter Ulfur broke his arm and could not work. And you see how it is with me. Besides my knitting I can do nothing that makes money. I borrowed from you—nearly seventy thousand kronur—and I have never been able to pay it back. I am most sorry."

Beneath Berglind's wide-eyed gaze I jumped up and kissed my aunt. The idea of being owed money by someone I loved was almost better than the idea of owning money.

THE NEXT MORNING ALL four of them came to see me off on the bus back to Reykjavik. My hand disappeared into first Ulfur's, then Gisli's large grasp. Berglind lifted me up and swung me round. "One summer Gisli and I will come to see you in Scotland," she said. "And you must come here. We will sail out to Flatey and visit the birds."

"I would like that," I said. "Please translate one more time."

I turned to my aunt. "Since my uncle died I've been a friend, a pupil, a maid, an au pair, but I've never had a family. Thank you for making me feel like a daughter again, and a niece, and a cousin."

Kristjana smiled and touched my cheek. "Berglind and Ulfur say you have your father's nose," she said. "And we all say you have your mother's spirit. Come and see us again soon, Fjola. Listen to the voice of Helgafell."

They stood waving as the bus pulled away. Only when they were out of sight and we hit the first pothole did I understand how she had dodged my question of the night before. She had foreseen my arrival; she knew about the voice on the wind.

chapter thirty-three

Besides the black stone and the scallop shells, and the photograph of my parents, I carried with me two copies—one in my notebook and one in the pocket where I kept emergency funds—of the details of my bank account, which, now that I was nineteen, was entirely at my disposal. Kristjana had explained that there were several branches of the bank and suggested I visit the one in the centre of Reykjavik when I got off the bus. I had never been in a bank before, and as I stepped into the lofty room, I kept expecting a policeman to tap me on the shoulder, but no one seemed to find my presence strange. The woman behind the counter beckoned me forward and nodded pleasantly at the sight of my passport.

"A minute," she said. "Please."

"*Takk fyrir*," I said as she disappeared into a back office.

She returned accompanied by a plump, cheerful-looking man wearing a tweed jacket with leather patches on the elbows. "Good afternoon," he said. "Can I be of service?"

"You're from Scotland," I exclaimed. His accent was much stronger than mine.

"No," he said, sounding pleased, "but I studied at Edinburgh University for three years. How can I help?"

I explained about the account, that it had money, that the money was mine, and that I hoped to take it back to Scotland. To my amazement he nodded as if this were all quite ordinary. Did I want cash, in which case he would have to give me kronur? Or would I prefer a cheque, which could be in pounds?

Although I had often seen Marian write a cheque, I was still not entirely sure how they worked. I said that I wanted the money to be safe. "If I fall through the ice," I joked, "or if someone steals my bag, I don't want to be penniless."

"The cheque isn't the money," he assured me. "It's the key to the door where the money is kept, and that key can only be used by you. Even if someone else gets hold of it, it won't turn."

Kristjana hadn't said how much money was in the account, and while I waited I made a bargain with myself that, whatever the sum, I would not be disappointed. If there was enough to pay back the Mac-Gillvarys and buy books for the first term of university, that would be wonderful. If there was more, enough, say, for a new winter coat and some boots, that would be even more wonderful. I could buy Robin a book about birds and get Marian the new kettle she'd said several times that we needed.

"Here," the man said, sitting down beside me, holding out a rectangular piece of blue paper, "this is your name. This is your passport number, for extra security. And here"—he set some notes on the table beside me—"is the extra money in kronur. Four thousand pounds is what you Scots call a nice round sum. After the fees, that left eighteen hundred kronur." He fanned out the brightly coloured notes. "I hope you can use it."

"Four thousand pounds," I whispered. "Are you sure you haven't made a mistake?"

"No. We are a very careful bank. The account has been gaining interest every year; little by little it grows. There has only been one withdrawal since it was opened."

I took the cheque—my parents' house, my father's boat turned into a piece of paper too small even to make a paper boat—and put it carefully in my purse. Then he held out another sheet of paper and said here was the name and address of the bank, my account number, and his name. "If you fall through the ice, write, and I will rescue you. When you return to Scotland go to a bank—there is a nice one in Edinburgh in St. Andrews Square—and open an account. Your money will be safe, with a view of the castle, and you can get it whenever you want."

If I had been Berglind, I would have lifted him into the air and carried him round the room. As it was I kissed him. "Oh, my goodness," he said. He took off his glasses and wiped them with a handkerchief. Then I asked if he could direct me to a shop where I could buy flowers. He walked me to the door and pointed, diagonally, across the street.

For the next half-hour I wandered in and out of shops, studying cakes and caviar, leather belts and jewellery, sweaters and scarves. Finally I chose a dozen deep red roses, a jar of caviar, a cake, and four jars of jam for Hallie's neighbours. I found my way back past the bronze statue overlooking the harbour and down the hill, past the former prison, to the bus stop. Once again following the map her niece had drawn, I walked to her house. Hallie answered the door dressed in her familiar black.

"*Rosavin*," she exclaimed as I handed her the roses. "No one has given me flowers since Eirikur died."

My little room waited; the table was laid. While we ate, I told her almost everything. She congratulated me on my three new cousins, although two, I explained, didn't really count. From Berglind's silences and Kristjana's dismissive gestures, I had understood that they were not close to the brothers in Reykjavik. Some branches on the tree, I explained to Hallie, were less sturdy than others.

"So you have posthumous cousins," she said, "but one good one is a lot. Did you remember your village?"

"The only thing I remembered was the kitchen floor of the house where we used to live. When I looked through the window, I remembered crawling across the linoleum." I asked if she knew about Helgafell, and when she said yes, I described how my aunt and father had lost their wishes there and how I had too.

"When I met you," she said, "you were wishing hard to find one relative and you found two. Maybe you got your wishes before you met the mountain." Her bright brown eyes looked into mine as if there was something more that she wanted to say, but when she spoke again it was to suggest we try the cake.

THE NEXT MORNING, ALTHOUGH it was only seven, Hallie insisted on walking me to the bus stop. "Don't forget," she said, "to take your ticket to my niece, Nanna. She is working today and she is anxious to know what happened on your quest."

I promised I would. And I promised to write and tell her when I was coming to Iceland next summer. That was another thing I had discovered money could be turned into: plans. "I couldn't have managed without you," I said.

"I think that is true," she said, accepting my thanks as she had the kronur I had handed her the night before. "Good luck at university, and with the people you meet. Next summer I will take you, or you will take me, to our famous hot springs."

As the bus pulled away, she stood waving her small, gold-ringed hand. Until yesterday no one had ever waved me off on a journey. Now here was Hallie, like my aunt's family, casting a blessing on my travels. Perhaps the curse I had carried for so long was, finally, loosening its grip.

At the airport all the desks were busy; I joined the queue at Nanna's. I wasn't sure she would recognise me, but when my turn came to offer my ticket and passport she said, "Hello, Scottish girl. How was your visit?"

"My visit was very good, thanks to you and Hallie." Quickly—people were waiting—I told her that I had found my father's family and my old home. "Could I sit by the window again?"

"It is already arranged," she said with a smile. "Come again soon."

In the lounge I stood looking out at the runway, the bleak lava fields, the distant mountains. Not far from Stykkisholmur, Berglind had told me, was the mountain of Snaefellsjökull, which the French writer Jules Verne had written about in *Journey to the Centre of the Earth*. "I did not like the story," she had added, "but it was nice to see our mountain in a book." I had promised to read it when I got back to Scotland.

The flight was announced, and I followed the small crowd through the doors, across the tarmac, and up the steps of the plane to my window-seat. In the row in front of me a woman and a girl sat down; their wavy hair was exactly the same shade of brown. Once again the seat next to me was empty. The day was clear and I hoped for a good view as we took off. Perhaps we would fly over the city and I would see the Hallgrimskirkja or even the little lake with the mallards. A voice said, "May I?"

Mr. Sinclair sat down beside me, fastened his seat belt, and, without another word, reached for my hand.

ONLY WHEN WE WERE safely airborne, when the roar of the engines had lessened, and we were out over the Atlantic, the city of Reykjavik and the smoky bay left behind, did he begin to talk. As he spoke, I examined him in sly glances, taking in his skin, so much paler than when we parted, his cheeks just a little thinner, his eyes, beneath their long lashes, at their darkest blue.

"I don't think you can imagine, Gemma, how I felt when I discovered you were gone. I'd been up all night thinking about what I could say to you."

He had caught a plane to Inverness and followed me as far as Pitlochry, then lost the trail. He had telephoned police stations, churches, and libraries. He had checked hospitals and—his grip on my hand tightened—morgues. People had reported seeing me in Glasgow, Dunblane, Perth, Aberdeen. Each time he had travelled north, only to find some other young woman. As the weeks passed he had tried to persuade himself that I was fine, but he knew that I had little money, few friends, no family, no—

"How is Nell?" I interrupted.

"Nell," he said. "She's flourishing. Thanks to you, she's doing well at the village school, and she's made friends. She asks about you every time we speak."

Involuntarily my free hand moved to the place below my ribs where her fist had landed. "I thought she hated me."

"No. She was sure it was all her fault you'd left. I told her it was mine."

I was still smiling as I asked how he had found me in seat 9A.

"I am sorry to be the bearer of bad news"—his voice fell and again his hand tightened around mine—"but your aunt has died."

My gasp was more of amazement than sorrow. After all my failures at telepathy, I had, it seemed, inherited a small portion of Kristjana's gifts. But there was no time to consider that now. Mr. Sinclair was already explaining that her death had set off a chain of phone calls. A woman named Mrs. Marshall had called Aberfeldy and, when she learned I was in Iceland, had—he didn't know why but was eternally grateful—called Blackbird Hall.

"Mrs. Marsden," I corrected. So even as we both endured Louise's conversation, she had sensed some of what I couldn't say.

"I knew how you felt about Iceland," he went on, "and I couldn't help hoping that meeting you here would be a second chance." He had flown to Reykjavik the day before and, like me, had asked people at the airport if they could help him: Did anyone remember the arrival of a Scottish girl, travelling alone, in the last week? After questioning him closely, Nanna had agreed to arrange our meeting. "Thanks to her and her aunt, I have nearly three hours to persuade you not to run away again."

I pulled my hand free of his and kept it, firmly, in my lap while I asked about Mrs. MacGillvary. Was she angry with me? As Mr. Sinclair said that he didn't know—he hadn't spoken to her directly—the air hostess set down trays of neat sandwiches. I couldn't help reaching for one.

"That's the easy part," said Mr. Sinclair. "How we both got here. The hard part is can we get to a different place from the one in which you left me. I've had nearly a year to think about how I might make amends."

I ate a delicious sandwich and then another while he told me that he was having the croft beyond the meadow rebuilt for Seamus. Maybe if he wasn't living in Alison's old home he'd be able to imagine a life without her. And Vicky was advertising for a couple to live in the house and help look after Nell.

"Can you afford all this?" I asked between bites. "Houses and jobs are expensive."

"They are," he said, sounding amused. "But when I haven't been looking for you, I've had my shoulder to the wheel. And this is still much cheaper than sending Nell to boarding school, which, you may recall, I promised not to do."

His emphasis on "promised" made me eager to change the subject. I announced that I had got into Edinburgh University. "At least I'm pretty sure I did. The exams results aren't out until August."

"That's terrific, Gemma. You must have worked very hard. If it weren't ten in the morning I'd ask the air hostess for champagne."

It hadn't occurred to me that one could drink champagne on an aeroplane. "I did work hard. Studying was the only way I could imagine my life getting better." It was the first hint I'd given of all I'd suffered since Maes Howe.

Mr. Sinclair nodded. "This is going to sound strange, but I had the feeling recently that you were in danger. A few months ago a minister in Pitlochry told the police you were safe and I stopped searching for you. But last week I dreamed we were back on the Brough of Birsay, standing on the edge of the cliff, watching the birds. Suddenly you announced you could fly. You kept moving closer and closer to the edge."

He had dreamed about me, I realised, the night before I visited Archie. "Did you cry out to me?" I asked.

"Not then, not in the dream, but after Vicky phoned, I stood there in my study, begging you to wait." He made a little noise and gazed down at his hands. "Were you looking for your father's family?"

"I was. And I found a cousin, Berglind, who's like Pippi Longstocking, strong and cheerful, and an aunt, Kristjana, who is blind but has second sight."

"And did they call you by your Icelandic name?"

"Fjola Einarsdottir. Hallie, the woman who helped me, told me that it means 'the violet daughter of he who fights alone.'"

"Fjola," he said, muddling the syllables as I had.

Back in his room at Blackbird Hall I had said I would tell him my Icelandic name on our wedding night. And, I now recalled, I had promised that nothing he had done could ever change my feelings. I remembered how insistent he had been in exacting the promise and how confidently I had made it, even—my cheeks burned—quoting

Shakespeare. Useless to say that I had imagined he would confess to a mistress, or two; I had given my word, and I had broken it, like Gunner with Helga. I was thinking how to frame my apology when Mr. Sinclair said, "Excuse me." With a click of his seat belt, he disappeared down the aisle.

Alone, I closed my eyes and let the roar of the plane carry me back to Helgafell. On that windswept mountain I had heard Mr. Sinclair cry out and I had answered him. Yet here he was sitting beside me, and my feelings were hidden away in a small dark room. My mother had made custard; my father had tied knots; despite their differences they had married and had a child. My uncle had married my aunt to save his brother's child. And Seamus—but I did not know how to finish that thought.

Ast. Love.

Perhaps—I had only just become a daughter—I was not yet ready to be a wife. Perhaps being a wife was not the only choice. Once a year, if the sky was clear on the winter solstice, the sun shone down the passageway of Maes Howe to the back wall. I opened my eyes to see an air hostess approaching.

"Excuse me," I said. "Could we have two glasses of champagne?"

When Mr. Sinclair returned I looked at him fully for the first time since he had sat down. I saw my own tiny silhouette in each of his pupils, and the creases in his forehead that mimicked his eyebrows. I saw the hollow above his upper lip where sweat gathered when he worked in the sun. He had been my age, a little younger, when the summons came to be a Bevin Boy; now he was more than twice my age. I watched as my hand touched his cheek. He seized it and kissed my palm.

"Here you are." Two tall slender glasses filled with golden, bubbling liquid appeared before us.

"My first champagne," I said.

"Does this mean—?"

"It means"—I raised my glass—"that I'm going to make a speech. I promised that I wouldn't let anything change my feelings for you and I broke my promise. I didn't mean to. I told myself you were no longer the same person, but that was a convenient sophistry." The last phrase gave me particular pleasure and I saw him register my pleasure. "Of course you were. My friend Miriam—"

"The girl with asthma?"

"The girl who was my friend. She told me that I would only understand certain things when I was older. I didn't believe her until I met Nell. And even then I didn't understand that I would go on changing. That life"—I waved at the rows of seats where our fellow travellers read or slept—"would change me. Since we parted I've learned that I too am capable of stealing and lying. I'm sorry I was so unforgiving. Here's my toast.

"Here's to living under our rightful names."

I drank my first fizzing mouthful and ducked his kiss. Through the window, far below, I saw several small islands in the grey Atlantic. I took a deep breath hoping, even here, to catch the scent of apple blossoms. In the seat in front of us the two brown-haired women were also leaning towards the window. "*Smavegis*," I heard one say. "*Himnariki*." Surely Kristjana would have told me if I too was about to fall on the rocks. I turned back to Hugh. He was still holding his glass, watching me intently.

"What I said at the registry office," I went on, feeling my way, "is true. We can be married next week. Or next year. I don't want a promise to govern my feelings; I want my feelings to lead to a promise. And there are other things I want too."

I began to list them: to be a student, to write cheques, to buy cakes, to make friends, to visit the hot springs, to see a lyre-bird—

Desires were springing up on all sides when Hugh interrupted. "You want," he said, gazing at me steadily, "to be beloved and regarded."

"I do." His eyes had grown lighter, or perhaps they were reflecting the sky. "You've been sitting at the adult table for twenty years. I want to sit there too, and sample a few of the courses. I want to see if I'm ready to spend ten thousand days with you, and ten thousand nights."

"But that's only thirty years."

He was arguing for more—fifteen thousand, twenty—as I raised my glass and drank again. Then I leaned forward and kissed him.

acknowledgments

𝕀 HAVE TRIED TO BE faithful to the geography of both Scotland and Iceland but have taken occasional liberties. Blackbird Hall does not appear on maps of the Orkneys, and the jetty where Gemma's father kept his boat may be hard to find. My thanks to the many people in both countries who stopped to answer my odd questions. I am especially grateful to the woman in the harbour shop at Stykkisholmur who talked to me about Mount Helgafell.

My main literary debt is obvious. The following books also helped to shape Gemma's story: *Tales of the Seal People* and *Fireside Tales of the Traveller Children* by Duncan Williamson; *The Mermaid Bride*, told by Tom Muir; *The Northmen Talk: A Choice of Tales from Iceland*, translated by Jacqueline Simpson; *Classics for Pleasure* by Michael Dirda; *Sagas of Warrior-Poets*, introduced by Diane Whaley; *Njal's Saga*, translated by Robert Cook.

My deep thanks to Jennifer Barth for her brilliant comments as she read and reread these pages. I also want to express my gratitude to Amy Baker, Jane Beirn, Jonathan Burnham, Jason Sack, Emily Walters, and all the people at HarperCollins who helped to make this book. Once again I am happily indebted to Amanda Urban.

My family plays a role, witting and unwitting, in all my novels. My thanks especially to Janet for driving me round the Orkneys, to Sally for revisiting the sixties, to my nieces for reminding me of what it is like to be a teenager, and to Merril for showing me Saint David's Well and teaching me the names of flowers. Eric Garnick endured many tedious dinner conversations. Susan Brison read the novel with wonderful empathy and attention to detail. Andrea Barrett read and commented and imagined and corrected Gemma's journey at every stage. Thank you seems a very small thing to say.

about the author

Margot Livesey is the acclaimed author of the novels *The House on Fortune Street, Banishing Verona, Eva Moves the Furniture, The Missing World, Criminals,* and *Homework.* Her work has appeared in *The New Yorker, Vogue,* and *The Atlantic,* and she is the recipient of grants from both the National Endowment for the Arts and the Guggenheim Foundation. *The House on Fortune Street* won the 2009 L. L. Winship/PEN New England Award. Livesey was born in Scotland and grew up on the edge of the Highlands. She lives in the Boston area and is a Distinguished Writer-in-Residence at Emerson College.